ADVANCE PRAISE FOR

MAKING IT HOME

"Presenting the Syrian refugee through fiction is a challenging task, but DeLory writes the Syrian characters in *Making it Home* with an understanding of the Syrian culture, minted with love and empathy towards the refugee experience. Her strong command of her tales stands out through the many engaging stories she tells. *Making It Home* is a testament that DeLory is a wonderful storyteller, as well as a hardworking researcher."

–Ahmad Danny Ramadan, award-winning author
of *The Clothesline Swing*

"From the broken streets of Aleppo to the quiet of Cape Breton Island, *Making it Home* follows two families scattered by grief and conflict. Though Canadians are familiar with the story of Syrians from the headlines, DeLory takes us into the heart of Aleppo and what it is that one family loses when bombs shatter their lives. Forced to flee on foot from their beloved home, they escape through collapsed streets with children in tow. Meanwhile, in Cape Breton, a community is whittled away by economic hardship as it seems an entire generation leaves in search of work. No matter where they are, characters discover that they are capable of more than they know, for both good and bad.

Told from a variety of perspectives, DeLory's novel explores family from all angles, from the strength of love to its selfishness, guilt, and resentment. *Making it Home* finds the intersection between cultures in our human need for more than just shelter, but acceptance too."

–Nicola Davison, author of *In the Wake*

MAKING IT HOME

MAKING IT HOME

a novel

Alison DeLory

Vagrant
PRESS

Vagrant Press is an imprint of Nimbus Publishing Limited
3660 Strawberry Hill St, Halifax, NS, B3K 5A9
(902) 455-4286 nimbus.ca

Printed and bound in Canada
NB1368

Cover Design: John van der Woude Designs
Editor: Stephanie Domet
Editor for the press: Whitney Moran
Proofreader: Penelope Jackson

This story is a work of fiction. Names characters, incidents, and places, including organizations and institutions, either are the product of the author's imagination or are used fictitiously.

Library and Archives Canada Cataloguing in Publication

Title: Making it home / Alison DeLory.
Names: DeLory, Alison, 1969- author.
Identifiers: Canadiana (print) 20189068612 | Canadiana (ebook) 20189068620 | ISBN 9781771087254 (softcover) | ISBN 9781771087261 (HTML)
Classification: LCC PS8607.E48865 M35 2019 | DDC C813/.6—dc23

Nimbus Publishing acknowledges the financial support for its publishing activities from the Government of Canada, the Canada Council for the Arts, and from the Province of Nova Scotia. We are pleased to work in partnership with the Province of Nova Scotia to develop and promote our creative industries for the benefit of all Nova Scotians.

*This book is dedicated to those searching for home,
be that a place or a state of mind.*

CHAPTER 1

Cape Breton, August 2014

THE WATER AROUND ITS STOUT BODY WAS STILL comfortably cold, but less so. It surfaced, blew spray upwards, dipped back down. The sand and seaweed on the ocean floor came into view, but others in its pod swam on either side and even in front of it, so it journeyed on. It heard the muffled sounds of crashing waves, not the comforting clicks that echoed in deeper water. Its fins grazed the sand as the ocean tugged it into shallower waters and then spat it onto the hard, cold shore. It waited for a wave to pull it back out. None came. It lay still, conserving energy. Waiting.

Meanwhile, driving along the squiggly road that traced the coastline, Tinker glanced out across the Atlantic. Seagulls wheeled and screeched overhead while whitecaps on the navy blue water mirrored cotton-ball clouds in the sky. Mainland Nova Scotia was visible on the horizon; a fine enough place to visit, but home for Tinker would always be here on Cape Breton Island. A scattering of small boats dotted the outer Canso Strait. Though he'd seen the view countless times from multiple perspectives, it never failed to seduce him. He breathed in the salty air through his open window, let the warm wind whip his weathered face, and turned the radio off, straining his ears to hear the distant rumble of the incoming tide.

Lulled by the beauty, Tinker's concentration waned and his Buick drifted seaward until he almost grazed the guardrail. He swerved to avoid busting through it and toppling down a rocky cliff. "Holy Mary Mother of God!" he blurted as his wheels made black skid marks on the road, jerking him to a stop on the shoulder. He sat motionless for a few seconds, his white-knuckled fingers glued to the steering wheel, until he snapped to and exhaled. His torso felt sore underneath the taut seat belt, and he rubbed his instantly aching neck. *I may be old,* he told himself, *but it's not my time just yet.* He wiped his sweaty palms on his jeans and placed them back on the steering wheel, then continued on toward home.

It was Tuesday, so his wife, Florence, would be in the kitchen patting out fishcakes. He pictured her heating oil in the cast iron frying pan and stirring a pot of brown beans. She'd have the table set with green tomato chow in a bowl draped with a tea towel to keep the flies off. He licked his lips thinking of it, but sadness tinged his excitement for supper, knowing he'd have to avert his eyes from the empty chair his son once occupied.

Approaching town, he glanced at the now-visible familiar sign, written in English and Gaelic, Welcome to Falkirk Cove: *Fáilte*. It needed a fresh coat of paint and was slightly off kilter, neglected. He was surprised to find his buddy Bob standing next to it, waving his arms.

"Bob," he called out, pulling over. "Need a drive?"

Bob climbed into the passenger seat. "Tinker, we've got to get down to the shore right away. Steel yourself. Apparently it's quite a scene."

"An accident?" Tinker asked.

"Of sorts," Bob said. "A mass beaching of pilot whales. Charlie called me to round you up so we could help rescue 'em. He and Nell are already down there."

They got to the beach quickly. As they raced through the dunes, the sharp marram grass slapped against Tinker's Levis. Over the sound of his own laboured breathing he heard people shouting and waves lapping. His grandson, Charlie, ran up the beach carrying two buckets.

"We need to wet them quick. They're drying out," Charlie said, tossing a bucket at Tinker, then the other at Bob.

Tinker froze when he saw the whales lying on the sand. There looked to be about a dozen, and a few people were pouring seawater over their glossy black bodies. Though in his past he'd seen migrating whales from his fishing boat, in all his seventy-three years Tinker had never seen one on land. His urge to get closer to them was strong, but when his feet started moving again he kicked off his shoes and instead ran into the cold waves to fill his bucket.

Nell was on her way up the beach, a full bucket in each hand. "Keep their blowholes clear so they don't suffocate. Wet them down, and if you see one on its side, whistle so we can roll it upright," she said.

He listened carefully to Nell, trusting she knew what to do. She could be a bit of a bossy boots but that girl was smart, no question; university educated on the mainland and now back in Cape Breton, trying to figure out how to put her science degree to use. Charlie was lucky to have her. Tinker hoped like hell they'd land permanent jobs here soon.

Charlie was off to the side on his phone. "Call yer grandmother—tell her we'll be late for supper, would ya?" Tinker yelled, wistfully thinking of the fishcakes he wouldn't get to eat for some hours yet. Charlie gave him a thumbs-up.

Tinker lumbered through the sand toward an unattended whale, about two metres long. It was so still and quiet he wondered if it was alive. It was on its belly, with its blowhole clear, so he angled around to look into its eyes. They were like small black bowling balls, and inside those eyes he saw not only intelligence but also pleading. It rattled him, and he waved his palm over the blowhole to confirm the whale was breathing. He felt it emitting warm puffs of air, then he stroked the whale a few times, not sure if he was comforting it or himself.

"Hey there, feller. What are you doing up here on land? You belong out there, in the Atlantic," Tinker said. Charlie hadn't been a baby for twenty-two years, but the soothing voice Tinker had once used to talk to his grandson came right back to him.

The whale wasn't used to the sound of human voices. It wanted to swim, but its flippers were stuck. It looked at the man, less than half his size and ten times its age. It had no choice but to accept his help.

"Tinker...keep running buckets. We've got to keep them wet until enough people arrive...that we can push them back into the water," Nell said, breathless. She was doing double duty, directing the bucket runners and checking the status of each whale.

Cold sand stuck like grit between Tinker's toes. "You look some fool-ish, Bob," Tinker said to his friend as their paths crossed. Bob's thinning salt-and-pepper hair flopped around his head and water sloshed out of his bucket. The two of them used to play on this same beach as boys, hauling water out of the waves to fill the moats in their sandcastles. Later, as teenagers, they'd made bonfires here on warm summer evenings and guzzled swish from Mason jars.

When he bent to fill his bucket Tinker stopped, hands on knees, panting. He'd fallen out of shape in the seven years since the arthritis in his shoulder had forced him to retire from fishing. He'd gone a bit soft and his skin was droopier by the day. He wore his pants low now and his belly flopped over his belt. His body startled him when he saw his reflection in the bathroom mirror. How could it be that he felt mostly the same on the inside and looked so different on the outside? He hoisted the bucket up and clambered back up the beach.

Charlie was still on that damned phone. Tinker shot him a "hurry up" look and Charlie met his gaze with a blank stare before turning his back to Tinker. Charlie had been coming and going at all hours recently, and even when he was home he seemed distracted. Tinker couldn't get a bead on him and had given up trying. Charlie was a man now, after all, even though he still acted like a boy.

Some of Charlie's buddies started showing up. Where once they'd run in a big pack, there was now just a handful left. Most youngsters had moved out west for work. Those who remained here, like Charlie, mostly worked seasonal or odd jobs trying to eke out a living. Despite his and Charlie's differences, Tinker felt lucky to have his grandson close. He was glad Charlie understood that if he moved away and left him and Florence alone it would break their hearts. Charlie belonged here in Falkirk Cove with him and Flo. He was their only family left.

Nell hollered for them all to huddle up. Other folks from town were now pouring in, buckets in hand, and soon they had a crowd of thirty-five or so. Nell reported there were thirteen whales, but four were already dead. Only one of the remaining nine—a baby—made any noise. Tinker had to fight the urge to clap his hands over his ears so as not to hear it whimper. He hoped its mother wasn't one of the corpses.

"We have to start pushing them back into the water. The tide's starting to pull out, so the longer we wait, the farther we'll have to go. Can you guys divide yourselves up and start pushing?"

They did as Nell asked. Tinker returned to the first whale he'd befriended, locking eyes with it every minute or so. Bob and his grand-daughter Catriona joined him. Grunting, bending their knees with arms extended, they could barely budge the whale, and it was small as whales go. Tinker's bad shoulder started to ache. He'd helped push trucks out of ditches with less effort.

"Why would they do this to themselves? I don't get it," Catriona said. Tinker saw bewilderment on her face. She was young—still a teenager. The random cruelty of the world was only starting to hit her. But she was holding it together as best she could.

"Whales are social animals. They travel in pods, which are like their families. Just like Cape Bretoners, their families are close. They look out for one another," Bob said. He straightened his body and, with his palms on his hips, arched his back until it cracked.

"This looks more like a suicide pact than a family vacation," Catriona said, her face whiter than sea foam.

"Well, sometimes a member of the pod gets off course. He might be sick and trying to rest on shore to breathe more easily. The rest follow him, whether to help him or keep him company, no one knows. They all end up beached."

Tinker looked up from the whale toward Bob. His old friend had always been a reader and a thinker, as long as he'd known him. While Tinker had hated school and left as soon as he was able, Bob had stayed much longer, even doing seven years away at university to train as a doctor before returning home.

They grunted, sweated, and pushed. The whale smelled faintly fishy, salty and sulfuric. Its firm, smooth skin was cool against Tinker's chapped palms. It barely budged. Tinker ran back to his car for a tarp. They tipped the whale onto its side, and then back onto the tarp. Then he, Bob, and Catriona grabbed corners and with small, laboured steps, managed to drag it into shallow water. Tinker's heart was thumping hard and his brow was dripping. The water churned around his legs as he felt the outward pull of the tide, but the whale stayed still and Tinker wondered if it was no longer able to swim. "G'wan, whale. Swim away," he said, to no effect. The whale hovered.

Other teams edged into the water with their whales. Tinker had watched his community pull together to help one another out plenty of times, whether it was to raise a barn or re-house a family after a fire or what have you, but he'd never seen anything like this. The floating whale still wasn't swimming away.

"What's going on, Grampie?" Catriona asked. Her eyeglasses were spotted with sea spray and her brown hair was falling in chunks out of its ponytail.

"It's waiting for the rest of its pod, darlin'," Bob said, draping an arm around her shoulders.

Just then Charlie waded over to Tinker. He dragged his feet in the sand. "Grandpa?" he said, looking past Tinker at some invisible spot on the horizon.

"Yeah, what?" Tinker looked exhaustedly at his grandson, his adrenalin giving way to fatigue. Charlie's hair was too long and he must've had the dullest razor in Cape Breton; as usual, his chin and cheeks were some stubbly. But his eyes were still big and brown, and if Tinker focused squarely on them and let the rest of Charlie's face go blurry, he could see his dead son in Charlie's face.

Charlie paused and shifted his weight back and forth between his feet. "You know that phone call I got earlier? It was from the oil sands. They're hiring again and offered me a job."

Tinker snapped to attention. "That so? What'd you tell them?"

Charlie kicked the sand and met Tinker's eyes. "I told them yes, I'll move to Alberta. I got a job fitting pipes, like I was trained to do." He said more words, but Tinker didn't register any of them. Charlie spoke quietly and with acceleration, words spewing from his mouth like he just wanted rid of them.

Tinker looked at the whales hovering near the shore. Some people were trying to rotate their stubborn bodies around so the whales would be facing deeper water.

"Like hell you will." Tinker knew he was being selfish and he didn't care. It'd been seven years since his son made a similar move, and five since the explosion that killed him.

"I'm not him, Grandpa. I'll come back. Promise."

"No. I'll not let you go." The breeze must have been picking up, for Tinker now felt chilled.

"It's not your decision. I'm going and you can't stop me."

All the living whales were in the water now. They hovered close to shore, their dorsal fins sticking out. A long minute passed.

"Look, they're leaving!" Nell shouted, waving both arms goodbye. Did she know about Charlie's plan to move out west?

Slowly, reluctantly, the whales regrouped and swam out and away from Cape Breton. Tinker turned and walked back toward his truck, brushing away tears, muttering under his breath about the damn wind making his eyes water.

CHAPTER 2

WALKING INTO THE LEGION, TINKER GLANCED around to see who'd turned up tonight. Florence was working in the canteen as usual. Only her head and shoulders were visible above the counter, but he knew she was adding up purchases and figuring out change without even needing a calculator. She'd always been good at sums. Every week she came to bingo early and stayed long after the last card was played to help close up, catching a ride home with her friend Jean. She'd climb into bed late, her hair smelling of hot dogs, but Tinker never minded.

Bob was sitting near the front of the room and Tinker thought for a second about joining his pal but then remembered how serious Bob's bingo friends were. They all had lucky daubers and superstitions about when to buy their cards and how to arrange them on the long, warping wooden tables. The worst case was when those folks asked Tinker to play their cards so they could go to the john. Some played a dozen cards at once. Tinker knew if his slow reflexes cost someone a bingo victory he'd be run out of town.

He grabbed a seat near the back of the room and waved to Catriona, who was walking up and down each row selling cards. He felt kindly towards her tonight, remembering how they'd rescued the whale together a few days earlier, and he gave her a nice tip with his card purchase. A full fifty-cent tip.

"B-7." Jean's voice rang out through the speakers. She'd been calling bingo for so many years that a robot would have spoken with more enthusiasm. A second of silence, then pound-pound-pound went the daubers. Tinker's dauber hovered over his single card without touching down.

CATRIONA WEAVED HER WAY THROUGH the rows of bingo players. Though she normally wished she had more curves and booty, at this moment, being shaped like a pencil meant she could turn sideways and squeeze behind the players who pushed their chairs away from the tables or leaned back.

"Over here. Four more cards please," called one of her grampie's friends.

She peeled the cards off her stack. "Eight dollars."

The customer waved away the change from his ten-dollar bill. "Hey Catriona, you finish high school in June, right? What's next for you?"

This again. She shrugged and walked to the next row, where a woman was waving.

"So I guess you'll be off to university next year, hey Catriona?" the woman asked. "What do you plan to study?"

"O-64."

Catriona pretended she hadn't heard the woman over Jean's voice and the thumping daubers. Bingo was supposed to be a distraction from these freakin' questions. Would they ever stop?

CHARLIE PUSHED THE DOOR OPEN and entered the Legion. He hated bingo but knew Tinker's routines and that he'd be able to find him here—and this might be his last chance to explain. He'd expected his grandfather to take it personally that he'd accepted a job fitting pipes in Alberta, but he hadn't thought Tinker would hold such a grudge. Tinker had been avoiding Charlie since they rescued the whales, and that took effort considering they lived in the same house.

"B-14." Jean's voice sounded like the teacher from Charlie Brown whose voice-over always translated to "wah wah wah" for the Peanuts gang. The pounding of daubers that followed intensified Charlie's tension headache. He searched his pocket for some pills to take the edge off but found none and wondered how they could be all gone already. He was thankful that at least the Legion was non-smoking now; as a boy he'd been regularly dragged here by his grandparents and had suffered through many hours in a blue haze while the bingo crowd puffed away. He glanced around but couldn't see Grandpa, only his grandma working in the canteen. Charlie considered charming her into buying him an Iron Brew, but that would prolong the inevitable confrontation with his grandpa, and he just wanted it over. He continued scanning the room.

Tinker's back was to him. Charlie recognized his shiny bald spot and the wisps of reddish-grey hair circling it. Thankfully he was sitting alone. Charlie approached and blurted out, "Grandpa, can I talk to you?" before he lost his nerve. Tinker didn't turn around and didn't answer. He was still pissed. Charlie's mind was made up, he was going to Alberta, but he didn't want bad blood between them. Other than Grandma, Grandpa was the only living relative he had. He had to try making amends.

"N-34." Pound-pound-pound.

"Grandpa, please. I need to explain," Charlie said in a loud whisper. Someone called out "shush" from two tables over.

Tinker used his foot to pull out another chair just an inch or so. "All right. Park it, Charlie."

Looking down, Charlie noticed his grandfather had hemmed his own pants with a stapler. He broke into a grin. There were lots of things about the old man he was going to miss.

"I know you're mad about Alberta, Grandpa." Charlie slid into the chair quickly. "But I need to work and it's not happening for me here."

Tinker didn't make eye contact but kept staring at his bingo card instead.

"Want a card, Charlie?" Catriona asked.

Charlie looked up from the ground past her long legs to her face. How did Bob's granddaughter get so tall and grown up all of a sudden? It seemed like yesterday she was a goofy girl with braids and braces. "No thanks, Cat," he whispered and watched as Catriona nodded and continued down the row.

"G-46," Jean called. Pound-pound-pound. Charlie glanced at his grandfather's card and saw a 46 in the G column, but Tinker didn't lower his dauber to ink it. He was about to tell him but thought better of it.

"Who knows how much longer this Alberta boom might last. I've gotta get out there now." There were other, more urgent, reasons Charlie needed to leave town, but he kept those to himself. "I've been looking for a job here in Cape Breton, you know I have, and there's nothing. Nothing. I've gotta go where I can be useful, Grandpa."

Tinker finally looked up from his bingo card. He lowered his fist onto the table with a dull thud. "It's the golden handcuffs, that's what Alberta will trap you with, boy. You'll get out there, all this money coming in, and you'll think you're all set. Buy yourself a truck, some flashy clothes, the latest iPhone-a-ma-thingy, and soon you're vacationing in Mexico rather than coming home."

Well, at least he was talking. Anything was better than the silent treatment. "That's not true, Grandpa. I don't want to leave forever. Just for now. To get some experience and pad my bank account a bit. But I'll come back. And I'll always be a Cape Bretoner."

Catriona walked by again selling cards and shot Charlie a sympathetic look.

Tinker finally looked directly at his grandson. "It seems like running away to me. Besides, there's talk the coal mine might reopen."

"Yeah, that's been the talk my whole life but it hasn't happened, has it?" Charlie watched his grandfather rack his brain for his next argument.

"Well there's seasonal work on the golf course. Or you could start a business."

"Doing what?"

A player next to them turned to face Charlie. "Take your argument outside, for the love of God."

Charlie ignored him. "Things aren't the way they were in your day, Grandpa," he said more quietly.

Tinker tilted his held. "If you tried, you and Nell could build lives for yourselves in Cape Breton the way your grandmother and I did."

"Well I'm not you and it's not the 1960s." Charlie stood up.

"It's not all that different. You've no patience, no long-term plan. When I was your age, your grandmother and I were planning our wedding and framing our house. We made our way staying right here because we were determined to."

"Shhhh," the people around them hissed.

"I-23," Jean droned. Pound-pound-pound.

"You'll stay at the camps? Come home on your weeks off?" Tinker asked.

That's what most Cape Bretoners did—lived in lodging right on site in the oil sands, banking their weeks off for trips home. Some employers even paid the workers' airfare back and forth. It was one of Canada's longest commutes.

Charlie sat back down. "Nah. I'm going to get my own apartment and stay up there awhile. Hopefully pick up extra shifts in my weeks off. Overtime pays well."

Tinker raised his eyebrows. "Is that right. What's Nell got to say about it?"

"It's my decision, not Nell's," Charlie answered.

"N-34." Pound-pound-pound.

"When do you leave?" Tinker asked.

"Day after tomorrow."

"Then you best go home and pack," Tinker said, turning away from him.

"BINGO!" someone cried out. A mixture of groans and cheers rose up from the crowd.

"Damn it all to hell," Tinker said, balling up his paper bingo sheet and tossing it on the floor. Everything felt as out of place as those whales on the beach.

CHAPTER 3

CHARLIE THREW HIS CLOTHES INTO A HOCKEY BAG and zipped it. He scanned his bookshelf, trying to decide if there was anything there worth taking. Certainly not his old school scribblers. Why was Grandma even hanging on to those? It wasn't like he'd been a great student. He'd only ever enjoyed working with his hands, not sitting at a desk. He picked up a stack and threw them in the garbage. Then he looked at the weathered baseball mitt that was now too small for his hand and remembered playing catch with his dad in the backyard. They'd start a few feet apart, then take a step backward each time one of them caught a toss until they were throwing clear across the lawn. He'd beaned his dad in the shoulder once so hard he fell down, but instead of being mad he'd sprung back up to his feet laughing and praised Charlie's strong arm. He'd been a good dad. Charlie pitched the mitt into his hockey bag and then reconsidered. What use would he have for a child-size baseball mitt in Alberta? The past was the past. He was ready for the future. Back on the shelf it went. In the end, packing didn't even take Charlie twenty minutes. His steel-toed workboots and hardhat even fit inside the bag no problem.

Nell sat on his bed with her legs crossed underneath her. Though she was usually chatty and quick to smile, her face was now drawn as she silently stared out the window at the distant woods. Charlie gazed at her profile, the bump on her nose and high cheekbones, wondering how many times he'd watched her pack during the past four years when she was heading back to Halifax for a new semester. Those were always sad but exciting afternoons, with the two of them fooling around on her bed knowing they wouldn't get to touch each other again for a few months, giggling then shushing each other while her parents or a brother or two or three puttered around downstairs. They'd lost their virginity together in the bed she sat on now, and Charlie knew they'd remain faithful always. Today though, the tension between them was as thick as Louisbourg fog. There was no teasing or messing around, but Charlie did want to comfort Nell, to tell her they'd be okay. They were CharlieAndNell, referred to mostly in the singular for going on six years. He drifted toward her and stroked her hair, then planted a kiss on the top of her head.

"I'll miss you, boo," Charlie said. Nell didn't reply except with a sigh. She probably never figured once she moved back permanently it would be his turn to leave. But he was leaving for her—for them. He needed to get his shit in order.

Grandma appeared at his bedroom door with a stack of his laundry in her hands. She was so short the plain white T-shirts folded perfectly on the top of the pile towered as high as her crabapple chin. "Here you go, luv," she said. He took the line-dried clothes and breathed in their meadowy scent before adding them to his hockey bag. Tears pooled in Grandma's blue eyes, but Charlie needed to keep it light.

"Bet you'll be happy to get your sewing room back once I've cleared out." He gestured toward the corner table with the Singer on it, once a state-of-the art electric and now a yellowed, plastic 1970s relic. They both knew it was unlikely she'd start sewing again. The quilt Nell now sat on was probably the last thing his grandmother had ever sewn. It was mostly reds and blues with some scraps of fabric depicting a baseball game and others, Mickey Mouse. She'd made it when he was about nine. He used to love staring at it and tracing his fingertips along the wavy seams, but he had no time to get sentimental now. His future awaited him. The quilt would still be here when he came back. The beauty and curse of this house and this community was that they were slow to change.

"That's not true, Charlie. I'm going to miss you hard. This takes me back to your dad leaving. You remember that day?"

Charlie shifted his weight from left to right foot. "'Course, Grandma.

I was sixteen." In Grandma's eyes he was always younger than his years. There were still Hardy Boys mysteries on his bookshelf.

Nell shot Charlie a look. "Tell me about that day, Flo," she said.

Charlie rolled his eyes. Grandma sat on the bed.

"Well, it was a Sunday, so we'd all gone to mass at St. Andrew's. Afterwards there was tea and coffee in the church hall, with sandwiches. I'd spent the entire day before mixing egg and tuna salad. Elsie—you know Elsie, Dr. Bob's wife? Well, she made ham sandwiches and brought plates of gherkins. Between us two, I think we brought enough to feed everyone in Falkirk Cove."

Charlie didn't remember the sandwiches or pickles, but he'd likely been too upset to eat, sitting in the hall unable to accept that his dad was about to move six provinces away without him. He understood it better now. After several years of unemployment, his dad had likely been as desperate to leave as Charlie was now.

"Father Dunphy announced just before the closing hymn that everyone was welcome to the hall for a special lunch and homemade squares in Russell's honour. I'd made some of those, too. Date squares, and those peanut butter–marshmallow ones Charlie likes so much." Charlie stood at the foot of the bed watching his grandma and Nell jabber like old friends and wished he were already on the plane.

Nell could be nostalgic, too, but now she was humoring Flo. She'd been at mass that day and at the reception. Charlie remembered her sympathetic eyes. It was the summer before they started high school, and though they'd long been friends and classmates, Charlie and Nell were only just starting to really notice one another. Back then, Charlie would direct his grandparents into the pew behind Nell's family and position himself so he could stare at the back of her head during mass. When she turned around during "Peace be with you" with her hand extended, he'd squeeze and grip it a second longer than was customary. Nevertheless, Nell let Flo tell her about the mass and his dad's reception like she hadn't been there.

"The hall was totally packed. Every seat was filled with parishioners wanting to see Russell off," Grandma said. "I think the whole town was there."

"G'way, Grandma," Charlie said. "There were empty seats. And you can be sure some people came just for the free lunch, not for Dad." Flo's smile dropped. "Though can you blame them? Your sandwiches and squares are the best in Cape Breton," he said, recovering with a wink.

Grandma rose to leave the room. "It was a nice tea party and a proper send-off," she said on her way out, pausing at the door.

Charlie understood that Grandma needed to believe it had been a happy time, but it had actually been tedious. The lights were too bright inside the hall. It was stuffy and a bitter, burnt smell wafted from the coffee urns. A small choir sang during mass, but there was no music in the hall, and only the sound of chair legs squeaking on the parquet floor punctuated the droning voices of the parishioners. Charlie had been uncomfortable because Grandma made him wear a tie, which felt like a noose around his neck, and a dress shirt and slacks. He'd rebelled and worn new Air Jordans instead of the too-tight loafers she'd wanted him to wear. He'd never been one for dressing up and still wasn't.

Charlie walked over to his grandmother, wrapped his arms around her waist, and lifted her off the floor. "My pocket grandma. So tiny I'm going to tuck you into my pocket and sneak you off to Alberta with me."

"Put me down, you rascal!" Flo said, swatting him playfully. When he lowered her, she grabbed his face with both hands, then stroked his cheeks with her thumbs. "What's that?" She looked down at the scribblers overflowing the garbage can. Sucking her teeth, she pulled the scribblers out and put them back on Charlie's bookshelf.

Now it was just Charlie and Nell in his room. "He's not coming to see me off, is he?" Charlie asked. Tinker had not been at the church hall the day his dad left, either.

"It's just too hard for him, Charlie. Try to give him a break." Nell stood up to hug him. He let her but felt tense even as he hugged her back. He pulled away and went to the bathroom to fetch his shaving kit. He opened the mirrored door and peered into the medicine cabinet. He snatched a half-filled bottle of his grandpa's prescription pain meds to help him transition, crammed it into his shaving kit, and walked back to his bedroom. He zipped up his hockey bag with a final look around the room that had been his for the past eight years. A room, a life, he'd outgrown.

TINKER ASSESSED THE TOWN'S WOODEN sign—WELCOME TO FALKIRK COVE: *FÀILTE*. He couldn't read or speak Gaelic so just stared at that part, approving of how the town's sign honoured its Scottish founders.

Late-summer goldenrod was growing high enough to reach the sign's lower edge. It swayed in the breeze, a green and yellow paintbrush coating the bottom of the sign, as though trying to touch up the fading and peeling paint.

"Home of Celtic music" was written near the top of the sign, flanked by two once-bright red fiddles, bows tilted diagonally across the strings as though in mid-jig. There was no person on the sign holding the fiddles or bows, so they floated there as though playing themselves. Tinker tried creating his own music by whistling, but the rumblings of cars and trucks on Highway 19 running up the west coast of Cape Breton drowned him out.

He set his toolbox down and walked around to the back of the sign. Sure enough, the nails fixing the posts to the billboard were rusting and the wood was splitting. The sign would soon need replacing, but until there was budget for that he would do his part to maintain it. The elements here were hard on everything and everyone—fog patches, rain, heavy snowfalls, and wildly fluctuating temperatures weathered and aged the structures and people alike. Tinker blamed a lot of his wrinkles and hair loss on time spent outdoors.

He took out a few five-and-a-half-inch nails and started hammering. Quickly, his arthritic right shoulder began to throb. Cars kept whizzing by as he rhythmically drove in each nail. Exhaust blew from their tailpipes, and the noise pollution was even worse. He shook his head at everyone's rushing around. What was the hurry?

Finished, he walked around to the front to check the sign's sturdiness. He grabbed the warping posts and shook them, not caring if he got a few splinters in his leathered hands. Yep, she was holding steady.

His task complete, Tinker kicked the goldenrod aside and started walking back to his Buick.

NELL WAS DRIVING CHARLIE TO the airport. They pulled off his grandparents' dirt road onto Highway 19. They drove in silence past St. Andrew's church, perched up on the hill, then past the small harbour and wharf at Moose Cove. Charlie gazed out the window, thinking he should really look at the landscape and try to soak it in—who knew when he'd be back—but he was too distracted by thoughts of leaving to try to imprint memories. Besides, he could never forget this place.

He could close his eyes and picture every house, barn, boat, person, and pothole.

Charlie saw him lift the hammer and swing it at the signpost. His grandpa's red hair, once flaming, had faded and thinned, but it was unmistakably him, passing his time as he always did: by tinkering with something, making small fixes to the community he loved. The community he'd accused Charlie of deserting.

"Want to stop?" Nell asked.

Charlie turned and stared straight ahead. "Nope. Drive on," he replied.

He wouldn't let her come into the airport, so they said goodbye at the curb. "Fare Thee Well, Love" was playing on the radio as Nell pulled away. Charlie didn't turn around to look back until after she'd driven out of sight.

CHAPTER 4

Syria, October 2014

AMIRA STOOD FACING A WALL IN HER BEDROOM, staring at jagged cracks in the plaster. She traced a finger down one. It was a few centimetres longer than it had been yesterday thanks to last night's bombing. Today, like most days for the past few months, she was confined to her family's apartment in Aleppo. She hadn't known how much she loved going places until it was no longer an option. Before the war, on a restless Friday like this, she would have taken her children on an after-school outing to the souk.

The bustling old central souk had been one of their favourite places in Aleppo. Although there were modern supermarkets and shopping malls throughout the city, Amira preferred walking through the vast stone corridors inside the enormous covered bazaar. The spices fascinated her son, Ahmed. Once, he got too close to the barrels and burst into fits of sneezing when airborne particles of cumin, turmeric, and nutmeg wafted up his nostrils. Amira stifled laughter at her son's misfortune and apologized to the grumpy vendor who raised his hands and shouted as Ahmed's spray hit him.

The silk shawls in rich purple, red, and green jewel tones with their ticklish tassels commanded her daughter Yasmine's attention. Amira loved the decorative plates and gold jewelry that glowed despite the souk's poor lighting. Taking her children in hand, she would walk through the dizzying labyrinth, stopping to chat if she happened to see friends from their mosque or neighbours, or to barter with vendors for items she wished to take home. She would often leave with fresh meat, vegetables, nuts, or small plates of the sweet baklava her children loved to share with their father, Sami.

But those outings were in the past. The souk, like so much of Aleppo, was destroyed. She heard estimates that fifteen hundred shops were burnt or damaged there and it would cost millions of dollars to repair them. She hadn't the heart to witness the damage first-hand, and besides, it was too unsafe.

So Amira stayed home and walked toward her living room window to gaze out at the desolate street. The glass windowpane had blown into the living room after an air raid the week before. The taut plastic sheeting that replaced it was turning milky and vibrated when the wind hit it. "Ouf!" she cried as she laid her hand on the sill and was poked by yet another glass splinter lying there. She plucked it from her fingertip and sucked away the drop of blood that appeared as she looked outside. The grey dust collecting on the sidewalk depressed her. A knobby-kneed boy about her son's age pulled a wobbly wagon carrying two jugs half his size around the loose bricks and bits of cement that littered the street. She supposed he was fetching diesel or water for his family. The war had turned many formerly middle-class children into poor child labourers. One of the wheels on his wagon was loose and he struggled to pull the wagon straight. It was a pitiful sight. Amira felt thankful that at least her son was still in school.

Though school was safer than outside, she still fretted. Would it one day also be bombed? The stress was giving her frequent headaches, and as she paced through the rooms she ground her knuckles into her temples. Her body sometimes felt as out of her control as this war—even her period, usually so regular, was overdue. Trips to her beloved mosque were off limits now, so five times a day she faced Mecca kneeling on a mat at home, praying to Allah that the war would soon end and life would somehow return to normal.

"It's not time to leave Aleppo yet," Sami had said to her as they sat in the dark the night before while bombs fell in the distance. She prayed silently the children would sleep through the reverberations, and they had. For their family's sake, she hoped Sami was right but it was getting harder to support his decision. Many of their friends and neighbours had already fled, and each time another one slipped away, a small piece of Amira left with them. Sami, though, didn't feel he could abandon his medical practice when so many needed his care. She fought against the feeling that Sami prioritized practicing medicine over his own family's safety.

There were no easy answers. Leaving the country would certainly be hard, especially considering her parents wouldn't budge from Azaz in northern Syria, but every day lately Amira felt more ready to go. She'd had a wonderful thirty-one years here, born into privilege, educated, and married to a man who loved and respected her, but she couldn't be optimistic about their future. She was a realist. Life as they knew it was gone forever. She could no longer go out for morning gatherings to drink coffee, talk, and eat sweets, read new novels by Syrians, ogle gold plates and jewelry at the souk, or gather with worshipers for Friday services at the mosque. Her parents hadn't been to Aleppo to visit in more than a year, and even phone communication with them now was rare.

Rather than just sit and listen to distant explosions become less distant, she had to prepare. She went to the bedroom and pulled two small suitcases out of her closet and opened them on her bed.

"What are you doing, Mama?" Yasmine stood at the doorway to Amira's bedroom with her hip cocked, one hand on the doorframe and a Barbie in the other. She wouldn't start school until next year and so was Amira's constant companion at home. Her brown eyes widened when she saw the suitcases. "Are we going on a trip?"

"Not today, Yasmine, but maybe soon. Don't tell Ahmed or Papa though. We will surprise them when it's time, okay?" Amira didn't like keeping secrets from Sami, but packing a few things in case they had to leave quickly seemed minor.

"All right, Mama. Pack some toys too, please," Yasmine said, skipping back to her bedroom.

Amira placed clothes and toiletries in the main cavity, then tucked cash and their identification papers into a money belt she placed in the zippered side pocket. Her temples continued to pulse as she browsed her bookshelf, dragging her fingers along the spines of books by her favourite Syrian authors that were too heavy to pack. Instead, she opened a photo album and began flipping through it. It was a treasure trove of memories from happier times. Her face relaxed as she turned the pages and drew her fingertips across the smooth plastic top sheet. There were she and Sami on their wedding day, standing in front of the white domes and elegant arches of their mosque. Though she was smiling in the picture, she could also see nervousness in her young face, and wished she were able to assure her younger self that Sami would be a good husband. Marriage hadn't always been easy, but at his core Sami was a decent man and she had no regrets. She peeled open the page and eased the photo off the sticky backing. She briefly pressed her and Sami's faces against her heart, then placed it, a photo of her beloved parents, and one photo of each of the children as babies into an envelope. Even if she lost every other material thing she owned, Amira would safeguard these four photos. Being a loving daughter, wife, and mother brought her life its greatest meaning and happiness. She had been so often blessed without always realizing it. Amira loved her family fiercely, and though times were difficult now, she would continue to believe they'd make new happy memories together in the future.

Once the suitcases were back in the closet, Amira went to the kitchen to boil water for her mid-morning coffee. Maybe caffeine could relieve her headache. She made several unsuccessful attempts to start the stove before trying to turn on the overhead lights. They, too, weren't working. She tried the television, radio, and a lamp, but nothing turned on. Power would regularly flicker, so Amira sat on the kitchen stool to compose herself. They had a generator for emergencies but a low supply of diesel and she couldn't squander it on a luxury like coffee. She stamped her feet in frustration.

"What's going on, Mama?" said a small voice from the hallway. Yasmine entered the kitchen and wrapped her small arms around Amira's legs.

"We've lost power again." Amira plastered a smile on her face, stood, and opened the cupboards. "Let's play a game called shopkeeper."

Yasmine, who loved role-play games, nodded her head.

"How many cans of food do we have left? This is called 'taking inventory.' Can you help me count them?" Amira strained to keep her voice matter-of-fact. Though they'd stocked up early in the war, today fewer than twenty cans remained. With the shops and markets closed or inaccessible, they relied on the occasional produce vendor who still appeared in the street, or patients who paid Sami with food. She lifted Yasmine onto the stool so she could reach inside the cupboards.

"Fifteen, sixteen, seventeen…" Yasmine stood counting when a familiar voice interrupted.

"Mama, where are you? Mama?" Ahmed shouted. He found them in the kitchen.

Amira looked at the clock. It was only ten o'clock, far too early for school to dismiss.

"What's wrong, Ahmed? Why are you home already?"

"School closed, Mama. There aren't enough teachers anymore. We were told to bring home our books and learn on our own." Ahmed dropped his heavy bag onto the kitchen floor with a thud.

Amira clenched her jaw and resumed massaging her temples. Her head was pounding. "Really. How do you feel about it, Ahmed?" Amira didn't want her reaction to scare her son, who was only ten, but the news was yet another blow, and possibly the most serious. Without an education, what future did her children have? This was unacceptable.

"I'll miss my friends. But my teacher said I'm lucky. She said, 'Ahmed, you are smart. You can already read and do math, and you live in a home with books and educated parents who can teach you now.'"

Was it bravado, Amira wondered, or had he truly resigned himself to this new reality that quickly? It was sometimes hard to tell with Ahmed. He always wanted to make things easier for others.

"Ahmed Ahmed Ahmed! Will you play with me?" Yasmine pleaded, climbing off the stool.

Amira envied her daughter's innocence and ability to find positives in any situation. Both her kids were coping better than she was. She would draw strength from them.

"It is a school day, Yaya. I have to do my lessons. How about this: We play school here at home. I'll be the teacher and you'll be the student. Don't forget, Yaya, I'm in charge. That means you have to do whatever I say, okay?"

Yasmine nodded. At five, she was always happy to get attention from her older brother and was also so eager to begin school she'd tolerate even Ahmed's bedroom as the classroom.

As the children scampered off, Amira went to the front door and locked it. She considered phoning Sami with the news but tried limiting interruptions to emergencies. This certainly wasn't that. It was hardly even a surprise. Schools, businesses, and offices had been closing for months now. She wasn't naïve enough to think her family wouldn't be directly affected, but that didn't stop her from feeling enraged when they were. Everything about this stupid war was unjust and unnecessary. She paced in circles and her breathing became shallower. Back in the kitchen, she grabbed the countertops and willed herself to slow her breathing.

She grabbed an olive to suck on in lieu of a cup of coffee and dampened a cloth to press across her forehead as her headache raged on. She found a moment to lie on her bed but knew it would be over when the children's game of school inevitably erupted into an argument. Inside or outside the home, there was never a long-term guarantee of peace.

CHAPTER 5

Cape Breton, October 2014

NELL HOPPED ON HER BIKE AND STARTED pedalling. The days were still fair, though it was mid-October and she knew what lay ahead. A spectacular explosion of colour in the surrounding forests would beckon busloads of tourists from near and far, only to be followed by an extended off-season during which hardly anyone came here.

It would be her first winter in Cape Breton in five years, and she feared it, especially with Charlie now gone. Most of her childhood friends had moved away, and she'd grown too far apart from those who stayed to pretend they still had anything in common. Moving back home, it turned out, was quite lonely and often boring, and the long winter ahead was only going to make it worse. Nell liked staying busy and spending time outdoors, both of which were antithetical to winter in Falkirk Cove. She'd need to figure out ways to stay busy, but for now reminded herself not to ruin this beautiful day by worrying about the cold and bleak ones ahead.

Her muscular legs set her bike wheels spinning along the packed dirt. She pedalled faster until her lungs filled to capacity with crisp air suffused with sea spray, crabapples, and pine needles. When Nell needed to clear her head, the best way was to exercise until her limbs moved by rote. She had used this same technique to get through final papers and exams at university, taking breaks from studying to go on long runs or swims that would settle and open her mind. It was often in these moments that her best ideas came to her, but today, despite her physical exertion, there were no moments of mental clarity. She remained unsure about her future, and the focus and determination that usually propelled her were threatened by uncertainty. She didn't know what was going to happen next, and that rattled her. She was a person who liked to have a plan. Her wheels spun out and she skidded off the path, touched her toes to the ground, and paused.

Charlie's leaving had been hard, no question. What hurt the most was that he hadn't discussed it with her at all. Nell thought they had no secrets from one another, but he'd obviously watched for job postings, sent resumes, made calls, and had interviews—all behind her back. He'd been cagey lately. In the course of their long relationship there had been times he'd withdrawn, so she'd decided not to over think it, but this time he'd crossed a line. If he'd really wanted to leave town, she would have considered going with him—but he'd never asked.

Nell resumed pedalling her bike down the portion of Highway 19 known as Main Street and stopped at the Kwikmart. She propped her bike against the building's side without bothering to lock it and unclipped her helmet with her right hand, smoothing down her flyaway dark blond hair with her left. The bells jangled as she pushed open the door and came face to face with Roger. He quickly averted his eyes and stared at her sneakers.

"Five hundred and seventeen. Five hundred and seventeen. That's how many shingles there are on the Kwikmart roof. Did you know that, Nell?"

"I didn't, Roger. Thanks for telling me. That's a lot of shingles. You count every one?"

Without pausing, Roger walked up and down the aisles with measured steps. His legs were always in motion, as was his brain. Nell wondered how long he'd been hanging around inside the store. He might wear out the floor tiles in here one day.

He didn't answer her question. "Five hundred and seventeen. Want me to come to your house and tell you how many shingles are on your roof, Nell? I can do that, Nell." Roger's arms hung limply at his sides. He was wearing a grey sweatsuit with the waist pulled high so that his ankles, covered in white tube socks, were exposed. He scanned the shelves, perhaps calculating the total cost of buying every item in the store.

"How about this, Rog? When I'm ready to build a house you come over and let me know how many shingles I'll need. Then I could buy just the right amount." Nell glanced at Jean, who was behind the counter. Jean peered over the top of the *Cape Breton Post* and smiled at Nell.

"That was nice work you did down there on the beach, Nell," Jean said. "The paper here is crediting you for possibly saving nine whales."

The attention was starting to embarrass Nell. A few people had tagged her in their Facebook pictures and updates, but she'd stopped acknowledging them. She grabbed an apple juice from the cooler and popped the cap. "Thanks, Jean. We couldn't have done it without the buckets you loaned us."

Jean flicked her hand in the air like it was nothing. Both women would have the day imprinted on their brains for life but wouldn't speak of it again. They'd done what was needed at the time and were ready to move on.

The apple juice slid down Nell's throat. She was thirstier than she'd realized. She downed the entire bottle and scanned the store unsuccessfully for a recycling bin.

Roger stopped pacing at the end of the aisle. "You going to pay for that, Nell? It's not free, you know. That apple juice costs two dollars. You can pay Jean at the front counter. Jean can't give away her apple juice, you know, Nell. If she let customers have their drinks and snacks for free she'd never make any money and then the Kwikmart would go out of business and Jean would have no job here and we'd have no store. It's $2, Nell. Plus fifteen percent tax so you'll need precisely two dollars and thirty cents."

Nell pulled change from the zippered pocket of her cycling pants and placed it on the counter along with the empty bottle. "Lucky you have this guy looking out for business, hey Jean?" She motioned with her thumb at Roger, who was halfway up the aisle staring at bags of bread. She walked toward the door. "See ya, Rog."

Roger stepped in front of her but continued staring at the shelves of bread.

"When's your birthday, Nell?"

"April 8. Why?"

"Year of our Lord…" Roger paused.

"1991."

Immediately, Roger blurted out: "Monday's child is fair of face."

Nell's brain raced to catch up. She hadn't known she was born on a Monday but didn't doubt Roger if he said she was. She'd heard the old Mother Goose rhyme but had never applied it to herself. Being fair of face wasn't important to her anyway—she'd rather be called smart or strong than beautiful—plus her nose was too big and her eyes too small for her to be considered traditionally pretty, yet it still made her blush to receive what felt like a compliment. "Thanks, Rog." She reached out to playfully punch his bicep, but he recoiled. Nell waved to Jean and hopped backed on her bike. As she was about to pull out of the Kwikmart's parking lot, a blue Buick was pulling in. The car slowed down and the driver's side window lowered.

"Hey there, Nell, how you keepin'?" Tinker asked her. He kept an arm draped over the top of his steering wheel and idled the engine when he stopped to talk. The rumbling of his Buick bothered her. Was it Cape Breton's idyllic scenery that made it hard for everyone here to remember that air pollution contributed to global warming?

"I'm doing just fine, Tinker. How're you?" She neglected to mention how poorly she'd been sleeping and how heartsick she'd felt since Charlie left. Nell hadn't forgiven Tinker for not saying goodbye to Charlie, nor Charlie for not saying goodbye to his grandpa. Those two. Always finding fresh ways to hurt one another. She'd resolved to stay out of it.

"I'm managing, dear. Florence and I sure miss having you over to the house. Don't be a stranger, you hear? You're still the granddaughter we never had."

"I know, Tinker. Thanks for saying that. I'll come by soon."

She wouldn't. Until she heard from Charlie and they sorted out a few things, she wasn't rushing over there for the third degree.

CHAPTER 6

TINKER STOOD DRUMMING HIS FINGERTIPS ON the Arborite countertop until the kettle reached full boil. He grabbed the teapot off the stove, still a quarter-full with the strong, warm tea he'd brewed at lunch, and emptied it into the sink. Flo hated when he left the old teabags in there, complaining they left brown smudges on the steel, so he fished it out immediately and tossed it in the trash. She'd trained him well. It was a routine he repeated many times each day. Tinker added a splash of milk to his "World's Best Grandpa" mug and sat down at the table with an egg timer to wait out the requisite two minutes for his steeping tea to reach the exact right strength.

He glanced outside to the yard where he'd soon be raking leaves. Having done so every fall for the past fifty-one years, he knew every knoll, squirrel hole, and tree root on the sprawling property. Sure it took a long time to rake, but what did he have but time these days? He was happy to find ways to keep his restless hands occupied, even if the work aggravated his shoulder.

"You're looking at that lawn, aren't you?" Flo asked. She added milk to her own mug and joined him at the table. Tinker nodded. Long ago there'd been a chicken coop on the flat, treeless patch. In winters past, after the foxes raided and the coop was dismantled, he'd stamp down the snow and flood it using the garden hose to make a skating rink for his son, Russell, and later Charlie.

"It's going to be a big job raking this year without Charlie's help," Flo said.

Tinker bristled. He hadn't spoken his grandson's name since Charlie left for Alberta. "I'll manage." The egg timer rang and Tinker fetched the Brown Betty and filled each of their cups. Flo blew on her tea while Tinker started taking slow, loud slurps.

Florence cleared her throat. "Tinker…."

He waited.

"It might be time to start talking about selling this place. It's a lot of upkeep for people our age, and besides, this house has too many rooms for just us two."

Tinker set his mug on the table more forcefully than he intended and some tea jetted over the rim onto the placemat below. "We're not going anywhere. Not yet and not for a long time." How could she even suggest it? "Maybe never. End of discussion."

"Well, hell's bells. Once again, Tinker gets to decide," Flo said. She stood and pushed back her chair, facing Tinker who, seated, was now at her eye level. Flo raised her index finger and pointed it at the bridge of his nose. "Let me remind you this is a marriage, not a dictatorship." She turned on her heels and stomped out of the room, her arms ramrod straight by her sides and her hands clenched in tight fists. Tinker was again alone with his sour mood until the ringing of the phone interrupted his thoughts.

"Florence? You answering that?" Tinker hollered after the fourth ring. She didn't respond and the ringing continued. He begrudgingly stood up and went to the wall where the phone was mounted.

"Hello?"

"Hey there. I'm looking, um, for, um, Alexander Gordon."

This woman's raspy voice wasn't familiar to Tinker. He also wasn't used to people calling him by his given name. He'd been Tinker for so long he often forgot he'd been baptized Alexander.

"What can I do you for?"

"Alexander Gordon? Born in Louisbourg in 1941? Husband to Florence?"

Tinker shuffled his weight back and forth on slippered feet. He wasn't sure whether to answer her. There were a lot of phone scams these days. He didn't want to be suckered.

"Who wants to know?" he asked. The cord on this phone wasn't long enough to allow Tinker to walk over to the table to retrieve his tea and he looked at it longingly. He saw steam rising out of the cup and wanted to enjoy it while it was still piping hot.

"You don't know me, Mr. Gordon. I'm Courtney. A former friend of Russell's." A long silence followed.

"A friend of my son's? What's your name again?"

"Courtney. I met Russell in Alberta. I live in Toronto now—that's where I'm calling from—but I spent a few years in the oil patch trying to find my fortune."

Tinker scowled at Courtney's mention of Alberta and a small muscle spasm in his face set his eye to twitching. "Go on."

"Well, that didn't work out great, but I did find Russell. He and I were friends when I lived out there. More than friends, actually...Russell and I were a couple."

"That so," Tinker said. He'd never really thought about his son having a social life in Alberta. In his mind it was the place Russell went to work and the place where he died in that jeezly accident. That Russell might have done anything else in the years he was out there hadn't dawned on Tinker. His closed his eyes to see if that would eliminate the twitch but it just felt more pronounced. "Okay, Courtney, what can I do you for? Is this a social call or have you got a reason for phoning here today out of the blue?"

"I know it's awkward, me calling like this. I wish I could be talking to you in person, but I don't have a way to get to Cape Breton."

Tinker suspected she was stalling. The steam stopped rising off his tea and he cursed silently that he'd now have to drink it tepid. "You've got my full attention. Get whatever it is off your chest. I'm all ears."

"Well, it's news I'm hoping you and your wife will welcome. I'm calling to tell you that you have a grandson and—"

Tinker cut her off mid-sentence. "That's not news. We know we do. Charlie. We raised him after Russell died."

"Right. Well, you have another grandson. Charlie's half-brother. Russell and me had a baby together, a boy. He's almost five years old now."

Tinker glanced around the room, then walked to where he could peer down the hallway, trying to spot Florence. She'd vanished. The nerve of her.

"Come again? Did you say you and Russell had a baby together? That can't be right. He never mentioned it."

Courtney repeated it a second, and then a third time, her voice more insistent with each telling.

Tinker couldn't take it in. As Courtney rambled on, he put his hand over the receiver and bellowed, "Florence!" How dare she take off and leave him dealing with this all by himself? His thoughts swirled and he didn't know how he was supposed to react.

"A grandson? And you're sure this boy is our blood, Courtney? Russell didn't tell us he had another baby. He didn't even tell us about you."

The tone of Courtney's voice carried an edge now. "Well, Russell and me never got married or nothing, but the boy is your grandson. We can do a DNA test to prove it if you don't believe me."

Was she calling his bluff? He'd order the DNA test if it came to that, no problem. "Perhaps we should do just that." His eye twitched even more rapidly.

There were several seconds of silence before Courtney spoke. "First I'd like you to meet him. It's time Alex got to know some of his people."

Alex? He and this boy, whoever he was, shared a name. Well, that could be rigged or a coincidence. Tinker looked out his back window and finally saw Florence. She must have slipped out the side door and was now standing on a stepstool, pulling sheets off the clothesline like it was a regular old day. The season for line-dried sheets was coming to an end, but it wasn't over just yet. Yes, soon they'd come out of the dryer smelling of Bounce sheets, but on this day he'd still be able to crawl into bed and envelope himself in the real fresh-air smell. Still, he suspected that tonight he'd not get the peaceful slumber he was used to having on laundry days. Florence was making her way toward the back door now with the basket under her arm.

"I'm going to need your number, Courtney. This is a lot to take in. Let me talk to my wife."

They hung up and Tinker returned to his tea, which was now cold.

"I saw you on the phone, Tink. Who called?" Florence asked.

Tinker looked up at his wife's face and his eye twitch suddenly stopped. He sighed. "Put the laundry down. We need to talk."

COURTNEY HUNG UP THE PHONE, lit a cigarette, and inhaled deeply. At least she hadn't lost her cool too badly. She'd order the damn DNA test if they made her, but if these people needed proof that Alex was their grandson, they'd have to foot the bill. God, it was so insulting. Step one was to get him in front of their faces. They'd love him—everyone who met him did, how could they not? She'd messed up a lot of things in her life, but Alex was the thing she was proudest of. He was sweet and smart, and had given her so much joy and purpose that now it was her turn to give something to him in return. Something that was rightfully his. He would not be denied.

CHAPTER 7

Syria, October 2014

S AMI PICKED UP HIS FORCEPS AND PLUCKED shrapnel bits out of the baby's cheek. The boy wailed and wriggled, but his mother clamped her hands tightly over each of his ears to steady his small head as he lay on the table.

"There now, just one more piece and I'll be all finished," Sami said. The shrapnel fragment clinked as he dropped it into a metal bowl. Sami peered inside the wound, dabbing at the fresh blood with his last roll of gauze to make sure no debris remained embedded in the tissue. He nodded and smiled wanly at the mother. "Great job. We're almost finished. I just need to stitch the wound." His suture supply was also dangerously low, but until it was completely depleted he'd keep using it. This baby was fortunate the shrapnel hadn't blown into his eye and blinded him, but also unfortunate for being born at the start of a civil war. Sami looked at his small patient and tried not to let the savagery unnerve him. He needed a steady hand for stitching.

Half an hour earlier, he'd been about to leave work when the frantic woman had rushed in with her son. Amira would be worried because he'd arrive home late, but how could he say no to a pair of ordinary Syrians caught in the crossfire? Becoming a doctor was the most important achievement of Sami's life. He'd pledged to help others to the best of his abilities and he honoured that pledge daily. As long as patients needed him, he'd be there for them. Amira would have to accept that.

He deftly wove the needle in and out of the baby's cheek. It took all his nerves and concentration not to flinch when yet another bomb dropped in the distance. The nightly raid had started early; it was only dusk. When he was finished, the woman held a small brown paper bag in her outstretched arm. Sami gently pushed it back at her. "It's not necessary," he protested.

"I insist," she replied.

Sami knew for dignity's sake she wanted to pay him so he accepted the bag and peered inside. His eyes widened when he saw three plums, four oranges, and a lemon.

"It's very little. I wish I had more to offer."

Fresh produce was rare and he practically salivated at the sight of the fruit. He knew it would also curry favour with Amira. "On the contrary, these beauties are more precious than jewels. I thank you sincerely." He escorted her out the door, locking it behind them.

Sami walked home quickly with downcast eyes so he could watch where he stepped. The soles of his shoes had thinned and a sharp object could easily puncture them and set off a chain of events leading to tetanus or even blood poisoning. He'd seen it happen. With so many buildings flattened, he felt exposed traversing the city streets and quickened his pace. There were a few scraggly trees left, but they offered no real protection, and the remaining street lamps that still lined this main boulevard hadn't been lit in six months. A group of young men hurried past him in the opposite direction, and though they gave him no real reason to fear them, he was relieved when they passed by without incident. He couldn't be sure anymore who were friends and who were enemies. The war had blurred all the lines.

The sun dropped behind the horizon and precious few minutes of partial light remained. He heard the crunching of track tires and looked up as a tank rolled by. It was the only moving vehicle he had seen for many blocks. He shuddered as it moved past him and then involuntarily running toward home. The sky was black by the time he reached his street.

"Hello?" he called out, stepping into the unlit foyer. He knew the apartment's layout well but in the darkness took small, cautious steps toward the hall with his arms extended.

He barely heard the opening of Yasmine's bedroom door and the quiet click of it closing. "Shush. The children are sleeping," Amira responded in a loud whisper. He was relieved to hear her voice even if he couldn't make out her face. "It took me an hour to settle them with all the explosions tonight."

Sami sought the comfort of Amira's lovely face. He felt in his pocket for his penlight, clicked it on, and swept it in the direction of her voice. "Good evening, my love."

Amira had dark circles around her eyes and a furrowed brow, but her lips were full and her cheekbones were even more prominent now that her face was thinner. After a day filled with ugliness, her beauty struck him like a blow. He handed her the paper bag.

"What's this? Penance for being late?" she asked, opening it and peering inside. Her frown turned into a smile as she lifted out the lemon. "Ah—fresh lemon juice for our olives. Okay, I forgive you." She moved slowly in the dark toward the kitchen.

He followed her there and fumbled in a drawer where he knew there was a pack of matches. He struck one and lit a tealight he set on the counter as Amira carefully set the lemon in a cupboard. He cut a plum roughly in half, spooned out the seed, and handed the larger piece to Amira. She closed her eyes as she sucked the sweet fruit by candlelight. A drop of juice leaked from the corner of her mouth onto her chin, an image so sensual Sami felt aroused.

As they climbed into bed, the air strikes intensified. Sami judged them to be at least several blocks away. Their immediate neighbourhood had been luckier than some others. Sami thought about reaching out for Amira, but with the war raging around them, intimacy felt off-limits. Instead, he and Amira lay on their sides facing one another in parallel lines, not touching, listening to voices shouting in the distance and the vases rattle on their living room shelves. In the morning they'd have to straighten the framed art hanging on their walls.

"Can we talk about what we're still doing here in this god-forsaken war?" Amira's voice pierced the darkness.

"You know my position," he said calmly, wanting to avoid a fight. "What would happen to everyone left behind if all the health-care workers left? Even the aid agencies are afraid to come to Aleppo now. The city needs doctors."

"I know it does. And I love that you're able to be of service. But," Amira paused, her voice sharper now, "I'm asking you not to risk your family's safety to help random strangers."

Sami sighed. He knew Amira wasn't cruel, and it was tension that made her speak sometimes as though he didn't consider her or the children's well-being important. Nothing could be further from the truth. But the sick and injured people he treated weren't any less deserving. They were all humans. "I have to help them, Amira. It's my duty."

Amira sighed and turned away from him, but when the building was rattled by another distant impact, she whimpered and backed up into Sami's warm chest, letting him wrap his arms around her. He pulled her into his body until they spooned, and as their minds and bodies finally relaxed, they both drifted off to sleep.

CHAPTER 8

Cape Breton, October 2014

CATRIONA SWALLOWED THE LAST BITE OF HER chicken, wiped her mouth, and stood up from the table. Her dad was out of town and thirty tense minutes alone with her mom, getting grilled about what all of her friends were doing next year, was all she could take. She wanted to be alone now. She swivelled on sock feet to turn and face the door to the hallway.

"Help clear the dishes before disappearing, miss," her mom said. "And a 'thank you for supper' wouldn't kill you, either."

Catriona doubled back and opened the dishwasher, mumbling, "Thanks."

"Finish your university applications?" Her mom carried dishes from the table to counter.

Catriona groaned and loaded the plates into the dishwasher. She knew her mom had been tiptoeing around this conversation while they were eating. She tried to be cool, but she was so obvious about stuff like this.

"Yep. Finished today," Catriona lied. She'd downloaded some applications off various websites but hadn't gotten farther than that. Had her mom been snooping on her laptop?

She put the last glass in the dishwasher and stood straight, her hands on her hips. "Can I be done? I need to go study for my test."

Her mom ignored her request. "Want me to proofread those applications before you send them?"

"Nah. I'm good. Stop being such a helicopter parent, Mom." Catriona went to the fridge and opened the door so the air inside might cool off her reddening face.

"Close that door. You're wasting energy. And if you haven't actually started filling them out, there's no time like the present." Her mom swung the dishwasher door shut and the cutlery rattled inside.

Catriona turned her back to the fridge and they faced one another across the kitchen's island. "Oh my God, Mom, get off my freakin' back!" Catriona stormed off to her bedroom. "It's my life. Let me live it!" she yelled before slamming the door, flopping facedown on her bed, and pounding her legs and fists on her mattress.

God, this year sucked. Her marks had slipped from straight As to a B average, everyone was hooking up except her, and it was all she could do not to bite the head off the next person who asked her what her plans were for next year. She'd tried meditation, yoga, and even smoking weed, but nothing helped her relax. She was constantly unsettled and jittery. It was draining. She went to the bathroom, dropped a bath bomb into the tub, and filled it with water, but she was restless even when lying in the fizzy pink water and afterward tossed around on top of her bed.

Hours later, Catriona stood on a stage staring at three doors. She twirled her straight brown hair with her index finger and pushed her glasses up higher on the bridge of her nose.

"Which door will it be, Catriona: door one, door two, or door three?" the game show host asked with a forced smile. A spark flew off one of his gleaming white teeth and she heard it make a high-pitched "ping" sound. "These are the doors to your future. Choose carefully so you can live out the rest of your life in the most fulfilling way possible."

They were identical plain grey doors. Catriona rolled her eyes at the game show host so hard that when the camera zoomed in for a close-up of her face, all that was visible to the television audience were the white parts of her eyes ribboned with red spider veins.

"I'd like to peek behind each of the doors, please."

"Sorry, Catriona. The rules don't allow it. But I can give you a hint, sweetheart. One door will take you off Cape Breton for school and then work and you'll never move back. One door will keep you here on the Island working at bingo indefinitely and growing more and more afraid of ever leaving. And the third is a trick door with more doors behind it. It leads to more choices about what to study, where to live, who to love…." The sound of corn popping interrupted the host. "Time is almost up, Catriona. What will it be?"

The studio audience started shouting. "Door one!" "Choose door three!" "Two two two!"

Catriona wanted all the noise to stop. The popcorn sound continued and the doors began to tremble.

"You have to choose. Choose now. Now!" The game show host was no longer smiling. His face was mere centimetres from Catriona's own and he was staring at her with glowing green eyes. Spittle flew from his mouth and landed on Catriona's shirt.

Pop-pop-pop-pop-pop. The grey doors exploded and shards of wood spewed all over the stage. Catriona bolted up in bed and threw off the covers. She reached for her iPhone on her bedside table and slid the power button off so the alarm would stop popping. She'd have to hurry or she'd miss the school bus.

"HEY," SEAMUS SAID. "'SUP?"

Catriona looked up from her social studies book and saw her friend weaving his way up the aisle toward her like he did every school day. There were no surprises on this route. Same kids, same shuffle and slump into the same seats, same lingering smell of Axe Body Spray and cherry lip balm, day after day. Catriona's was a window seat close to the front. When she leaned back she felt the familiar ragged crack in the backrest scratch her spine. The only mystery for Catriona each day on the bus ride was what everyone would be wearing.

"Study for the test?" Catriona gestured at her ragged social studies book as Seamus slid into the seat next to her. They were learning about the Middle East, and the long, complicated history of conflict there. It sounded like a hot mess, especially right now in Syria with air raids and innocent people being bombed and fleeing their homes. She thought talking over a few of the key points might help her cram, especially since she hadn't studied last night like she should have. She pulled out her recipe cards to review.

"Study? You know me, right? I'm a straight-C student. Why change now?" Seamus started scrolling through texts on his phone. Catriona, suddenly embarrassed by her tidy printing, lowered the cards onto her lap and laid her hands over them. After a few minutes of her and Seamus not talking, she got over herself and started reviewing them. Reading while the bus bumped along the road sometimes nauseated her, but she had to try. Since they'd consolidated high schools, the Falkirk Cove kids now had to ride fifty minutes each way back and forth to school. With focus, she could get a lot of studying done, but today she was struggling to concentrate.

Seamus tucked his phone into his pocket and Catriona could feel his eyes on her. "You wanna come to my hockey game this Saturday night, Cat? Lots of kids from school will be there. We'll probably hit up a party afterwards."

"Sorry, wish I could. I'm working at bingo." She was happy to have an excuse that was at least true.

The school bus hit a pothole and Catriona's body butted against his. Seamus grinned. "Suit yourself. Will I see you at the dance on Friday?"

She and Seamus had been buddies forever, but lately there was some awkwardness between them. He'd never asked her on a date, but would mention these group things and say that she could come along. She wasn't really one for hanging around in a pack, and plus, she was an awkward dancer, even more so since she'd had a late (and hopefully final) growth spurt and was a lanky five-foot, ten inches tall. She'd practiced dancing in front of a mirror recently and concluded that she looked like one of those inflated air tube people that dealerships had on their car lots, bending and flopping erratically in the wind.

"Maybe."

Seamus shrugged and put in his earbuds.

She felt squirmy. Even though she didn't want to do the things Seamus suggested, she didn't want him to stop asking her. That would be even worse. She yanked out one of his earbuds. "Have lunch with me today?"

"You bet." He gave a lopsided grin that made one dimple appear, and reinserted the earbud.

Catriona stared at the water spots on the bus's window as the familiar scenery rolled by in a blur. A barn. An abandoned house. A field of cows.

Would she miss them if she left? She wasn't sure. Many people here said you had to leave Cape Breton to get training and experience, while others insisted that keeping young people at home was the community's best chance at recovering. In her lifetime more people had moved away from Falkirk Cove than into it, and there was a real possibility that one day the town might only be a memory. Maybe even in Catriona's lifetime. It was still on Catriona's mind as she made her way into school.

CHAPTER 9

Cape Breton, November 2014

NELL SPRAYED VINEGAR ON THE GLASS COUNTER-top and reached for the paper towel. It squeaked as she rubbed away the fingerprints and dust, which was temporarily satisfying, though the smell made her crave salt-and-vinegar chips. She caught her own reflection in the glass and it made her think of Roger blurting out, "Monday's child is fair of face." What a laugh. She'd been called pleasant-looking and fresh-faced before, but not pretty. She'd never worn make-up other than lipstick, her dark blond hair was usually in a ponytail, and she had a bulge on the bridge of her nose, the result of a break she suffered when the boom on her sailboat swung into her face one gusty day out on Bras d'Or Lake. She'd been surprised and flattered when handsome Charlie Gordon started paying attention to her. Lots of girls had crushes on Charlie, but he chose her. Maybe it was her confidence or athleticism that was attractive? She also smiled widely and often, which lit up her eyes and showed off her straight white teeth. She'd had other suitors at university, guys and girls, but her heart still belonged to Charlie and always would. It was he who made her laugh with his silly dances, who held her for a whole weekend when her family's cocker spaniel died, who'd sprung to his feet, fist pumped, and yelled "Wahoo!" when she crossed the stage with her degree last spring.

She'd already mopped the floor and restocked all the Ashley MacIsaac CDs this morning. Her shifts were dragging now that it was November and the start of the slow season. She yearned to be putting her environmental science degree to use but this was the best job she could find here. The pinging of her cellphone broke her thoughts. She reached into her pocket to see who was texting her.

"What's shakin', bacon?" There was an emoji of bacon strips instead of the word.

Charlie. Finally Charlie. A flood of anger mixed with relief overtook her and she grabbed the glass countertop she'd just cleaned, adding fresh fingerprints to the formerly spotless surface. She took a deep breath and made herself wait a few seconds before replying. Charlie didn't need to know how eager she was to communicate with him. She'd never been clingy and didn't want to be now.

"It's strange here w/out U but I'm managing. Can U call me? I want to hear all about Alberta," she texted.

"Sorry luv, can't call now. Just on a short break @ work. I'm at Tim Horton's."

A text while he waited in line for coffee? This was the extent of his efforts at communicating?

"Right. Well, R U happy there? R U safe?" she typed with her thumbs.

"Yes & yes. Gotta go, almost @ the counter. Can U drop by 2 C my grandparents? They keep asking after U. TTYL."

Nell stared at her phone screen waiting for more, but it remained black. So Charlie had been in touch with Tinker and Flo, but not her. TTYL…talk to you later? Later when? She wanted to ask but also wanted to show restraint. She was a strong, independent woman, she reminded herself, not a whiny, needy girlfriend.

"Sure. Call soon, K?" she typed. She resisted adding a heart emoji at the end.

"Yup, promise. XOXO. Love you lots."

Nell put her phone back into her apron pocket and sat on a stool, gazing out at the parking lot. Two cars with Maine license plates were pulling in. She walked to the front door, relaxed her face, plastered on her winning smile, and welcomed the customers as they entered.

FLO SAT AT THE KITCHEN table, pen in hand. A blank notepad lay in front of her, but she didn't know where to begin. She wrote "To Do" at the top left and underlined it. There was much to prepare for this party and many expenses to incur, but she didn't mind. If ever there was a reason to celebrate, this was it. A new grandson! Her life had been filled with so many goodbyes and so few welcome homes. She planned to invite the whole community around to meet this boy and his mother, Courtney. It would be the soothing balm Tinker and she needed to ease the pain of Charlie's departure.

She hadn't yet broken it to Tinker about the party, but she knew how to manage him—she'd been doing it for most of her life. Plus she'd already scored one small victory when she'd persuaded Tinker to buy both Courtney and Alex plane tickets from Toronto to Sydney, despite his grumbling about the price. Being married to Tinker hadn't always been easy, but Flo knew he was like a beetle. A hard shell protected his inner self. When flipped over on his back, he needed someone to come along to right him, and for more than half a century now that someone had been her.

Choose a location.

Invite friends.

Order a cake.

Hire musicians.

Flo worked on her list until she heard Tinker's Buick roll into the driveway, and put down her pen.

"Florence, you home?" he asked upon entering.

"In here." She got up and poured water into the kettle. All news, good, bad, or indifferent, was better digested with a cup of tea. She loved her custom kitchen, handmade for her by Tinker with its low counters and cupboards so she could easily reach her things. She grabbed them each mugs and plated a couple of oatcakes she'd baked that morning as the kettle whistled.

Tinker took his usual seat facing the glass door to the back porch that overlooked their large yard. "What've you been doing, dear?" he asked her.

Flo sat across from Tinker and feigned nonchalance. "Planning a little shindig. Seeing as we have a new grandson coming to visit, I'd like to show him off a little." Flo kept her voice calm and spoke at a measured pace. She poured their tea.

"You're getting ahead of yourself, Florence. We've never even met these people. How can we be sure he's our own blood?"

Unlike Tinker, Flo had no trouble believing that Russell had fathered another baby and not told them.

"Oh Tink, can't we just be hopeful for once? Accept good news at face value? Why do you have to doubt everyone and everything?" Flo broke her oatcake into small pieces but didn't put any of them into her mouth.

"Because this woman, this Courtney, might be playing us for fools. Maybe she wants our money."

Flo would not let Tinker ruin this with his negativity and doubts. She'd been talking to Courtney on the phone every night. They were sometimes bumpy conversations when Courtney got defensive, but eventually Flo had pried enough details out of her about her relationship with Russell, and where and when they'd met, to feel sure that Courtney was telling the truth. And Flo knew Russell had always been a tomcat, whether Tinker liked to admit it or not. Russell had had a lot of girlfriends and lived pretty loose. Plus there was the matter of the boy's name being Alex, same as Tinker's. Courtney told her Russell had suggested it.

"Why do you always have to be such a doubting Thomas? Let me have this happiness, Tink. I want to be excited about something for once." Flo looked at her husband and placed her tiny soft hand over his large weathered one. Her gold wedding band caught the sun coming in through the window and gleamed. Tinker looked from it into her eyes and sighed. She knew that meant *yes, proceed*.

NELL SAUNTERED OVER TO THE ringing phone. Being bored was making her uncharacteristically lazy. "Celtic Interpretive Centre, how can I help you?"

"Nell, sweetheart, is that you? It's Flo calling."

After those unsettling texts from Charlie, she didn't really want to talk to his grandmother, no matter how lovely Flo was. "Yes, Flo, it's me. It's wonderful to hear your voice. What can I do for you?"

"I'm planning a big party and need a place where I can hold it. Can you check a date for me in your books there? The centre is the perfect spot."

"Certainly, I can do that. What are you celebrating?"

Flo paused. "Our new grandson."

"Come again?"

"I likely should be telling Charlie first, but I can't reach him and I'm just bursting to share the news! We've learned Russell had another baby who now lives in Toronto—Charlie's half-brother. I'm throwing a welcome party when he comes to visit."

Nell dropped the phone on the countertop.

"Nell? Nell? You still on the line, dear?"

She regained composure. "Sure am. What date do you have in mind?"

CHAPTER 10

Syria, November 2014

A MIRA WALKED TOWARD THE OLIVE TREE ON HER balcony with a wicker basket in her hand. Above its strong, twisted trunk the slender branches extended as gracefully as a ballerina's arms. The tree was starting to bear fruit as though to spite the turmoil in the air enveloping it. Amira planned to pick the hard, green olives until they covered the bottom of her basket. She needed to be quick; she felt like she was wearing a target each time she stepped outside, but this should take no longer than fifteen minutes. Then she would go inside and wait at the window with the children for Sami to come home from the office for his midday break.

She tucked her chestnut brown hair behind her ears so it cascaded down her back. Amira considered it her best feature and was proud that it was still lustrous even though she'd been rationing shampoo and was down to using a small dollop once a week. She pulled her pale blue silk hijab up over her head. Although there was a partial wall enclosing her balcony and it was unlikely anyone could see in, it was her habit to cover her head any time she stepped outside. The fabric also offered some protection from the sun and kept dust out of her ears. Washing was a luxury these days given the frequency of power outages and resulting lack of hot water, so she tried to stay as clean as possible. She abhorred being dirty.

The tree sat in an enormous planter and had grown to about eight feet tall, but Amira could still easily reach most of the olives. Though briefly dismayed by the grey dust that dulled the green leaves, she deftly plucked an olive and rolled it around with her fingertips, delighting in its firmness. They'd lost so much recently that even a single olive seemed like a gift now. Raw olives weren't edible, but she'd soak these for seven days, adding precious fresh water daily, before draining and stirring them with salt and a little oil. She'd saved her lemon to squeeze into the olives, and the anticipation of its tart juice on her tongue made her tingle. Olive picking gave her day purpose, and the anticipation of serving her family a bowl of their own olives in a week's time pleased her. They were also down to their final three cans of food and even low on bread, so the olives would offer nourishment.

Their neighbourhood had not been shelled as badly as some other parts of Aleppo where whole streets had been levelled. She wasn't sure why they'd been spared the worst, but that could also mean it was yet to come. Ahmed hadn't been to school in a month and she had both her children now confined with her at home. Electricity was increasingly intermittent and their diesel was gone. As she dropped the olives into her basket, she racked her brain to think of new ways to convince Sami to leave. He'd accepted none of her arguments or pleas about putting family first and was still arguing that patients here needed him. Their circular conversations were getting them nowhere except more estranged from one another. Last night after they rehashed it again, she climbed out of their bed and into Yasmine's, finding comfort in her daughter's sweet breath and cozy body. It was the first time she and Sami had slept apart in their marriage. He had dark circles under his eyes when he entered the kitchen in the morning.

The satisfying sound of the olives rhythmically plopping into the basket like large, intermittent raindrops soothed her nerves temporarily. She glanced around the expansive balcony, trying not to feel depressed by the waterless pedestal fountain, or the loosened and cracked tiles in their patio area where they used to sit and drink tea in the evenings. She found reassurance in her children's faces in the window, but then she thought of Sami at work. He told her his medical clinic wouldn't be targeted. No regime, no matter how evil, would stoop so low, he said, telling her that even in wars some places were invulnerable to attack. Amira was skeptical.

As she stood at the olive tree, a sudden shift in the air gave her pause. Though most birds had by now flown to safer skies, a crow streaked past the clouds overhead, and an inexplicable dread rose up inside Amira. The bird's caw as it flew over her yard sounded to Amira like, "Go! Go! Go!"

A chill crawled up her spine and she dropped the basket, olives spilling onto the hard dry dirt. "Go! Go! Go!" rang in her ears. She stared up at the bird flying north until it was a tiny dot in the sky, then out of view. Amira knew the crow was a harbinger of imminent danger. She'd been patient and deferential long enough and it suddenly became obvious to her that Sami would never leave unless she insisted. If the absence of food, safe shelter, and even hope weren't enough, what would it take? It seemed Sami would be standing alone in the middle of a rubble pile that was once their home and he'd still be saying, "It's not time just yet. Patients need me." Amira knew they had to follow that crow out of this city. Not next week or tomorrow—today. She ran back into the apartment with new resolve. She'd have to be the one to get them out.

"What is it, Mama, what's wrong?" Ahmed asked. Yasmine hid behind his back.

"I must call your father right away. Where's my phone?" Amira scanned the dining table and then ran into the living room, tearing pillows off the couch in her frantic search.

Ahmed handed it to her. Amira hadn't used it in weeks to save battery power and was relieved when she was able to still turn it on and punch in Sami's number. "Sami? You must come home right away. It's urgent."

"Why, my love? It's only one thirty and I still have patients in my waiting room. You know my midday break starts at two," he said.

"Please close early. Now, in fact. I beg you to trust my instincts. Something terrible is about to happen." Her voice trembled. Amira took the phone with her into her bedroom and closed the door so the children wouldn't see her panic. She was close to hyperventilating now and having trouble speaking. "Go! Go! Go!" The crow's squawking echoed in her mind. She paused, trying to regulate her breathing. She put her left hand on her chest to try to calm her heart. Her breasts were swollen and so tender she withdrew her hand.

"Are you still on the line, Amira? Tell me what's going on. What will I tell my waiting patients?"

She didn't mention the crow or her premonition of imminent danger. It seemed absurd even to her although she trusted it. "Tell them… it's an emergency…your family needs you. Please, Sami. I don't ask for much. Do this one thing for me."

Neither spoke for several seconds. Sami heard something in his wife's voice he'd never heard before. An edge, an insistence, and a certainty he couldn't deny. "All right, I'm leaving now."

SAMI HUNG UP.

"I'm sorry everyone, the office is closing right now," he told the crowded waiting room.

The patients, some who had been waiting several hours already, began grumbling and complaining to one another.

"I realize it's inconvenient. I apologize, but you must leave at once. I have an emergency at home. My family needs me," Sami said, ushering them out the door. His staff had been whittled down to one receptionist who eyed Sami in frustration, knowing the patients would make their displeasure clear to her when they returned later.

Sami glanced quickly around at the empty clinic, devoid of potted plants, magazines, medical supplies, and now even people, shaking his head as he locked the door behind him. Amira's hysteria was out of character and he was trying to grasp the reason for it. The nightly air raids were still hours off.

When he was a block away from his practice he heard a whistling sound pierce the air and dove for shelter behind a pile of broken bricks. He looked back in sufficient time to see the first rocket land and rubble fly into the air then crash to the ground in plumes of dust. He shielded his head with his medical bag and muffled his ears with his hands. He tasted grit in his mouth. Was it the cement that fortified his former office? When the explosions stopped he counted to one hundred before opening his eyes, standing up again and assessing the devastation. Most of the block where his clinic had stood was flattened. His medical practice was demolished. It was just past one thirty in the afternoon. Nothing was predictable anymore. How had Amira known?

He heard a person yelling for help somewhere behind him, back in the direction of his practice. In shock, he stumbled forward, away from the voice, toward home. In future days, he'd think of that person he'd forsaken, and wonder if they'd survived.

AMIRA PACED AROUND HER BEDROOM, trying to compose herself. She'd been frustrated and nervous for months but this was different. It was so hard to breathe it was like hands were tightening around her throat. She was terrified yet empowered and saw with a clarity she hadn't had in long time. They'd leave today.

"Amira, where are you?" Sami shouted, bursting through the front door. She and the children ran to him, collapsing into his arms. "We must leave Aleppo, Amira," Sami said. "I don't know how you knew, but the time has come. We'll leave at once." Sami looked at his wife with incredulity, his love and respect mixed with awe and a tiny bit of fear.

"What happened?" Amira was able to take a few deep inhalations now that Sami was home.

"My clinic's been bombed. Our home could be next."

Her instincts had been right. "Children, gather a few things in bags you can carry. We're going on a trip and it's not certain when we'll be back." She forced enthusiasm into her voice. "Pack some clothes. No toys, books, or extras. Just essentials."

Yasmine started clapping and jumping up and down. "We're finally going on our trip. Yay!" she said. "Wait. No toys? None at all?"

Amira nodded and watched her strong-willed daughter stomp off to her room. She glanced back at the wicker basket on the kitchen counter, wondering if she would ever fill it again with olives from her tree. She carefully took the envelope of family photos and inserted it into her beloved Quran, then wrapped the divine book in a piece of white linen and added it gently to the items already in her suitcase. Sami opened his suitcase to discover clothes already packed.

"You did this?" he asked.

Amira was worried he disapproved. "Yes, weeks ago. Just in case, Sami. I hope you're not mad." She approached her husband cautiously and he wrapped his arms around her.

"Mad? I owe you my life and the lives of my employee and waiting patients for making me close the clinic today when I did." He let go of her. "We have to hurry."

Amira helped Yasmine fill her backpack but had to trust Ahmed to look after himself. They all scurried around their home like mice in a maze.

"Ready?" she asked, again pulling up her hijab. "I've got our passports. Do you have money?" Sami nodded, grabbing his medical bag. After eleven years of living here, they were ready to leave in less than eleven minutes. Amira longed to do a final walkthrough but didn't want to waste precious seconds, so she stood at the front door and gazed at her living room and into the distant kitchen. She'd moved from the protection of her parents' home into this one as a naïve young bride, never doubting the privilege and comforts she'd enjoyed her whole life wouldn't continue indefinitely. With her family now by her side, she gathered herself and her meagre belongings and closed the door behind them. Was there even any point locking it? Would they ever return?

They rushed to their car parked in a small lot several blocks away. There were distant sirens wailing and they had to step over scattered bricks and chunks of concrete. "Keep your heads down, children," Amira cautioned, sneaking a few final glimpses of her neighbourhood as she left it. There were blank, expressionless faces in the windows of some buildings on their block. Other windows were missing their glass panes and the black apartment interiors suggested they were empty. The lack of colour anywhere struck Amira. No bright curtains blew in windows, no flowers or grass grew, and cars were parked curbside. Everything was overwhelmingly grey and crumbling. The dust in the air was thick, and Yasmine began to cough as she ran to keep up with her older brother and parents. Amira wished she had some water to offer her daughter but they had to press on. When they got to their car they found it buried under a pile of rubble. The concrete roof above it had caved in. Amira couldn't believe how close the destruction was to their home. "What now?" she asked.

Sami draped his arm around the children and turned them both away from the car. "We walk," he replied. They set off on foot, all muttering prayers to Allah to get them, somehow, out of this warzone and across the border.

CHAPTER 11

Cape Breton, November 2014

TINKER PULLED HIS BUICK INTO THE PARKING LOT, grabbed a fresh toothpick to chew from a packet inside his glove compartment, and began his regular walkabout through the graveyard behind St. Andrew's Church.

He glanced up at the steeple and walked away from it. He hadn't been inside the church in a decade. That he left to Florence, who went weekly and prayed hard enough for the two of them. His church days were over. Tinker's faith had been tested time and time again throughout his life and at some point had simply blown out of him like an exiting nor'easter.

Tinker made a perfunctory stop at his mother's grave. As he laid some pink carnations beside her small headstone, he pictured her pinched face at the window of their small saltbox home in Louisbourg the day of the accident.

His brothers had been at school that long-ago day, so it was only young Tinker and his mother at home when it happened. Tinker, as usual, was tinkering around with his toys, taking them apart then attempting to rebuild them. It was a habit bordering on an obsession that had earned him the nickname Tinker. His mother's days were typically filled with cooking, cleaning, and mending, so her stillness puzzled Tinker. He attempted to fill the silence.

"Chugga chugga chugga chugga chugga chugga chugga chugga CHOOCHOOOOOO!" he yelled, pushing his train engine across the wood floor and bumping it into his mother's Oxfords.

She lifted her foot, annoyed. "Go down to the root cellar and fetch some bread-and-butter pickles, Tinker. I'll serve them with fish for supper," she ordered, and Tinker promptly obeyed. He scoured the shelves of preserves without any luck. When he came up empty handed his mother sent him back into the cellar for another look. Only years later did he realize there had never been pickles there—his mother was merely thinking up ways to keep him out of sight. When no lunch appeared at 11:30, Tinker took his grumbling tummy outside to play in the spitting rain and wind. When his father wasn't home by two o'clock he knew in the pit of his still-empty stomach that something terrible had happened.

They learned that Tinker's father had drowned quickly when his lobster boat overturned. The swell had been strong that day, and despite having lived on the ocean his whole life, like so many other fishermen at that time, he had never learned to swim.

After they buried Tinker's father in Louisbourg, the family had to move to the opposite end of Cape Breton, where his mother, despite only having her grade eleven, got work teaching in the one-room schoolhouse in Falkirk Cove. Tinker later became her pupil, and from the first day he hated calling her Mrs. Gordon and role-playing as her student instead of her son. She wasn't a popular teacher, rarely smiling, meting out lessons and discipline in equal measure, never afraid to drag Tinker or one of his friends by an ear if she found them in the school-yard when they were meant to be behind a desk. To his mother's bitter disappointment, Tinker left school in grade ten and never returned to formal education. He'd found work on various fishing boats and broke his mother's heart when he saved up enough to get his own boat and fishing license. Like his father before him, Tinker never learned to swim.

He chewed his toothpick until it splintered in his mouth and continued on to Russell's grave. Here, he knelt on the dirt, inhaling the scent of damp earth and decay, and pulled a hanky from his pocket. His bad shoulder ached thanks to all the raking he'd just completed, and he'd been unable to find his Percocets in the medicine cabinet. He winced as he lifted his right arm to wipe down the mottled grey granite:

RUSSELL GORDON, 1968–2009,
SON OF FLORENCE & ALEXANDER 'TINKER,' FATHER TO CHARLES.
R.I.P.

He wallowed in his losses for a moment, and then asked himself if he'd really had more than his share in his lifetime or if he was just feeling sorry for himself. Sure, there had been happy moments too—falling in love with Florence, her agreeing to marry him, Russell's birth. But then heartbreak and disappointment inevitably followed. His and Florence's inability to have the big family they'd wanted. Off and on money worries as market prices for fish and seafood fluctuated and catches became less plentiful. Fishing moratoriums and mine closures forcing his brothers and most of his friends off Cape Breton Island for opportunities abroad. And then, worst of all, the accident out west, a freak explosion that sent a fireball straight at his son and fractured Tinker in some fundamental way he'd been unable to repair.

"What day in 1968 was he born?" a voice from behind him asked. Still crouching, Tinker turned around and came face-to-knee with grey sweatpants. He raised his eyes to Roger's face. Roger stared at the treeline.

"Oh, Roger. What's that you asked?"

"What day Russell Gordon was born. Your son. What month it was and what day. That is what I'm asking you, Tinker Gordon."

For such a tall fellow, Roger sure had soft footsteps. Tinker hadn't heard him approaching. Today was the anniversary of his Russell's passing—five long years since they got the call that his son had been killed. Though Tinker kept waiting, he hadn't recovered from it yet, and maybe he never would. Maybe he didn't want to. He dreaded this day every year, and now that it was upon him, he'd planned on keeping to himself. It took him a few seconds to adjust to having company.

"He was born on November 13."

"November 13, 1968, was a Wednesday. Eleventh month, thirteenth day, year of our Lord 1968. Wednesday. Middle of the week. Sometimes known as hump day. Mid-distance from the weekend before it and the weekend after it. Gotta get over the hump of Wednesday to have the majority of your work week behind you."

Roger could have been right about it being a Wednesday. Tinker couldn't remember what day it had been. He remembered being at the hospital in Sydney, the smell of bleach wafting up from the freshly mopped floors as he paced the hallways waiting for a nurse to come tell him whether Florence had birthed a baby girl or boy. He remembered entering the room and getting his first glimpse of Russell in the bassinette, a squinty, brown-haired infant who'd not inherited his own red locks or, hopefully, the quick temper Tinker believed accompanied them. He remembered welling up with hope and happiness, but he didn't remember if it was a Tuesday, a Friday, or a Wednesday.

"You could be right about that, Roger. I can't honestly say I remember." Tinker stood up and felt an unexpected comfort in Roger's presence.

"Wednesday's child is full of woe," Roger said to the sky.

Tinker spat the remaining shards of his toothpick onto the ground.

"That marker over there is for Grace Libbus. Grace was born and died on the same day, March 20, 2007. That would have been a Tuesday, Tinker. Born on a Tuesday, died on a Tuesday. The same Tuesday. Tuesday's child is full of grace, just like her name."

Tinker remembered Grace's passing well. She'd been Bob and Elsie's granddaughter but so briefly, suffocated when her umbilical cord wrapped around her neck during delivery. She would have been Catriona's younger sister.

"That so? How about me? I was born in 1941 on April 10," Tinker said.

Roger crouched down and started peering at a patch of clover growing near Russell's grave. "Thursday."

This one Tinker knew to be true. He remembered his mother telling him he was born on Holy Thursday after evening mass and how she'd missed observing Good Friday that year but was back in church for Sunday's Easter celebrations.

"Thursday's child has far to go," Roger said.

Tinker let that comment hang in the dank late-afternoon air. He'd never journeyed much beyond Cape Breton and didn't expect to. He'd gone almost nowhere, and it suited him fine.

"Put out your hand, Tinker Gordon." He did as Roger told him. Roger pressed something almost weightless into his palm then folded Tinker's fingers over it before he could see what it was. Then he swiftly turned and walked away.

Tinker watched him walk out of the graveyard, past the church, and down the shoulder of the country road. They were three or four kilometres from Roger's house and though it was only four thirty, the mid-November sky was already darkening. But Tinker knew better than to offer him a drive. When he opened his palm, he discovered a four-leaf clover.

CHAPTER 12

Alberta, November 2014

THREE MONTHS INTO HIS NEW JOB, CHARLIE HAD found his groove. The shifts repairing and laying pipe were long and physical, just as he had hoped. He'd caught on quickly and made no major errors, thus earning a shot at overtime shifts. He'd foregone most of his days off to pick up extra work, and if he didn't think about his grandparents, Nell, or life back in Cape Breton, he hardly missed them at all. Out of sight, out of mind was Charlie's plan for staving off homesickness, and it was working—mostly. He hadn't kicked all his bad habits or saved money just yet, but he would in time. Today was payday and he'd deposited it all except three hundred dollars he'd resolved to make last. He tucked three crisp hundred-dollar bills into the back pocket of his jeans and crossed the parking lot.

"C'mon, Charles, it's beer o'clock. Move your ass," his buddy Rex shouted from the window of his pickup truck. They'd just finished a ten-hour shift and had a rare weekend off in front of them.

It never took much coaxing to get Charlie to go out partying. Back in Falkirk Cove there were no bars close by, so he and his friends played rock-paper-scissors to determine who would be designated to drive them back and forth to town for the night, or instead they partied in one another's homes or a boarded-up old house, often crashing there overnight. Here in Fort McMurray everyone could drink as much as they wanted, and there was always a cab to call at the end of the night.

Rex and Charlie grabbed stools at the bar and ordered drafts from the bartender. Charlie noticed a stocky guy in a leather biker jacket with a horseshoe mustache sitting at the opposite end. He locked eyes with Charlie and raised his shot glass, mouthing, "Cheers." Charlie looked away.

Country music poured out of the speakers. Charlie looked down at his dusty workboots, wishing he owned cowboy boots. The styles here were growing on him, but a new wardrobe wasn't cheap. His right upper arm throbbed and he rolled his sleeve up to take a look at his new tattoo. It was a Celtic family knot; interwoven endless paths that Charlie had chosen to represent his infinite love, faith, and loyalty to his family and home. He adored the design and got it to motivate him to stick to his plan of straightening out and manning up for Nell and his grandparents, but right now it was flaking and peeling like an itchy, sore sunburn. It looked glassy and felt tight, but he was told to expect this. He lowered his sleeve and popped a couple of Percocets in his mouth, chasing them with beer.

"Hey, you know the guy down there at the other end of the bar? He's been checking you out. I think he's into you." Rex flicked his head toward the biker.

"Ignore him," Charlie answered.

They ordered a couple of sixteen-ounce rib-eyes with baked potatoes. When the waitress leaned over to set down their plates on the bar they each got a good look at her cleavage down the front of her tight black tank top. Charlie averted his eyes while Rex gave her a big tip with a wink and a smile.

"Looking's free y'know, Charles."

"I told you I have a girl back home. My one true love," Charlie replied.

"Yeah? You never talk about her. She have a name?"

"Nell." Charlie grinned. They were a few beers in and had just done a round of tequila shots. He was starting to have to concentrate on his words so as not to slur his speech. "I don't need to talk about her all the time. We're solid."

"If you say so," Rex replied.

They grabbed pool cues when the table opened and started a game with two guys they'd just met. They went down fifty dollars each when they lost, then another hundred when they tried to win it back in a double-or-nothing rematch. Charlie had already spent two of the three bills in his pocket.

He kept feeling his phone buzzing but ignored it. "I gotta piss," he told Rex, weaving his way to the bathroom. Once there, he pulled out his phone to finally check it. The calls had been from Grandma and Nell. There were texts, too. He scrolled down. Grandma's sweet little face was in a tiny circle on his screen. "Charlie, dear, call me back please. I have news."

Next he saw Nell's face; her blond hair, twinkling eyes, and prominent nose next to an all-caps message, "CALL YOUR GRANDMOTHER. NOW."

Grandma: "Charlie? Charlie? Dang it this texting business. Nell tried showing me how but I don't know if I'm doing it right. Can you see this message, Charlie? Are you there?"

Nell: "Charlie, I don't know what UR up to or why you've been so hard to reach. I respect UR need 4 space. But this is important. Call your grandparents."

He sighed, held himself up with one hand on the bathroom wall, and pointed his penis at the urinal's drain with the other. Once his bladder was empty, he deleted all the texts and felt considerably better. Then he dialled his grandparents' number.

"Hello?" said his grandmother's groggy voice after the fifth ring. Shit. It was three hours later there. That'd make it well past midnight.

"Sorry, Grandma," he said in the soberest voice he could muster. "I just finished work. Whazzup?"

"There's been a development here. Brace yourself, Charlie: We've learned your dad had a baby he never told any of us about. That makes you a big brother."

Charlie's head started spinning. He asked his grandmother to repeat what she'd just said. A brother? Couldn't be. Were the booze and Percocets playing tricks on him? Someone opened the door to the men's bathroom. He turned around and came face-to-face with the horseshoe mustache. "Grandma, I gotta go. I'll call you tomorrow," he said, hanging up on her. He tried to dart around the man's broad shoulders but could only manage to weave and lurch. The man was built like a refrigerator and was just as heavy. He grabbed Charlie, put him in a headlock, and pressed his fingers into Charlie's sore tattoo. Charlie winced in pain and felt the steak climb back up his throat. The man's baritone voice, carried on breath smelling of warm onions and tequila, poured into Charlie's ear: "Charlie, we meet again. You avoiding me?"

Charlie squirmed but the man's grip was too tight. "Lemme go," Charlie slurred.

"I don't think so, fuckface. You and me got some unfinished business. Got my money?"

"Some of it." Still in the headlock, he managed to pull his remaining hundred-dollar bill from his pocket and hold it out in front of him.

"You're shittin' me, right? Where's the rest?"

Charlie tried to think of an excuse. His brain was too compromised to come up with anything believable. His regular Charlie-charm routine didn't seem likely to work on this guy. "You'll get it soon. Really soon." He tried to regain his footing, but the man held him off balance, then quickly pulled back his arm and decked Charlie with an uppercut to the chin. The last thing Charlie heard before hitting the cold tile floor and losing consciousness was his jaw snapping shut and teeth smashing together.

The man kicked him in his ribs on the way out, before plucking the hundred-dollar bill off the floor.

CHAPTER 13

Syria, November 2014

"MAMA, PAPA, CAN I PAT THE KITTY?" YASMINE asked. The mangy orange cat stood at her feet meowing. It was emaciated and missing an eye, but Yasmine didn't care. It was the first living thing the family had seen thus far on their journey. Behind it a small fire burned in the street with no one trying to extinguish it.

"No, Yaya. Keep walking," Sami said, urging his daughter on. "Don't touch the cat. It could make you sick."

Amira kept her head mostly down but snuck the occasional peek, scanning about for other people or any signs of human activity. There were none. This part of the city felt deserted, like a post-apocalyptic wasteland.

She felt overexposed and anxious walking through the crumbling streets of bombed-out Aleppo after having spent all her time recently inside her home and yard. As badly as she'd wanted to leave her home, now Amira missed it.

Streets once so familiar were almost unrecognizable. She couldn't quite process what had happened to her historic, beloved city. She knew battles between government forces and insurgents had razed great swaths of its ancient history—she'd heard the Great Mosque of Aleppo, once so elegant and inviting with its marble-floored, arched hallways, was now a crumpled heap of stones—but they'd also decimated symbols of day-to-day life. Tree-lined boulevards where people lived and worked and markets where they'd come to socialize and trade for centuries simply no longer existed.

Amira's eyes travelled up crumbling pillars that once supported a second storey. There were no walls, and whoever lived or worked here was likely long gone. Poking out of the ground next to it, exposed steel beams bent at odd angles were oxidizing and turning green. The sidewalks and streets were littered with rubble, and Amira felt the dirt accumulating on her body.

Sami looked less shocked, but he'd been walking to and from his office and making occasional house calls to patients unable to travel there. He'd known how grim it was first hand.

"You never told me things were this bad." Amira hadn't meant to sound accusatory.

"Was I supposed to come home from work and tell you and the children over dinner about almost getting lost because the streets I've walked along my whole adult life had become so unfamiliar to me?"

They passed a white wall with black lettering spray-painted on it. "The Islamic caliphate on behalf of the prophet," Ahmed read aloud.

"Keep walking, Ahmed," Amira said. The message made it clear ISIS had been here. What prophet did ISIS think it served? Islam was not about destruction and death.

Yasmine would have no understanding of what was going on, but Amira worried Ahmed might be old enough to process some of this. Still, how does one explain a civil war, or any war for that matter, to children? There's simply no sense to be made of it.

Before long Yasmine began dragging her small feet and whimpering. Her coughing continued, prompting Sami to retrieve a white mask from his doctor's bag. He double-knotted the straps at the back of her head so it fit snugly over her mouth and nose. He then picked up Yasmine and her backpack in his left arm, slung his doctor's bag over his right arm, and dragged his wheeled suitcase through the rubble with his right hand. Amira held Ahmed's hand as they each carried their own suitcases in their outside hands. She frequently stopped to pat their passports, all four of which she'd wrapped securely into a moneybelt that was tight around her waist, hidden under her skirt.

"Mama, Papa, how much farther?" Ahmed asked after hours of walking. Amira saw fatigue on his dusty brown face and suspected he was hungry. She'd lost touch with her own appetite. There were very few other people walking on the streets, and only occasionally did a car or minivan drive by. But Amira didn't know whom they could trust and they pressed forward without a clear plan.

"We have to ask for help, Amira. We cannot make it to the border on foot," Sami said. Amira nodded. Fleeing like common criminals making a getaway, begging for a ride from strangers. How quickly and drastically their status had dropped even since that morning. Sami began trying to wave down each vehicle that drove by. Most drivers didn't make eye contact. None slowed down.

Amira's anxiety rose as the sun began to set. It was nighttime when the fighting intensified. They had no shelter and no plan. Amira and the children sat on a curb and watched until Sami was finally able to get the driver of a black van to stop. After a short conversation, he waved the family over.

"This gentleman will take us to the Turkish border. Quickly, get in the car," Sami said, sliding open the panel door. Amira had no idea what their transaction had involved or how much cash they could afford to pay, but she knew he wasn't driving them for nothing. Capitalism reigned even in times of war, maybe more so. The underground economy was strong. She also accepted that at this point, they had no other options. They piled into the van.

"There's a case of water on the floor. Each of you may take one bottle. Only one," the driver said.

"Thank you, friend. We are very grateful," said Sami, tipping a bottle into Yasmine's mouth before drinking deeply from his own.

The van left Aleppo, and because the highway was now closed, they drove along a potholed farming route. The children dozed off but Amira was completely alert. She told herself to focus on the road ahead; there was no point in looking back, the past was the past, but restraint failed her. Amira glanced over her shoulder behind the van. The city was so much flatter than it once had been, and almost completely dark due to the power outage. Stars were starting to emerge in the sky. It briefly looked peaceful, if decayed. Then a faint grumbling from above became louder.

"Look!" Ahmed, now roused, stretched his skinny arm in the direction of three planes beelining in a triangular formation toward the opposite corner of the city. The family watched the planes drop a series of barrel bombs and heard the shrapnel spew as they hit the ground.

"Children, look at me," Amira said urgently. She put a hand on the back of each of their heads, feeling the heat coming off Ahmed's coarse hair and Yasmine's glossy curls. She drew their heads down to her lap, and pressed a hand against their exposed ears. The ground tremors radiated as far as the road under their van. Amira snapped her head forward. She hadn't known one could grieve a place but she regarded Aleppo now like a dying person on no form of life support. Its pulse was slipping away.

THE VAN PULLED OFF TO the side of the road. Amira looked around to see a barren wasteland. If there were any landmarks here she might once have recognized, they were now demolished.

"This is as far as I take you. From here you'll walk about twenty minutes to the trenches. After you get through those you'll see a barbed-wire fence and the Bab al-Hawa checkpoint. There will be armed soldiers there."

Amira could hardly believe her ears. She was dragging her children directly to confront soldiers with guns. What kind of mother was she? She'd promised her children when they were infants that she'd love and protect them forever.

"Approach one of the soldiers with your hands up," the driver continued. "Identify yourselves as refugees. Plead with them and, *insha'Allah*, they will let you in."

Amira and Sami pulled their suitcases and the children, now whimpering from fatigue, out into the night air. Sami pulled out his wallet and counted out several bills before handing them to the driver. They watched him turn and drive away. There may have been others doing the same trek in the darkness, but with such limited visibility they saw no one and heard no voices, just explosions behind them. Sami extracted the penlight from his pocket and projected a narrow triangle of yellow light onto the hard ground at their feet. They took cautious, measured steps, following each short stretch lit by the penlight before casting it a little farther into their future.

They held on to one another and wove a trail over hard and unforgiving ground toward the border. The sound of barking dogs grew louder. What was supposed to be twenty minutes felt like hours before they saw the fence under glowing lights in the distance. There was a trench to cross before they reached it, as their driver had warned them, but he hadn't told them it was filled with loose and sharp rocks.

"Yasmine, Ahmed, look how close we are now," Sami said with forced gaiety. "Our adventure will soon be over."

The children, looking dazed and fatigued in his penlight, were silent.

They all began scrambling down with their hands and feet, pulling their belongings along with them. Sami managed to carry Yasmine and drag a suitcase while Amira held Ahmed's hand.

"Mama!" he cried out as his hand slipped out of Amira's and he stumbled to the bottom.

"Be brave, Ahmed, I'll catch up." The sharp rocks under her feet slowed her down and she heard her skirt rip when it caught a sharp edge. It was a long few seconds before she grabbed Ahmed again. The indignity of it all enraged Amira, but she turned her anger into the energy she needed to pull Ahmed and herself up the incline while Sami carried Yasmine. Amira smoothed her skirt and hijab when they all reached the top, panting. Her hands felt sticky, and under Sami's penlight she saw both she and Ahmed were streaked with blood from Ahmed's palms. He'd cut them in his fall and not told her. She pulled him close and whispered, "My poor child." She pointed the beam of light at Sami, who was still holding Yasmine and looked ready to collapse.

"Ready?" he asked. Amira took a deep breath and nodded.

They approached a shelter no larger than a tin hut and patrolled by an armed guard and stepped under the glare of the light from a nearby lamppost.

"Stop! Not one step farther. Identify yourselves," the guard shouted in stilted and heavily accented Arabic, pointing a rifle at them. He was poised and ready, having heard them scuffling through the ditch.

Sami urged them to drop their bags and raise their hands high above their heads. "Please, have mercy. We are a family of innocent refugees fleeing Aleppo. We mean nobody harm. We are seeking asylum," he said.

Amira was unable to speak. All her bravado from earlier in the day had drained away. When the guard lowered his rifle, Amira dropped her arms and pulled her children close to her. Sami and the guard spoke to one another in hushed tones before he stepped back and spoke to them all.

"Open your bags," he barked at the family, flicking his square chin up as he spoke.

They opened their suitcases and backpacks and he rifled through them, mussing up the neatly organized clothes Amira had packed. He spat on the ground then picked up her Quran. Amira held her breath, but he flipped through and then returned it gently without damaging it. "Papers?" he said in a deep and condescending voice. Amira fumbled around her waist and unlatched the moneybelt, pulling out their passports with trembling hands. The guard snatched them and retreated into his post.

"What's happening, Mama?" Yasmine asked.

"He's learning who we are before letting us into Turkey," Amira said. He'd have to admit them...wouldn't he? There was no turning back now.

He emerged from the hut with a second guard who held their passports. They spoke to one another in Turkish, and then turned to the family with blank faces. Amira felt every muscle in her body clench.

"You're through."

A wail travelled up Amira's throat and her knees buckled. From the ground, she extended her arms. "Praise Allah."

CHAPTER 14

Cape Breton, November 2014

NELL TOOK A DEEP BREATH AT THE FRONT DOOR before pushing it open. This afternoon she would be a guest at a party here at the Celtic Interpretive Centre. Normally that would please her, to be served rather than serving others, to be out socializing and celebrating, but today's circumstances made it so awkward she'd hesitated about coming at all. In the end her curiosity won out. She blotted her lipstick on a tissue, tucked her hair behind her ears, and walked into the reception room.

"Hi Flo," Nell said, bending to give Charlie's tiny grandmother a hug. "Everything looks so lovely." Flo was wearing a periwinkle blue angora sweater set that complemented her complexion and brought out the blue in her eyes. Nell had never seen Flo looking so lovely, nor so jittery. "Thanks for inviting me."

"Nell, I hate to complain, but the tea biscuits aren't flaky. And the chowder's too thick with potatoes."

"They'll never be as good as yours. I warned you about that when you booked," Nell said with a wink. Most people praised the food at the Celtic Interpretive Centre, but Flo's standards were predictably sky high. As sweet as she was, she could be hard to please.

"At least the balloons and welcome banner are a nice touch, don't you think?"

Nell nodded. She'd always found the Gordons tight with their money, but Flo had spared no expense today. "I do. Where's Tinker?"

"On his way. He went to Sydney to pick up Courtney and Alex. Their plane landed at three."

Nell could not imagine a more uncomfortable car ride. Tinker was not someone she'd send out in a welcoming party. Other guests arrived and Flo scurried off to greet them. Nell turned to mingle.

"Hi! You're Catriona, right, Dr. Libbus's granddaughter? I'm Nell. Maybe you remember me from rescuing the whales?"

Catriona was swirling ice cubes around in a plastic glass filled with ginger ale. She looked up but her shoulders remained slumped forward. "Yeah, I'll never forget that day. It's nice to see you again."

"You too. Good turnout, right?"

"For sure. It seems the whole community's been rounded up, 'cept Charlie, of course. You must be disappointed."

Nell tried to play it cool but her face gave her away. She'd been holding out faint hope he'd surprise everyone and show up at this party to meet his half-brother; it would be a Charlie sort of thing to do to make a big entrance. Now she knew for sure that was a fantasy. What a fool she'd been.

Catriona sensed her gaffe. "You didn't know? Geez, sorry. I thought he was your boyfriend. I'm such a boob. Forgive me?"

Nell reassured her it was fine. She saw Roger pacing the room and excused herself to step in his path.

"Seventy-six. There are seventy-six square tiles on this floor. Thirty-eight are grey. Thirty-eight are green. Only fifty-eight are visible to the naked eye."

"Is that so, Roger?"

Concern coloured his face. "Area calculations lead me to conclude there are another twelve under the bar and sixteen under the raised stage, Nell. Unless the builders knew those areas of the floor would be invisible and didn't waste precious tiles there that would never be seen. Do you think that happened, Nell? Do you?"

Nell shrugged. She noticed he wasn't wearing his regular grey sweatsuit but had on a stiff white dress shirt and a tie that was knotted high up on his neck, obscuring his Adam's apple. A bit of toilet paper stuck to a shaving nick on his cheek. Roger was muttering as he gathered his thoughts. Then he spoke up. "But you work here, don't you, Nell-Fair-of-Face? Could you ask? Could you find out for me?"

Nell agreed to ask, though she wasn't sure what value such information could possibly hold for Roger. Maybe that wasn't the point.

Bob walked by, arm in arm with his wife, Elsie. When she was a child, Nell had known him as Dr. Libbus, the town physician. She'd later gotten to know him as Bob, Tinker's closest friend. Like her, he'd left Cape Breton to attend university and had come back. Nell thought she'd like to speak with him about life as a come-back-from-away. Coming home was harder than she'd imagined it would be. She hadn't expected to feel so isolated in her own community. She'd felt like a hayseed when she first moved to Halifax, and now, back in Falkirk Cove, she felt like a city mouse stuck in the country. Nell maneuvered through people, but before she could reach Bob the front door opened and a gust of cold air blew in. There, in the door's frame, stood Tinker. Next to him was a tall, thin woman in a black leather bomber jacket, and a redheaded boy who barely reached her waist, pressing his body tightly against her legs.

Nell watched Flo rush toward the door but stop short of reaching it for a good head-to-toe look at the boy. His mother pushed him forward. He had nervous green eyes underneath eyebrows so pale they were barely visible on his face. His freckles were so numerous it was impossible to say where each one started or stopped. They spread right across his lips, which he chewed. Nell moved around to his side. His red hair shot up at strange angles, especially around his protruding ears and again at the back of his head where it appeared he had a double-crown. His narrow shoulders sloped forward as he stood there in the doorway, dressed in a long-sleeved T-rex shirt and jeans.

"You must be Alex. I'm Flo, but when you're ready, hon, you can call me Grandma," Flo said in a cracking voice. Tears pooled precariously in the corners of her eyes.

"Okay. Thanks," he mumbled.

"And you must be Courtney," Flo said, approaching her with open arms. Courtney backed up and extended her hand. They shook awkwardly.

Nell waited her turn, and then approached and introduced herself to the newcomers too. Her sharp nose caught a whiff of perfume and spearmint gum off Courtney, and she was struck by how cold, dry, and slender Courtney's hand felt in her own. Nell felt for her. Falkirk Cove was a friendly place on the surface, but true acceptance here had to be earned.

TINKER WALKED AWAY FROM FLO, Courtney, and Alex and toward the bar. Though he was usually a teetotaller, on this day he needed liquid courage. Being courteous to Courtney and his supposed grandson during the ninety-minute drive from the Sydney airport had worn him out, and he was glad now to be among people who accepted him for the curmudgeon he was.

"Whisky, rocks," he said to the bartender, easing onto a barstool.

The bartender poured from a bottle of Glen Breton and slid the glass toward Tinker. He lurched forward when a hand slapped him from behind. "Love of God, that's my bad shoulder you just walloped." He twisted to see his oldest friend in the world beside him and felt relieved for the first time that day. "What's the big idea, Bob?"

"I can't let you skulk over here by yourself. You've a room full of guests to entertain." Bob smirked.

Tinker wanted no part of this party. "Florence'll have my head if I don't do the rounds." He made no move to get up off his stool. He followed Bob's gaze to Flo, who was talking to Roger now while Courtney chewed her fingernails. He'd taken an instant dislike to her. The boy just puzzled him. Tinker couldn't remember how to talk to a kid that age. And Alex was funny looking.

"You know that kid is the spit of you as a boy, right?" Bob was clearly enjoying this.

Tinker bristled. Courtney's deep and gravelly laugh pierced the room. In their car ride she'd laughed a few times, even when Tinker wasn't saying anything funny: once when they were talking about Russell, like his life was a joke. Tinker finished his whisky and indicated to the bartender with two raised fingers that he'd like another.

The band started setting up on stage. Two fiddlers, a father-and-son duo Tinker had seen many times, picked up their bows and a woman sat at the piano. They started playing "Beautiful Lake Ainslie," a lilting tune that usually helped Tinker relax but wasn't working its magic today. Not only had Flo used his credit card to buy plane tickets for Courtney and Alex, she'd spared no expense for this party—and what for? They didn't know this Courtney woman or her son, and it wasn't their job to feed and entertain the whole town. Besides, no matter how much entertainment, food, decorations, and friends Flo had managed to pack in here, it could never be complete without Russell and Charlie.

CHAPTER 15

Alberta, November 2014

CHARLIE SMASHED TWO PILLS ONTO HIS KITCHEN counter with the back of his spoon, swept the powder into his glass, and sipped his dinner through a thick bubble-tea straw, telling himself he'd never take chewing for granted again. (He would.) His jaw was still wired shut, but at least he was out of the hospital and recovering at home. The doctors said he was lucky the break was clean and he didn't need surgery to reset his jaw. The police said he was lucky his assailant didn't have a gun or a knife. Rex said he was lucky he didn't bust his perfect nose or screw up his handsome face too badly. But Charlie didn't feel lucky—far from it.

In the two weeks since the attack his swollen cheeks and neck had been a kaleidoscope of colours: black, blue, green, yellow, brown. The pain was bearable with narcotics, but the bleeding, drooling, and his inability to speak wore him down. He was also recovering from two cracked ribs. He'd lost two weeks' wages and his return to work was a ways off yet. If he were able to open his mouth, he'd scream about it.

He set down the glass on the floor and stared at it from the couch. Usually he made fruit and yogurt smoothies, but today he'd tried something new and puréed boiled chicken and brown rice with stock in a blender. How did babies tolerate this crap? It looked like vomit and tasted only marginally better. But he sunk into his battered old couch feeling some relief, knowing the drugs would soon take the edge off the ever-present throbbing in his face and neck.

The wires would come out in four weeks, and then he'd need to have his broken and cracked teeth assessed. He was scared to see the inside of his mouth and flat-out dreaded going to the dentist, not to mention the bill that would follow. He hadn't been in his job long enough to qualify for dental benefits, so it would all come out of his own pockets, which weren't deep to begin with. He stared at the chunky beige mush in his glass on the floor and though he knew he needed the calories, he couldn't bring himself to take another sip.

When he was a boy and sick, his grandmother doted on him even more than usual. She'd flatten ginger ale to calm his stomach and cook chicken soup from scratch when he had a cold. If he tried hard, he could almost smell that soup simmering now.

Jeopardy played on the TV, but Charlie only glanced at it occasionally. "I'll take Speedy Recovery for five hundred, Alex," he said in his mind, unable to vocalize the words. He lay in his basement apartment staring at the ceiling, noticing bubbling and peeling caused by water damage that some previous tenant had unsuccessfully tried to mask with paint. There were a hundred other things he could and should be doing but wasn't. The police were urging him to come down to the station with more details about the guy from the bar, but there was zero chance Charlie would do that. There were also messages from his grandma and Nell, old friends and new—voice mails, texts, and emails, asking him over and over again what was going on. It seemed everyone in his life thought he owed them an explanation—everyone except his grandpa, who was the only person not trying to reach him. For once Grandpa's icing him out was a blessing. As for the rest of them, Charlie could see no reason to burden anyone with his problems. There wasn't anything they could do to help, anyway. He'd gotten himself into this mess, and he'd get himself out. In two quick texts to Nell and his grandma he said he was just taking some time for himself to mull over the news of his new brother and they shouldn't worry about him. Honestly, he was doing them a favour. And besides, Alex could be a shiny new distraction if they needed one.

His doorbell rang. He ignored it. A fist pounded.

"Charles, you there? Let me in."

Charlie slowly rose off the couch and walked up the stairs to open the door for Rex. He appreciated the visit, but being unable to talk made it hard to entertain.

"Hey, bro. You feeling any better?" Rex asked, pushing a bag of groceries towards Charlie. Charlie shrugged and took the bag into the kitchen. He emptied bananas, oatmeal, and homogenized milk onto his countertop. He wanted to say thanks for the baby food, but the words were literally trapped in his mouth. He grabbed a notepad and pen and joined Rex in the living room.

Wanna watch the hockey game? he wrote.

"How about we watch it at the bar? Get you out of this rabbit hole for a few hours." Rex looked at him hopefully. Charlie couldn't blame him for asking. His sheets and towels hadn't been laundered in weeks, and his hamper was overflowing with dirty clothes. His apartment must have smelled funky, and he supposed he did too. They both needed airing out.

Not ready yet, Charlie wrote in reply. He hadn't been able to shave, was still bruised, and couldn't remember the last time he'd showered. The days were a blur. He slept fitfully and at random hours, waking each time his body rolled onto his left side where he'd been kicked in the ribs, or when his face made contact with the pillow. But it wasn't just his appearance, pain, and fatigue keeping him at home. He didn't want to run into horseshoe mustache again.

"Okay man, I'll lay off for now. But soon I'm going to get you off your lazy ass," Rex said, grabbing the remote and settling into Charlie's sole armchair.

They watched the game in mostly companionable silence interrupted only by the sound of Rex chewing Doritos and cheering when the Oilers scored. At the end of the second period, Charlie reached for the notepad. *Thanks for the food, bro. I'll pay you back. Promise.*

"Don't worry about that now," Rex said. "I need you recovered and back at work ASAP. Just get better. The new guys aren't as chill as you." Rex and Charlie were hired and trained together, but already they'd been displaced as the junior guys on the crew by even newer hires.

Can you do me one more solid? Fill a Rx? Charlie wrote. He pulled a fresh prescription from his pocket, and then shook the empty pill bottle on his side table.

"What the fuck, man? That was supposed to last you four to six weeks. You need to slow down, Charles. That shit's addictive."

Please? The pain's brutal, Charlie wrote. He tilted his head to the side, widened his eyes as big as they'd go, and pressed the palms of his hands together in front of his chest like he was praying. He desperately needed more narcotics.

"I'd whack you upside the head if you weren't already so pathetic," Rex replied. "All right. I'll fill it tomorrow."

Thx man. You're a good friend, he wrote, and then laid the notepad and pen on the floor. The narcotics had kicked in. Charlie relaxed into his couch for the third period.

CHAPTER 16

Turkey, November 2014

YASMINE DIDN'T GO TO SCHOOL IN THE REFUGEE camp. When she and Mama walked Ahmed there, she got to peek inside at the rows of desks.

"What's school like, Ahmed?" she asked her brother after his first day at Al Salam School.

"It's hard, Yaya. There's no time for playing. We have to concentrate on the lessons. Plus it's cold and we have to read books together two or three at a time because the library is so small."

A library? Friends? It sounded fantastic to Yasmine. But the school at Reyhanli Refugee Camp was overcrowded already and besides, she was too young. Yasmine was five, or "only five" as her mother liked to say. (Five wasn't a small number! Her hand looked like it had many fingers attached to it. And once a long time ago in Aleppo when it was her fifth birthday, she'd eaten five kibbeh balls and they made her tummy very full.)

Instead of going to school, she mostly stayed inside her family's tent with her mother. They'd go to the latrine or line up at the water spigot or for their food rations, but after that Amira always hurried them back to their tent without stopping to talk to anyone. Yasmine wanted to ask her mother why she wasn't friendlier but didn't want to upset her. Mama was probably just shy, but Yasmine wasn't shy. She liked meeting new people and they liked her.

When they first came to Turkey and began living at the camp, staying inside the tent was fine even though they had no toys or books. They'd make up their own games. Yasmine and Mama would play house, pretending they were princesses and their tent was a palace. They'd sing while they tidied up, and then Yasmine would crawl in her mother's lap and they'd talk about which tasselled silk gowns they would wear that day (always purple for Yasmine) and what colour jewels they'd like in their crowns.

When Ahmed got home from school he would sometimes play with her, too. She'd often hide under the blankets when she knew he was coming and he'd look for her, calling out, "Yaya, where are you?" Their tent was small and she was always hiding in the same place, but Ahmed was so silly he'd lift up the floor cushions and look for her there first. Then sometimes he'd lie on top of her and say, "I can't find my sister anywhere. Has anyone seen her? I better lie down and have a nap. I'll look for her again later once I'm rested." Yasmine would squeal because she was right there underneath him. If Papa were home, he'd caution Ahmed not to squish her but Yasmine never minded.

But lately staying in the tent with her mother while Ahmed went to school hadn't been good. Her mother didn't want to play the pretend-palace game anymore, and Yasmine wasn't allowed to crawl on her lap now. "You're too big," her mother told her while holding her own lower back. They didn't talk about pretty clothes and jewelry. Her mother tidied up by herself now without singing. She had always been quiet when she was praying, but now that quietness lasted for long stretches even after her prayers ended.

It was also cold outside, and some days Yasmine found it hurt to breathe. Papa said it was dust getting into her lungs and when that happened it was better not to walk around camp because her asthma would get worse. Today she wanted to get up and walk Ahmed to school so she could see the students and desks and dream about sitting at her own desk some day. She would be a star student who listened to the kind teacher and worked hard and earned lots of gold-star stickers. But this morning her body wouldn't stop shivering.

"Stay in bed, I insist," her mother said. Yasmine tried to sit up but was weak and her shaking got worse. Amira piled all their blankets and even two coats on top of Yasmine. They were heavy, and Yasmine opened her mouth to object, but then reconsidered when she saw the tension in her mother's face.

Ahmed whispered in her ear on his way out. "Look around you, Yaya, and find five good things. That's what I do when I'm sad or sick and it always makes me feel better."

He left and Yasmine looked around the tent. First, she noticed their water jugs were full, so she'd be able to get a quick drink if her coughing started again. That was good. Second, she had new-to-her sneakers and had learned to tie the pink shoelaces. Third, her mother, whose back was to her, wasn't wearing a hijab and Yasmine admired her pretty hair. Hmmm. What else. She hugged a ball of socks she pretended was a teddy bear. The socks could be fourth. This game was getting hard. She scanned around for a fifth good thing but fell asleep before settling on anything.

Now, she lay awake under the weight of the covers and tried to imagine what Ahmed was learning at school. Was he writing stories or making art? Counting to high numbers? Talking with his friends in other languages? She missed playing school with Ahmed the way they used to in Aleppo.

AHMED HELD FOUR COLOURED PENCILS tightly in his hand. His new school, *Al Salam,* or Peace School, was at the centre of the Reyhanli Refugee Camp. Today's assignment was to draw a picture of the thing that made him happiest. His pencils hovered over the page while he thought of his options: books, soccer, the spice stores at the old souk in Aleppo, visits from his grandparents who always brought gifts, climbing trees.

"What's the matter, Ahmed?" His teacher, Ms. Hussain, spoke in Arabic as she paused at his desk. Though they were in Turkey now, the dominant language spoken throughout Reyhanli Camp, populated as it was by Syrians, was Arabic.

"I can't decide what to draw. Can you please tell me what my picture should be?" Ahmed answered.

"But I don't know what makes you happiest. Only you know that," Ms. Hussain said. "Knowing what makes you happy is important, Ahmed. You can only find happiness when you know what it is you are seeking. Think about what thing makes you smile the widest. Take a few more minutes and then begin, please. Other students are waiting for their turn to use those coloured pencils." She moved on. Because Ahmed was new Ms. Hussain was giving him extra attention, but that would be short-lived. New students arrived at Al Salam School every week, and the class bulged with almost fifty students. Soon Ms. Hussain would have to close enrollment.

Ahmed picked up a brown pencil and began outlining his family. He filled in the background and focused on adding details. Passing the pencils to the child next to him, he felt pleased with how it had turned out and put it in the plastic grocery bag he used as a school satchel to take home to show his family. He was looking forward to his language lessons next. Ms. Hussain had been a pharmacist in Canada before returning to her native Turkey to help the refugees here, and she was teaching them to speak both rudimentary Turkish and English. She praised Ahmed's aptitude for learning new words, and the attention pleased and motivated him to try hard and take chances. Too bad no one else in his family spoke Turkish or English so he could practice at home. He especially enjoyed the challenge of English and training his throat to make smooth new sounds.

The next hour flew by, and soon Ms. Hussain was dismissing them.

"Goodbye, Ms. Hussain," he said in stilted English when school was dismissed. He pointed to his bag and said slowly, "Hap-py...pic-ture."

"Show me." She smiled when Ahmed showed her what he'd sketched. "Goodbye, Ahmed. See you tomorrow."

Ahmed would have liked to stay longer, but students came to Al Salam in two weekday shifts so the maximum number could be educated in the space. He was elbow-to-elbow with other students but his parents told him he was fortunate to even go to school and he shouldn't complain about the crowding or lack of heat. Lately he'd been so cold at school in the mornings it was hard to grip his pencil.

Ahmed began his walk back to his family's temporary shelter in one of the thousands of white tents erected in parallel lines at Reyhanli Camp. His mother and sister had walked with him to school at first and picked him up, too, but today Yasmine wasn't well and Mama made him walk alone.

"Sixteen, seventeen, eighteen..." Ahmed quietly counted each tent he passed. He had done the same thing on his way to school, counting twenty-seven tents plus one right turn and one left turn between his home and school. It was his plan for finding his family's tent after school amidst the sea of identical dusty white tents.

"Watch out!" A soccer ball thumped Ahmed's back just as he heard the warning. He stumbled forward on the rutted, hard-packed dirt lane but managed not to fall. For this he was grateful, as he was trying hard to keep his clothes clean. Laundry was an onerous task here, one that made his mother grumpy since she washed it all by hand. Their water came from a central spigot their whole row of tents shared, and accessing it wasn't always easy—nor was there always supply. Sometimes the water tank ran dry and it would be hours or even days before a truck came to refill it. His mother had said several times already that one of the things she missed most was a washing machine. If she were to draw her own happiness picture, Ahmed imagined she'd draw a house with appliances in it.

"Is this yours?" he asked, turning around with the soccer ball in his hands to face a boy who looked to be about ten, like himself, standing about three tents' distance away. The boy's face was dirty and the knees of his pants were threadbare.

"Yes. Kick it back?" the boy replied, his face breaking into a smile.

Ahmed dropped and kicked the black and white ball, noticing it was low on air. The boy ran towards it and, to Ahmed's surprise, kicked it back to him. Ahmed placed his plastic grocery bag on the ground underneath a rock to prevent it from blowing away as he got into the passing game. The land here was entirely flat and barren, providing few obstacles along the laneway save for older children on their way to school for the second shift. Adults also walked up and down the lane without smiling, their faces less carefree than those of the children in the refugee camp.

"I'm Ahmed. What's your name?" Their passing game had taken them up and down several laneways now and around a few corners where fraying and tautly pulled ropes anchored the tents into the hard earth. Ahmed had to pay attention not to trip on them but the other boy moved deftly around obstacles with light steps. He was a natural athlete.

"Abdo." He picked up the soccer ball. "I gotta go home now. I've got chores. Want to play again tomorrow?"

"Sure, after school. How come you're not in my class, Abdo?"

"I don't go to school. There's too much to do at home. I'll meet you there when you're done though. See ya, Ahmed."

Ahmed watched his new friend leave and, despite the chill in the air, he had a warm feeling in his body. He hadn't had a friend in a long time. If he'd known this was going to happen today, he might have made it the subject of his happiness drawing. His footsteps felt lighter as he set off for his family's tent. The drab camp even looked a little brighter despite the overcast sky. He tried counting again but couldn't remember at what number he'd previously stopped. Twenty? Twenty-one? It probably didn't matter anyway, he reasoned; he was no longer where he'd been standing when Abdo's ball first hit him. He was properly lost. Ahmed walked up lanes searching for any familiar landmarks. There were none. The warm feeling left his body and he began noticing his hunger, too.

He kept walking, trying to retrace his steps. His breaths quickened but he didn't panic. Ahmed had taken much scarier journeys than this one in his life. The night he and his family fled Syria and crossed the border into Turkey, for example. If he was brave enough to get through that, he could surely manage this. He stopped walking aimlessly and looked up. It was time to think. He gazed all around, searching for clues. In the distance he saw a line of laundry hanging between two tents. He remembered the same pants and shirts flapping back and forth above his and Abdo's heads as they ran and kicked the ball. He walked until he was underneath the line and looked around again, now spotting his plastic grocery bag on the ground a ways off. With relief he moved the rock that was anchoring it and picked it up, back where he started, and walked to his family's tent.

When he got there he opened the flap, excited to tell his mother about his day at school and his new friend.

"Ahmed, where have you been?" Amira snapped at him. Yasmine was lying on a mattress and coughing behind her.

"I was playing soccer with—" Ahmed began, but Amira interrupted him.

"Soccer? I told you to come straight home from school. Don't make me worry like that."

Ahmed then remembered that his father was not around that day. He had left camp to treat patients in a nearby village. He'd done this a few times before and, though he'd always returned safely to Reyhanli

Camp in the late evening, sometimes with food or other small household items his patients had given him, his mother was nervous each time he left. When Ahmed asked her why she didn't want his father seeing patients, she told him it wasn't about that. She admired and resented his dedication to his patients all at the same time. She said Ahmed would understand it better when he was older, but he felt like he was old enough to understand it now. He also liked and hated things at the same time, like this refugee camp.

"I've been holding my bladder for hours, Ahmed. Watch your sister while I go to the latrine."

Yasmine's coughing continued and Ahmed went over to sit on a small yellow pillow beside her mattress. "Hey, Yaya, how are you feeling?" he asked, taking her hand. His sister had been ill often since they fled Syria. Papa said it was the dust and weird temperatures affecting her asthma. Even underneath all their blankets and coats, Yasmine's hand was cold in Ahmed's. "Hey, want to see a picture I drew today?" He reached for his plastic bag and pulled out the happiness drawing. "This is me, this is you, and this is Mama and Papa," he said, pointing at the figures. "You have a little cat like you've always wanted, that grey blob in your arms. And see this flag above our heads? It's a freedom flag. The war is over. There aren't any more bombs in the sky, just birds and the sun. We're all smiling because we can go home. Do you like it?"

"No," Yasmine said, before coughing some more. "I love it."

CHAPTER 17

Cape Breton, December 2014

TINKER CREPT OUT OF BED AS QUIETLY AS HE could so Florence could sleep longer. He'd always gotten up before sunrise; it was the fisherman in him. He no longer had early morning demands on his time, but his body's clock was permanently set to wake him at five o'clock.

The house was still dark as he made his way down the hallway and stepped on something sharp and blurted, "Jesus Murphy!" Good thing Florence was a sound sleeper. He shook his foot and a LEGO block dropped off his sock onto the carpet. Could that kid not learn to put away his toys when he was done playing with them?

He continued into the kitchen to make a Thermos of tea. He'd take it to the wharf as he did every day. Where once he'd enjoy it on his boat as he briskly cleaned the deck and prepared the lines, he now sipped it slowly sitting in his car while thinking about the past. He'd loved fishing—the sense of purpose, the routine, the physicality, the camaraderie with the other men on the wharf—even when the weather was poor or the catch disappointing.

Thermos in hand, Tinker was striding toward the back door when the floor gave way beneath him. He tumbled and fell on his side onto the linoleum, stunned. A plastic yellow dump truck rolled away from him. He was too old for this bullshit. He couldn't move.

"You okay?" Alex peered down at him.

His hip was sore, but he tentatively moved his joints and they all still seemed to work. He hauled himself onto his knees before needing another second of rest.

"What happened?"

"You! You happened. You left toys scattered about and I tripped on them. Put them into the toy box when you're done playing from now on."

Alex's lip quivered and he scurried back to bed, forgetting that he'd gotten up to pee. An hour later Flo would be changing his soiled sheets.

THE MOOSE AMBLED DOWN THE west side of North Mountain. It was simultaneously awkward and graceful. Its enormity lent it a lanky gait, yet it still walked briskly through grasslands and sure-footedly through forests. Its antlers were bare of their velvety coating now, but the moose habitually rubbed them against the trees it passed anyway. It would shed these antlers in January, but for now they could be useful to clear a path or intimidate any potential predators or even fellow moose.

It travelled alone, consuming twigs, leaves, and pondweed. It noted the shift in air temperature and hardening of the earth beneath its hooves of late and was gorging on as much food as it could find to bulk up for winter. Its foraging took it farther and farther down the mountain until it came to a final small embankment. It stumbled, ending up on the road, where it wove a haphazard track along the painted yellow line in the middle like a giant drunk driver trying unsuccessfully to walk straight before being ordered to take a Breathalyzer.

Tinker rounded a blind curve in the road and slammed on the brakes as he came face to face with the moose's large brown eyes and broad snout. He was snapped back into his seat by his seat belt. The moose stared at the car nonplussed, while Tinker's right arm instinctively shot out across the passenger seat, giving Bob a proper thumping on his chest.

"Mother of God, are you okay, Alex?" Tinker shouted, turning toward the seat behind his own. He felt a sharp pain in his chest and tried to slow his breaths. Stress could kill a man his age.

"Yup. Why's that humongous horse on the road? Good thing you didn't hit it."

It was a close call. Cape Breton moose were becoming both plentiful and bolder in recent years. They were spotted on the roads semi-regularly, and hitting one, or swerving off the road to avoid one, had resulted in some bad accidents and more than a few deaths. Tinker said a silent thank you to the God he thought he'd stopped believing in that he wasn't another statistic. Especially not with Bob and Alex in the car. Needing to regroup, he carefully drove around the moose and pulled over to the shoulder, where there was a small parking lot and look-off point.

"That's not a horse Alex, it's a bull moose. Do you see his antlers?" Bob asked, rubbing his sore chest where Tinker had clotheslined him. The moose was leaving the road now, scrambling back up the small embankment and disappearing from sight.

"I did see those! Where'd he go? I want to see him again." Alex had his face pressed up against the window glass.

"Back up the mountain, Alex. Bet you don't see that every day back home in Toronto, do you?" Tinker asked.

"Nope. But I've been to the zoo and saw lots of animals there. Even tigers," Alex replied. "They were in cages." He rebuckled his seat belt and looked ready to resume their journey. Nothing fazed this kid.

They were on a day trip in the Cape Breton Highlands National Park. It had been many years since Tinker had played tour guide, but Flo insisted he take Alex on an adventure, and when Flo had an agenda there was no dissuading her. It was only two days since his fall in the kitchen, when he'd yelled at the boy, and Tinker's hip was still as tender as his relationship with Alex. Tinker knew this outing was Florence's cunning way of trying to turn them into friends. Thankfully he'd convinced Bob to join them. Tinker still felt uncertain about how to talk with a five-year-old boy, or if he even wanted to, so Bob, who loved to both ask and answer questions, could help with that. It actually wasn't proving too difficult yet, as Alex wasn't the kind of child who prattled on endlessly. In fact no one seemed bothered by silent stretches as they drove along the winding Cabot Trail. Now they got out of the car so Tinker could recover his breath and so they could all stretch their legs and look around.

The air was crisp and as fresh as peppermints, and Alex quickly noticed he could see his breath. He found a twig to serve as a cigarette prop, pursed his lips, and exhaled streams of vapour. "Look at me, I'm cool like Mommy."

"Smoking's not cool, Alex. It's a nasty habit that can give you cancer. Put that stick away," Tinker said. Alex dropped it and ground his toe into the tip like he was extinguishing it. Tinker scowled. He and Florence had both quit smoking twenty years ago and had come to despise it. Tinker and Alex regarded one another defiantly.

Bob changed the subject. "People hunt moose here in Cape Breton, Alex. Once upon a time they hunted them until they were all gone."

"They killed them all? That's sad," Alex said.

"Yup. Every last one. But that was almost a hundred years ago."

"How'd they come back?"

Bob said, "That's a great question. The government actually brought in eighteen moose from Alberta in the late 1940s. All the thousands of moose here today, including that bull we just spotted, descended from those eighteen."

"I was born in Alberta," Alex said. "Mommy says it's pretty there with lots of mountains like these. Maybe even bigger than these." He gestured with his small arms at the mountain range stretching far in either direction.

"Alberta, Alberta, Alberta," Tinker mumbled under his breath.

"My dad died there, you know. He exploded."

Tinker tried not to flinch. Since Russell died, talking about him had never been easy. He gazed up at the sky where a cirrus cloud formed a shape resembling a submarine. The leaves were off the trees now, but it was a dry day and still fine for sightseeing.

Bob made eye contact with Tinker, then wandered off to the far end of the parking lot with his binoculars.

Tinker forced himself to break the silence. "Your dad was a good man. He worked hard and helped others. He made Grandma and me laugh every day and he had lots of friends. I think you would've liked him."

Alex pulled a Ziploc baggie of cheddar Goldfish crackers from his pocket. He shoved a handful in his mouth. When he started talking, crumbs the colour of his hair spewed into the air. "Mom put a picture of him and me in my bedroom. I'm tiny and all wrapped up in a blanket. Dad's holding me like a football."

Tinker kept waiting to feel lousy, but he had to admit it was sort of nice to be talking about Russell with this boy. He couldn't resist asking:

"What does your dad look like in the picture?" He was still waiting to be convinced that Alex's dad was indeed Russell, though he was coming around to the idea. He could now see the resemblance between himself and the freckle-faced boy that everyone kept bringing up. He'd decided not to push Courtney to order the DNA test. It just seemed like another expense and not a necessary one.

"Curly brown hair. Smiling. He has a funny scar over his eyebrow like a zipper."

Tinker remembered well the day Russell had cut his face. They'd had so much snow one winter when Russell was about ten that he could climb onto the roof of their garage and slide off. He was playing up there with his friend until the other boy slid his Crazy Carpet right into Russell's face. The snow was quickly soaked red with Russell's blood. It had given Tinker a bad fright to see all that blood, but he pressed a towel to Russell's head and drove him to Bob's house, where Bob stitched him up. It might not have been Bob's best work—the scar was jagged—but then it had been a deep cut that required two levels of stitches, and who was Tinker to criticize? He wasn't a doctor and couldn't even hem pants let alone flesh wounds.

"Did your Mom tell you that you have a brother, too?" Tinker asked.

Alex put the baggie of Goldfish back in his pocket and took out a small box of raisins. He pried them apart one by one and nibbled them with his front teeth. Tinker waited for him to reply.

"No, but Grandma told me. Charlie. I'll meet him another time. He's too busy working right now."

Too busy me arse, Tinker thought. *Too self-absorbed is more like it.*

"Can we go for lunch soon? I'm hungry."

Alex ate a lot for such a little runt. Florence had been fixing him a seemingly endless supply of grilled cheese sandwiches and bowls of cereal since he'd been staying at their house. Courtney had an appetite on her for such a skinny mini, too. They'd been shopping just about every day since their guests arrived. Tinker figured their grocery bill had at least doubled, but managing household expenses was Flo's department and she hadn't said.

Bob wandered back. "Want a turn?" He passed his binoculars to Alex.

Alex awkwardly pressed the large binoculars against his small face. "It's all blurry."

Bob slowly turned the dials. "Say when."

"When! Stop! Everything is so close up. I'm looking for the moose but he's nowhere," Alex said from behind the binoculars.

Bob swivelled Alex's small shoulders so he was gazing south. "What do you see through the binoculars when you look that way? That's where Falkirk Cove is. Can you see your mom or Grandma?"

"Nope. I just see home," Alex replied.

FLO STOOD AT THE WINDOW looking for Tinker's blue Buick. She was anxious for Alex and him to get home from their day trip to the Highlands. She'd been wondering all day how it was going. She was also tired of being trapped alone in the house with Courtney. The awkward-ness between the women was mounting.

Resolving to be a good hostess, Flo forced cheerfulness into her voice and called out, "I'm making myself a cup of tea, Courtney. Will you join me?"

"Sure. I'll have a cup with you," Courtney's gravelly voice replied from the den. "Want some help?" Flo knew Courtney didn't want to get up off the couch and she didn't want her in her kitchen anyway.

"No, stay where you are." Flo walked from the front window to the kitchen, where she plugged in the kettle and readied the tray. Courtney took sugar in her tea, something Flo could not get used to. Everyone she knew had his or her tea—always orange pekoe, nothing fancier—with just a splash of milk. She also laid some homemade tea biscuits and gooseberry jam on a plate and brought the tray into the family room. Flo and Tinker drank their tea at the kitchen table, but Courtney hardly ever moved from the couch. Flo accommodated it, but no one said she had to approve of it.

"Here you go." Flo tried to set it on the oak side table Charlie had made for her in Tinker's workshop, but it was covered with bottles of nail polish, nail polish remover, and soiled cotton balls. That explained the smell of alcohol in the room. Who was Courtney trying to impress here anyway with red fingernails? Once Courtney had swept the items onto her lap and Flo was able to lower the tray, she walked away and opened a window widely to get fresh air moving through the room. Courtney put an extra teaspoon of sugar in her tea when Flo turned back around.

The TV blared, though it was only three o'clock. Flo enjoyed after-noons visiting or, if alone, busying herself in the kitchen or with a book or her knitting. She never turned on the television before the supper-hour news. When, oh when, would Alex and Tinker return? She'd uncovered Charlie's old Snakes and Ladders game in the basement and was hoping to have a game or two with Alex before she had to start supper.

"Flo, can I ask you something?" Courtney said. She brushed biscuit crumbs off the afghan covering her torso onto the floor as she sat up.

Flo resisted the urge to fetch the hand vacuum and suck them up off her clean rug. Instead, she grabbed the remote control and switched off the TV. "There. Much better. Ask away."

"You know Alex and I are booked to go back to Toronto on Saturday."

Flo knew it well. She only had two days left with her new grandson. "Sadly yes. We've sure loved meeting Alex, Courtney. I'll never be able to thank you enough for reaching out to us."

"I'm thankful to you and Tinker for the plane tickets," Courtney said. "And Alex has enjoyed it here. It's nice for him to have family other than me."

Flo glowed. She'd noticed how much Alex had begun opening up in the last couple of days. He was withdrawn when he first arrived and clung pretty close to his mother, but last night he'd let Flo read him a story and tuck him into bed.

"In Toronto it's just him and me. Things can be pretty lonely there, even in a city so big. *Especially* in a city so big."

Flo nodded but could only imagine. She'd lived in rural Cape Breton her entire life. The traffic in Sydney some days overwhelmed her.

"Plus, raising a child there is so expensive. I work full-time and can still only afford to pay the minimum on my credit card bills."

"It sounds like you do work hard, dear." Flo sympathized with her predicament but was also treading carefully.

"But still my paycheque never stretches far enough." Courtney worked as a veterinary assistant. It paid poorly, but she said it was the best job she could find without a university degree.

Flo bit her tongue to stop herself from mentioning Courtney's smok-ing. If she'd quit the dastardly habit, she'd have an extra fifteen dollars a day. "Well you're both welcome back here at any time. No promises, but we might be able to help you out some with travel costs."

Courtney raised her eyebrows with interest. This was going just as she'd hoped.

"Plus we'll talk—every day if you like," Flo continued. "And we can Skip each other. That's when you call over the computer and look at each other at the same time." Flo had recently replaced her old Singer with a computer. It occupied the former sewing table in Charlie's old bedroom.

Courtney laughed. "You mean Skype. Sure, we can do that. But it's not really as good as being in the same house, you know?"

"What are you getting at, Courtney?"

"Well, I have an idea. What if just I went back to Toronto on Saturday? I need to get back before work fires me, but I could leave Alex here with you and Tinker for a little longer. It'd save me the cost of childcare. You could keep him through Christmas if you'd like. That is, if Alex wouldn't be an imposition. What do you say?"

Flo could barely believe this was happening. She wanted to jump up and do a little jig. Charlie had emailed her last night to say he'd be unable to come home for Christmas, and this was just the thing that might help her get over that disappointment.

"I'll have to speak to Tinker, but it's certainly all right with me." Flo had to quell her excitement. She'd never been good at hiding her emotions and was sure Courtney could see that inside she was squealing.

"Excellent," Courtney said, grabbing the remote and turning her attention back to *The Ellen Show*.

The Buick pulled into the driveway and Tinker helped Alex out of his booster seat. They walked in the front door.

"We're home and guess what guess what guess what, Grandma? We saw a moose!" Alex announced as he opened the door. Tinker walked in behind him.

"Oh how exciting," Flo replied. "Was it big?"

"It was ginormous. Where's my mommy?" Alex peeled off his jacket and dropped it on the floor.

Flo picked it up and hung it in the closet without mentioning it. "In the den, dear. Go tell her about the moose you saw. I want to talk to your grandpa for a minute."

COURTNEY, TINKER, AND FLO WERE talking in the kitchen and Alex couldn't hear what they were saying. He recognized when adults were using their inside voices and sensed that this conversation was important, but didn't include him. He decided to go to the backyard. In Toronto, they lived on the eleventh floor of an apartment building. Although he loved pressing the buttons on the elevator, it was also nice to be staying in a house with a big yard like this one. There were lots of trees here and even an old tire swinging on a rope hanging from one of them. He climbed onto the tire and tried to figure out how to make it move.

"Want a push, Alex Gordon? I can push you. I know how, Alex Gordon," a voice asked from behind him. "It's basic physics. For every action there is an equal and opposite reaction. It's Newton's third law."

Alex turned around. "How do you know my name?" he asked the lanky man in the grey sweatsuit who'd approached him with soft steps.

"I was at your welcome party. Did you know there are seventy-six tiles on the floor at the Celtic Interpretive Centre? And six hundred and thirty-four tiles on the roof of your grandparents' house? And ninety-four headstones in the cemetery behind St. Andrew's church?"

"Nope. You're good at counting. You can push me now."

Roger put his hands on Alex's small back and walked forward as far as the rope would allow. When he let go and stepped out of the way, Alex began swinging like a pendulum. His red hair stood up on end, and to stop himself from screaming he squeezed all the muscles in his face together so that his freckles crowded even closer. The people here were all so nice to him; he wasn't ready to go back to Toronto in two days. After a while he stopped swinging and Roger grabbed his shoulders and turned him around and around and around in circles.

Alex looked up. "The rope looks like Twizzlers! Red licorice is my favourite treat."

When Roger let go he untwisted faster and faster and faster. Alex spun around, screamed and laughed. "Again," he requested. Their game continued until Alex's belly began to hurt.

"Want to go look for pinecones?" Alex asked his new friend.

Roger didn't answer but immediately wandered over to a wooded area and began scouring the ground. He removed his ball cap, exposing brown hair sticking out in tufts in different directions. It reminded Alex of his own spiky hair, which his mother was always trying to pat down—sometimes with her spit. Gross! They wandered from tree to tree, picking the best pinecones and putting them in Roger's hat.

"When's your birthday?" Roger asked.

"November eight. I'm five." Alec opened his palm, flashing five fingers, then picked up another pinecone and added it to Roger's hat.

"You were born on a Sunday. The child that is born on the Sabbath day is bonny and blithe, and good and gay."

Alex wrinked his nose and laughed.

As the woods became thicker the pinecones became more plentiful and soon Roger's hat was full. Alex was having the very best day.

"Alex! Alex! Where are you?" he heard in the distance. Uh oh. He recognized his mother's angry voice.

"In here," he shouted. He started to run and Roger trailed him. They emerged from the woods one after the other. Alex wasn't smiling anymore. He knew he was in trouble for wandering off without telling his mom where he was going. That was against the rules. She'd also warned him about stranger danger. His pale face full of fear, he ran right up to her legs and wrapped his arms around her waist. "Here I am. See? I'm fine. Sorry, Mommy. Sorry."

"Who are you?" Courtney shouted at Roger. "Stay away from my son!"

Roger turned on his heels and walked back into the woods.

"Come back here, you! What were you doing alone in the woods with my son? I'm talking to you. Answer me!"

Roger walked faster. Courtney tried to go after him but the dead weight of Alex clutching her legs prevented her from moving any faster than a slow lurch. Flo and Tinker came out their back door just as Roger disappeared out of sight and earshot.

"Who was that creep? What did he want with my boy?" Courtney turned and asked them. Alex hugged her tighter, scared by the panic in his mother's voice.

"Courtney, calm down. That's Roger. He wouldn't hurt a horsefly," Tinker said.

"Don't tell me to calm down. Why were they together in the woods?" Courtney reached into her pocket for her cigarettes, lit one, and inhaled deeply.

Tinker and Courtney stood at the end of the yard facing one another. Tinker's voice was clipped. "You've had a fright, Courtney, but you're overreacting. Roger's no threat."

"Says you." Courtney replied. "I don't want that man coming near my boy. He looks like a perv."

"Come with me, Alex, I've a new game to teach you," Flo said, grabbing him by the hand. "Snakes and Ladders. Would you like to learn?" He shook his head, but Flo leaned down low to Alex's level and asked again in a calm voice. She pried him off Courtney and escorted him into the house.

Tinker made a point of waving his hand in front of his face to deflect the smoke from Courtney's cigarette. "Pervert? You pump them brakes right now, miss. Don't throw accusations like that around about an innocent man you don't even know."

"I know what I saw! The village idiot chasing my boy out of the woods." Courtney dropped her cigarette and ground the butt into the grass with her toe.

"How dare you come here and disrespect our people," Tinker said. He felt sharp pains in his chest for the second time that day.

"I've known creeps in my day. I'm half-tempted to change my mind and take Alex back to Toronto after all."

"Please don't do that." Tinker knew he had to back off if he and Flo were to keep their grandson a while longer.

"Can you promise me you'll keep him safe if I leave him here with you?"

"Yes. You jumped to the wrong conclusion about Roger. Alex'll be completely safe here. You have my word," Tinker said, surprising himself with how badly he wanted the boy to stay.

CHAPTER 18

Alberta, January 2015

"AS WE PREPARE FOR LANDING, PLEASE TAKE YOUR seats and fasten your seat belts. Also make sure your seat backs and folding trays are in their full upright position."

Nell closed her eyes. It had been a long day with three separate flights, layovers, and too much overpriced airport food. Though her feet were sweaty in her boots, her body felt cold, and she wished she hadn't put her jacket in the overhead bin. Worse than physical discomfort, though, was her nervousness. While this trip had seemed like a good idea when she was booking it back in Cape Breton, now that she was almost at her destination she wondered what she'd been thinking. Nell loved science precisely because it was evidence-based, but there was no evidence to indicate that Charlie wanted her to come. He'd never said he did. She had uncharacteristically acted on emotion rather than reason. She clutched her nervous stomach and glanced toward the washroom, regretting she hadn't used it while she was still allowed.

The touchdown was smooth, and as they taxied along the runway to the gate she turned her cellphone on. "Hi, Charlie. Surprise! I'm here in Fort Mac. I'll grab a cab and arrive at your place in an hour or so." She stared at the text and her finger hovered over the send button, then pressed delete instead.

CHARLIE'S JAW WAS HEALING. His surgeon had removed the wires last week so he could open and close his mouth. Movement was coming back slowly and painfully, but it was coming. The bruising and swelling had almost disappeared and Charlie could finally bear to look at his face in the bathroom mirror again.

The razor made a satisfying scratching noise as he dragged it up his cheeks. He was relieved to see even skin tones underneath and that his jaw looked squarish once again. Done, he walked to the kitchen, grabbed all the bags of peas he'd used as ice packs out of the freezer, and threw them in the garbage. The pity party had to end. Yes, he'd had a setback, but it was time to turn things around for himself and to prove to his grandfather and the rest of the world that he could make it here.

He pulled on sweatpants, tightening the drawstring around his thinner waist. He was weaker, too; six weeks lying around would do that to a guy. He wanted to join a gym to start rebuilding his strength but didn't have money for that so was working out a plan to rehabilitate at home. He'd found some half-full paint cans his landlord had left behind in a closet. They'd have to do as weights. It wasn't much, but it was a start. He longed for his grandpa's well-equipped workshop, where he would have been able to build himself a workout bench, but he'd sit on an armchair and curl paint cans instead. What a life.

When he finished three sets of reps on each arm he lay on the floor and began doing push-ups. Twenty, thirty, forty, and then Charlie heard the doorbell. He sat back on his knees, catching his breath before standing up. It had to be either Rex or his landlord and he hoped like hell it was the former, since he owed his landlord rent money. He threw open the door.

Nell. There she stood. The girl he'd fallen in love with in the pews of St. Andrew's Church. His best friend. He stopped breathing for a few seconds. A cab pulled away from the curb.

"Hi, Charlie. Happy New Year." She stood between snowbanks with a small suitcase at her feet. Her hands were stuffed into the pockets of her parka. A striped tuque with a pink pompom on top sat high up on her head, and her dark blond hair fanned out over her shoulders. "So this is Alberta, huh." The tip of her nose was red. Charlie fought the urge to press his own nose against it.

He had trouble speaking. Not only was he out of practice, words escaped him. After the longest ten seconds of his life he managed to get just one out: "Nell." Charlie opened his arms. Nell walked into them and her cheek found the familiar groove in his clavicle, now deeper than before given his new gauntness. They stood there on the porch, on a frigid winter's night, for a full minute before pulling apart.

"Are you going to ask me in? I can't feel my toes."

"In a minute. Look up."

A streak of emerald green cut across the indigo sky. It quivered and widened, then peaked into the shape of a mountain range before arcing.

"Are those the northern lights?" Nell had never seen an aurora before, and its beauty was mesmerizing. She stood still and forgot the discomfort of being cold.

"You bet. Ford McMurray is in the auroral zone. Isn't it something?"

A second green wave appeared and undulated in time with the first. They pulled apart from one another, then rushed together and pushed vertically upward. It was a graceful dance between partners, light waves bouncing off each other, retreating and then rushing back together before merging into one luminous mass of electrons and protons.

Then, as quickly as the light appeared it disappeared, and the sky was black again.

"Where'd it go?" Nell continued staring at they sky, searching.

"It'll come back. It always does. Maybe not tonight, but it'll come back."

Nell righted her head and smiled at Charlie, who escorted her inside.

AFTER SETTING DOWN HER SUITCASE and having a look around, Nell couldn't resist asking any longer. "What happened to your face?"

"It's a long story," Charlie answered.

"I've got time."

He told her about getting decked in the bar. She suspected she wasn't getting the full picture—the guy who'd beat him up must have had provocation, though Charlie made it sound like a random attack—but in due time she hoped to be able to piece together the tale. For now, though, after four months apart, it was enough just to be able to touch him again. They sat on his couch and Nell pulled a Tupperware container from her suitcase. "These are from Flo."

Charlie opened it and peeled back waxed paper to find the marshmallow peanut butter squares he'd loved as a boy. He was still having trouble chewing, but his grandma's thoughtfulness was sweeter to him than any squares.

"How'd you get time off to come here? Don't you have to work?"

"Laid off for the winter. You know how it goes for us Capers."

"That sucks. How'd you scrape together the money for a plane ticket, then?" Charlie was breaking a square into tiny bites and chewing them with his molars. They tasted like home.

"Flo helped me out with the ticket. I'm going to pay her back. She wanted to come too, but we decided I'd make the trip for both of us. Everyone's worried about you, Charlie." Not only did his battered face concern Nell, Charlie was jumpy. He fidgeted constantly, tapping his feet and drumming his hands on his leg.

Charlie tilted forward until his forehead touched hers. He had tried so hard not to think about Nell and his family back home, but seeing her now made him realize how much he missed them all. "How's Grandpa?"

Nell pulled away and shrugged. "I don't really know. He was grumpy at first but now seems to be warming up to Alex. That's something."

"Right. Alex is still there." Charlie just couldn't picture a young boy living with his grandparents. And it had been over a month now.

"His mom's gone, though. Went back to Toronto. No one in Falkirk Cove took to her."

Charlie knew what it was like for your only parent to leave you behind. Poor Alex.

"Charlie, I don't want to presume anything, so I have to ask: is it okay if I stay here with you?" Nell cast her eyes around the apartment; the paint cans propped by an armchair, the overflowing trashcan, the bare beige walls.

"In this shithole?" Charlie was smiling.

"Yeah, imagine. What do you say?"

Relief flooded Charlie's face and once again the words caught in his throat before tumbling out of his injured mouth. "Stay as long as you want. Or as long as you can stand it."

CHAPTER 19

Turkey, January 2015

A MIRA WALKED PAST ROW UPON ROW OF WHITE tents, gripping her cellphone. It had been raining lightly for weeks, so she trod carefully around puddles. Staying clean and dry was difficult at Reyhanli Camp. With few places and opportunities to wash, most children ran around wearing mud-encrusted clothes. For Amira though, after having already lost so much, keeping her pride was essential—and for her, that meant staying presentable. Her parents would have never allowed her to run wild and dirty, nor would she allow her own children to do so, no matter the circumstances.

The damp, chilly air matched her mood. She got to the edge of the camp that was closest to Syria. Her Turkish SIM card usually worked for calls up to ten kilometres inside Syria, and she hoped to reach her parents who still lived in Azaz, just south of the Turkish border.

Amira dialled and waited. The call failed to go through. She made two more attempts. A man walked by smoking a cigarette, and the smell of tobacco revolted her. She turned her back to him as her nausea passed.

"Hello?"

"Mother, hello? Can you hear me? It's Amira." Relief spread through her like butter on toast. She rarely managed to connect with her parents and lived in constant fear that she'd lose contact with them completely.

Reception today was poor so she slipped her phone underneath her black hijab and pressed it directly against her ear to see if that helped.

"Amira, Amira, are you well? I thank Allah every day you're safe at the refugee camp, and I pray every day that He keeps you healthy," her mother said.

"Yes, we are safe now far away from the bombs. The Turks are taking good care of my family and there are humanitarian aid agencies here, too."

"What a relief. I am so glad."

Encouraged, Amira didn't stop exaggerating the positives for her mother's benefit. "And Ahmed goes to a school funded by Canadians. He's doing so well there, Mother. He's learning to speak Turkish and English. You would be proud." The words tumbled out of Amira's mouth in a hurry. She had much to say and little time.

"He's a clever boy. And Sami? Yasmine? How are they?"

Amira didn't want to concern her mother with their news. Yasmine had days where she wheezed constantly and hardly got up from the mattress, and because Sami had started seeing patients in the camp as well as in nearby camps and villages, he was often absent. The tension his career caused still strained their marriage.

"They're fine, too. Yasmine has started going to the nursery tent, where she likes to paint and play with putty. We are all trying to make a life here." She originally thought they'd be at Reyhanli Camp temporarily, but it had already been two months and there was no talk of returning to Syria any time soon—if ever. Amira didn't know what would become of them. She tried to keep her spirits up, but hopelessness loomed always, and lately she'd been turning away from Sami on their mattress and crying herself to sleep. Seeing patients again gave him satisfaction, but her sense of purpose was shaky. Without going to their mosque to pray with others, without an hour here or there on the sofa with a good book, without dressing up and rimming her eyes with kohl to celebrate Eid, without the ability to cook her family their regular foods, it felt like she was only just surviving, not living.

"Tell me about you, Mother. How are you managing?" Amira was nervous to ask. Many of Azaz's residents had fled to Turkey when it came under siege by rebels. Amira had begged her parents many times to leave, but they repeatedly told her they were too old to start their lives over anywhere else. She knew they'd already lived through bombings and massacres, but yet they resolved to stay in Syria even if it meant they would die in this war. Their stubbornness frustrated Amira, but she was raised to be deferential and respectful so hid her feelings from them.

"Your father and I remain alive and uninjured. We are more fortunate than many."

Amira wanted to lighten the mood. "Mother, you would laugh. There are Syrian businesses opening up in the nearby town of Reyhanli. There's a new store called The Revolution Bakery selling Syrian-style bread. Some people even call that area Little Syria." Amira and her mother knew this was both a positive and negative thing. Familiar services and products were a comfort but also made life here more permanent.

The phone kept cutting in and out and they knew they could lose connection at any second. Amira rubbed her free hand in circles over her belly. "Before you go, Mother, I have to ask you again. Please come join us. It's safer here than in Azaz. We have our own family tent. It's not grand, but it can fit two more—you and Father. Say you'll come."

Her mother replied without pause. "We will not, my darling daughter. Give our love to Sami and the children. Call back when you can. *As-Salaam Alaikum.*"

"Bye, Mother." Though she didn't know it at the time, it would be the last time Amira would speak to her mother in Syria.

Tears slid down Amira's face and mixed with raindrops on her walk back to the tent. She composed herself before opening the door flap, wiping her cheeks with a handkerchief. Inside, she found Ahmed sitting on pillows, carefully chopping parsley on a small cutting board. This was a good sign. It meant Sami had bartered medical care for fresh produce with a local farmer or one of the vendors who came to the camp. Amira thanked Ahmed for helping and gave him permission to go find Abdo to play soccer so she could take over. She liked having help but wasn't ready to relinquish her role as homemaker and still wanted to be in charge. She began peeling a cucumber to add to the chopped parsley. A tomato and lettuce leaves were already washed and sitting on the cutting board. These simple vegetables were a bounty. It was a relief to once again be able to access fresh produce occasionally, and though it also shamed her to have more than her neighbours, who were likely eating rationed lentils and rice, she knew she needed the vitamins, particularly now.

"Did you reach your parents?" Sami asked from the mattress, where he was sitting with Yasmine.

"Yes, I spoke to Mother."

"How is she?" Sami had his stethoscope pressed up to his daughter's chest.

Amira, suddenly exhausted, sat on a pillow. "Her voice wavers. She tells me nothing about day-to-day life in Azaz. I know it's dangerous." In fact, she suspected her parents were housebound. She'd heard there were men fighting in the alleys of Azaz and soldiers shooting out of windows, but she didn't want to voice these details in front of Yasmine.

Amira rose again to continue preparing their meal. It was a challenge in this makeshift kitchen to cook food so that it would all be hot at once, and tonight they may eat in stages. But they would be together and eating, Amira reminded herself. Not everyone was so lucky. She filled a pot with water so she could boil rice for kabsa.

"What are we having tonight, Mama?" Yasmine asked.

"Tabbouleh and kabsa." Amira was pleased that her daughter had an appetite today. She wished that she was offering fried kibbeh, too, but such a special dish was just a memory from her former life.

She began mixing spices for the kabsa, measuring and pouring pepper, cloves, cardamom, saffron, cinnamon, and nutmeg into a bowl. As she stirred, the flavours wafted into the air. Suddenly Amira had to vomit. She ran from the tent but only got as far as a nearby ditch before her stomach contents blasted up into her throat and out of her mouth. When she finished, she looked around to see who'd witnessed it. Thankfully it was dinnertime and people were inside their tents preparing or eating their meals. She grabbed the tear-dampened handkerchief from her pocket, wiped her mouth, and returned to their tent, embarrassed but also feeling better.

Sami was smiling weakly as she entered. "Poor Amira. Night sickness is always worse than morning sickness. But this too will pass." He lowered to his knees in front of her and began whispering to her stomach.

"What are you doing, Papa?" Yasmine asked, giggling.

"Telling your future baby brother or sister to be easy on your mother. She's already dealing with enough."

CHAPTER 20

Cape Breton, February 2015

FLO STARED AT THE COMPUTER SCREEN.

"Whatcha doing, Grandma? Playing Minecraft?" Alex was lying on the bed in Charlie's old room, where he'd now been sleeping for more than two months. The things in the room were still mostly Charlie's, but Alex had started adding items of his own. Rocks and shells from the beach, acorns and pinecones, and a postcard of the CN Tower from his mother were now scattered in between Charlie's baseballs and Hardy Boys mysteries on the bookshelf.

"No, I'm going to the bank, if you can believe it." Flo was slowly getting the hang of her new computer, but today she must have made a mistake. She yawned and rubbed her eyes. As much as she loved Alex, caring for him tired her out.

Maybe that had led to a careless banking error. Her and Tinker's bank balance was lower than it had ever been. "This is how people manage their money these days." Flo clicked on the refresh button to see if a new number would appear in the bank balance. It did not. "Do you have a bank account?"

"I don't think so. One of Mommy's boyfriends gave me ten dollars once, but later Mommy made me give it back to her when we needed milk. Want to play Snakes and Ladders?" Alex grabbed the game from the floor.

Flo had a hard time saying no to him. "You bet I do. Why don't you set it up on the kitchen table and I'll be right down." She did some mental math. Courtney and Alex's flights, their party, half of Nell's plane ticket to Alberta, this computer, and higher-than-normal grocery bills had added up—and then there were the secret payments to Charlie. Goodness. The low balance was correct. Tinker would pitch a fit. They lived on a fixed income and couldn't spend extra without consequences. She turned off the computer.

Alex was rolling the dice as soon as she entered the kitchen. "Nine," Alex said, rolling a four and a five and sliding his blue player over nine squares. He landed at the bottom of a ladder. "Up up up up up up I go."

Flo loved hearing him chatter. He was opening up more and more every day. "How will I ever catch up?" she said, grabbing the dice. "Help me add those dots up, now. How many squares should I move?"

"Five plus six equals eleven," Alex answered automatically. "Haha, you're about to land on a snake already." He knew the board by heart. "Can I have a snack?"

Flo went to the fridge and grabbed a block of hard cheddar and an apple. She chose a paring knife from the drawer and began slicing both.

"Grandma, is Mommy ever coming back for me? I miss her."

Flo looked at the knife in her hand and wondered if stabbing herself in the heart with it would be any less painful then coming up with more excuses for Courtney's prolonged absence. She gingerly placed it on the counter and took the plated snacks to Alex.

"Of course she is. Her work's been really busy, that's all. She's been taking extra shifts at the clinic. Aren't you happy she's helping all those sick animals?"

"I guess. I just wish Mommy were here too. Like when I first got here. That was my favourite time." Alex chewed as he talked. "Everyone all together." Apple spittle flew from his mouth and Flo saw masticated orange cheese in his baby teeth. It was adorable.

Tinker walked through the front door, removed his overcoat and boots, and entered the kitchen. "Hello, family," he said, nodding at Flo and laying his hand briefly on Alex's spiky hair. "Is there tea on?" He laid a newspaper on the table next to Alex as Flo rose to plug in the kettle.

Alex slid the newspaper toward himself and stared at it. His mouth started moving. He pointed at the headline. "What's that word?"

"Ceasefire," Tinker answered, his mind on the cup of tea he craved.

"Ceasefire fails in…S….S…S…What's that word?" Alex asked, pointing.

"Syria."

"Ceasefire fails in Syria as war ra-ra-rages on," Alex read aloud.

Flo and Tinker stared at one another. Flo had been reading Dr. Seuss board books with Alex at bedtime, but this level of literacy was beyond rote memorization of *Green Eggs and Ham*. "How'd you do that?" she asked.

"I sounded it out, just like you taught me. What's a ceasefire? Is it like a bonfire? Do you roast marshmallows?" Alex was staring at a picture of a bombed-out building. The caption said it had been a hospital in northern Syria.

"No," Tinker replied, sliding the newspaper across the table where Alex couldn't read any further. "It's when soldiers stop fighting."

"Oh. So they did or they didn't stop fighting?"

"Didn't."

"They kept on fighting? Why?"

"Why indeed," Flo said. "There's a war happening in Syria. It's hard to explain, sweetie. The good news is that we live in Canada, far, far away from that war. Go get the globe and I'll show you how far." She placed a cup of tea in front of Tinker and a juice box in front of Alex's seat, then grabbed her own seat at the table.

Alex retrieved the globe from the den and Flo showed him where they lived, how close by his mom was in Toronto, and how far Syria was. "That's good. But I'm still sad for the people who live in Syria. Are there kids there, too?" Alex poked the straw far into his apple juice. Juice arced out onto his Batman shirt.

"Only the soldiers fight, Alex. They're all grown-ups. No kids are hurt," Tinker said. The newspaper was telling a different story, but why fill Alex's small head with worry about people half a world away intent on killing one another? Besides, those people weren't like them. Tinker had never known a Muslim, and the ones he saw on the news didn't seem worth getting to know. Bombing hospitals, for Christ's sake.

"But maybe some of the soldiers have kids? Maybe their dads get blown up just like my dad was blown up. That would be sad." With one long, slow suck Alex finished his juice box. "I hate 'splosions. Want to finish our game, Grandma?"

Flo grabbed the tissue she had wedged underneath the cuff of her sweater and used it to dab the corner of her eyes. "Sure, honey. It's your turn." She slid the dice toward Alex while Tinker blew on his tea.

CHAPTER 21

Alberta, March 2015

THE ALARM ON CHARLIE'S PHONE RANG AT FIVE IN the morning and he woke instantly, hitting it off before it woke Nell. Too late. She rolled over and switched on the lamp propped up on a cardboard banana box currently serving as a makeshift bedside table.

"So this is the new normal? You head off to work while I stay home and keep house all day like some 1950s housewife?" Nell rubbed sleep from her eyes.

"Sounds marvellous, darling," Charlie drawled.

"Should I file my nails and prep a pot roast while you're gone?" Nell teased. "Now that you're chewing again you're eating like you've never seen food before."

Charlie picked up his jeans off the floor and pulled them on. "Pot roast sounds fantastic. Grandma makes it with soft potatoes, peas, and carrots, and pours thick gravy over everything before serving it. Text her if you need any cooking tips. I'll be home at six. Have a highball ready and your face on, would you, doll?"

"Ha! Dream on." Nell sat up and grabbed the corners of her pillow. She swung it at Charlie, but he ducked out of the way and she hit the lamp instead. It toppled off the cardboard box and shut off. "Oh shoot, now look what I've done."

"Not to worry, Little Missus, soon we'll be able to afford real furniture, seeing as I'm gainfully employed again." Charlie's feet hit the floor and, despite a lingering ache in his jaw, he was full of energy and relieved to have finally gotten medical clearance to return to work. He flicked on the wall switch and the ceiling fixture flooded the room with a harsh yellow light that made Nell squint. Her hair was mussed up in a dishevelled way Charlie found adorable, and he couldn't resist jumping back into bed, pinning her down, and covering her neck and face with sloppy kisses. He stopped when he kissed her on the mouth and made an exaggerated wave of his hand in front of his nose. "Morning breath. The worst breath of the day. I'm outta here," he said, lacing up his boots. "Ever heard of mouthwash?"

"Haha, you're one to talk about oral health, Charlie. When do you plan on getting to the dentist for an estimate on your teeth, anyway?"

"Soon as I can afford it, Nell." Their inventory of needs and wants was long. Charlie was already building a mental list of what he wanted to buy once he was getting paycheques again. He didn't know what to prioritize: a better place to live, real furniture, a car, or a dog for him and Nell. But first he'd have to start paying back his grandma and his more threatening debts. Cosmetic dentistry still seemed like a far-off luxury.

"What are your plans for today?"

"I have to start looking for a job myself. I can't freeload off you forever, Charlie."

The horn honked again. "That's Rex. I'll mention to him that you're looking. Maybe he knows about something." Charlie grabbed an apple and polished it on his jacket as he walked toward the door. He bit into it with a loud crunch and felt enormous satisfaction in being able to eat whole apples again.

"Is that all you're having for breakfast?"

It felt good to have someone worrying about whether or not he'd be hungry. "We'll grab drive-thru on the way. I'll be home at six. Smell ya later, swamp mouth."

HE ALMOST SKIPPED OUT OF the door. Even though he was wearing steel-toed boots, Nell had never seen Charlie step more lightly.

She tried falling back asleep but at six thirty gave in and got up. Even after she made the bed, showered, and ate a bowl of cereal, dawn had barely broken.

Nell grabbed a folder with copies of her resume inside it and stuffed it into a backpack. She hadn't brought fancy clothes with her to Alberta and couldn't afford to buy any yet, so she dressed in the best things she had— black pants and a red turtleneck. She added small gold hoop earrings, dried and styled her shoulder-length bobbed hair until it was sleek and smooth, and rubbed Vaseline into her chapped lips. Feeling more hopeful already, she pulled on boots and her jacket and walked to the bus stop.

The hair in her nostrils froze instantly and her fingertips began to tingle. Winter here was much colder than in Cape Breton, and it was drier. Her eyes began to water as she looked down the road hoping to see an approaching bus. She did a little self-talk to stay focused. She was young, healthy, and university educated, looking for work in Alberta. The economic boom here had definitely slowed since oil prices had dropped, but heck, she was a Cape Bretoner and bred for adversity. How hard could it be?

Her bravado waned when she arrived downtown and wandered around aimlessly, unsure of where to begin. She knew no one here other than Charlie and had no clue how to begin a job search without any connections or leads. She saw a "Free WiFi" sign on a coffee shop and decided to go in and search for jobs from her phone.

Wrapping both her cold hands around her coffee, she sat down at a table where the local newspaper was splayed out in front of her. ENERGY INDUSTRY COLLECTIVELY LOST $600 MILLION IN THE FIRST QUARTER OF 2015, blasted the front-page headline. Nell read on. *There are now 25,000 fewer jobs in the oilpatch. The oil market, which was already slumping due to oversupply, is officially in freefall.* Oh no. This didn't bode well for her and Charlie. The environmentalist in her would love to see Canada wean itself off fossil fuels, but the practical side knew that right now the country needed them and Charlie needed his job. She pushed the paper aside, staring out the window at the steady stream of trucks and gas-guzzling SUVs that drove by instead. Charlie was at work right now, at least. His job was safe. There was no need to panic.

She cast her eyes around the coffee shop. There were others seated at tables like her, flipping through the classified ads or scrolling through their phones and laptops. Were these the people she'd be competing with for jobs? Assuming there even were jobs to compete for? What could she offer that they couldn't?

"This seat taken?" a gruff voice asked.

Nell glanced up to see a stocky man in a leather biker jacket and black cowboy boots standing across from her. He didn't fit in here. "Sure, take the chair. I don't need it." She assumed he wanted it to drag it off to another table.

"Actually I want to sit here with you. Have a little conversation. Nell, isn't it?" His horseshoe moustache dropped vertically down his face deeper than his frown.

Nell glanced around the crowded coffee shop. She was nervous now, but what could he do to her in here? "How do you know my name?"

"I'm a business acquaintance of Charlie's. You gonna let me sit down or what?" he asked again.

Nell nodded and cleared the newspaper off the tabletop.

The man lowered himself onto the seat and crossed his arms in front of his chest. "You know who I am?"

"No. Should I?" Nell was struggling to keep her voice steady.

"So Charlie's kept you in the dark. How is Charlie, anyway?" He raised his thumb and index finger to his face and began stroking his moustache. "His jaw fixed yet?"

"Charlie's good. He's actually gone back to…" Nell paused, suddenly aware it might not be wise to give this man too much information. The cheerful guitar music filtering through the shop's sound system was at complete odds with the dread welling up inside her.

"Gone back where? Don't tell me Cape Breton," the man said.

"No. I misspoke. Look, I should go. I'll tell Charlie hi from you. What's your name?" Nell stood and put on her coat.

"What's your hurry? Sit down," the man said, ignoring her question. Clearly he would be asking the questions and she would be answering.

Nell sat back down.

He propped his elbows on the table with a thud and leaned forward until his face was inches from Nell's. "When you see Charlie, you tell that little fuckity-fuck I haven't forgiven the rest of what he owes me. Those pissy little transfers from his grandmother don't cover the interest."

Nell's mind was racing. She opened her mouth but no words came out.

"He can't avoid me forever. Tell him, too, that our little smackdown in the bathroom at the bar was only a warning. And sure, tell him hi from Lou."

Nell watched him swagger away. As Lou held the door for someone else on his way out, he turned back to Nell once more and locked eyes with her. It gave Nell cold shivers. She tried to finish her coffee, but the cup shook so badly in her hands when she lifted it she looked like an addict in the grips of withdrawal. She lowered the cup back onto the table and forced herself to take some deep breaths. What in the hell had Charlie gotten himself mixed up in?

AT TEN O'CLOCK THAT EVENING Nell was home with the door deadbolted and chained. It had been almost twelve hours since the incident at the coffee shop. She paced the apartment, had diarrhea several times, and bit all her fingernails off as she waited.

She texted Charlie for the seventh time: "U R 4 hours late. Where the hell R U???????????" She sat at the small table they'd dragged home from Goodwill and stared at her phone, willing Charlie to finally reply. He didn't. She heard Rex's truck pull up.

Charlie tried opening the door, then pounded on it. "Nell, you here? Lemme in." His voice slurred.

Nell climbed off the couch and opened the door. Charlie walked past her into the kitchen without saying anything. He grabbed a beer from the fridge and opened it, plopping into a chair.

"Sorry, no pot roast. I got a bit sidetracked. Let me tell you about my day and the pleasant man I met in a coffee shop," Nell said, sarcasm dripping from her voice.

Charlie looked at her and opened his mouth as if to speak, then closed it while he appeared to be thinking. "Can it wait?" Charlie asked. "I'm not in a great mood."

"Yeah? Join the party. Neither am I." Nell looked closely at Charlie. The sparkle that had been in his eyes that morning was gone, replaced with a dull glaze. His pupils were small. He was breathing slowly between deep gulps of beer, and after each draw, wiping his mouth with the back of his dirty hand.

"Oh God, Charlie, what happened?" Fear seized Nell's body and nauseated her.

Charlie turned his head slowly to Nell and she was shocked by how droopy his eyelids were. "Laid off. First day back and I was laid off." He belched loudly and downed the rest of his beer.

CHAPTER 22

Cape Breton, March 2015

"CAN I PLAY WITH THESE, GRANDPA?" ALEX WAS dragging a wooden box with yellow rope handles into the den.

Tinker lifted the lid off it and released a whiff of cedar. Inside were variously shaped wooden blocks. "Where'd you find these old things?" He picked up an equilateral triangle and rubbed his thumb along the sanded sides, admiring the smooth finish.

"In Charlie's closet. What are they?"

Tinker thought it self-evident, but checked himself before pointing out the obvious. "Exactly what you see. Wooden blocks."

"What for?"

"They're toys for building. I made them for your dad when he was a young boy like you. Your brother, Charlie, liked to play with them, too."

"I thought toys came from the toy store." Alex held two rectangular blocks and began tapping them against one another like drumsticks. Clack-clack-clackety-clack.

"The best toys are homemade. I made these from scraps of wood in my workshop. You can stack 'em into towers or even build castles. Why don't you try?" Tinker was trying to redirect him so he'd stop that incessant tapping before it gave him a headache.

Alex dropped to the floor with the box, pulling out piece after piece. Tinker was home alone with Alex while Flo was at Sunday mass. Flo stopped asking Tinker to accompany her years ago, knowing it was pointless, and she wasn't allowed to take Alex to church on Courtney's orders. Tinker could've used the morning off from grandparenting. He wasn't accustomed anymore to the energy of a child. It was many years since Charlie was a young boy and he didn't have the energy now that he did even in his fifties. Full-time grandparenting wore him down. He could see that Alex tired out Flo, too, especially as she was the one getting up with him in the middle of the night when he woke, though she'd never complain.

Alex stacked the blocks into a tower as high as himself. When it crashed to the floor he turned to Tinker. "I wanna see your workshop, Grandpa."

"It's awfully dangerous there for a boy." Couldn't he just relax here with his tea for five more minutes? The boy had trouble sitting still and, since retiring, sitting still was one Tinker's favourite pastimes. He saw that he'd miscalculated and his warning only made the workshop even more alluring.

Alex's eyes lit up. "You'll protect me. Let's go." Alex walked toward the basement stairs, turned and waved Tinker toward him. "C'mon!"

So much for his lazy Sunday morning in his armchair, drinking tea and looking out the window at the snow piles. Buddy MacMaster was playing on the radio, and Tinker had been tapping his right foot along with the fiddle music. A man his age had earned his armchair time. He sighed and stood up.

Tinker's basement workshop was well stocked. On one wall he stored only nails, sorted by quarter-inch length, in neat cubbies. He had gleaming saws of various sizes hanging off S-hooks on another wall. A polished tree stump sat in the corner with several axes driven into the seat for winter storage. Neat pine boxes with rope handles that Tinker, Russell, and Charlie had built over the years held assorted hand tools, while on high shelves electric tools were safely stored with their cords wrapped tightly around them.

"Wow. This place is awesome-sauce!" Alex's eyes were wide.

It had been years since Tinker had had anyone join him in his workshop. He gave Alex his lightest hammer and a small smooth plank and taught him how to drive nails into it without smashing his fingers. Tinker's shoulder was throbbing today and he couldn't help but wince. Plus being here with Alex brought bittersweet memories flooding back of times he'd spent here with Russell and Charlie. Under Tinker's careful watch, his son and first grandson had likewise been taught to hammer nails and twist screws into boards before graduating to small woodworking assignments. Russell had approached any new project with gusto but grew restless with the tedium of precision work, and Tinker often had to finish what he started. He glanced down at Alex and felt sad for him that he was fatherless; he knew first-hand what growing up with a stern mother and no dad was like. Tinker would have traded his own life for Russell's in a second if such a deal could have been struck. It should have been Russell here in the workshop with Alex today.

Charlie had been a more natural and patient learner. In his teens he'd become such a good builder that Tinker taught him to make door signs, cutting boards, step stools, and shelves. His creations were scattered throughout the house, many still in use.

"See that sign? Charlie made it." He gestured above the workshop door where a wooden plank into which Charlie had burned TINKER's TIME OUT hung.

"Haha. You have timeouts and you're a grown-up."

"Sometimes I am still a naughty boy." Tinker mussed Alex's hair.

"Let's make something for Grandma. How about a ladder since she's so short?" Alex asked.

Tinker pretended to consider it. "That's pretty difficult for a beginner. Why don't I teach you to make her a coaster for her teacup instead?"

"Why does a teacup need a roller-coaster? Won't the tea splash out?"

"I mean the other kind of coaster. A small, round placemat you put under drinks." Tinker figured a clean cut through a dry log with a bit of sanding would do the trick, and they'd be finished before they had to pick up Flo at church. He could teach Alex to count the rings to estimate how old the tree was. Alex nodded and the two got down to work.

FLO TOOK COMMUNION, THEN RETURNED to her pew and dropped slowly to her knees for a final few minutes of prayer in God's house.

Please keep Charlie on the right track in Alberta. I'm scared he's mixed up in something bad, she said without speaking out loud, squirming slightly to try to reduce her discomfort. The red vinyl cushioning on the kneeling bench wasn't enough to keep her legs from cramping.

Should I have sent money to that Alberta bank account? Charlie said if I didn't a bad man would hurt him. I wouldn't have been able to live with that. I had to send it, God.

Attendance at mass had been dwindling for many years, and the once at-capacity congregation now was spaced sometimes two or more pews apart. It looked to Flo like a bingo card early on in the game, when only a few dots were inked. There was no longer a choir and rarely a coffee service in the hall after mass anymore. Father Dunphy was old and semi-retired, his doddery pace prolonging the service. His sermons rambled these days, and Flo had trouble connecting them back to the scriptures. She sometimes got annoyed but didn't dare complain to the diocese, knowing Falkirk Cove was lucky at this point to even have its own parish.

And dear God, if you could help us find a way to keep Alex in our lives without him feeling abandoned by his mother, well, that would just be the ultimate blessing. Flo couldn't envision how this could come to pass, but God must have a plan, and she'd have to accept whatever it was. Though Flo was glad Courtney had left Alex with her and Tinker, she was at the same time mad at her for the hurt and confusion this had caused in Alex. She'd given none of them any indication of when she would return and it seemed selfish—but Flo didn't want to be uncharitable and judgmental in church. She reached for her hymnal to prepare for the closing hymn and looked up at Father Dunphy, waiting for him to sit so she could do the same. His first name was Simon, and as a boy Charlie used to joke that mass was like a giant game of Simon Says. Back at home over Sunday lunch Charlie would re-enact the service for Tinker, casting himself in the role of Father Dunphy. "Simon says kneel. Simon says stand up. Simon says sing a hymn. Simon says pray. Stop praying. You stopped praying! You're a bad Catholic. Simon didn't say to stop praying." Tinker would laugh at Charlie's antics, but Flo would smack him gently with her missal.

Father Dunphy was still wiping the chalice. With a sigh so tiny no one would hear it, Flo set the hymnal back down and returned to praying. It occurred to her that all her prayers this week had been for her own family. She needed to think of others.

Also look over those poor souls involved in that war in Syria, please God. She lifted her right hand and with her index and middle finger touched her forehead, chest, and each shoulder in the sign of the cross, signalling the end of her prayer. She quietly said *Amen* and pulled herself up as Father Dunphy retreated to the presider's chair, the hymn thankfully drowning out the loud cracking of her knees.

TINKER OPENED THE BACK DOOR and Alex climbed into the Buick and onto his booster seat. As Tinker scraped frost off the car's windows, the interior began to reveal itself, and he saw Alex fastening his seat belt and then pulling the coaster out of his jacket pocket. Tinker had promised him they could stain it together later that afternoon after they showed Florence. He was glad they had a plan to fill the hours. Days spent entertaining a child often seemed long.

Tinker backed out of the driveway and drove down the road that would take them to Highway 19. The spring melt was not yet upon them, and the snow that had looked so pretty twinkling on the tree branches and barn roofs back in January was now a dreary, grey patina. It was a wearisome time of year, the end of winter, and Tinker had to fight to keep his spirits up in the weeks before Easter. He wondered what it was like in Alberta. He'd heard about their Chinooks bringing blasts of warm weather in the dead of winter and thought once again that Alberta seemed to get more than its fair share of lucky breaks.

Tinker kept driving. No cars passed driving in the opposite direction.

He drove past a property with a FOR SALE – REDUCED sign on the lawn. They continued driving down Highway 19 past the Kwikmart, the only business left in town. When Tinker was a boy there'd been a large general store with a soda counter, a barbershop, a gas station, and a pharmacy here too. One by one they'd all closed.

"See that there? That's where I went to school. My ma was the teacher." Tinker pointed to the one-room schoolhouse. The black trim had faded and white paint was peeling off the clapboards. An old brass bell turned green still hung over the front door.

"Wow. Cool. Can I go to that school?" Alex asked.

"No, it's boarded up," Tinker said. "There aren't enough kids here anymore to fill it up."

"Oh. Where'd they go?" Alex asked.

"They grew up and moved away. The kids that live here now take buses to different towns with bigger schools." Tinker pulled into the church parking lot as the doors opened and people started dripping out like water droplets from a leaky faucet.

"There she is," Alex said, undoing his seat belt and hopping out of the car. "Hi, Grandma!" he shouted, running to greet her, his unfastened boots clomping on the slushy gravel and the coaster clutched in his outstretched hand.

"What's this?" she asked, receiving her gift.

"It's a roller-coaster for your teacup so it doesn't leave rings on Grandpa's good wood furniture."

Flo raised her eyebrows at Tinker, nodding slightly to acknowledge him.

"Count the rings, Grandma. The tree is five like me. Me and Grandpa made it for you in Tinker's Time Out workshop."

"Thank you, dear. I love it." Flo dragged her fingertips across its smooth surface like she was affectionately patting a cat. "I'll use it every day." She slipped it carefully into her purse as Bob, Elsie, and Catriona approached. "Alex, you know Bob, right? And his wife, Elsie, and this is their granddaughter Catriona, in case you forgot."

Alex, suddenly shy, nodded and looked at the ground. He slid behind Tinker's legs.

"I'll call you about that meeting, Flo," Bob said. "Better yet, why don't you and Tinker and Alex come over for supper this week? Come Tuesday. I'll make the famous Libbus family cabbage rolls—my mother's recipe. No one knows cabbage rolls like the Lebanese."

"Sounds delicious, thank you, Bob." Flo replied for them all. "If there's tabbouleh, too, we'll be there for sure." They all said goodbye.

"What are you and Bob meeting about now?" Tinker asked.

"We got talking about the Syrian crisis after mass. We might revitalize the old parish committee. See if there's some way us here in Falkirk Cove can help."

"For cripes' sake, Florence, do you really need to take on this cause? Those people are not our problem—we have our hands full with our own." Tinker gestured toward Alex with a small wave of the back of his hand.

"It's him that got me thinking of the Syrians, Tink. There are kids there, too, you know."

"Do you hear this nonsense, Alex? Your grandma thinks she can save the world."

"Great plan, Grandma," Alex said. "Can I help?"

"Of course." Flo reached out her hand and further mussed up Alex's red hair.

As they made their way back to the Buick, Tinker sighed.

"What is it now, Tinker?"

He knew that despite being half his size, Flo was the boss. If she said they were having supper at Bob and Elsie's on Tuesday, then it was to be, but he didn't have to like it.

"I hate foreign food—especially cabbage rolls."

Flo swatted him with her purse. "You'll come to Bob and Elsie's and you'll eat cabbage rolls and you'll listen to our conversation and maybe even join in. And I'll enjoy a night off from cooking."

Tinker never knew Florence to complain about cooking before. She loved fixing him meals.

"Now take us home. I've got a new coaster in my purse that's in need of a cup of hot tea to sit on it." Flo winked at Alex.

CHAPTER 23

Turkey, April 2015

IT WASN'T A BIRTHDAY CELEBRATION LIKE THEY used to have back in Syria, when her parents would travel from Azaz to Aleppo with sweets, toys, and books for the children. No, there would be none of that inside the refugee camp, but still Ahmed was turning eleven and Amira was trying to make it as special for her son as she could. He was relieved of his chores and free to play with Abdo all afternoon. They'd kicked Abdo's old soccer ball through the refugee camp, knowing the lay of the land so well now that getting lost was no longer a concern. After weeks of the same plain starches, Amira had splurged and visited the vendors who came to the gates of the camp to hawk their wares, buying a few extras to make approximations of Ahmed's favourite foods. She invited Abdo to join the family for *maklube,* a rice dish with beans and chicken, and pickled eggplant. After they ate, Amira washed the dishes and the boys grabbed the clean rice pot and banged on it with wooden spoons, singing a birthday song.

"Quiet, boys, you'll disturb the whole camp," Amira scolded. She reached out to grab the spoon from Ahmed, but her husband stepped in front of her.

"Let him drum, Amira. You only turn eleven once," Sami said gently. She relented and let the noisemaking continue. She didn't want to nag and argue on Ahmed's birthday, when everyone's spirits were high. She sat on a pillow, rubbing her taut stomach. It itched as her skin stretched over her growing belly.

In an unusual burst of energy, Yasmine rose to her feet, jumped up and down, and clapped her hands, excited by the exuberance inside the family's tent. When the children calmed down, Amira stood and walked to a dark corner of the tent where she'd hidden Ahmed's gift. She dug underneath a small pile of blankets and clothes and pulled out a paper bag with handles.

"For you." She handed it to Ahmed. His eyes lit up and she clasped her hands on either side of his head, pulling him in and planting a kiss on his forehead. There'd been no gifts since they arrived in Reyhanli Camp months earlier, and she could see from the shock on his face Ahmed wasn't expecting anything on his birthday. Sami had gone to a lot of trouble procuring this item from the black market.

Ahmed peered inside the bag and his eyes lit up. "Thank you, Mama! Thank you, Papa!" he said, placing the bag on the floor and pulling out his glossy new soccer ball bearing the Real Madrid crest. "I can't believe it. An official Real Madrid soccer ball! Can we go play with it?"

"For a short time only, Ahmed. It's almost dark. Don't be too long," Amira cautioned as the boys tore out of the door.

Sami took Amira's hand. "He's doing just fine, my love," he said, offering one of his regular reassurances that their family was managing well under the circumstances. "Can I make you some tea? Then there's something we need to talk about."

Amira nodded. Her eyes closed as she waited, the din of pot-banging and singing now a distant ringing in her ears. Fatigue hovered around her constantly, like the cooking odours she was never able to properly fan from the tent, or the dust in the air outdoors. She was always moving through a fog of some kind.

"Doctor, doctor, is this your tent? Doctor, can I speak to you?" an unfamiliar small boy's voice beckoned from outside. The sense of community was strong at Reyhanli Camp, and news had spread that there was a doctor in the camp. Sami looked at Amira with raised eyebrows and a tilt of his head as if seeking her permission, but they both knew he would go. In addition to what he considered a moral obligation, he was now receiving a stipend from the Turkish government for providing on-call medical help. So, whether Amira approved or not, he couldn't really refuse.

"Doctor, are you there? Please answer. My sister is sick," the boy pleaded.

The spread of infectious diseases was a major concern here, with thousands of refugees living in close quarters, but so far there'd been no outbreaks, and Sami most often saw minor ailments or hypersensitivity, fear, and panic attacks borne out of post-traumatic stress disorder. Nights seemed to be the worst, with people either unable to sleep or, if they could, suffering night terrors when memories of the war came rushing back into their subconscious. It had made for many disrupted sleeps of late when people came to their tent at all hours seeking Sami's help.

Amira sighed. "Go. As usual, someone else needs you more than me." She tried not to resent Sami's helpfulness. At least he could still be useful here, and the family often benefitted from his small salary and the random objects or foods patients gave him, but her old resentment lingered. Would he always be a doctor first, even above being a husband and father? Sami grabbed his doctor's bag and left the tent just as Ahmed returned.

After Ahmed and Yasmine crawled under the blankets together and Amira kissed them goodnight, she prepared for her nightly prayers. *"Bismillah ar-Rahman ar-Raheem,"* she said quietly at the beginning of her ablutions. *In the name of Allah, most gracious, most merciful.* She plunged her hands into a stainless steel mixing bowl she'd filled with water and washed them three times with a surgeon's precision, making sure she cleaned thoroughly even between her fingers.

God is most great, Amira said to herself. She needed to believe this. Things in Syria, and particularly in Aleppo, had become desperate. She thought she'd seen the worst but had learned that even when things seem to be at rock bottom, there are often greater depths to which they can fall. The government and rebel factions were fighting for control of the city and, as far as anyone could tell, no side was winning. What victory could there be if what was left of Aleppo at the end of all this were bricks and bones? She wondered if she'd even find her beloved city recognizable when they moved back. Was their home still standing, and would they ever be able to return to it? She kept the key to their front door in her suitcase just in case, sometimes clutching it in the palm of her hand like a talisman, hoping their home would be magically protected, though in her logical mind she knew it was likely already demolished. In Azaz, where her parents lived, things were reportedly also dire. Her calls to them had gone unanswered for two months now.

Isha'a, the night prayer, was the last of five prayers Amira performed each day. The children now lay sleeping on their mattress as she unfurled her prayer mat and laid it on the floor beside them, directing it toward Mecca. Though her patience with the children grew short in the day, they were easy to love at night as they slept. Yasmine, wheezing faintly, lay on her side like a kidney bean. A stray brown curl flopped across her cheek and Amira gently swept it behind her daughter's small ear. Ahmed, too, slept on his side, spooning his little sister. His busy day turning eleven and chasing soccer balls had finally caught up with him.

Normally Amira stood and recited the Quran from memory before beginning her deep bends, but considering she was pregnant she was allowed to perform the whole praying ritual while kneeling. From the mat, she raised her hands and then folded them under her swollen breasts. She felt gravity pulling her stomach down onto her thighs, and attempted to focus on her prayers and not the lead weight in her abdomen or the ache in her hips. She groaned despite her efforts.

Once finished, she sat on a pillow and waited for Sami to return. Oh, how she'd love to have a book and some light to read it by. She heard families talking in adjacent tents, people reciting their own prayers, feet scuffling along in the dirt outside. The lack of privacy here was wearing on her.

"Mama, are you okay?" Ahmed mumbled sleepily. She'd woken him with her groaning.

"Yes, go back to sleep," she whispered, touched by his concern for her. He barely looked or acted like a little boy anymore, and she was suddenly wistful for his rapidly disappearing childhood.

SAMI FOLLOWED THE YOUNG BOY to his tent at the edge of camp. He heard wailing as they approached. Sami steeled himself as the boy held the door flap for him. He did a quick headcount and saw there were eight people living here. The mother appeared to have seven children and no husband, as was so often the case in the camps. Many men were fighting in the war or already dead. The tent was the same size as Sami's own, about eight by twelve feet—roughly the same dimensions as his former carport in Aleppo. He did his best not to flinch in reaction to the screaming, glancing around quickly, noticing the same basic set-up as his own tent: two mattresses, a small kitchen area with a makeshift hotplate on the floor currently topped by a kettle, jugs for water in the corner next to piles of clothes and linens, and a small floor space with fraying pillows for sitting on. There was only sufficient height to stand in the tent's centre. Certain tents Sami had entered had small televisions wired to outdoor satellites, and occasionally a laptop computer plugged into a socket secured to a tent pole, but not this one. This tent was as basic as they came.

"As-Salaam Alaikum," Sami said in greeting, nodding to them quickly one by one. In turn they waved or nodded, though most were too busy coughing to speak. Only the boy who had fetched him didn't appear distracted or beset with a virus. The mother looked up and Sami noted her red-rimmed eyes were almost swollen shut with conjunctivitis. She dabbed them constantly with a yellow-streaked, whitish face cloth.

"It's the littlest one. She won't calm down." Exhaustion was evident in the mother voice.

Sami sat on the mattress next to the toddler while her siblings stood behind him. "Hello there, friend. What troubles you?" he asked calmly. Her wailing persisted.

"It started late this afternoon when a small tractor rumbled by to flatten the ground for more tents," the mother said. "I think it reminded her of the tanks that rolled down our street in Syria. She started screaming and hasn't stopped."

Sami did a quick physical examination and noted nothing of major concern. Her breathing and pulse were rapid but that could be explained by stress.

"What's her name?" Sami asked, touching her forehead with the back of his hand. It was warm but not burning with fever.

"Jamila."

"Hello, Jamila. You are safe here, Jamila. What a lovely girl you are. What a brave girl. So many people love you, Jamila. They are worried about you. Let them know you are all right, won't you, Jamila?" Sami spoke evenly, trying to model simple techniques her family could use the next time she had a panic attack. He took her hands in his own and looked into her eyes and smiled. It took effort not to flinch as her ragged screams pierced his eardrums and snot ran from her nose into her O-shaped mouth. He began to hum a lullaby. Her screams turned to whimpers and her eyelids dropped. Soon her breathing became regular as she fell asleep. Sami's medical bag lay beside him, still unopened.

"I must go." He cast his gaze around the room. "Jamila will be better in the morning, but the rest of you have terrible colds. You must take care to cough and sneeze into your sleeves." He demonstrated proper technique. "And wash your hands often." He looked now at the mother. "Mom, you must go to the dispensary in the morning for antibiotic eye drops."

The woman nodded and rose to her feet, then walked to a drying rack of dishes. She pulled out a bowl with a hairline crack through it and a chipped rim, and pushed it into his hands. Sami didn't want the bowl but nodded, smiled, and said, "Thank you, it's lovely. My wife, Amira, will appreciate this."

Walking back to his tent, Sami counted his blessings. He'd seen people maimed, killed, and—what was sometimes worse—with spirits broken by the war. Yet other than Yasmine's low energy and asthma, his family was well. Amira's pregnancy was on course. They had gotten out of Syria in time and he was grateful to Turkey for this camp and the temporary situation it provided. But it was clear to him it was just that—temporary. Here they were biding time, not advancing with it. They needed to find a place to live safely, peacefully, and permanently. They were vulnerable at Reyhanli Camp to everything the rest of the camp suffered and while it was colds today, what if it were malaria or cholera tomorrow? They couldn't have escaped a war only to die from an infectious disease. Leaving would mean overcoming major hurdles, not least of which was convincing Amira to leave the Middle East. Even as a married woman she'd remained deferential to her parents, and Sami knew she would not want to emigrate without them. But there would be no going back to Syria now. They must look to the future.

FINALLY, THE WHITE CANVAS DOOR parted and Sami's silhouette filled the frame. "You're still awake?" he whispered.

"I can't fall asleep when I'm worried," Amira hissed.

"All this worrying isn't good for the baby, Amira."

"You make it sound like I worry by choice. I can't control my emotions that way." She spoke curtly yet quietly so as not to wake the children.

She missed sleeping on her stomach and rolled from side to side trying to find a comfortable position. The firm mattress did little to absorb the pressure on her hips. Sami crawled in beside her.

"How is the patient you saw?" she asked.

"Barely more than a baby. Traumatized and screaming—she's likely never known a day without tanks or gunfire. But for now, at least, she's okay."

Amira was sympathetic, but also glad their tent was far enough away that she hadn't had to listen to the toddler's screams.

"I wish we were home, Sami. I know I should be grateful that we're together and safe here, but it's not our home. What will become of us?"

Sami began massaging the muscles in her lower back, which were constantly knotted. "Please don't get mad, Amira, but I think it's time to consider emigrating."

Amira shuffled further toward the edge of the mattress, pulling her back out of Sami's reach. "Emigrate? We already did that. We're in Turkey now."

"I mean for us to leave this part of the world altogether. To start over in a new country far away where we'll live for the rest of our lives."

Amira flipped over to face him. It was the first time Sami had articulated these thoughts. Even though he was speaking quietly, she detected trepidation in his voice. In the dark tent, she could see only the outline of his familiar face and feel his warm breath on her cheek. She had the simultaneous urge to reach out and embrace him and also to push him away. She knew he wanted what was best for them all, but to introduce it now, on Ahmed's birthday when they'd set aside their problems for the day to celebrate, felt wrong. And despite the living conditions and the total lack of privacy here, she still didn't accept the idea of moving anywhere else. "I don't want to leave while my parents are still in Azaz."

The tables, it seemed, had turned. Now it was Sami who wanted to go and Amira who wanted to stay. Would they never think as one? They used to be so in sync before the war. Silence hung in the darkness between them. It extended so long Amira hoped Sami had dozed off. This was a conversation she didn't want to have.

"I know. I don't want to upset you, Amira. I pray for your parents every day. But it's been two months since you spoke to them. We can't put our lives on hold hoping they're still alive, and that they'll change their minds and leave Syria. They told us unequivocally they'd rather die there than leave."

A sob travelled up Amira's throat and her shoulders lurched forward. "What are you saying, Sami? You think they're dead? We should give up on them? Run away from them, from here?"

"I know you love your parents, Amira. But I'm asking you to put your children first. To ask yourself where they'd be best off. The two children you have *and* the one on the way."

"Are you accusing me of being a bad mother?" It was the worst insult Amira could imagine.

"Never. But moments ago you asked me what will become of us. Well, we can have a life—a future, Amira—but not here. I think in your heart you know that, and you also know Syria is lost to us."

Amira couldn't listen to another word. She turned over and shuffled to the farthest edge of the mattress. The only thing that had made this living situation bearable until now was her faith. Faith in Allah. Faith that she'd see her parents again. Faith that the war would one day end and after Syria was rebuilt they'd return to live there again. She had not lost that faith—not yet. When her pillow became damp with tears, she flipped it over and dampened the other side, too.

CHAPTER 24

Cape Breton, April 2015

CATRIONA WAS STRUGGLING TO OPEN HER STICKY locker door when she felt a tap on her back.

"So, hey, Catriona, there's something I want to ask you."

She swung around and came face to face with Seamus, grinning from one side of his mouth. His hands were in his jeans pockets, but his shoulders were raised. "Yeah?" She was almost late for third-period English and hoped he'd get right to the point.

"Prom's coming up. Wanna go together?" He now swung his long arms by his side.

It wasn't a big showy prom-posal, but heck, it was an invitation, and Catriona hadn't had another. Many seniors were already paired up, and all the talk in the cafeteria these days was who was going with whom and what they were wearing.

"Sure. Why not," she replied, leaning her back against her locker to put an arm's distance between her and Seamus.

"Cool. We'll have a blast." Both corners of his mouth were raised now. He did look a little cute. A few of his buddies walked past and one thumped him on the back, vaulting him into Catriona's personal space.

"Me and the boys are drinking rum, but I can also get us a bottle of bubbly. Sound good?"

Seamus was backing away from her down the hallway now, his face lit up.

She'd sensed a shift between them on their bus rides lately. He looked at her a second longer than he used to when he sat down. Sometimes he pressed his muscular shoulder against hers. Lots of girls would've been happy if he asked them to prom, but he'd asked her instead. She wished she felt some of the giddiness she'd seen on other people's faces when they'd just been asked to prom.

"Sure. As friends though, right, Seamus?" She was practically shouting as he was halfway down the hall by then. What was wrong with her? She would like to have a boyfriend, and he'd be considered a catch for a nerd like her. Maybe if she just hooked up with him then she'd start like-liking him...but maybe she wouldn't and then she'd have ruined their friendship.

"Whatever you want. No backing out, k?" He slipped into the boys' bathroom.

Catriona nodded to no one and headed toward English class. With that one question settled, she felt a measure of relief. It was temporary. She picked up speed as she walked past the guidance counsellor's door, but he poked his head out just as she was passing by.

"Catriona! Come into my office for a minute."

"Can't. I'll be late for English," she replied without missing a step.

"I'll write you a note. No more excuses. You've missed our last two meetings."

Catriona grimaced and entered his office. He pointed at a chair, which she lowered herself into.

"So talk to me. What's going on with you?"

"Nothing." She tried not to sound hostile.

"Your mom called me. She's worried about you and frankly I am, too."

It pissed her off that her mother had called the school. She was always up in Catriona's business. "Why? I'm not doing drugs or flunking out." Her own rudeness surprised her. She was so bad at controlling her emotions lately.

"No, you're a smart girl with good grades, but you missed all the college and university deadlines. What're your ambitions?"

Therein lay the problem. She had none, as far as she could tell. She didn't feel a strong interest or pull toward anything. Maybe she'd never figure it out and would live a meaningless life. "I'm taking a gap year to figure them out." Catriona came up with that on the spot and it sounded decent rolling off her tongue. She'd use it again the next time someone asked.

Her guidance counsellor sighed. "Don't squander your life away. You'll be letting a lot of people down—most importantly yourself." He wrote her the late note and dismissed her.

THE NEXT DAY WAS SATURDAY, and Catriona had made a date with her grampie at their favourite bench. It faced west, just between the Flyer Trail and the harbour. It was simple in form and function, with four pine planks for its seat and four more for its back. It greyed and warped a smidgen more each winter but was still a comfortable place for a rest or a conversation, or to quietly watch the tide pull in and out of the cove.

Behind the bench sloped rolling hills thick with maple trees. Though it was a warm day for April, their leaves were still furled buds on otherwise bare branches. Clear streams ran down from the hills, coalescing into waterfalls and feeding nearby brooks, rivers, and apple orchards. After a prolonged winter's sleep, many things were finally waking up and charging forward into the future. Not Catriona.

She allowed her arms to languish across the width of the backrest, extending her long legs in front of her. "Did you used to come here when you were my age, Grampie?" Catriona asked.

"Sometimes. I'd watch the fishing boats leave the harbour if it was daybreak, or watch them return in the early afternoon. I wondered if fishing was my destiny, too, like most of the other boys my age." Bob pulled a couple of butterscotches out of his pocket and handed one to Catriona.

"But it wasn't. How come?" Catriona asked, sucking on the candy and twiddling the gold wrapper in her fingers.

"I wanted to be a doctor."

"Did you always know that?"

"I suppose I did. The same way my best friend Tinker always knew he'd become a fisherman, I always knew I'd become a doctor. I don't remember either of us ever considering anything else."

Catriona envied their certainty. "Was it hard work?"

"Yes, but I liked helping people."

"Why'd you stop being a doctor if you liked it?"

Bob's eyes scanned a thicket. "After forty-five years of long and erratic hours, I owed it to your grammie. It was hard retiring, though, knowing there's no longer a doctor in town." Bob stopped talking and put his index finger to his mouth as though to keep Catriona from speaking. A faint "kak kak kak" could be heard in the distance. Bob pulled binoculars from his jacket pocket and scanned the nearby trees to their south. "It's a bald eagle. Here, Catriona, take a look." He passed the binoculars.

Catriona held them to her face and soon found the regal bird perched a few hundred metres away. Its yellow eyes spooked her, but she found its grumpy face comical when it cocked its head to the side, and she laughed out loud.

"Unlike me, a bald eagle sighting never gets old. Now what about you? Any plans yet for next year?" Bob asked. "You've got plenty of options."

"Not if I want to stay here. There aren't any jobs or universities in town, but I'm not sure I'm ready to leave home," Catriona answered truthfully. Even though it felt like all she and her parents ever did was fight lately, she still wasn't ready to move away.

"Well, that's okay. No one says you have to leave right away. And if you do go, it wouldn't have to be forever. Look at me: I left and came back. Some people leave and fall in love with a new place. And other people come here from away and fall in love with this place and stay."

"Like who?" Catriona had never known anyone to move into Falkirk Cove. All they seemed to do was leave.

"Well, my parents—your great grandparents—immigrated from Lebanon. Can you imagine what a culture shock that must have been? But they made this place their home and loved Cape Breton dearly. Anything's possible."

The "kak kak kak" sounds resumed and the eagle took flight, circling the blue sky. They both watched it plunge suddenly into the water and snatch a wriggling mackerel with its sharp talons. Its broad wingspan cast a shadow over the bench as it flew away. The sudden aggression startled Catriona, and she turned and buried her face into her grandfather's shoulder. She started shaking and messy crying, streaking snot on her grandfather's jacket. Couldn't she ever have even one nice afternoon without wrecking it?

"Catriona, what is it?" Bob asked.

She kept her face buried in his jacket and her voice was muffled. "Nothing. Everything. Why is life so hard? And mean?"

"Aw, my love, life is all kinds of beautiful, too. This situation you find yourself in is temporary. You'll see." He wrapped his arm around her back and waited for her to be the first to pull away, then wiped the tears off her cheeks with the bent knuckle of his index finger.

Catriona managed to smile. "I want to be wise like you, Grampie."

Bob laughed. "It's the only perk of old age, m'dear."

As they walked back to Bob's car, they passed Roger shuffling by in the other direction. Both nodded and said hello, but he passed briskly without acknowledging them.

"What's wrong with him, Grampie?"

Bob started the car and waved to Roger as they drove past him. "Wrong? Nothing. Roger's exceptional."

CHAPTER 25

Cape Breton, April 2015

"IS IT TIME YET, GRANDMA? IS MY MOM HOME FROM work finally?" Alex sat at the kitchen table, colouring. He'd been moping around the house all day, not even interested in eating. At suppertime, he'd only pushed his spoon through his stew in figure eights. Flo didn't think he'd taken even two bites.

"Soon, love. Let me finish these dishes then we'll call her." She plunged her hands back into the sink and began scrubbing a pot. Often Alex pulled up a stool and helped with the washing, but he'd been keeping his distance today and Flo had given him space.

Alex's hand aimlessly dragged a black crayon back and forth over the page. "I want to talk to my mom. Now." His words had unfamiliar sharp edges.

Flo knew something was brewing. When she dried her hands and turned around, he stopped colouring and snapped the black crayon in half, dropping the broken pieces on the floor. She could see the outlines of birds on the page in his colouring book, but he'd only scribbled over them with ragged lines. Then Alex lifted the green crayon and snapped it too, then a yellow one. He picked up speed and confidence until he broke every crayon in the box, letting the pieces plop onto the tiles below him. Then he looked defiantly right at Flo.

"Well, look at that. Now you have twice as many crayons as before. Better pick those up before Grandpa walks in and gets cross," Flo said with a forced light tone. "You don't want to poke the bear." She opened her arms wide and made a fierce face like she was an attacking bear to see if she could improve Alex's mood.

"I don't want those stupid crayons! I hate them! I hate it here! I want to talk to Mommy! I want to go home!" Alex ran from the room.

Flo heard the bedroom door slam, put down her dishtowel, swept up the crayons, then walked to the den. There sat Tinker in his armchair, hand resting on the remote control while the CBC evening news played in the background, bringing more bad news from Syria—there was speculation that a chemical attack had maimed and killed civilians. Meanwhile, Tinker reclined without a care in the world, his eyes closed and mouth open a crack. His cup of tea was growing cold at his side.

Flo glanced at the television and felt even more derailed. "Wake up, Tinker. Alex's pitching a fit. He said he hates it here." In her logical mind Flo knew he didn't mean it, but her grandson's words stung all the same. She wanted Tinker to reassure her that what Alex said wasn't true.

"What's gotten into him all of a sudden?" Tinker asked, stirring.

"Where do I start? Missing his mother, I'm sure. Having no friends here his own age." Flo grabbed the remote control from Tinker's limp hand and snapped off the TV. "Being five and living with a couple of senior citizens. It's really a surprise he's been so good for so long."

"Still doesn't give him permission to sass you." Tinker's droopy eyelids closed once again.

"He's just grumpy. I wonder where he gets that from." Flo drummed her fingers and stared at Tinker.

His eyes reopened. "Give him time to cool off," Tinker said, snapping the TV back on and turning up the volume on the news. "He'll come back down when he's ready."

"I think he deserves some answers, and so do we. Does he live here permanently now?" Flo watched Tinker mull it over.

"I'd be okay with it if he did." Alex tired Tinker out, but he'd grown accustomed to the boy.

Flo took a seat on the couch but couldn't focus on the TV. "I'm going up there to check on him."

"Need backup?" Tinker asked.

"No, you stay put. I'll go," Flo said. She went upstairs, steeling herself. She knocked on Alex's door, and when he didn't reply she pushed it gently and let herself in. He lay prostrate on Charlie's old Mickey Mouse quilt, his face buried in the pillow. It made her flashback to Charlie lying in the same position in the days after Russell left. These poor grandsons of hers, both abandoned by their only parent. And here she was now, raising a third child in her early seventies. It wasn't the life she'd imagined leading, but God's will was sometimes a mystery. Flo touched the back of Alex's head, flattening down the red hairs that sprung out at all angles from his double crown only to watch them pop right back up when she raised her hand. It comforted her, and perhaps also Alex.

"What say we call your mom now? Should we use Skype?" she asked.

Alex flipped over. His face was damp, red, and puffy. "Okay, I guess." Flo sat at the sewing-table-turned-computer-desk and positioned the mouse over Courtney's name in her small Skype directory. The beeps and swooping sounds the computer made when connecting seemed to perk up Alex and he moved to Flo's side.

COURTNEY STARED INSIDE HER FRIDGE. A jar of mustard, some wilting carrots, a quarter-loaf of old bread, and a tub of margarine. She wouldn't be able to offer her date dinner, but what was he still doing here anyway? They'd had a fun afternoon hooking up, but it was time for him to scram.

"Babe? Where you at?" a voice called from the bedroom.

Courtney sighed and didn't respond. If Alex were here, she'd scrape together change for pancake batter and make him a big stack. Alex loved having breakfast for dinner. She closed the fridge door and turned to see Rick now at the kitchen door. He was shirtless but wearing jeans. She'd found him attractive when he came into the veterinary clinic with his Jack Russell Terrier puppy, but now, on his own, she wondered if it was his tenderness with the dog that had made him seem cute.

"Take me out for a burger?" she asked. A girl had to eat, and she wouldn't be paid until Friday. Alex loved burgers too, especially cheeseburgers. She wondered if Flo and Tinker made him burgers. If they did, theirs were probably better than hers, though Alex wouldn't say so. He always protected her feelings. Was he just as sweet with them? He'd been with Flo and Tinker long enough now to charm them like he did everyone. Courtney needed the bond between Alex and his grandparents to be unbreakable before she played her next card. It might be time now.

"Sure, I'm famished," said Rick as her computer started beeping from the kitchen table.

"Gimme a minute." Courtney sat at a kitchen chair and clicked the Skype button. "Hello? Is that my best boy, Alex?"

His face was too close to the computer. Flo pulled him back by the shoulders so Courtney could see both their faces.

"Yeah, Mommy. It's me. Me and Grandma. How's Toronto?"

"Toronto's good except it's missing the one thing that would make it great—you," Courtney said, pointing her index finger at Alex from two thousand kilometres away.

ON THE MONITOR, FLO COULD see a man walk behind Courtney in her kitchen. He appeared to be shirtless.

"Hello, dear. I'll give you and Alex some privacy," Flo said, before leaving the room. From the hallway she overheard Courtney and Alex chatting. Flo sometimes forgot that Alex had had a whole other life before entering hers. It seemed, in her mind, that he only started existing when he arrived in Cape Breton in November. It was like he was born five years old and dropped off on her and Tinker's doorstep. When she allowed herself to think about it, she resented Russell for not telling them about Alex when his son was first born, though in his defense, Russell hadn't had much time; he'd died when his second son was only a month old. Still. She had been praying to find forgiveness in her heart, but it hadn't arrived yet. Russell's thirty-day secret had robbed them of five precious years with their grandson.

Flo lingered in the hallway looking at framed photos hanging along the wall. She'd had Tinker hang them five feet above the floor, just the right height for her to enjoy at eye level and well below Tinker's gaze. Whereas she found comfort in the pictures, Tinker found only pain. There was Russell in his grade nine graduation photo wearing his first suit, peach fuzz on his lip and his tobogganing scar obvious on his shiny forehead, but still handsome as all get-out. Flo reached out her hand and touched her fingertips to the photo's glass. Next to it hung a picture of Russell throwing leaves onto baby Charlie, sitting in their backyard one fine fall day twenty years ago now. Charlie was laughing with his arms raised over his head, trying to catch the downpour of leaves, wearing an Aran cardigan she'd knit him for his second birthday. There was a portrait of Tinker and her on their wedding day in 1964, next to another of them at their fiftieth wedding anniversary last year posing with Nell and Charlie. She made a note to add a photo of Alex to the gallery, to let him know he was officially in their clan now. Her family was small compared to many, but she wondered if she loved them all with extra intensity because of it. It was like she had enough love in her heart for ten children and twenty grandchildren, but because she had only one child and two grandkids they got ten times the prescribed amount. She hoped she wasn't smothering anyone.

"Grandma? My mommy wants to talk to you," Alex shouted from the bedroom.

Flo entered the room as Alex was leaving.

"Can I have a snack now?" he asked.

She was relieved his appetite had returned and he looked like himself again. "G'wan downstairs and ask Grandpa." She shooed him from the room.

She sat at the desk and tried to remember where the camera was on her computer screen. "Hello again, Courtney. How's life treating you?" Flo asked, moving her face around in a clockwise fashion, bringing it closer then further from the monitor.

"For Christ's sake, can you stop moving, Flo? You're making me dizzy. Just pretend I'm sitting across from you. Try to relax." Courtney raked her fingers through her black hair. The shirtless man reappeared behind her. Courtney motioned him to leave with the back of her hand.

"Sorry, dear. I'm still a telephone talker at heart, but I know this is the way of the future. I've gotta keep up with the times. And if you could refrain from using the Lord's name in vain again I'd appreciate it." Flo did her best to remain polite.

Courtney sighed and nodded. "So Alex was pretty upset tonight. I think he's homesick."

Flo chose her words carefully. She didn't want to appear accusatory. "He misses you. But overall he's doing just fine here with Tinker and me. He's growing like a dandelion and even has his first wiggly tooth."

"Oh yeah?" Courtney didn't ask which tooth. "Listen, I think maybe I better come get him. It might be time for me to take him back to Toronto."

They were the words Flo dreaded. She didn't respond.

"Or maybe you'd like to keep him a while longer?"

"We'd love that, dear, but he's your son. As his legal guardian, you get to decide." Flo was incredulous she had to point this out.

"He's doing good with you. My life's a little complicated right now. It might not be the best time for him to come home." Courtney lit a cigarette and inhaled deeply.

"Sorry to hear that. Can I help?" Flo asked cautiously.

"Do you think you could spot me a bit of money? Just so, you know, I could fix up my place nice and start a little nest egg for Alex before bringing him home."

Flo paused. "I'd need to talk to Tinker about that." She's been hiding their bank balance from him. It was uncharacteristically deceitful of her. It had to stop. But maybe she could make this one withdrawal first.

"Could you? It sure is expensive raising a child, as you know. I'm not a rich woman."

"Neither am I," Flo replied. A pregnant pause followed.

"Well, I'm wondering, you know, if Russell's company settled with you after he died? There must have been a payout right? It was a workplace accident, after all."

And there it was. The blow Flo didn't realize she'd been waiting for. Her shoulders rounded forward and her stomach caved in, as if she'd actually been punched.

"What are you getting at, Courtney?"

"Just that if there's money in an account somewhere, maybe part of it is owed to me. For Alex, of course. I wouldn't want more than my share. But I've had no support the whole time Alex's been alive. It doesn't seem fair."

Flo neither agreed nor disagreed. She felt cornered. She hoped their Skype call would freeze the way it sometimes did, but of course on this night they had a perfect connection.

"I'm not comfortable having this conversation without Tinker. Let me go get him." Flo stood up.

"Wait!" Courtney called after her. "Let's keep this between just us for now. You know how Tinker can be. Just think about it and we'll talk again in a few days. Kiss my boy goodnight for me, will you?"

They hung up, but Flo didn't rush to leave the bedroom. She moved to the bed and sat there alone, feeling backhanded and trapped, racking her brain for what her next move should be.

CHAPTER 26

Cape Breton, May 2015

AFTER HIS PORRIDGE WITH A SLICED BANANA ON top and two cups of tea, Tinker retreated to his workshop in the basement. He wouldn't have much time to himself today, as he and Florence had a long list of things to do in Sydney. But before they left for the city, he wanted to complete his daily ritual.

On his way into the long, narrow workshop, he glanced at the "Tinker's Time Out" sign, then inhaled. Some people loved the smell of roses and others, coffee. But for Tinker, the most enticing aroma in the world was sawdust. Plain old sawdust, swept into small, organized piles in the corners of his workshop. The smell of it brought back memories of sanding a pinewood derby car with Charlie.

He pulled a sharpened pencil out of his shirt pocket. Charlie used to tease him because he wore pencils down to the tiniest nubs, and, sure enough, this one was no longer than an inch, but it still wrote just fine if he pinched it between his thumb and forefinger. He grabbed the calendar out of the drawer in his corner desk, slowly marking a large X across today's square. It was the end of April and the eighth month he'd been marking a calendar this way. Eight months since Charlie left home, eight months since they spoke. The longest they'd ever gone without communicating. He was still trying to learn to live with this hole in his heart, and there were days it threatened to open wider than the Canso Strait.

He didn't ask Flo about Charlie but she'd been letting little details slip now that Charlie and she were talking regularly again. Tinker knew Nell was out in Alberta now, and he let himself hope for a moment that perhaps Nell would bring Charlie home; that those two might get married and start a life together here. But like a fool his hopes were dashed again. It seemed that damn huge magnet of a province had pulled Nell out west, too, and apparently she was staying.

"Whatcha doing, Grandpa?" Alex leaned against the doorjamb with his jacket and sneakers on, a piece of toast in his hand and crabapple jelly glowing pink from the corners of his mouth.

"Just gathering up some paperwork to take to the bank. You excited about our day trip?" Tinker asked, opening a filing cabinet. Flo had been managing their accounts lately on the computer, but he still liked an old-fashioned face-to-face meeting at the bank and that's what he'd booked for them today.

"Yup. Grandma said if I'm good I can have a Happy Meal for lunch. C'mon," he said, beckoning with his arm.

Tinker followed him upstairs and out to the car, rubbing the jelly off Alex's mouth with his pocket hankie as they walked. Flo was already buckled into the passenger seat. "I invited Roger to come along. Keep an eye out for him," she said as they pulled out of their driveway.

"Now you tell me? Thanks for asking," Tinker said.

"I don't need your permission. You know Roger enjoys walking through the city. The change of scenery is good for him."

They found Roger plodding down the shoulder of Highway 19 in the direction of their house and stopped the car. He climbed in wordlessly and sat next to Alex. In the rear-view mirror he looked like the boy's opposite—tall where Alex was small, dark complexioned where Alex was pale. Neither one looked at the other, instead staring out of their respective windows. It had been awkward ever since Courtney caught them coming out of the woods together that day last fall.

Alex finally broke the silence. "Want a Twizzler?" He had two red licorices in a Ziploc bag. "There's one for you and one for me."

Roger didn't reply.

Tinker flipped on the radio to break the awkwardness inside the car. "Sonny's Dream," a song he adored, was playing. He gazed out the window. They were driving on the Cabot Trail now next to the Margaree

River, a stretch that brought back happy memories of fly-fishing for salmon. He started whistling along with the lyrics. Tinker was a decent whistler and equally good at playing the spoons, but these were the extent of his musical talents. He added a few trills for effect until Flo told him to hush, saying she wanted to hear the radio.

The lyrics told the story of a man, Sonny, who spent his lifetime watching the waves roll on the sea from his room by the stairs, dreaming of leaving his oceanside home for the wider world outside.

"'Sonny's Dream' by Ron Hynes. Singer-songwriter from Newfoundland. Born December 7, 1950, in St. John's. That was a Thursday." Roger had found his voice.

"I almost forgot we brought the human encyclopedia with us," Tinker said.

Flo turned her head away from Tinker as the song finished. "I know I can't hold him though I've tried and I've tried," Flo sang quietly as the song faded to silence. She reached for the dial and switched the radio off. Her shoulders began to tremble and Tinker caught her reaching for a tissue in her purse. She dabbed her eyes and blew her nose with it.

"What in heaven's sake has gotten into you?" he asked.

"Tinker, you know I love you, but you're really pigheaded sometimes."

Tinker had no idea what had triggered this, but he couldn't disagree, so he just kept on driving.

THEY ARRIVED AT THEIR FIRST stop in Sydney, the doctor's office. As soon as Tinker turned off the car, Roger opened the door and began walking. Tinker shouted after him to return to the parking lot by three o'clock. Roger didn't acknowledge but he had exceptional hearing and a steel-trap memory, so Tinker didn't worry.

The news at their first stop was good and bad. Tinker's arthritis hadn't worsened and he didn't need his pain medicine refilled. His last prescription wasn't even half gone and the doctor praised him for cutting back so drastically. He must've been taking fewer narcotics lately without even realizing it. He'd never been one to dose regularly or count his pills so this was a pleasant surprise.

Flo's blood pressure was high. The doctor looked concerned as she wrote a prescription for a low-dose antihypertensive medication and told Flo she'd need to check her blood pressure every day until it dropped.

"It could be situational," Flo said, with a flick of her hand that suggested it was not that big a deal. "Stress-related." She shoved the prescription in her purse.

What was stressing her out, Tinker wondered to himself.

ALEX, FULL FROM EATING NOT just one but two Happy Meals for lunch, waited on a couch in a small reception area at the bank. He had his Happy Meal toys, two Hot Wheels cars, in either hand, and he drove them along the couch cushions and armrests. He was under strict orders not to leave the couch for any reason.

Inside an office down a short hallway, Tinker bit his lip as Flo opened a new account to help the Syrian refugees that Falkirk Cove was sponsoring. At last Sunday's mass a second collection was held specifically for this cause. It netted a modest ninety-six dollars.

"Well, at least it's a start." Flo handed over the envelope, drooping with loonies and toonies, over to Gail.

"I still don't know why you're taking up collections for warring Arabs," Tinker grumbled.

Flo turned to face Tinker and snapped. "You do realize that Bob is Lebanese, thus also of Middle Eastern descent, right, Tinker?"

He thought about that for a second. "Well, that's different. He was born here. Plus I know him."

Gail busied herself sorting the money while they cooled off. She looked up and clasped her hands. "I've been reviewing your long-term investments and they show moderate growth so I don't think we need any adjustments there."

"Well, that's good news." Flo's pinched face began to relax.

"But I also have some bad news."

Flo's face tightened once again and she squirmed in her seat.

"Your primary savings account has been depleted. This is serious. You need to stop spending from that account altogether until you can build it back up a bit. You don't want to go into overdraft."

"What do you mean depleted? I like to keep at least twelve thousand in that account for emergencies," Tinker said.

Gail turned her computer monitor around to face Tinker and Flo. She pointed at the balance: $2.46.

"So where'd the money go?" Tinker barked at Gail.

Flo fidgeted in her seat. "Lower your voice, Tinker. Where are your manners?"

"I don't know how you spent it, Mr. Gordon. I only know the account is practically empty."

"Check the balance again. Something's off." It didn't make any sense to Tinker. He and Florence lived on a budget, they always had. They didn't take expensive trips, eat in restaurants, or drive a fancy car. Something didn't add up and he guessed it was the numbers in that column. Computers weren't to be trusted.

Gail turned her computer monitor in Tinker's direction and pointed at the screen. "There have been a series of five-hundred-dollar electronic transfers over recent months, and some for two hundred as well. See? It doesn't take too many like that before an account is drained."

Tinker glanced at Flo. She reached into her purse for her travel rosary beads and clutched them discreetly in her partially closed left palm.

"Electronic withdrawals? Aha. We were hacked and robbed!"

Florence's lips were moving in prayer and she used her right thumb to rub the beads.

"I knew that damn computer banking was going to foul up one day." Tinker looked smug.

"It's no error, Tinker," Flo said. "I withdrew the money. Don't get angry with Gail. She's only the messenger. I'm responsible."

Tinker's mind raced. "Is this about our selling the house? Your way to force us to get rid of it and move into an old-age home?"

"What? For heaven's sake, Tinker. I said we could keep the house. This isn't about the house. I'll figure out a way to get the money back."

Gail cleared her throat. "I don't want to be alarmist, but your Old Age Security just isn't enough for you to be spending like you have, Florence. You have to rein it in immediately."

Tinker was speechless. He looked at Flo like she was a stranger. She stared at her feet.

ALEX'S STOMACH BEGAN TO HURT. The second Happy Meal might have been a mistake. He needed to poop. With his toes on the seat cushions, he crawled on the floor using his hands until his body stretched across the hallway like he was in a push-up position. He then backed up and climbed to stand on the couch's backrest. Alex couldn't get anyone's attention to ask about going to the bathroom and he'd been told not to leave the couch under any circumstances. He tried to ignore the sharp pain in his lower tummy and his urge to push. A few farts slipped out and he looked around in embarrassment but nobody seemed to hear. The lingering sour smell surrounded him and he tried fanning the air with his hands, then returned to playing with his cars, trying to ignore his body's urges.

ROGER STOOD OUTSIDE THE BANK. He spotted Tinker's blue Buick, license plate AJP 194, in the parking lot. He paced back and forth across the front of the building waiting for them to exit.

Roger stopped walking. It was an overcast afternoon, and the yellow lamplight emanating from inside the bank beckoned him closer. As he stepped off the sidewalk and crossed the crabgrass his white trainers squeaked. His long arms dangled at his sides.

He'd been walking for most of the day, and although his legs were strong, they wanted a break. When he was not in Falkirk Cove, Roger didn't normally stand still in case people tried talking to him. Here in the city, no one knew him.

He walked straight up to the window, where he could get a closer look at the lady inside. She glanced up from her float then went back to her task sorting bills into neat piles.

Roger tried adding up the money, but she was too far away and her flying hands obstructed his view. It frustrated him to be unable to calculate how much money she had, but the way the lady sorted money into neat, organized piles impressed Roger. She worked briskly and purposefully. His stomach growled as he'd missed lunch, but he ignored it.

Roger shoved his now-cold hands into his pockets and shifted his weight back and forth on his size fourteen feet. He could see breath leave his open mouth and fog up the window. As that happened the bank lady stopped touching the money and looked up, meeting his eyes briefly. Her mouth was moving but Roger couldn't hear her words, only some crows cawing in the trees nearby. The lady wasn't smiling, and her eyebrows were scrunched up like wriggling caterpillars. She raised her hands and flicked them like she was shooing flies. Roger looked away, frozen, not knowing what to do.

The lady talked with another woman inside the bank then picked up a telephone, glancing at Roger. He stood there for another few minutes, alternatively rubbing the condensation off the window, then pressing his face against it to try and focus on the teller's money. He heard a car approach from behind him.

"Sir, I want you to step away from that window. Now, please," said a man's gruff voice.

Roger turned to see it was a policeman. He was walking away from his cruiser toward Roger.

"I said step away from that window. You've no business standing there. You're alarming the people inside the bank."

Roger willed his feet to move away from the window and the scary voice.

"You. Sir. Stop. I want to talk to you. Turn and face me, please."

Roger began to run. He heard more shouting and footsteps behind him getting closer. Then something hard whacked him across his back, and he was knocked to the sidewalk, breathless. He felt the policeman yank his arms together and felt cold metal on his wrists. The handcuffs went click.

ALEX SAW THE POLICE CRUISER from inside the bank. He jumped on the couch to try to get a better look. His stomach pains worsened. When the police put Roger, handcuffed, into the back of the police cruiser, he lost control of his bowels. His underwear filled quickly and a turd rolled down his leg and onto the floor. "Grandpa, Grandma, help!" he yelled. He stepped off the couch and onto the turd, then burst into tears. "I need help!"

CHAPTER 27

Alberta, May 2015

N ELL AND CHARLIE SAT ACROSS FROM ONE another in the counsellor's office. Charlie scratched his itchy forearms in long, continuous lines while Nell stared out the window.

The appointment was in the evening and Charlie was drowsy, but not because he'd had a busy day. He'd done nothing more than lie around the apartment. Fatigue also showed on Nell's face. Things were tense at home, and her new job doing environmental assessments in the oil fields had created a dynamic neither had settled into. Charlie had tried to argue that they should cancel this appointment and talk it out at home, but Nell wouldn't hear of it. She'd booked it and made his attendance non-negotiable.

"Why do *you* think you keep secrets from Nell, Charlie?" the counsellor asked. She had what some might consider a soothing voice, the kind Charlie imagined a yoga instructor might use. If it was supposed to relax him, it wasn't working. It grated on his nerves. He wanted to catch Nell's eyes to flash her a discreet, "Can you believe this woman?" look, but Nell was looking out the window. He tugged at a hangnail on his thumb instead.

There was a long, awkward silence during which Charlie and Nell shifted in their chairs.

"I guess I was embarrassed. And I wanted to protect her, I suppose. She doesn't need to suffer all my problems," he said, slouched over his chair and speaking slowly while focusing his gaze on the diagonal purple stripes on the grey carpet. "I got myself into this. I'll get myself out." The second hand on a wall clock ticked quietly, but otherwise the room was still and silent for several seconds until Nell sighed.

"Will you? And did it ever occur to you that maybe I want in on your problems, Charlie? That your problems are my problems too? That I'd like to help you?"

Nell's voice sounded shrill. Charlie looked up from the carpet into her brown eyes. Usually Nell still looked to him like the teenager she was when they first fell in love, but when he looked at her objectively now her freckles were faded, and her hair was no longer pulled into a ponytail but cut into a stylish bob. She looked like a woman. A woman with her shit together. Out of his league. She was leaning forward with her hands clasped together on her knees, waiting for his answer.

"I wanted to get control of the situation first," Charlie said. The hangnail got longer as he peeled it backward. It now poked him like a thorn.

The counsellor was nodding in his direction. She meant well, but God, was she patronizing. "Are you referring to your narcotics dependency?"

He squirmed in his chair but nodded. Was it a dependency? He thought of it as a recreational habit. A habit that had led him down a reckless path, it's true—especially after he started buying Oxy on credit off that biker, Lou.

"Charlie, are you willing to commit to being more open and honest with Nell?" the counsellor asked. "This is an opportunity to prove it." Of course she was taking Nell's side. He was the fuck-up. He was the one who'd started skimming his grandpa's pain meds back in Falkirk Cove. When he was high he didn't have to think about being the kid whose mom abandoned him at birth, or whose dad moved away and then died. When he was high he didn't care about disappointing his grandfather. He could just be Charlie, the fun, easy-going guy everyone liked. Charlie finally nodded. "I want to try."

"Then start by telling us about the pills."

"What is this, confession? Bless me father for I have sinned? Can I just say a bunch of Hail Marys and be absolved?" Charlie pressed his hands together as though praying.

"Cut it out, Charlie. This isn't a joke," Nell said. "I know you're using." Her voice broke on "using."

He rotated his head to release a kink in his neck and sighed deeply. "All right here it is. It started when you were in Halifax. Grandpa's arthritis was getting worse and he brought narcotics home. I found them in the medicine cabinet."

"You stole from Tinker?" Nell asked.

She made it sound so bad when she put it like that. It wasn't like he'd held up a pharmacy at gunpoint or anything.

The counsellor raised her index finger. "Nell, please reserve judgment. You said you wanted the truth. Charlie, go on."

Charlie was having trouble concentrating and choosing the right words. "One night I was going out with the guys and I didn't have any money for beer. I skimmed one of Grandpa's Percocets. I had a good time. No hangover the next day. It was only going to be once."

"But it wasn't once," the counsellor said in an even voice.

"Obviously not. It wasn't daily or anything. Just a weekend thing at first." He looked at Nell, who raised her eyebrows and gave a tiny nod as if urging him to continue. "I was flat broke. Not working. Not doing much of anything. I'd finished school and was waiting for something to happen but I didn't know what—you to come home, Nell, a job to materialize, a plan." He clasped his hands and squeezed until his knuckles turned white.

"You took drugs because you were bored?" Nell asked.

"More restless, maybe. I started spending money I didn't have on gas to get out of that town for a few hours every day. There's nothing to do in Falkirk Cove. Not a damn thing."

Nell interrupted. "Not true. You're making excuses."

The counsellor shot her a look. Nell stopped talking.

Charlie continued. "Everyone knows you and all your business, and other than the odd ceilidh, Saturday's bingo at the Inverness Legion is the highlight of the week."

Nell's shoulders dropped. "You forget how beautiful it is there, but go on."

Charlie felt the heat rise up his face. "Anyways, I got into debt—a few thousand dollars. I was tired of borrowing and begging. I made a few calls, sent out a few resumes, and got offered the job out here. Doing what I was trained to do, fit pipes. Things were looking up, except with Grandpa and you, Nell. Both of you didn't want me to move—"

Nell cut him off. "I never said I didn't want you to move. I just wished I were consulted. You were being so selfish."

The counsellor turned to Nell. "Please let Charlie talk now. You wanted him to open up. It's your turn to listen."

Nell, admonished, mumbled, "Sorry."

"I figured once I had a bit of money I'd iron out those personal problems."

Charlie's throat was dry and a deep tiredness was overtaking him. Getting all this out was much harder work than laying pipe. He tried to ignore his hangnail but couldn't.

"It started out great. I met Rex. We were hanging out on our days off, especially after we got paid. I became a regular at this bar and started going there even when Rex wasn't free. I met some bikers, played a few rounds of pool with them, and then one of them, Lou—who you met at the coffee shop, Nell—asked me if I wanted to score. I hadn't been high for months at that point." Charlie's denial sounded desperate, even to his own ears. "Can I get some water? My mouth's so friggin' dry."

While their counsellor was out of the office Charlie lost his willpower and pulled the hangnail off. Blood started trickling down his thumb toward his wrist. Nell shot him an exasperated look. When the counsellor returned she handed Charlie a glass of water and a tissue box.

"So like an idiot I said yes to Lou and one night led to two which led to three and pretty soon half of every paycheque was going to him. I wasn't talking to you, or to Grandma, just working and getting high. When I got behind on the money I owed Lou he broke my jaw."

"And that didn't scare you into quitting?" Nell asked.

"It might've, but I got more narcotics to deal with that pain, prescribed to me this time in my own name. It was my medicine. Doctor's orders." He set the glass of water, now half-empty, on the coffee table. When he lifted it he discovered a water ring on the wood that he wiped with the bloody tissue.

"And now?" Nell asked.

"I swear, Nell, when I saw you on my front porch that cold night in January I was done with drugs forever. And for weeks I was...until I got laid off. I started taking again."

The counsellor glanced at the ticking clock and closed her file. "Thanks for telling Nell that, Charlie. You've got some work ahead of you learning how to deal with life's disappointments sober, but I'm guessing you know that."

Charlie nodded.

"Nell, what's your reaction?"

Charlie was prepared for whatever came next. If Nell decided to leave him he wouldn't blame her. But if she decided to stay he'd vow to do better.

Nell sat forward on the edge of her chair and extended her arms. Charlie did the same and took her hands in his own. They looked into the other's eyes and started breathing in time together. Nell chewed her bottom lip.

"Loving you isn't always easy, Charlie Gordon, but nothing worth having ever is. I've invested years in this relationship, and I'm not giving up on it this easily. If you quit taking drugs and go to Narcotics Anonymous, I'll stay with you and we'll work on our relationship together."

"Withdrawal is difficult, I'm sure you both know that," the counsellor interjected. "I can see that you're physically addicted, Charlie. There will be many discomforts to endure."

"I can do it. Nothing would be worse than losing Nell." Charlie had never been more sincere. He squeezed Nell's hands and she squeezed back. It stung a little where he'd torn off the hangnail but also felt fantastic. "I don't say it enough and don't always act like I do, but I've always loved you, Nell, and I always will. I'll do whatever it takes. You're my cup and I'm your saucer."

CHAPTER 28

Turkey, May 2015

"OKAY, AHMED, IT'S TIME TO PUT AWAY YOUR book," Ms. Hussain said.

It was something she prompted him to do almost every day at *Al Salam* School. He didn't mean to disobey but always wanted a few minutes more to read before he was dismissed. Ms. Hussain had brought a small bag of books with her from Canada, and Ahmed had read the simple English picture books dozens of times each. The English alphabet was challenging, but he'd been studying the letters in his free moments and could now recognize some short words and understand simple stories as long as they had pictures. When immersed in a book he could be freeing genies from lamps, fighting pirates, or befriending jungle animals. Once he got home he was more likely to be fetching water, hanging laundry on the clothesline, or sweeping the floor of their tent.

"Just one more minute," he said, without looking up from the page. "Teacher, can monkeys really be pets? Is there such a thing as a magic cave? If you had three wishes what would they be?"

"Now, Ahmed. Put the book away." Ahmed could hear in her voice that Ms. Hussain meant business. She stood over him with her hands on her hips. "I want a lunch break before the afternoon students arrive."

Ahmed closed the pages on *Aladdin*, which Ms. Hussien told him was the English name for Alaa Al-Deen, wishing he could take it home to read to Yasmine. (It was funny to read the English equivalent of her name in the book: Jasmine.) He also wanted to read to her about the market because how it was pictured in the book reminded him of the souk in Aleppo. "Thank you, teacher. See you tomorrow," he said, re-shelving the book and standing to go.

Ms. Hussain smiled and laid her hand on his shoulder before giving him a playful shove out of the door.

It was already a hot, dry day, and Ahmed had ignored his thirst for the past half hour, but he was suddenly parched. The sun was beating down from a cloudless sky onto the refugee camp as he walked home. There were no trees among the lines of white tents to provide any shade, and he dragged his sandals through the dust lethargically. Ahmed thought back to the olive tree on his balcony in Aleppo, with its wispy green leaves, scratchy bark, and strong branches. It didn't offer much shade but it did look alive and he missed it. Nothing much grew here. A family in a neighbouring tent was trying to keep an olive tree alive that they'd transplanted into a large plastic bucket, but the leaves were turning brown and dropping. Talk inside the camp was that it would never work and was a foolish waste of space and water, but Ahmed admired that family's effort, and he prayed for that forlorn little tree.

When he arrived at his tent he went straight to the water jug to pour himself a glass of water. At air temperature it wasn't refreshing, but he drank to the bottom anyway.

"I need you to beat the dust out of this carpet, Ahmed." Amira did not say please, or ask about his morning at school. All she ever seemed to do anymore was order him around.

"Fine. In a minute," he replied. He tried to walk past his mother but she was twice her normal size now, and he bumped into her belly.

"Careful, Ahmed!" she said.

He lifted the rug off the floor and dragged it outside. He heaved and slung it over their makeshift clothesline, which was no more than a fraying yellow rope tied between the front pole propping up their tent with another pole on an adjacent tent. He grabbed their straw broom and started whacking the rug. Plumes of dust rose off it and fell onto him. He spluttered and coughed. He wished it was magic like Aladdin's carpet and could fly him out of this refugee camp to someplace spacious, lush, and cool. He swung the broom back to hit the rug even harder. He began counting his strikes in English. "Four, five, six, seven, eight, nine, ten," he said aloud, picking up speed and strength with each strike. Now he was shouting the words. He didn't know how to count any higher than ten in English so switched to Arabic and continued counting up to twenty, then thirty. He stopped, panted, and rested, propped up on the broom handle.

"Here. Is this clean enough for you now?" he said to his mother, hauling the rug back inside and pushing it toward her.

"What has gotten into you, Ahmed?" she asked. She and Yasmine sat on one of their two sleeping mattresses, sharing a large piece of pita bread. No one had offered him anything to eat. His father was not home to remind him to respect his mother.

"Nothing. Leave me alone." He flopped down face first on the opposite mattress. He craved his old bedroom where he could shut the door and be by himself. He was never alone in Reyhanli Camp. There were probably fifty people in shouting distance at this very moment. He heard people scuffling by outside, the rumbling of conversations, the distant motors of tractors clearing even more land for even more tents. It had been half a year now that they'd lived here. Months since he'd seen his grandparents, sat beside his olive tree, or read a book quietly in his bedroom. Abdo had already been here for more than a year. He'd had two birthdays at Reyhanli Camp.

Ahmed looked at the happiness picture he'd drawn months ago, which Yasmine had pinned to the tent wall. He remembered drawing each of his family members as best he could. His mother had a flat stomach then. Yasmine was holding the cat she always dreamed of having. They were returning to their home in Aleppo, and a peace flag was flapping in the air above them. "Mama, when are we going home?" Ahmed asked.

Amira grunted loudly as she got up from Yasmine's mattress and repositioned herself next to Ahmed. She rubbed his sweaty back. "We can't go home, Ahmed. There's a war happening in Syria, you know that."

"So next month? Next year? It has to end sometime, right?" Ahmed was being naïve and he knew it but wanted to see if his mother would be honest with him.

"Our country is destroyed, Ahmed. Your father thinks we are going to have to make a new home in a different country." Ahmed heard the pain in his mother's voice. It was probably just the baby pressing against her ribs again.

"Another new country? Which one?"

Amira paused before answering. "Your father thinks somewhere in Europe or North America. We don't know yet who will have us." She smiled at Ahmed but only with her mouth. Her eyes didn't crinkle the way they did when she was truly happy.

Ahmed thought about never going back to Syria and shared his mother's sadness. But he decided to trust that wherever his father chose, it would have to be better than here.

CHAPTER 29

Cape Breton, May 2015

F LO PUSHED THE SWINGING GLASS DOOR INTO THE reception area of the Sydney police station. "I demand you release Roger," she said, approaching the desk. "Now." Tinker and Alex followed at her heels.

The clerk stopped tapping on her phone, looking up from her game of Candy Crush Saga with bored eyes. "Who?"

"Roger! Your officer had no right to haul him away from outside the bank. He wasn't doing anything illegal."

Tinker pulled her aside. As concerned as he was for Roger, Flo had just been diagnosed with high blood pressure and this conniption fit wasn't going to lower it any. "Florence, you know you catch more flies with honey than you do with vinegar."

"Well, isn't that rich advice coming from you."

He gazed down at her red face and took her elbow, directing her to an armchair. "How 'bout you sit here for ten minutes while I deal with Alex?" The boy stunk to high heaven and was whimpering. Flo relented and Tinker escorted Alex to the washroom, where he stripped and wiped him down with scratchy paper towel inside a crowded stall.

"Ow. Ow." Alex squirmed. "Ow."

"Hold still!" Tinker was too old for this kind of hands-on childcare, but he had no choice. He put Alex's skid-marked pants back on him.

He shook the soiled underwear over the toilet and flushed, then pitched them in the trash on his way out.

Roger was standing next to Flo, rubbing the welts on his wrists when Tinker got back to reception.

"Sorry about the misunderstanding, sir. Your wife, here, explained Roger's situation. He's free to go," the officer said.

Just like Florence to take matters in her own hands. After brusque thank-yous and good-days, the four of them left the station for home. What a day.

SIX WEEKS LATER, MUCH STILL remained unsaid. Tinker and Flo didn't know how to fight. They'd always just given each other space and let things blown over. When Tinker stopped going to church Flo was disappointed but accepted it. When Flo helped Russell pack his bags and move away, and then did the same for Charlie years later, Tinker took his hurt and anger outside of the house. They'd sometimes disagreed, but when they did, they set their differences aside by evening and climbed into the same creaky bed together, where Flo warmed up her cold feet by tucking them under Tinker's hairy legs. It had been that way for fifty-one years. Neither of them could adjust to the new tension between them, and neither wanted to broach the subject and have it out.

Tinker poured a glass of water and grabbed a vial of pills from a high shelf in the pantry. He struggled with the childproof bottle but ignored the pain in his shoulder and managed to pop it open. With two pills in the palm of his hand, he grabbed the water glass and found Flo sitting in the quiet living room, staring out the window at the recently bloomed lilac bush in their front yard.

"Here. Take these," Tinker said, placing the antihypertensive pills and water on the end table beside her. She picked them up and swallowed them, forcing her mouth into a weak smile. Tinker walked over and opened the window to bring the sweet smell of the lilac's blossoms inside. A breeze blew as if on cue and the floral perfume swept in.

"Want me to cut a few boughs and put them in a vase?" he asked.

"No, they'd only bring ants inside the house. I can enjoy them well enough through the window."

"All right. Should we go to town this afternoon? We could double-check your blood pressure at the pharmacy." He began walking toward the bathroom to fetch her arm cuff for the first reading.

"I'm feeling fine. You and the doctor are worked up about nothing." Flo sounded annoyed. "Plus your fussing is making me edgy. I'm not used to being nursed."

"Florence, your pressure's been elevated for more than a month now." No one had voiced the word "stroke" aloud, but Tinker knew it was a risk at her age. It remained in the back of his mind all day long. She'd even complained of smelling burned toast that morning and he thought, *That's it, she's having a stroke,* until they saw black crusts in the garbage and figured out Alex had actually burned some toast.

"It's probably just elevated because of caffeine. I'll be happy when it stabilizes and we can drink regular tea again." Tinker had switched them to decaf as a precaution, but both of them found it unpalatable. They still brewed it out of habit but tossed most of it down the drain.

"When's Alex expected back?" Tinker asked. The house was eerily quiet with him out and the tension between Tinker and Flo was even more intense.

"In a bit. Catriona's taken him to the beach."

"It's good she agreed to babysit. Gives us a little break," Tinker said.

They sat in silence for a few minutes until Tinker said, "Then I guess we better talk about the money. We've avoided this conversation long enough." The events of their chaotic day in Sydney, starting with Flo's diagnosis and ending at the police station, had left them both reeling and exhausted. Tinker was desperate to find out where their money had gone, but he was also mad as hell that Florence had spent it without asking him first, and afraid that if they talked about it he'd blow up and push her blood pressure higher still.

"Yes, I suppose it's time. You deserve some answers," Flo said. "You won't like what you're about to hear."

"NO TAG TODAY, ALEX. I'M too tired." Catriona sat down on a log on the beach.

"Okay. Whatcha want to do then?"

Catriona passed him a bucket and a list she'd drafted at home of things for him to find. There were small sketches by the words: starfish, razor clam, periwinkle, smooth rock, and sea glass. "Find all these things and put them in the bucket. We're making a collection. Don't go where I can't see you."

Alex ran off and Catriona sat motionless, glad she'd thought of making the treasure hunt. She had low energy. Normally she enjoyed babysitting Alex and the pocket money it provided but today she had her first full-blown hangover and, she hoped, her last. (It would not be.) Drinking so much at last night's prom had been a mistake. She'd even played a few rounds of beer pong at the party after the dance and lost badly. Seamus had been really nice and held her hair back when she threw up later. She vaguely remembered telling him he was her best friend. She'd stressed *friend*; there was no use leading him on. She couldn't fake a crush that wasn't there. He'd taken it as well as she could have hoped.

"Got 'em all. Ready to head back?" Alex pushed the bucket toward her face. The smell made Catriona dry heave.

"Sure, buddy. Let's go show your grandparents." Catriona stood up off the log too quickly and got the spins. "Just gimme a minute."

"I GAVE SOME MONEY TO Courtney. She asked for a loan," Flo said.

"For what?" Tinker barked. The mere mention of that woman's name set him on edge. He'd figured she was behind their financial problems somehow.

"She said to fix up her apartment and start a small savings account for Alex. I was afraid that if I said no we'd lose Alex forever."

The boy had grown on Tinker, too, and he couldn't imagine their lives now without him around. Still, he didn't like this power Courtney had over them, or being played.

"So all the money went to Courtney? And what are the repayment terms for this so-called loan?"

"We haven't discussed repayment. Plus she didn't get it all. Expenses at home started adding up this winter with Alex coming here and Nell going west." Flo laid her hand on top of Tinker's. "I helped pay for Nell's plane ticket."

Tinker was speechless. Florence had kept this secret from him for months. Nell's parents had money. Why didn't they help her? He closed his eyes and counted backwards from ten to calm his nerves. What he really wanted was a strong cup of tea—caffeinated tea.

"Okay, is that all?"

Flo started chewing her bottom lip. "I sent money to Charlie, too. He got beat up, Tinker. A man broke his jaw and then he lost his job. People were coming after him for money. Bad people. He needed me."

"Who'd he owe money to? For what?" Tinker yelled.

Flo dropped her head into her hands. "I don't know! He wouldn't tell me. He said it'd be dangerous for me to know. And he begged me not to tell you." A sob caught in her throat.

As Tinker had predicted, Charlie found trouble in Alberta. The nerve of Florence, keeping this secret from him. He seethed. Just then the door flew open and Alex came blowing in with Catriona right behind him.

"Grandma, look what I found at the beach!" Alex kicked off his sneakers, then walked straight towards her to show her his plastic bucket filled with shells and rocks. The bottoms of his pant legs were damp and sandy and he smelled like a clamshell.

Flo lifted her head from her hands and collected herself, slipping Catriona ten dollars before waving her goodbye. She turned her attention to Alex. "Did you wade into the water?" Flo asked. "Tell me the truth: did j'duck?"

Alex was used to Flo's manner of speaking now. "No way did I duck. The waves were fr-fr-fr-freezing," Alex said, chattering his teeth. "I couldn't hardly feel my toes. I thought they falled off, but I counted and they're all still attached."

Tinker was amazed that Flo could play the doting grandmother in this moment. He couldn't calm down.

"Oh, wow. Look at all these treasures," Flo said, peering in the bucket. "Show me your favourite."

Alex dumped out the bucket onto the carpet. Drops of salt water, sand, bits of seaweed, and damp rocks and periwinkles splayed around Flo's dainty feet. "Oh, whoops. Am I in trouble?" Alex asked, lifting up a small starfish to show his grandma.

"It's okay, sweetie; Grandpa will clean it up later," she said, looking around the room for Tinker, to let him know she was only teasing. She knew they hadn't said all they needed to about their finances and Charlie's troubles, but she was grateful for the reprieve. "Where'd Grandpa go?"

"I dunno. Maybe downstairs to Tinker's Time Out."

Tinker's car pulled out of the driveway.

TINKER DROVE ALONG THE HIGHWAY, his mind racing. It had been twenty years since he smoked a cigarette, but he could sure use one now. Florence had crossed a line. Drained their bank account and kept secrets from him. Jeopardized their futures. Betrayed and angered him. This wasn't the woman he'd married. Flo had always been strong-willed but never sneaky and she'd never double-crossed him. How dare she?

CHAPTER 30

Alberta, June 2015

ALTHOUGH THEIR BASEMENT APARTMENT WAS cool, Charlie lay in bed sweating. He pulled off his white T-shirt and Bart Simpson pajama pants, but even naked, his body was a furnace. The red numbers on the alarm clock beside him burned into his retinas like a branding iron: 2:23, 2:48, 3:16, 3:36, 4:05. Though his energy had been low all day and he'd gone to bed early, he now lay between the crumpled sheets unable to sleep. He turned the clock around to face the wall so it only emitted the faintest glow and then flipped himself back over to stare at Nell's silhouette in the near-total darkness. She lay beside him asleep, her dark blond hair fanned out on her pillow and her plump, damp lips parted as she breathed rhythmically. Not too long ago staring at her like this would have made him want to jump her bones, and he would have nibbled her ear or stroked her hair to wake her up gently and get her in the mood, but they hadn't had sex since before he lost his job, and he sure as hell didn't feel like it now. His desire was for sleep only. Charlie squirmed and flopped, trying new positions to see if that was the answer. Nope. His eyes began watering, so he grabbed the corner of their top sheet to dab them, yanking it off Nell in the process.

"Can't sleep?" Nell sat up and yawned. "The doctor said this might happen."

"That doesn't make it any easier when it does." Charlie's temperature dropped rapidly now, and the sweat on his body turned cold. He began to tremble and it quickly escalated until his body shook.

"Maybe take a shower. If you were more comfortable you could relax."

"Don't tell me what to do, Nell. You've no idea."

"You're right, I don't."

Nell climbed out of bed, and Charlie was glad. Irritability was a side effect of withdrawal, and he didn't have the willpower to be nice right now. He tossed Nell her pillow and envied her the extra sleep she'd get on the couch before she had to get up at six. He lay on his back awake until he heard Nell's phone alarm beep on her side table, then pulled his sour-smelling pajamas back on and walked into the living room. His hair stuck out in every direction and dark circles ringed his puffy, bloodshot eyes. "Wake up. You have to go to work," he said, leaning over Nell.

Her eyelids flew open and she looked scared to see him. "Good morning?"

Charlie grunted and walked past her to the kitchen and started rummaging through cupboards.

"Where's the goddamn coffee press?"

Nell appeared in the kitchen, where she grabbed the Bodum from the drying rack and handed it to Charlie.

"Of course, right in front of my friggin' face. Nell to the rescue again," he mumbled.

Nell backed out of the kitchen and Charlie heard the water turn on in the shower. He plunged his coffee while she was still showering. Usually she was careful to conserve water, but this morning her shower lasted until after he'd drunk his first full cup. She eventually appeared in the kitchen dressed in work clothes and poured herself a bowl of whole-grain cereal and topped it with skim milk.

Charlie was so tired that even formulating words in his brain was an effort, but he knew he had to try. "What do you have going on today?"

"A site visit. We're starting to collect data in a proposed new drilling area." Her voice betrayed her excitement.

"You like this job, eh?" Charlie finished his second cup of coffee and worked at focusing on Nell's words. "Active listening," their counsellor called it.

"I kind of do. You think I'm a hypocrite to be working in the oil sands?"

Charlie shook his head. The reality was that at least one of them needed to make money, and it seemed the work itself—sampling soil, looking at forestry management plans, writing reports—suited her. Charlie let there be silence between them. He thought about his former job, and how he, too, used to get excited about going to work.

"I really hadn't imagined myself working within the oil and gas industry, but maybe I can make small changes from within."

Charlie wondered why success seemed to come so easily to Nell and not at all to him. "You can do anything, Nell. Hey, sorry I've been such a grump lately. Detox ain't all it's cracked up to be."

Nell cupped his face in her hand. "So what are you doing today?"

"I have a meeting at Narcotics Anonymous this morning." Why couldn't he just feel happy for Nell rather than sorry for himself?

"Hey, I'm proud of you, I hope you know. What you're going through is tough. Tougher than anything I've ever done," Nell said.

She was probably trying to be supportive, but her words sounded condescending. Charlie stood at the counter while Nell put her bowl in the sink. Their shoulders touched, but they didn't embrace.

Nell turned to face him. "Why don't we take a break this weekend? We could rent a car and drive to Jasper National Park. I hear Athabasca Falls is beautiful."

Her face was hopeful, but he didn't want to string her along. "I'm just not up for it, Nell. Sorry to be such a drag."

"Whatevs," she said, kissing Charlie's cheek. "Another time. And shave, would ya? I just exfoliated my lips on your stubble."

Charlie washed the coffee cup and Nell's bowl, then waited for his sponsor to pick him up. The pain in his jaw was finally gone, but the memory of it lingered. Making matters worse, he had random joint and muscle pain now. He seized up the way his grandfather did mid-arthritis attack. Some days he felt like a seventy-year-old man. The doctor said this, too, was part of withdrawal. He was to take it one day at a time. He was almost through the first month, considered the acute phase, which was supposedly the worst. He seriously hoped so. Today, at least, he had distractions. He was going to make a nice dinner to atone and thank Nell for her patience. He'd also been mulling over an idea he wanted to float by her. He'd need to find time to rest today before exhaustion overwhelmed him.

NELL WAS BACK AT HER desk entering data on her computer, her site visit having finished hours earlier. Her phone beeped.

"Ready?" Rex texted. She was lucky they'd been able to line up their work schedules so she could commute with him.

"5 more mins?" she texted back.

Rex sent a smiley-face emoji.

Nell could have left then or even earlier, but lately she was stretching out her work hours by every extra minute she could. She enjoyed her rides home with Rex; the more she got to know him, the easier his company seemed. It was the not knowing what version of Charlie waited for her once she arrived at home that she dreaded.

CHARLIE TURNED THE ELEMENT DOWN to let the spaghetti sauce simmer. He lit candles and spread garlic butter over sliced French bread. Nell would be home in five minutes. He poured her a glass of red wine and himself a glass of water and then tossed a Caesar salad.

He'd managed to have a nap today, and in the few moments after he woke up, when both his mind and body felt a temporary reprieve from their discomforts, he pledged to follow his instincts and suggest to Nell that they move back to Cape Breton. He was more than ready; he was suddenly desperate to go home and finally meet his half-brother. He popped the garlic bread into the oven as he heard the door opening.

"It smells fantastic in here," Nell said, entering the kitchen. She stirred the spaghetti sauce with a wooden spoon she then touched to her lips. "Spicy, yum. Where'd you learn to cook like this?"

Charlie turned to her. "A wonderful teacher called YouTube." His smile was genuine. "How was your day?" He noticed the red sauce on her lips. Adorable. He kissed it off and put his arms around her.

Nell didn't hug back but she didn't stiffen, either. "Great, actually. I got to ride in a helicopter. The views looking down at the treetops were amazing."

Charlie pulled the pot of pasta off the stove and poured it through a strainer. "I'm glad you like your job."

Nell snorted. "Yeah, an environmentalist finding happiness working on a drill site. I must be delusional." She sat down and sipped her wine.

Charlie plated their dinners and sat across from her. He lifted up his water glass to clink Nell's wine glass. "To delusions."

"That's strange. How about to health? And happiness."

They both sipped their drinks and started eating.

"Are you happy here?" Charlie asked, genuinely curious. He wasn't sure whether he wanted her to say yes or no.

"Some days I am. Alberta's not what I expected," Nell said, twirling noodles on her spoon.

Charlie swallowed a gulp of water. "What did you expect?"

"To fetch you and bring you back to your grandparents. Then we'd both be come-back-from-aways. That was the plan and why Flo paid for half my plane ticket." The wine was loosening Nell's tongue.

Charlie began clearing the table even though Nell had barely touched her plate. He had a fidgety energy and wanted to keep his hands busy. "You still want to move back to Cape Breton?"

"Not anymore." Nell smiled. "I have to admit that you were right about Alberta. It's pretty great."

Charlie went silent and felt his body temperature rise. The night sweats, waiting in the wings for hours, were about to take centre stage once again.

CHAPTER 31

Cape Breton, June 2015

THE SYRIAN BRIDE WAS LEAVING THE HAIR SALON before her wedding when a suicide bomber on the sidewalk walking past her pressed a button on his vest, detonating his backpack full of explosives. She lay dead on the street, her once-white wedding dress turning red as it absorbed her blood. Flo had to turn away from the scene on last night's evening news. Not only was the senselessness confounding, she found the war confusing. ISIS, Syrian Armed Forces, Kurdish YPG, Arab tribal fighters…and there were even more groups involved than that. She couldn't remember who was attacking whom or why. It made her feel hopeless and powerless—but not entirely so. She couldn't save the world, but if she could help even one Syrian family or even one innocent person, shouldn't she? Wasn't that what God wanted her to do?

"It's a massacre," Bob said. His role in the Falkirk Cove Refugee Project was to update the committee members about current events in Syria.

"Preach, preach, preach," Tinker mumbled from the chair next to Flo's. "Feels like we're upstairs gettin' a sermon."

"Shhh!" Flo said sharply, turning in Tinker's direction with her index finger in front of her pursed lips.

"Arabs aren't our problem," Tinker mumbled under his breath but loud enough that Flo and a few others around them heard. It was his first time inside St. Andrews in over a decade and he wasn't happy about it.

Bob ignored the chatter. "Mortar shells and rockets are falling from the sky onto cities, towns, and villages," he told the small group gathered in the church's basement. "Plus there are ground attacks. It's estimated six thousand people were killed last month alone. One thousand of them were civilians. That's more than all the people living in Falkirk Cove."

After a few seconds of silence Catriona asked, "So what can we do from here?"

It did Flo's heart good to see Bob's granddaughter here. They needed young people stepping up.

"Not a damn thing. If they're hell-bent on killing one another, there's nothin' we can do to stop them."

No one acknowledged Tinker's outburst.

"I propose that we privately sponsor a family. If we raise enough money, we can resettle them right here in town," Bob said.

Chair legs squeaked on the basement floor as the group considered this.

"Resettlement is the government's job," Tinker said. "Assuming we even want those people here."

Flo had been surprised Tinker relented and came to the meeting but now she just wished he'd shut up. She knew it was un-Christian to think like that, but she couldn't help it.

"It is, and it's ours too. There'll be public and private sponsorships." Bob kept a cool head. Flo had always admired that about him.

There was some twittering among them before Flo spoke up. "How much will we have to raise, Bob?"

"Well, it's not going to be cheap. About $35,000 to bring a family," Bob said. He let it sink in. That was more money than many people here made in a year.

Tinker let out a high-pitched whistle, then took a loud slurp of coffee from his Styrofoam cup.

Jean spoke up. "That's a lot of money. Even if we manage to raise it and the refugees do come, where will they live? Where will they work?"

"Exactly!" Tinker stood up. "There's no jobs here for locals, but we want to bring in foreigners?"

Flo was appalled. She glanced around the room, but Tinker seemed to have no allies. People were looking away and fidgeting as he spoke.

Bob remained calm. "For sure there are lots of details to iron out. This isn't going to be easy. That doesn't mean it can't be done. I think if we face one challenge at a time, it'll feel less overwhelming." Bob winked in Catriona's direction.

Tinker stood up. "It's foolish. We can't afford to be bringing in outsiders. We should be looking after other Cape Bretoners first. Jesus H. Christ, there's enough of us here unemployed and broke already."

Flo bristled at Tinker's use of the Lord's name, and at his attitude. Some days Tinker was bitterer than the free coffee he now sipped. She sprang to her small feet and stood as straight and tall as she could. "Where's your humanity? This is a real opportunity for us to pull together." She wasn't seeking an argument, but she wasn't afraid of one either. "Why'd you even come here today, Tinker?"

"To talk some sense into the lot of you. These people could be dangerous—terrorists, even. We don't know. They're not like us." Tinker was towering above Flo, peering down his nose into her face. Flo felt the eyes of the others on them. Bob opened his mouth to speak, then thought better of it and motioned with his hand that Flo should continue. She wanted to scold Tinker. But instead she searched her soul for mercy and dug deep into her internal reservoir of calm.

"Actually, Tinker, I suspect they're a lot like us. People who love their families, who want to breathe clean air and feel safe in their homes." Flo was proud of herself for finding self-control. "I think we can raise $35,000 and we should try. Who's with me? The naysayers are free to leave."

Everyone stayed seated. Tinker looked around the room, turned on his heels, and stormed out, tossing his coffee in the metal trashcan and kicking it as he left. When it stopped rattling, Flo sat down to catch her breath.

Jean broke the tension. "We'd better start fundraising. I'll put out a collection jar at the Kwikmart and bring a second one to bingo on Saturday night. Catriona, you'll help spread the word as you're selling cards, won't you?"

"You bet," Catriona said. She nodded at Flo. "We got this."

TINKER NEEDED TO COOL OFF. He found Alex in the church nursery, where he'd been amusing himself with LEGO. He didn't want to infect Alex with his bad mood but Florence was sure pushing all his buttons lately. They climbed into the Buick and drove to the Kwikmart where Tinker bought them each ice cream sandwiches. They sat in the car licking the sides and bit through the cookie exterior in unison. He was risking hell from Florence for spoiling Alex's appetite before supper, but he didn't give a sweet damn. He finished and sat back, staring vacantly out the window.

Florence would need a drive home from St. Andrews, but she could ask Bob or one of the others for a lift. Or he could go back and get her. As the minutes passed his anger abated, making space for a small measure of regret. His behaviour at the meeting, especially fighting with Florence in front of their friends, might have been a bit much. He had felt their judgmental eyes on him and knew they were on Florence's side. He smacked the steering wheel with the palms of both hands.

"What's the matter, Grandpa?"

"My hot-headedness might have got me into some trouble."

"Can you fix it?"

"I can try."

They circled back and walked into the graveyard behind St. Andrew's. The unmown grass was alive with grasshoppers. "What's that noise?" Alex asked of the buzzing and clacking.

"Have you never heard a grasshopper, boy?"

"I dunno. I guess not. Can I see one?"

"Look close and you'll see them jump. Maybe you can even catch one. Give it a try."

Alex started stretching his skinny arms out at the insects darting up at random intervals. He was a second or two late each time but kept trying.

Tinker stopped at his mother's headstone. She'd lain here thirty years now. Someday Tinker would be buried in the family plot next to her and Russell, and Flo would be buried with them, too. In his mind he would die before Flo; there could be no other way. He'd simply not survive without her. That realization made him even more remorseful.

"Mary Gordon," Alex said, approaching Tinker from behind and reading the tombstone. "She was your mommy?"

"Yes, she was. Your great-grandmother."

"Was she nice?"

This was a deceptively complicated question for Tinker. "She worked hard her whole life. She was tough, I guess. Strong and fair. Disciplined."

"So not nice like Grandma?"

"Just different. Not everyone can be as sweet as your grandma."

"Yeah." Alex thought about it for a moment, chewing his lips. "My mommy works really hard, too. It makes her tired and cranky sometimes."

"But you love her all the same?" Tinker asked, then immediately regretted the inflection in his voice.

Alex extended his arms and started spinning around. "'Course. She's my mommy. I miss her all the time, too. All. The. Time." Alex stopped spinning and tumbled to the ground where, after shaking off his dizziness, he started pulling blades of grass out of the dirt.

Tinker crouched down next to him and felt his hips start to ache. He worried he wouldn't be able to get back up. "She misses you too. You'll get to see her soon." Tinker and Flo were supposed to give him this news together, but the moment seemed right and Tinker seized it.

"I will? She's coming here to see me?" Alex stopped pulling grass and looked at Tinker, wide-eyed.

"Not just to see you but to take you back with her to Toronto. You're going home next month."

"For real?"

"For real."

Alex sprung up to standing. "Hey, can you help me catch a grasshopper, Grandpa?"

Tinker couldn't gauge how Alex had received the news he'd be leaving. Certainly more casually than he and Florence had. Or perhaps he needed to just sit with it for a bit. "Sure, if you'll help an old fella back up onto his feet." Tinker extended a hand, but Alex walked around him and then pushed upwards on his bottom, like he was giving him a boost. Curiously, it worked, and Tinker was again upright.

He showed Alex how to cup his open hands and hover silently in the grass looking at the ground. Alex spotted one greenish-brown body and pointed at it. Tinker raised his palm to indicate Alex must wait. When it jumped, Alex clasped his cupped hands around it mid-air. "I got it! I caught a grasshopper!" He made a small space between his thumbs to peek at the bug. "It's tickling me," he said, giggling.

The church door opened and Flo walked through it and toward Alex.

"Grandma, Grandma. I caught a grasshopper. Come see!" Alex ran toward her too fast and tripped over his feet. His hands flew open reflexively to break his fall and the grasshopper dropped to the ground, then jumped away.

"Oh dear. Are you okay?" Flo asked.

"Ouch. Yeah, I guess." Alex stood up, brushing off his knees. "Where'd my grasshopper go?"

"He grass-hopped away. I guess it was time for him to head home, too." Flo didn't look at Tinker.

"Hey, Grandma, did you know my mommy's coming to get me this summer? She's taking me back to Toronto."

Flo shot Tinker a look. "I did know that. Are you happy?"

"Happy and sad. Let's go home. See ya later, grasshopper." Alex waved and started walking to the car.

Flo stared at Tinker, but his eyes were downcast.

"Do you have anything to say for yourself?"

"I might've been out of line in there." He gestured at the church.

"Oh, you think?"

Tinker was caught off guard by Florence's sarcasm. "I'll try to behave better."

"You might want to do a little soul-searching to see what's behind your outrage. I won't stay married to a bigot, Tinker. Don't test me. This is your last warning."

The look on her face told Tinker she meant it. "Sorry," he mumbled.

Florence sighed and shook her head. "You exhaust me sometimes, Tinker Gordon."

"I exhaust me sometimes too."

CHAPTER 32

Turkey, July 2015

MEMBERS OF THE UN REFUGEE AGENCY WERE visiting Reyhanli Camp. Peering from one open eye, Amira watched Sami get up well before sunrise to register their family. He wanted to beat the crowd.

"How did it go?" she asked when he returned to the tent mid-morning, strain showing on his tired face.

"They brought an interpreter who helped me fill out the paperwork. It was onerous, but we're all registered. You, me, and the children—including the unborn one." Sami reached out and touched Amira's large belly.

She felt a flutter as the baby began to stir inside her. She looked down and saw a bulge appear in her lower left abdomen. "He's kicking."

Sami moved the palm of his hand over the bulge and grinned. "Hello, baby. Aren't you a feisty one."

"He's going to need to be." Amira tried to ignore the pressure on her bladder. She'd just been to the latrine and surely didn't need to pee again. "What happens now?"

"Our names will be sent to various embassies around the world. I'm certain some generous country will approve us." Sami flopped on the bed and yawned.

Would they? Amira kept her doubts to herself. Their names would be listed with presumably thousands of other names, a roster of the world's most desperate. Who's to say whether they would be distinguishable from the masses? Amira knew they weren't that special. But she wouldn't let despair overtake her today. Today they had an outing. They were leaving the refugee camp to go into the Turkish city of Reyhanli. Amira sometimes forgot there was a city here separate from the tent city. Some even dubbed it "Little Syria" because the population of about sixty thousand had now more than doubled with so many Syrian immigrants living there. Amira's ankles were swollen and her back ached, but she didn't dare complain. It wasn't often she was able to leave camp, and she was excited. While washing dishes at a spigot she'd overheard good things about a bakery in town, plus Sami had recently treated an injured woman whose cousin opened a barbershop there. The woman paid to have her leg wound disinfected and stitched with three free haircuts. Amira wanted Sami and the children to cash in these I.O.U.s before her appointment at the health-care centre.

"Shall we hire a driver now?" Sami asked as they walked along the road away from camp. Amira nodded. She wanted to save money by walking farther but knew her limits, and though it was early, the morning sun was already intense. Yasmine's energy, too, waned quickly and they needed to preserve it to complete their errands.

A car drove by and slowed down when Sami waved his arm. Sami opened the passenger door for Amira and helped her maneuver inside before climbing in the front seat. *"As-Salaam Alaikum,"* Sami greeted the driver.

"As-Salaam Alaikum. I'm Tareq. Where are you headed?"

Amira wanted to speak but, unable to find the confidence, deferred to Sami. He gave directions and set about getting to know Tareq. Amira envied his ease with new people. He'd always had a long waiting list at his medical practice, and she could see why. Sami was likable.

"I'm ex-military. I defected from that corrupt war back home. Now I make a living doing this and that. Driving a taxi, selling cellphones or small appliances, exchanging money." Reyhanli camp got smaller and smaller in the distance as Tareq spoke.

"Won't the Syrian army kill you if they catch you?" Sami asked.

"They might, but if I'd remained a soldier I'd have been killed anyway. I'd rather die on my own terms than for Bashar al-Assad," Tareq replied. "Hey, did you hear the latest news from Aleppo? A bomb went off in a tunnel outside the outer wall of the Citadel two days ago. It's basically destroyed."

"Oh no. I heard it had become a military base. What a shame," Sami said.

Despite the heat and discomfort of her swollen body, Amira faked cheerfulness and initiated a game of "I Spy" to distract the children in the backseat of the taxi from the conversation underway up front. They'd visited Aleppo's Citadel before the war and had a wonderful time exploring in the large castle and saying their midday prayers in its excavated Hadad Temple among the etched stone pillars the archaeologists had uncovered. Amira wanted Ahmed and Yasmine to hold onto that version of the Citadel in their memories. She didn't want them to picture only the bombed-out version of the city every time they heard the word "Aleppo."

Sami and Tareq exchanged numbers when they arrived in town, already thinking the other could be useful if they needed to barter medical care for goods or services in the future. Friendships were too expendable these days to be built on simply liking another person; there had to be mutual benefit to both parties for them to make time.

The family poured out of the car onto a commercial street. "There's the barbershop." Amira pointed for Sami's benefit. "Take the children with you and get everyone a haircut."

"Even me, Mama? I want long hair like yours," Yasmine said. Amira wore a hijab today as she always did in public, but her daughter had seen her often in their home without it on. Amira's hair trailed halfway down her back in glossy, chocolate brown waves. Back in Syria it had been Amira's favourite feature, and she enjoyed washing it every other day and brushing it at bedtime while Sami complimented her beauty. In the refugee camp, though, she was lucky if she got to wash it every other week. During the day she kept it braided and out of the way and found when she undid her braid and shook out her hair at bedtime, cooking smells were released.

"It's too hard to keep clean and tangle-free." Amira gently pulled Yasmine's long curls and watched them recoil like springs. "Just as short as your shoulders, please? I'll meet you in one hour right here."

As her family crossed the street hand-in-hand, Amira slipped into a lingerie shop. While once upon a time in Syria she'd enjoyed buying lacy bikini briefs, today she needed to focus on comfort. It irritated her to be the size she currently was and to have all her dresses, once loose, now stretched across her abdomen so she could see the outline of her protruding navel. The elastic waistbands of her underwear cut a red line into her lower abdomen and she sought relief in several new high-waisted pairs, size extra-large. They were decidedly un-sexy, but she didn't care. The idea of wearing actual lingerie seemed laughable now. She used to wear provocative underwear, sometimes even all day while Sami was at work. It was her own little secret until he came home and she could giggle and whisper, "Guess what I'm wearing under this," into his ear as they put the children to bed, knowing where it would lead. Such flirting seemed a lifetime ago.

She watched her family members leave the barbershop and make their way toward her. They all had smart haircuts, and she found herself jealous of them. She'd wanted to have her eyebrows threaded like she did in her previous life, but there wasn't money for that, nor time. They had no mirror in their tent, but when she caught her reflection in a pot or spoon she was appalled by how bushy her eyebrows had become. Sami had become hairier too, but today his cheeks were the smoothest she'd seen them in ages. "I splurged on a shave," he told her when she grazed her fingertips across his face. "My barber was a thirteen-year-old Syrian boy barely bigger than Ahmed."

They stopped at a falafel stand for lunch. Now that Amira was used to living in the refugee camp, things in town seemed civilized and gloriously clean by comparison. Reyhanli didn't have the elegance of old Aleppo and it, too, was vulnerable to terrorism, but the streets felt calm today and the Turks and Syrians seemed to get along here well enough.

Could this ever feel like home for them? Amira wondered. No, she decided, that was magical thinking. Living here permanently would likely mean her children would work rather than go to school, Sami would provide unlicensed medical care in exchange for cellphones and drives, and she would always worry that ISIS might strike. She and Sami had ambitions for their children beyond this, and wanted them to grow up somewhere quiet and peaceful. They would not sell these dreams short just for the convenience and marginal gain moving from the camp permanently into town would offer.

Sami had arranged a prenatal check-up for Amira at one of the local health-care centres. He had been monitoring her pregnancy himself but wanted her to deliver the baby in a clinic. Her other births had been uncomplicated but that didn't guarantee this one would be too, and besides, Sami didn't feel the refugee camp was sufficiently sanitary and neither did he want the sole responsibility of delivering his own child. He was too emotionally invested to act as a clinician.

"Thirty-four weeks and growing well," the doctor declared. "How's mom feeling?"

"Huge, hot, tired, and uncomfortable all the time. The usual," Amira replied. The baby kicked her in the ribs as she spoke, as though objecting to Amira's words. "Oof. There he goes again," she said.

"He *or* she. And you'll come here for the delivery?" the doctor asked.

Amira nodded and tried to be grateful. She preferred the clinic to her tent but was still coming to terms with her baby being born in Turkey. Technically, according to his birth certificate, he wouldn't even be Syrian. He might not get to see Syria for decades.

Yasmine was examined and declared stable and prescribed an inhaler for her asthma. Sami agreed with the treatment plan. Yasmine wasn't one hundred percent, but she wasn't worse.

They had arranged to have Tareq drive them back to Reyhanli Camp. As the white tents pulled into sight, Amira's mood plummeted. It had been such a welcome break to leave camp for the day. Her old sense of freedom and purpose had returned. Now the monotony and rigor of camp life stretched in front of her as endlessly as those white tents.

Sami's phone rang as they climbed out of Tareq's car. Amira was reminding the children to thank their driver.

"Who called?" Amira asked, when Sami was finished.

"The United Nations Refugee Agency. They just needed to confirm something with me about our registration. They were confused by the birth date of our third child, which I estimated will happen one month from today."

Ahmed overheard his parents' conversation. "What's happening, Papa?"

"An agency is sending our file to embassies around the world. Those embassies select families from a list to interview. If we pass, we're invited to go live there."

"So it's really happening? We're moving far away?" Ahmed's eyes darted from his mother to his father, and Yasmine was now looking at them expectantly, too.

Amira took a deep breath. She turned around, her back to her family, and rubbed her large belly. Once composed, she faced them. "It appears we are. Or at least we're going to try. There are no guarantees we'll be selected, but let's hope so."

Ahmed noticed that this time, when his mother smiled, her eyes smiled, too.

CHAPTER 33

Alberta, July 2015

CHARLIE SURFED CHANNELS WHILE NELL LACED up her sneakers, then filled a water bottle. She hummed as she pulled her hair into a ponytail.

"You sure you don't want to come to flag football, even just to watch?" Nell shifted her weight from her left to her right foot, then pulled her arm back like she was about to throw a football.

"Nah, you go on. Is Rex picking you up?" Charlie replied from the sofa.

"Nope, I'm cycling. Warm up my gams a bit." Nell slapped her thighs. She'd recently bought a second-hand mountain bike that took up most of the space in their hallway. "You should take the bike out someday. It's a smooth ride," she said.

Charlie nodded noncommittally. Nell wanted him to get better so badly that it felt like extra pressure. Her cheerfulness and nudging grated on his nerves. Other than his Narcotics Anonymous meetings, he preferred staying home these days. He felt a random ache in his hips, and his watery eyes were making the TV screen blurry. His symptoms were more infrequent now but still reared occasionally and with no warning, like a rogue wave that burst out of the ocean, knocked him down, and sucked him in with its undertow. He was trying to tough it out without methadone, but some days he just plain hurt. He switched the TV off and laid his head back on a pillow.

"You okay?" Nell asked, glancing over.

It took all Charlie's effort not to snap at her. "Sure, peachy. You go on." He wanted her to leave so he could focus on what he needed to do.

"All right. I'll do my best not to catch any footballs in the face. I don't need to break my nose *again*."

Charlie mumbled goodbye without lifting his head off the pillow. He adored Nell's facial imperfection, but he didn't feel like teasing her about it today. Nell leaned down to kiss his cheek, and his eyes fluttered open. She looked like the old Nell again, with her hair up and wearing athletic shorts and a team jersey. He felt a surge of affection for her.

"Later, gator." She heaved her bike up the stairs to their front door and cheered "touchdown!" when she got to the top.

Charlie made some toast and tea and sat at the kitchen table. "Hi, I'm Charlie and I am an addict," he said out loud to the empty room. The words didn't roll easily off his tongue. "I am an addict." He made a few more attempts, trying to modulate his voice so it didn't sound so robotic, then picked up the phone and dialled.

"Hello?"

"Grandpa, it's Charlie." He felt his armpits dampen. The world's longest five seconds passed before Tinker replied.

"To what do I owe this honour?" Tinker spoke loudly when calls were long distance, and Charlie had to pull the phone away from his ear.

"Is Grandma home?"

"She's just putting Alex to bed. Want me to get her?"

"No, let's you and me chat first." Charlie asked after Alex and the other people he missed in Falkirk Cove. Tinker's answers were brief, but he didn't hang up on Charlie. Then he asked about the weather in Alberta and how Nell was doing. Each stuck to safe topics. Neither was yet prepared to discuss the schism between them. Tinker introduced the next piece of news, telling Charlie about Grandma's new cause sponsoring Syrian refuges.

"She wants to bring a family of Syrians to live in Cape Breton?"

"Yep, you heard me right. Hard enough for Cape Bretoners themselves to get jobs, yet your grandmother thinks it's a good idea to bring outsiders in."

Charlie let that lie. What was taking Grandma so long to get to the phone?

"They probably won't even speak English."

Charlie didn't want to argue so switched subjects. "Is her blood pressure still high?" He couldn't allow himself to feel responsible for that, but in the back of his mind he worried that this phone call wasn't going to do anything to bring it down.

"A bit, yes. Here she is now." Tinker bellowed even louder now. "Pick up the phone in the living room, would you, Florence? It's Charlie calling from Alberta."

The line clicked. "Charlie! It makes me some happy that you two are talking. What'd I miss?" Flo said.

His grandma's sweet voice and cheerfulness weighed heavily on Charlie. But this admission was important. He swallowed.

THE FOOTBALL FLEW THROUGH THE vast Alberta sky. A guy on the opposing team caught it and began running in Nell's direction. In a split second she saw the entire field before her and mapped out a jagged line to reach him. She made a few cuts as she ran and then surged toward her opponent's waist, reaching for a rectangular piece of yellow cloth hanging from his belt as she fell forward. Nell stood up quickly and thrust her arm into the air, waving the yellow flag as the ref's whistle blew and the play ended.

"Nice grab, Nell!" Rex said, giving her a high-five as they got off the field and let the offensive line take over. "You're a natural."

"Oh, right! I just got lucky." Nell didn't know why she said that. She'd always been athletic and proud of it. "Having three older brothers meant lots of backyard football when I was growing up." Now she was crediting boys for her talent? Ugh.

She watched a family walk down the path adjacent to the football field. One dad pushed a double stroller and the other dad walked next to a boy on a scooter. For the first time since she arrived, she had a pang of homesickness and longed for her own family. She'd been so mired in Charlie's problems and family drama recently she hadn't had much contact. She was the last of her parents' children to leave Cape Breton, but they had neither made her feel guilty for going nor for her infrequent check-ins. Her mother's advice when Nell announced she was heading to Alberta was two-fold: "Don't lose yourself" and "Pack only what you can carry." Nell appreciated both her wisdom and pragmatism, but reflecting on the advice now she wasn't certain she'd followed it.

It was their line's turn to play, and Nell ran to her position and bent forward, ready to sprint. The field had recently been aerated and the stubby brown soil cylinders she kicked with her cleats looked like turds. She laughed out loud.

"What's so funny?"

Nell looked up at Rex, broad-shouldered and tall standing next to her. She breathed in the crisp air, and in her peripheral vision saw a red kite bobbing in the sky. She felt a lightness she hadn't in a long while. "Nothing. Focus on the football, not me."

The whistle blew and the play began. Nell used her agility to her advantage, grabbing yet another flag on the next play.

"We make a good tag team, you and I," Rex said as they huddled with their teammates on the grass at the end of the game. They cheered hip-hip-hooray for the team they'd just beat and shook their opponents' hands, and Nell began walking toward the bike rack. She dumped the remaining water in her bottle over her head to cool down.

Rex caught up to her. "Aren't you joining us for a beer?"

She must've looked a mess. She needed to get home to check on Charlie.

"C'mon. The whole team's going. I can throw your bike in my truck and take you home later." Rex pulled off his shirt and grabbed a clean one out of his kit bag to change into. Nell snuck a peek at his six-pack abs, then averted her eyes by looking up at the big sky, brush-stroked with muted pinks and purples behind a sun now plunging into the Athabasca River on the horizon.

"All right. A victory beer sounds great. Thanks, Rex."

"I'VE SOMETHING TO TELL YOU both. Something important. It's hard to say, but here goes." Charlie swallowed and tried to project his voice, but the words still got caught in his throat. "I'm an addict," he finally croaked. He waited for his grandparents' reaction.

"What's that? You're in the attic? I thought you and Nell lived in a basement," Tinker said.

He wasn't going to make this any easier for Charlie. "No, Grandpa, I said I'm an addict. I was hooked on narcotics. I became physically dependent on them. I'm in recovery now."

Flo spoke gently. "How did this happen, Charlie?" She thought about how quickly Tinker's pain pills used to disappear. And about the money she'd given him recently.

"Like a damn fool, I started taking pills back in Cape Breton to get high when I couldn't afford booze. Hillbilly heroin, right? I thought I'd kick it when I came to Alberta, but then I started using here, too. It got worse until I couldn't stop. But six weeks ago I did stop." Charlie was pacing around the apartment and his hand felt so slick against his phone he risked dropping it. "I'm done with it now. It's behind me." He switched the phone to his left hand and wiped his right palm on his jeans.

"Does Nell know?" Flo asked.

"Yeah, she's been great. Supporting us both with her new job, putting up with my bullshit. It's more than I deserve. Sorry 'bout the cuss word, Grandma."

"God love that Nell. She's a good egg." For once, Flo didn't scold him for swearing.

"I asked her not to say anything to you guys. I had to tell you myself. They say at Narcotics Anonymous that admission is an important part of recovery. I'm determined to beat this." It sounded cliché even to Charlie's ears, but he meant every word. He waited for Tinker to respond—to say anything at all. That he'd known trouble would find Charlie in Alberta. That Charlie had brought it upon himself. That he'd disappointed them, broken their trust, broken their hearts. Charlie sat on the couch and placed the phone on the floor. He dropped his head into his hands and sobbed.

Tinker voice finally boomed from below him. "I'm awfully sorry to hear this, Charlie. What happens now?"

Charlie tried to pull it together, but his voice warbled and broke. "I want to come home."

CHAPTER 34

Turkey, July 2015

THE DRIVER PARKED HIS WHITE VAN AT THE GATE, walked around to its side, and slid open the panel doors. Passengers spilled out, eager to exit the cramped vehicle and start their new lives in the relative safety of Turkey. A petite woman was the last person left sitting inside, breathing the hot stale air. Her liver-spotted hands were folded on her lap, and her slick back stuck to her seat.

"Could someone help me, please?" she asked. The passengers stopped walking away and turned back now, surprised to hear her speak. She hadn't uttered a word during their drive together. One man extended his hand and asked her, "May I touch you?" The van's driver did the same. She didn't answer but, nodding, grabbed their wrists instead. "Pull me out. I haven't any strength in my legs."

Malnourishment and injury had aged her prematurely. Though slight, she was limp, and the men still had to bend their knees, count to three, and heave in unison to get her up off her seat and propped upright on the packed dirt. The driver put his arm around her back with his hand tucked in her opposite armpit to prevent her from collapsing onto the ground.

"Thank you for this kindness," she said with effort.

"Of course, ma'am. How will you manage?"

She didn't answer. He had also helped her into his van, at which time she had assured him there would be someone to greet her at their destination. He'd assumed that meant right here where they pulled up, but now could see that wasn't so. He stood there perplexed. A lame woman could not attempt to search this vast camp alone. Whoever her people were, they would need to be found and brought to her. But he couldn't do it; he had to get back to fetch yet another group of refugees.

"You had no bags, is that right?" the driver asked.

Again, she ignored his question.

He used hand signals and acted out carrying bags like they were playing charades.

"No, no luggage. I have nothing. Everything's gone," she said.

Some children ran by and the driver called to them. "Find this woman a cane or crutches, would you? Anything to help her walk. As quickly as you can. Go!" They scuttled off and he remained with his arm around her. The woman's gaze concerned him. Though she stared straight ahead, her eyes focused on nothing. She again fell mute.

When the children returned with two aluminum tent poles, he thanked them and awkwardly handed the poles to the woman. She reached out and wrapped her hands around the tops of poles and shifted her weight off the driver so she could stand on her own, leaning onto the poles for support.

"I have family here in Reyhanli Camp. When I find them, they will care for me." She gazed ahead at the rows upon rows of white tents. "I'm not your responsibility. Go."

AMIRA KNEW ONCE THE BABY arrived that Yasmine would get much less attention, so she wanted to make her feel special now. They spent the morning at the nursery, where Yasmine did fingerpainting and played. Amira rested on a cushion close by, gritting her teeth through cramps and the relentless pressure of the baby bearing down on her pelvis. She drew inner strength to stop herself from nagging even when her daughter smudged blue paint on her dress.

Next they headed to the swings. They took slow, small steps, and Amira forced herself to make eye contact and smile at the people they passed. After so many months at Reyhanli Camp she still had few acquaintances but was making an effort to be friendlier and overcome her shyness in preparation for emigrating.

They reached the swings and waited for their turn. When one became empty Yasmine ran toward it. "Push me!"

Amira stood behind her but was too scared to push her daughter for fear the swing would pendulum back into her large belly before she had time to retreat. She stepped aside. "Try pumping your legs like the other children."

Yasmine pouted, but then another mother stepped in and offered to push her.

"Thank you, friend. I'm afraid I'm rather useless these days." Amira winced as another sharp pain seized her from inside. When it released its clench she exhaled.

"Nonsense." The woman had kind eyes and large-knuckled, mannish hands she placed on Yasmine's back. "You're growing a baby inside you. I know what that feels like. I have seven children."

"Seven? Praise Allah." Amira willed herself to continue their conversation. Her interpersonal skills were dull. "I'm Amira."

"Pleased to meet you, Amira. I'm Noor. Where are you from?"

Wiry black hairs slipped out of Noor's hijab and stuck to her round face. She was heavyset and what Amira would call handsome rather than feminine. Amira envied the easy way she moved her body and made small talk.

"Higher, please!" Yasmine pleaded.

"She can be demanding, Noor, watch out. And to answer your question, we're from Aleppo." She offered a half smile and shrug.

Sweat beads formed on Noor's forehead. She was doing double-duty now, pushing Yasmine and her own daughter, darting back and forth between swings. "We too are from Aleppo." When the girls were both midair, Noor glanced at Amira. Although it was only for a microsecond, Amira felt completely seen.

Amira grabbed the swingset's frame to balance herself. "Do you think you'll ever return?"

"It depends. My husband stayed to fight in the war. If he's still alive at the end of it we might." Noor spoke matter-of-factly and stepped away from the swings now. It was time to give other children a turn.

"I'm sorry about your husband. I'm more fortunate than many here. My husband, Sami, is with us." Amira fanned her face with Yasmine's fingerpainting of a cat.

"Dr. Sami?"

"Yes. You know my husband?"

"Indeed I do. He calmed down my Jamila when she was suffering the worst of her night terrors, and he diagnosed my pink eye. I am honoured to meet you, Amira. I hold your husband in highest regard and now you, too."

My people skills must be improving, Amira thought. *I've just made a friend.* The warm feeling it brought distracted her from the seizing tightness in her lower belly.

THE WOMAN INCHED FORWARD ON her poles. The sun scorched her leathery skin, but she appeared not to notice. She limped along in a mostly straight line, with the posture, fatigue, and determination of a climber summiting Mount Everest. Those walking by tipped their heads in greeting or moved out of the way. She acknowledged nobody.

IT WAS MIDDAY AND AMIRA craved shade and rest. Yasmine, too, was fading, and Amira heard a faint wheeze creep into her breathing. "You know what's a nice thing to do? Take a nap," Amira said.

"No, Mama, I'm not a baby, I'm five. No nap." They were walking back to their tent after saying goodbye to Noor and Jamila. Amira had to stop regularly to catch her breath.

"Then let's just lie down together on my mattress and close our eyes and tell each other stories. We can play the princess game and imagine what colour tassels and jewels we would choose to wear," Amira said. Her ulterior motives were so obvious she wondered if Yasmine would resist, but she knew her daughter well. Yasmine loved to play pretend.

"Okay, but I won't sleep."

"Of course not. You're five. Too old for naps."

A hunched woman approached them with her head down, leaning on tent poles as she walked. Her clothes were dirty and her hijab was coming loose.

"Why's that lady walking like that?"

"Don't stare, Yasmine. Lots of people at Reyhanli Camp have been injured. She's doing her best." Amira got a faint whiff of urine as the woman passed them.

THE WOMAN COULDN'T WALK any farther. Her legs were throbbing and her throat was parched, but most concerning were the black spots that kept appearing in front of her eyes. She feared losing consciousness. She straightened out one arm and grabbed the next person who walked close enough to her. The tent pole clattered as it hit the hard ground. "Help?" she asked. Her body was rotating in slow circles, though her feet remained planted.

The young woman she grabbed stayed with her and sent her friend to get a cushion and some water. Once seated, the old woman drank and closed her eyes.

"Ma'am, where are you going? I'll help you get there."

After a long pause, the older woman spoke. "I need to find my daughter, Amira. She's here with her children and her husband, Sami. He's a doctor. Do you know them?"

The young woman nodded her head. "I've heard of Dr. Sami. Together we'll find them." She put her arm around her and bore most of her body weight as they walked together.

AMIRA AND YASMINE LAY ON the dank mattress in the stuffy tent. Amira felt heaviness within her, like she had swallowed a watermelon whole, but Sami told her this was to be expected because the baby was big and that was a blessing. When Sami had palpated her lower abdomen the night before he declared the baby's head was pointed down and in the birthing position. It wouldn't be long now.

Amira thought back to readying her home in Aleppo for Ahmed's and Yasmine's births. She'd painstakingly picked out paint for their bedrooms, deliberating each time over colour. Ahmed's room ended up being a grassy green, Yasmine's, a buttery yellow. Both times she had a change table stocked with diapers and creams, and a dresser full of baby clothes and receiving blankets. The bookshelves were lined with early board books, dolls, and stuffed animals. There were no such preparations to be made in the tent. With no crib, the baby would have to sleep with her, and once she was back on her feet she would carry them in a makeshift sling rather than pushing them in a stroller. She already felt guilty that this baby would have so much less than her other two children, but Sami assured her that babies all over the world were born into uncertain conditions, and all they needed were breast milk and love to thrive.

Yasmine dozed off as Amira hummed in varying octaves and tempos. Amira also felt the tempting tug of sleep, but the tightening inside her was keeping her awake. When the tent flap pulled back and a silhouette appeared in the doorframe, she sat up. "Who is there? What do you want?" she asked.

The young woman escorted the older woman and her tent poles into Amira's tent. "Is this your mother?"

Amira rose to her feet, staring at the shrunken, dishevelled woman she and Yasmine had walked by on the path earlier. It was so obvious now that it was her mother despite how much she'd changed that Amira felt ashamed she hadn't recognized her earlier. She cried out, "Mother! What are you doing here?" Shock and distress overtook her, but relief also flooded through her body. She helped her mother onto a cushion on their rug. "I've been so worried. I can't believe you're here." She saw how weak her mother was and made an effort to calm herself down. Yasmine was now awake, too, and staring curiously from the mattress.

Through tears of joy and relief, Amira thanked the woman who had brought her mother to them. After she left, Amira pulled out her prayer mat and squatted at her mother's feet. Her belly dropped as low as her ankles.

"I've prayed so hard to see you again and my prayers have been answered. Thank you, Allah."

Amira's mother laid her hands on Amira's head. Yasmine walked over to her grandmother's side and stared skeptically into her face before breaking into a smile. "It *is* you! You found us. That's so nice." She threw her small arms around her grandmother and pressed her cheek into her shoulder.

"Where is Father? Why isn't he with you?" Amira asked.

Her mother cupped Amira's face in her wrinkled hands and looked into her eyes, finally focusing her pupils so it was clear she was actually seeing now. She pointed at her ears and shook her head.

"You can't hear?" Amira asked.

Her mother shrugged her shoulders.

Amira locked eyes with her and slowly said with exaggerated mouth movements, "Where is Father?"

Her mother gently shook her head, opened her mouth and then closed it without speaking. The words didn't need to be said. Amira knew he was dead. Her body seized in grief and sudden white pain, and she cried out.

"Mama, what's happening?" Yasmine asked.

Amira looked between her feet at the small puddle now lying there. "The baby is coming! You must find Ahmed and your father. Go!"

CHAPTER 35

Cape Breton, August 2015

B OB UNWOUND THE ROPE FROM THE CLEAT AND
shoved the boat off the wharf with his foot.

Tinker wanted to captain but it was Bob's boat, so while Bob took the wheel, Tinker settled into the cushioned passenger seat beside him. Tinker hadn't had a boat of his own since he stopped fishing so had seized the invitation to get out on Bob's motorboat, even if he didn't get to be in charge. He hoped they'd make a full day of it and had packed a small cooler with sandwiches just in case.

The men didn't attempt to talk over the roar of the motor as they pulled away. Tinker tilted his chin upwards and let the sunshine warm his weathered face. He'd had so much on his mind recently and took extra pleasure in the contentment this provided.

When they got far enough out that the rolling green hills of Falkirk Cove were mere bumps in the distance, Bob cut the motor and turned to Tinker. He looked directly into Tinker's eyes in a way he rarely had in all their decades of friendship.

"What is it? Need me to pitch in somehow? I could steer. Just say the word."

Bob shook his head. It was the first time the old friends had been together since Tinker's outburst in the church basement. "This isn't a pleasure trip, Tinker. I brought you out here for a conversation. You're not going to like it."

Tinker squirmed in his seat. They'd always had a breezy and cordial relationship, not complicated by disagreements, yet Bob now seemed intent on ruining this perfectly lovely day. Could he not get a moment's peace?

"All right then, spit it out. What'd I do now?" The boat rocked gently on the twinkling waves. The fine day now seemed at odds with the tension in Tinker's gut.

"I've known you almost seventy years and have considered you a friend that whole time. I know at your core there's a decent person." Bob paused. "That's why I'm hoping your recent behaviour is just bluster."

First Florence gave him the gears, and now Bob? "This is about the Syrians, I s'pose?" Tinker sneered. This sponsorship business aggravated him to no end.

A seagull hovered and screeched above the boat, hoping they'd have trash fish or guts to toss overboard, before giving up and flying on.

"Not them personally, but about your attitude toward them, yes." Bob's face, usually so open and contented, now was stern. He sat with his knees open, hands clasped between them. "I've seen you act badly in the past and I've looked away. But this time it's different. It's mean-spirited and I won't be a bystander to it."

Tinker wanted to walk away. He looked over the gunwale at the water lapping around them and realized he was trapped.

"I'm set in my ways, Bob. Too old to change."

Bob snorted. "That's nothing but an excuse. No one's ever too old to change. You have to try."

Tinker didn't know if he could—or if he wanted to. His stubbornness was a core part of who he was. But Florence was still mad as hell at him, and now Bob, too? "Well I don't like that they're coming here and taking jobs away from Cape Bretoners—or worse, living off our charity. Plus, I just plain don't trust 'em."

"Because they're Middle Eastern?"

"That's part of it."

Bob looked crestfallen. His voice softened. "Imagine how that makes me feel for a minute. I'm Lebanese."

Tinker sucked his teeth and shook his head. "Your parents were. You're Canadian. It's different."

"It's not!" Bob stomped his foot on the boat's floor. "We're both of us descendants of people who were once immigrants—yes, even you. Your ancestors were Scots, mine were Lebanese. Neither group was entitled to this land we both call home. The island's in fact unceded from the Mi'kmaq."

Tinker wasn't in the mood for a history lesson, but it was impossible to stop Bob once he got going.

"I'm a proud Libbus just like my parents were. Did you hate them?" Bob asked.

How ridiculous. Tinker had spent lots of time at Bob's house when they were boys. Bob's parents were always welcoming and jovial. They loved music and hosting home concerts. They'd also had a range of businesses in and around town, and for a time owned the fish plant Tinker supplied. They paid a fair price for fish even when market prices dropped, assuming the reduced margins themselves rather than paying the local fishermen less. Tinker had been a pallbearer at both their funerals, for Christ's sake. "You know I didn't. Your parents were good people."

"And what's to say these new immigrants won't be good, hard-working people, too? Wouldn't you rather assume the best of them, instead of the worst?"

Tinker didn't answer. The boat was drifting, and he suddenly felt bone tired and wanted to return to land. "Think we could head back now, Bob?"

"In a minute. I need to know that you're done making xenophobic comments. That's step one."

Tinker sat still and didn't say anything. He'd look up "xenophobic" when he got home but knew it was bad.

"And then that you're going to examine your prejudices and make amends. These are my terms. Take 'em or leave 'em." Bob fell silent.

Tinker stared over the bow at the horizon until he spotted something breaking the water's surface in the distance. "Hand me your binoculars."

Bob retrieved them from a shelf below the steering wheel and passed them to Tinker with a sigh.

Tinker stood up and pressed them to his face, adjusting the dials until the pilot whale's dorsal fin came into focus. It was swimming toward town. He watched until it dipped below the surface. The boat listed and Tinker felt wobbly and sat back down.

"I'll think it over, Bob," he said, handing him back the binoculars.

"Let me say just one more thing, then. You could probably live without me in your life, Tinker, but I'm not sure if you could manage without Flo."

As they sped back, Tinker took stock of his bad fortune. Russell was dead. Charlie had messed up his life with drugs. Alex was going back to Toronto. Flo and Bob were all he had left and those damn Syrian refugees could take them away from him, too. His life suddenly seemed to hold very little value to anyone at all.

CHAPTER 36

ALEX STOOD AT THE RED WOODEN GATE UNSURE how to answer.

"Let me ask again. Are you a British spy?" the soldier in the blue uniform and funny pointed hat asked him.

Alex looked to his grandfather for help. The soldier had a friendly face, but he was holding a rifle by his side. It was confusing.

Tinker gave him a light poke. "Answer him, Alex. You're not a spy, are you?"

"No?"

"You don't sound certain. Are you planning to lay siege to the Fortress of Louisbourg?" the soldier now asked him. Tinker was chuckling, which helped Alex relax.

"I just want to visit, please."

"Why didn't you say so? You may enter. *Bienvenue, mon ami.* This way." He waved them into the walled fortress. As the thick fog burned off, the interior buildings started to become visible.

"Whoa," Alex said, unsure where to begin. There were dry moats and cannons perched on top of walls, and long and short buildings made of stones. The reconstructed town stretched out before them. As they walked around getting their bearings, a cluster of townsfolk, followed by a goose and some ducks, marched a criminal to the public shackles to punish him for stealing bread. All around them men, women, and children walked past wearing strange clothing. Alex couldn't help staring at the men with their wooden shoes. Their pants were short and looked scratchy, but Alex liked how they used pieces of rope for belts. Their puffy white shirts looked like his mommy's fancy tops. "Why are they dressed so weird?" Alex asked.

"We've stepped back in time. That's what people wore three hundred years ago, Alex. And they might have only changed their clothes once a year."

A man introducing himself as a cod fisherman invited Tinker and Alex into his home. "Do you know what this floor you're standing on is made out of?" he asked Alex.

"Dirt?"

"Nope. Horse manure. That's right: poop. At this house you wipe your shoes on the door mat not when you're entering, but when you're leaving." The fisherman chuckled.

Alex quickly pinched his nostrils closed before he began smelling the poop but then noticed his grandpa laughing so dropped his hand to his side and laughed, too.

Tinker checked his watch. Charlie should be arriving at the house right about now. Flo insisted it was best to let Charlie settle for a few hours before introducing him to Alex. Plus it gave Tinker some alone time with Alex, who only had a week left in Cape Breton before Courtney came to take him home. And then who knew when or even *if* they'd see Alex again. It was a rotating door of grandsons at Tinker and Flo's, and it was giving Tinker the spins.

Tinker pointed at a cannoneer preparing to light a cannon flanked by two soldiers pointing rifles at the open water.

Alex tore off toward them with Tinker at his heels, trying to keep up.

CHARLIE WALKED AROUND THE HOUSE, noticing all the changes. Small canvas sneakers with Velcro fasteners were lined up on a mat next to Grandpa's workboots and Grandma's petite green-checked Phentex slippers. His old building blocks were spilled out on the living room floor. Board games were stacked on the coffee table, with Snakes and Ladders on the top of the pile. His grandma was now using sanded wooden discs for coasters, and they were scattered around on various end tables between Hot Wheels cars. Drawings of stick-figure people were stuck to the fridge with alphabet magnets. He opened its door to see what was inside.

"Jeet?" Grandma asked him from her chair at the kitchen table.

It had been a long time since anyone asked Charlie "Did you eat?" with a Cape Breton accent. He replied in kind. "No. Ju?"

"Not yet. Let me fix us something," she said, rising to her feet.

Charlie walked to the window and looked out at the yard. His tire swing swayed in the breeze. The thick grass, mowed close to the ground, glowed like a green carpet against the fog. When he turned around again his grandma was placing egg salad sandwiches on the kitchen table.

"Come, have lunch. You're some skinny. I have a plate of squares for when you're finished your sandwich to fatten you back up."

Charlie chewed his food, self-conscious about his broken teeth. Flo didn't mention them.

"So Grandpa's avoiding me? For how long, you figure?" he asked between bites.

"He's not avoiding you. Him and Alex just went to Louisbourg for the day. They'll be home for supper. We thought you might want to unpack and rest up first."

They drank tea and ate Flo's squares. "Thanks again for the plane ticket, Grandma. I know I owe you so much already. But add this to my tab," Charlie said.

Flo laid her hands over his and then stood to clear the table.

"I'll do it," Charlie said, rising beside her. He'd forgotten just how short and cute his grandma was. He couldn't resist. He wrapped an arm around her, clasped her hand, and began waltzing her around the kitchen while singing Rita McNeil's "Flying on Your Own."

"Stop! You're making me dizzy, you rascal," Flo said between squeals. "I missed you something awful, Charlie. How long are you staying?"

Charlie looked down at his grandma, wishing he had a definitive answer. She tilted up her face to his, her blue eyes twinkling, the wisdom lines across her forehead deeper than Charlie remembered. "TBD, Pocket Grandma. To be determined."

TINKER'S BUICK PULLED INTO THE driveway. He parked and watched as Alex unbuckled, climbed out, and raced into the house. He sat in the driver's seat with his hands on the steering wheel, gathering his thoughts. *At least Charlie came back to me alive*, he reminded himself, *not like Russell did, in a box. Charlie's broken, maybe, but still breathing.*

Alex ran upstairs. He was eager to tell his grandma all about their day in Louisbourg at the fortress and driving by the old house where Grandpa lived when he was a boy, but first he needed to go pee. It was a two-hour drive from Louisbourg on the east coast of Cape Breton to Falkirk Cove on the west, and the hot chocolate he drank earlier wanted to come out. He tore into the bathroom, urinated, and then walked by the spare bedroom. The door was open and there was someone in the bed. He slowed his pace and tiptoed into the room to see who it was. He walked right up to the head of the bed and stared at the sleeping man's face. Alex had been told Charlie was arriving today, but this man looked different than the Charlie he'd seen in pictures. He looked a little sick. The man opened his eyes.

"Are you Charlie?"

"Yep."

"Hi. I'm Alex." His missing front teeth added a faint lisp to his speech, so "Alex" sounded more like "Alexth."

Charlie closed his eyes again.

"We're brothers, you know."

Charlie stuck his fist out from underneath the quilt and Alex bumped it with his own.

"Wanna get up and come downstairs?"

Charlie did not but knew he couldn't hole away in the spare bedroom forever. He threw off the covers and stood up and they walked through the hallway past the family photos and down the stairs slowly. Alex ran ahead to find Flo, but Charlie paused on the bottom step. He craved something chemical to take the edge off his tension and dread. Was he ever going to get used to never-ending sobriety? Sometimes it felt like a life sentence. He'd done a quick check in the medicine cabinet earlier just to see what was there, and his grandparents had cleared out all the medicines—even Tylenol. Charlie didn't blame them. All that remained in the cupboard was a box of Spiderman bandages.

Tinker was sitting on the couch reading the newspaper. Charlie saw only the top of his balding head and thin crown of reddish-grey hair.

"Hi, Grandpa."

"Charlie." Tinker lowered the newspaper and gazed at Charlie over his glasses. "I could use some help sawing and sanding a piece of lumber down in my workshop. Think you could help me after supper?"

Charlie's stomach unclenched and his face broke into a smile. "Not home five hours and you've already got jobs lined up for me. So that's the way it's going to be, is it?"

"Sounds 'bout right," said Tinker.

CHARLIE LAID HIS FORK DIAGONALLY across his plate and wiped his mouth with a napkin. "Grandma, that was the best blueberry pie I ever tasted."

"Credit belongs with Alex, too. He helped me pick the berries yesterday. He's a pro." She winked at Alex, who was eating his second piece of pie.

Charlie remembered picking wild berries with Grandma when he was a boy. He used to whine about how long it took to fill an ice cream container. He hated picking blueberries, though he'd always enjoyed eating the spoils after Grandma had removed the green ones and leaves.

"Wanna play catch, Charlie?" Alex's mouth was ringed with purple pie filling and he had pastry flakes on his T-shirt.

"Sorry, bud. I gotta help Grandpa in his workshop."

"No, you two g'wan." Tinker flicked his hand toward the backyard. "I can wait."

Tinker plugged the kettle in while Flo cleared the table. Alex ran upstairs, emerging seconds later with a small mitt on one hand and gripping a ball in the other.

"Where'd you get that mitt?" Charlie asked.

"From my room. It was on the bookshelf."

"You mean my room. That's my old glove. Hand it over."

"Watch your tone, Charlie," Tinker said.

Alex did as Charlie asked. Charlie held it in his palm and squeezed it. Some of the criss-cross stitching had popped. The brown leather was faded and any printing on it had now worn off. "What'd you do to it?"

"Nothing. Just played with it some. Are you mad?"

"It was my dad's when he was a boy. He gave it to me. That's all."

Florence sat down with her tea and shot Charlie a look with her eyebrows raised. "He was Alex's dad, too. There's nothing wrong with sharing with your brother."

Charlie knew he shouldn't be jealous of a little kid. He looked at Alex, standing pigeon-toed in front him with his eyes cast down and flaming hair sticking up, and tried to think what a better person would say in this situation. "Okay, let's go" was all he could come up with.

Alex's chin tilted upwards and, grinning, he threw open the door to the backyard and ran onto the grass.

CHAPTER 37

Toronto, August 2015

COURTNEY STRUGGLED TO CLOSE THE ZIPPER ON her suitcase. She wasn't going to let the airline sucker her into paying for checked baggage, so was cramming everything into a carry-on. She flipped open the top and dumped everything out on her bed, forced to start over. God, could she never catch a break? She tucked socks into shoes, filled every nook and cranny with underwear, and sat on the lid. Grunting, she tugged on the zipper and then heard the telltale pop-pop-pop of a seam. Looking down, she saw an expanding hole where the zipper was detaching from the suitcase's frame. "Damn it all to hell," she muttered. "Cheap piece of shit."

"What's the problem, babe?" a voice from the other side of the bed mumbled.

"Go back to sleep. I'll fix it." Then she paused to think. Rick had gotten sex twice last night, plus a blowjob. Certainly that earned her a present? "Unless you felt like going to the mall to buy me a new suitcase? Something with wheels, please, that'll work as a carry-on. And fast. I need to leave for the airport in an hour."

He sighed and got up. Though Rick was growing on her, Courtney was glad to watch him go. She could use the hour without him to straighten up the apartment. She didn't want Alex coming home to a bunch of clues that there had been a man having sleepovers here. Alex might figure it out anyway—he was clever—but she wanted to keep him in the dark for as long as she could. He always had so many questions. But she was also anxious to have Alex home, even if it did mean being more discreet.

"Soon, baby, soon," she said out loud to no one. She couldn't believe Alex had been gone for nine months. At this point she just wanted to sweep him up into her arms for the world's longest hug. They'd been apart too long, even with their Skype calls, but she'd saved nine months of childcare fees while Flo and Tinker looked after her son. Courtney could tell they'd become attached to Alex and was glad that he had more family to love and look after him now. Her plan was working. She sat down at her kitchen table and quickly wrote Flo and Tinker a letter she slipped into her purse. This was one she'd hand deliver.

Courtney opened the window to try to get some air moving through her apartment and looked up at the cloudless sky. A hot gust hit her like a hairdryer blowing at her face and it carried with it the sound of a toddler screeching from the apartment next door. She closed the window in defeat, craving air conditioning. Courtney felt a bead of sweat trickle down between her breasts as she cleared ashtrays, emptied garbage cans, stacked dishes in the sink, and started putting away all the clothes she'd dumped on Alex's bed in his absence.

The light pouring in from his small bedroom window was illuminating dust, and she grabbed a damp rag and ran it over the framed picture of Russell with a newborn Alex in his arms. If Russell were still alive, he'd hardly know her now. She'd settled down a lot and was currently only dating Rick. Monogamy took some getting used to, as did protected sex, but she made damn sure he always wore a condom. Alex was the biggest blessing in her life, but one unplanned pregnancy was enough for her. She could barely afford to care for him—scratch that; she couldn't afford to care for him. Daycare in Toronto on her measly salary had bled her dry. If she got knocked up again, she'd really be screwed.

It was a real mindfuck when Russell died. He'd only just accepted that he was Alex's father and was coming around to the idea of co-parenting when the explosion happened. It seemed like her destiny to have anything good in her life snatched away.

The door opened. "How's this?" Rick asked, pulling a red, wheeled suitcase behind him.

"It'll do. Thanks for that." Courtney walked over and kissed him. His mouth tasted like coffee and she liked it. Rick was a sweet guy. One day she might even let him meet Alex. She kissed him some more and began to feel a familiar longing when he swept his tongue through her mouth.

"Nooooooooo, I don't have time," she said, already knowing resistance was futile. Rick grabbed her hand and pulled her into her bedroom. He ripped off his shirt and flopped backwards onto the bed. Courtney crawled on top, straddling him with her knees, and kissed his chest, his neck, and his earlobe. He ran his hands underneath her shirt, and hoisted it over her head. She felt her nipples harden. She reached into her bedside table, grabbed a condom, and ripped the package open with her teeth. It would be a mad dash to the airport.

ALEX WOKE UP HAPPY. His mommy was coming today. Today! He climbed out of bed smiling, and went down to the kitchen to see who he might find there. He hoped it'd be Charlie. Charlie was so cool, and sometimes would play with him. Yesterday they'd found an old magnifying glass in Tinker's workshop. It was Charlie's idea to use it to play detective. He'd dressed up Alex in one of his old coats, tucked a notebook and one of Tinker's stubby pencils in the pocket, and put a funny hat on Alex's head. Grandma and Grandpa laughed when they saw him and took some pictures. Charlie told him about Sherlock Holmes, the most famous detective ever, and called Alex "Mini Sherlock." It might have been Alex's favourite day yet in Cape Breton, and he'd had plenty of good ones. Maybe Charlie liked him for real now and not just because they were brothers. Sometimes Charlie got sweaty and felt sick and then they had to stop playing, but as long as he was feeling well, Charlie said yes to lots of things. Even Snakes and Ladders.

Alex heard voices in the den, so he stopped outside the door and pressed his back up against the hallway wall. He was gathering clues to see if he could figure out what Grandpa and Grandma were saying. They were speaking with their inside voices but he was a good detective so could make out lots of their words.

"...entitled to a portion. How can we deny her that? She could sue us if we're not careful," Grandma said.

"After all we've done for her these past months, looking after Alex? She wouldn't dare," Grandpa said.

Were they talking about his mommy?

"She mightn't have a choice, Tinker. I don't think she can support him on what she earns. If we can help, we should."

"With what? Some sort of allowance?"

Alex knew what allowance was. He'd never gotten it but he knew some other kids did. Free money—it sounded awesome. It would make Mommy happy to get allowance. Alex strained his ears, but they were saying things he couldn't understand no matter how hard he tried. Words like "trust fund" and "compensation" and "wrongful death" and "custody" were confusing.

"Whatcha doing, Mini Sherlock?" Charlie asked, sliding up alongside him against the wall.

Alex dragged the tips of his thumb and index finger across his lips like he was zippering them shut. They both stood still and listened together.

"We need to cash it out, Tinker. It's time. Our chequing account's in overdraft and our credit card is racking up a big balance. I take some responsibility for that, but I'm not truly sorry. Family needed our help," Grandma said.

"That money's supposed to be for Charlie and Nell's wedding. And to help them buy their first house here." Tinker's voice sounded sad.

"That's your dream, Tinker. You might need to let it go."

Charlie grabbed Alex by the arm and dragged him along the wall and towards the kitchen. It hurt Alex a little and he felt scared. Charlie had never been rough with him before. Charlie turned on the kitchen radio, which drowned out their grandparents' conversation.

"Listen, Squirt, there's a difference between playing detective and eavesdropping. I should have explained that to you yesterday."

"What do you mean?" Alex felt his bottom lip shaking.

"That was a private conversation between Grandma and Grandpa. If they wanted us to hear it, they wouldn't have been off on their own," Charlie said.

"Are we in trouble?" Now Alex felt worried. He hadn't meant to be bad.

"No, we're not in trouble. But stick to looking for clues that you can see. Like those grey clouds in the sky," Charlie pointed out the kitchen window. "What do they mean?"

"That it's going to rain later?"

"Yup, looks like. What say we pound back some cereal then play outside while it's still dry?"

"Okay."

Charlie poured their cereal and they chewed quietly. The song finished on the radio and the announcer's voice boomed: "A traffic note from the Inverness RCMP: Be advised there are cows on Route 19 between Falkirk Cove and Port Hood. Please take care driving through that area."

Charlie and Alex looked at one another and started to laugh.

"You know what we should do? Go looking for those cows and when we find them say, 'Moooooooove over cows. You're blocking our road,'" Charlie said.

Alex giggled even harder, his head hanging low and mouth still full of Cheerios. He looked up when Catriona walked through the back door into the kitchen.

"Hey, Charlie, I didn't know you were home. What's so funny?" she asked.

"Cat! It's good to see you again. What's so funny? Just some udder nonsense," Charlie answered, pretending to milk a cow.

In the throes of his giggling fit, milk leaked out of Alex's nostrils.

Catriona didn't get the joke but couldn't help herself from laughing along with them. "Am I still babysitting you today, Alex?"

Alex knew it was time to settle down, but he couldn't stop laughing. How could laughing hurt your belly but also make you feel so good, both at the same time?

"Charlie and me are gonna save some cows. Wanna come, Catriona?" His head dropped forward again and his shoulders shook as he was overcome by yet another fit of laugher.

Catriona raised her eyebrows at Charlie, who merely shrugged his shoulders and waved them both out the back door. Alex extended his hands and both Charlie and Catriona clasped one. Linked together, the three of them strolled casually toward the road swinging their arms back and forth as they walked.

FLO AND TINKER PAUSED THEIR argument long enough to hear the door click.

"Feels like all we ever do is fight about money these days." Flo sighed.

"Maybe if you'd stop spending it like we're millionaires we wouldn't have to."

"The settlement is no good to any of us sitting there untouched in the bank." Flo cocked her head toward the window. "I think I hear a baby bird in distress. You hear that?"

Tinker strained his ears. "I don't hear anything."

"Sounds like 'cheap, cheap, cheap.' Oh wait. That's you I'm hearing." Flo stared at Tinker. He held her glare as long as he could, then scowled and slunk off to the kitchen to console himself with a cup of tea.

CHAPTER 38

Turkey, August 2015

THE BABY CROWNED IN THE BACK OF TAREQ'S TAXI.
Amira wailed. The folds of her full skirt tented around Sami, whose head was between her splayed legs.

"Try not to push," he told Amira. "Tareq, can you drive any faster?" He quelled the nerves in his voice for Amira's sake but couldn't slow the adrenalin coursing through his veins.

Tareq maintained a forward gaze. "I'm doing my best, brother. I'll get you to the clinic as fast as I can." His tires squealed as they rounded a corner.

Amira writhed and sweated, intermittently groaning then screaming. Sami admired Tareq's ability to even keep the car on the road. He'd surely have driven into a ditch with such a distraction. Fluids leaking out of Amira were soiling the taxi's backseat and Sami made a mental note to offer to clean Tareq's car after things settled down.

"Sami, let me push! The urge is too strong," Amira sobbed.

"We're almost there." He squeezed her hand. The clinic was in sight now.

"Why is this happening now? I want Mother," she wailed.

"Shhhh. She's back at the tent. Ahmed and Yasmine are with her." Sami hadn't believed Yasmine when she found him in Reyhanli Camp an hour earlier. She was running down the laneway screaming "Papa!" when he heard her small voice and broke away from the patient he was treating. Ahmed also heard her call and came running. Yasmine said her grandmother was there and the baby was coming, but it seemed too incredible to be true. She'd been right on both counts.

Sami helped Amira hobble into the clinic and collapse on a stretcher. Twenty minutes later a healthy, strong, eight-pound boy emitted an ear-piercing yell.

HE HAD A SLEEPY FIRST month, waking to nurse and then drifting back to sleep. Now, at five weeks, baby Omar appeared to have gained weight and grown several centimetres and was becoming more wakeful and fussy. Sami gazed at him feeding at Amira's breast as they both lay on a mattress and pondered the circle of life; the death of his father-in-law, baby Omar's namesake, just days before the birth of this precious boy. Tragedy followed by triumph. Sami made a quick prayer asking Allah for less of the former and more of the latter in the future.

Sami hoped their emigration would happen quickly so baby Omar would have no memory of life in the refugee camp. He wanted his son to grow up proud of his Syrian heritage but also part of the culture of wherever it was they ended up living. Sami was certain Omar could succeed almost anywhere. Fatima, however, was another story. She'd needed a different application and to be registered separately with the United Nations Refugee Agency. They promised to do their best to link her registration to Sami's, Amira's, and the children's, and the most promising scenario Sami and Amira could envision was that she would be approved by the same embassy as them. Given Fatima's infirmity, however, Sami worried about how she might perform in the required interview. Would some merciful country take them all? Fatima remained as despondent as she was the day she arrived at Reyhanli Camp. She could ruin their chances of emigrating if her file couldn't be attached to their own; Amira wouldn't leave the Middle East without her mother. Sami told himself it was a blessing to have Fatima alive and with them, but sometimes it felt like a curse.

"How is my little man?" Sami asked, taking Omar in his arms now that his son had finished nursing. He held Omar against his neck and breathed in his baby scent. "Let me have a good look at you." Sami repositioned the infant to lie in his forearm so he could gaze at Omar's face—full lips, prominent nose, and long black eyelashes. Naming Omar after Amira's father fit. The baby had his grandfather's strong Arabic features. "How is my son today?" he asked.

"Shush, don't wake him," Amira cautioned from the mattress. Finding calm and quiet in the tent these days had become her near obsession. Sami knew it was because she was exhausted and grieving her father, but the tiniest noise or movement could provoke a rebuke. It wasn't easy on Yasmine and Ahmed, who were also sleep deprived and irritable.

In Syria Sami had never participated in housework, but here in the camp circumstances left him no choice. He changed Omar's diaper on the children's mattress without waking him and laid him back down beside Amira for, hopefully, an extended nap. Fatima sat in her usual spot on a cushion doing nothing, and the children were, thankfully, occupied. Ahmed was at school and Yasmine was at the nursery with Noor and Jamila. Sami seized the opportunity to sneak away.

AMIRA DRIFTED OFF FOR a few minutes but awoke with a start after she stretched involuntarily and bumped baby Omar. She was still not used to co-sleeping and had regular nightmares about rolling onto and suffocating him, and this felt like a warning signal. She gasped but then relaxed when she saw Omar open his eyes and raise his own hand to his mouth. He made loud noises sucking his thumb, and Amira looked up to her mother so they could share in this amusement, forgetting for a moment that Fatima couldn't hear. Fatima gazed blankly at them. Amira was persistent in her attempts to get her mother to bond with her newest grandchild the way Fatima had with Ahmed and Yasmine; she lifted the contented baby into her arms and took him to her mother. She laid him gently onto Fatima's legs and tickled his chin, eliciting one of Omar's lopsided grins. Fatima turned her head away and made a sweeping motion with her hands to gesture that she wanted Amira to take the baby off her. Although Fatima barely spoke, she had little trouble communicating.

It had been five weeks since she had arrived in Reyhanli, and Amira was able to piece together that an explosion had hit her parents' apartment building, causing their roof to cave in and killing Amira's father. Though Sami couldn't get her to submit to a medical examination, he suspected Fatima's eardrums had shattered given the proximity of the blast, and that she'd never hear again.

Amira retrieved baby Omar and nestled him into her neck. She pondered how she might start preparing fattoush for her family's lunch with a baby stuck to her. If the stale bread started soaking in the dressing now, it would be tender by the time they ate. She laid Omar on the mattress, where he immediately began crying. She had to ignore his wails, and in less than a minute had placed precious radishes, a tomato, cucumber, and bread on a cutting board and laid a knife across it diagonally. She retrieved the baby and gestured to her mother. "Your turn to make lunch. Chop those up, please," she said. Amira lifted the knife and extended it toward Fatima. Fatima raised her hands and shook her head as though puzzled. "Please, Mother, don't play dumb. I know your legs were trapped by a beam and are still recovering, but your arms are just fine."

Fatima crossed her arms in front of her chest.

Amira was growing increasingly frustrated. The tent was a mess and her mother, always so proud about her appearance, looked dirty and sat with her legs splayed in an uncouth manner. Then the smell of urine reached Amira's nose. She checked Omar's diaper but it was dry. It was her mother's diaper that needed changing.

SAMI COUNTED THE MONEY in his pocket. Their savings were long depleted, and the small amount he was paid by Turkey for providing medical care hadn't stretched quite far enough this month. He should walk to Reyhanli, but he wouldn't have time to get there and back before the children got home. He called Tareq for a drive.

"Where to?" Tareq asked.

"The internet café in Reyhanli, please," Sami replied. His phone wasn't internet enabled, offering only basic calling options.

"Sure thing. How's baby Omar? Have you told him he gave me quite a scare in this taxi? I've never had a more demanding customer than that guy, insisting to be born immediately."

"You'll be Uncle Tareq to him for his whole life, I promise," Sami said. "With Amira's screaming I don't know how you stayed focused on the road."

"Experience, my friend. Have you forgotten I was a soldier? I've driven through many tenser situations than that. I'm glad yours had a happy ending."

Sami arrived at the crowded internet café and had to wait for a computer to become free. He badly wanted tea but didn't have money for it, so he waved the server away when he came around taking orders. He began researching which embassies were currently accepting Syrian refugees. More and more refugees were taking their chances in ocean rafts and arriving in Europe illegally. He understood the desperation, but the risk was enormous, and Sami had pinned all his hopes on a country issuing them a visa for legal entry. He wanted to do this the safest way possible.

Tareq drove him back to camp. Sami fidgeted when the white tents came into view. "I'm embarrassed, Tareq. I don't have money to pay the fare. Can I owe you, or is there anything I can do in exchange for you or your family?" Sami felt deep shame. He'd never incurred debts before.

"Forget about it, brother. Remember, you said I am Omar's uncle now. That means we are family. There's no debt amongst family members, only favours."

Sami clasped his hand on Tareq's shoulder, climbed out of the taxi, and walked back to his family's tent. He desperately wanted to leave Reyhanli Camp forever, but even amid the crowding and desperation there was goodness in this place.

"Where were you? You can't just take off like that. I needed you," Amira said when he entered the tent. Though fall was coming and the nights were blessedly cooler, the days were still hot and even more scorching inside the tent when no one opened the flaps. The smell of baby poop hit his nostrils.

"I had to go into town. What can I do to help?" Sami spoke loudly over the baby's cries. He glanced at Fatima, sitting still on a cushion, and briefly envied her deafness.

"Here." Amira straight-armed the baby at Sami. Omar's diaper was droopy with yellowish stool that seeped out at the legs and stained his pajamas. Yasmine scuttled by Sami's legs, plugging her nose, and ran to hide behind Fatima. Sami held the baby away from himself.

"Town? How nice for you. Off to drink tea with Tareq, were you?" Amira's voice oozed with accusation. "How lucky to have that kind of freedom when your wife is trapped here looking after everybody."

Sami laid the baby on a plastic bag and opened his diaper. "Yaya, get me a wet facecloth, please. I need to clean up your baby brother." Omar continued to wail as Sami wiped him but settled once he was in clean pajamas and in his father's arms. "There you go, my son. It's only poop. We all do it. Nothing to be upset about."

Ahmed returned and was immediately sent out again to dispose of the diaper in the dumpster.

"No really, Sami, tell me. What urgent business took you into Reyhanli?"

Sami gazed at his wife, who'd now risen and begun spooning fattoush into bowls. He forced himself to smile. "Research. We need to know who is accepting refugees and how to ace our interview, should we get one." Sami wanted a bowl of fattoush but held on to Omar so Amira could eat first. His family sat eating as his stomach rumbled and Omar burped up milk onto his shirt.

CHAPTER 39

Cape Breton, September 2015

IT HAD BEEN THREE WEEKS SINCE CHARLIE'S HALF-brother went back to Toronto. Though he'd had to adjust to having Alex around, now that he was gone Charlie missed the little squirt. Sure, he was no longer tripping over Hot Wheels cars or stepping on random LEGOs, but so what? The house was too tidy and quiet; the only sound Charlie heard now as he walked down the carpeted hallway was the relentless ticking of the mantle clock. It was presumed he would move back into his old bedroom once Alex vacated it, but Charlie continued sleeping in the guest room instead.

Tinker and Flo had withdrawn to their own corners. Tinker was holing up in his workshop alone, and Flo had thrown herself into fundraising and resettlement work for the Syrian refugees. The tension and sadness at home was a daily reminder to Charlie that he'd caused them similar pain when he left abruptly for Alberta. What an asshole he'd been.

Charlie buttered a raisin tea biscuit and ate it as he wandered to the basement, mentally mapping out his day.

"Whatcha working on, Grandpa?" he asked, poking his head into Tinker's workshop.

Tinker was standing at his drafting table with a calendar in front of him opened to September. Charlie could see three weeks' worth of large Xs through the squares.

"Nothing much." Tinker flipped the calendar over and pushed it aside. Underneath were drawings in his neat handwriting. "I'm about to start building a table for the Syrians we're expecting."

"I thought you weren't too crazy about their coming."

Tinker grabbed the edges of his drafting table. "I'm not. But my objections have been overruled. Plus I've been told I need to keep an open mind and make amends for certain things I said or there will be severe consequences."

Charlie found his grandfather's contrition amusing. "Okay then."

"You hear they're moving into the vacant house next to Roger's?"

"The McCormacks' old place? Hasn't it been empty for years?" Charlie feigned ignorance, for he knew it had. He and some of his friends had broken in and squatted there on occasions when they were too drunk or high to go home.

"Yeah, it's run down some since the last McCormack moved out a decade ago. They're willing to deed it to us for nothing, but we have to fix it up. Care to help? There's plenty of work to go around."

Charlie didn't have to mull it over for long. He'd always enjoyed working with his hands and knew he was good at building things. A project—a distraction—was just what he needed. He was avoiding old friends, worried he'd fall back into substance-using habits. Though according to his sponsor Charlie's recovery was progressing well, it was yet tenuous, and Charlie didn't fully trust himself.

"Sure, why not. I'll be like Joseph from the Bible. The people's carpenter." Charlie touched his index and middle finger to his forehead, chest, and either shoulder in the sign of the cross.

"Don't you let your grandmother hear you comparing yourself to Jesus Christ's father. She'll be left praying for your salvation after she wrings your neck." Tinker stood and walked toward a neat pile of lumber stacked against the opposite wall.

"Good point. Besides, I'm more like the prodigal son, right?"

"You best stop while you're ahead, Charlie," Tinker said.

FLO SAT IN THE MUSTY church basement with Bob, Catriona, and the rest of the Falkirk Cove Refugee Project. It was encouraging to see attendance growing, though Tinker hadn't been invited back, but the money wasn't piling up fast enough. Roger tapped her shoulder from the row behind.

"When were you born, Florence Gordon?"

"Now, Roger, you don't ask a lady how old she is. All I'm saying is that it was a Saturday a long time ago."

"Saturday's child…" Roger began. He and Flo finished together, "works hard for a living."

Flo continued, "And ain't that the truth. Though I've never had a salaried job in my life, the work never stops. On what day were you born, Roger?"

Without answering, Roger stood and began pacing across the back of the room, staring at his feet.

With a few thousand now in their bank account, they still had miles to go to reach thirty-five thousand dollars, and there were only so many collection jars that could be placed along the southwest coast of Cape Breton. They needed a new plan. Jean had one.

"Chase the Ace. I can sell advance tickets through the Kwikmart and we can hold it as part of Saturday bingo in Inverness. Who's heard of it?"

No one replied.

"Well go on then, Jean. Tell us about this Ace Chasing thingy," Flo said. She'd consider anything at this point. Days were turning into weeks, and weeks into months. They needed to accelerate their fundraising. A Syrian family was counting on them.

Jean handed out a sheet of paper to each of them explaining the details. "Here are the highlights. Each week players buy lottery tickets. The funds from ticket sales are divided into three parts. Typically the organizers keep fifty percent. The winner of the lottery takes twenty percent and thirty percent goes into the jackpot. The jackpot grows each week till it's won, then the game is over."

They all read the handout and mulled it over.

"How do you win the jackpot?" Bob asked.

"Each week the lottery winner also then draws a card from a deck of playing cards. If they draw the ace of spades, they win the jackpot. If they don't, their card is tossed. The deck of cards, now smaller, is kept for the following week's game and the jackpot grows bigger as the likelihood of pulling the ace grows better."

Flo was a tinge skeptical because it sounded a bit like gambling which she knew to be addictive, but then again so was bingo if you were to get technical about it.

The squeaking of Roger's sneakers as he paced the church basement floor was like a backbeat to their discussion. It became noticeable only when it stopped. Roger stood still and cleared his throat. They all turned to face him.

"Chase the Ace. Chase the Ace. Chase the Ace. Also can be played as Crown the King or Jig the Joker. A popular way to raise money with terrible odds. Slim odds. Razor-slim odds. Chase the Ace."

A silence descended on the room until Bob broke it. "Mathematically it doesn't favour the player. But what about the fundraiser?"

"Terrible odds for the player. Terrible. Often excellent returns for the organizer. Better each week the longer the game lasts. Money piling up every week that Ace isn't pulled." Roger resumed his pacing as the committee worked to decipher Roger's words.

"So let me get this straight. The longer it takes for someone to pull the Ace, the more that money pile grows?" Catriona asked.

"Yup," Jean replied. "It's possible if that jackpot gets big enough we'll pull in people from other parts of the island and maybe even the mainland, too. You never know."

They took a vote on whether to take their idea to the Inverness Legion. It was a unanimous yes save for Roger, who abstained.

CHARLIE AND TINKER WORKED SIDE by side for two hours finalizing the plans, then measuring and cutting long wood blanks for the table's legs. Charlie did most of the heavy lifting under Tinker's orders and critical eye.

Charlie had forgotten what a taskmaster his grandfather could be, yet he relaxed into the jobs he was assigned. He worked steadily but didn't rush, making sure to measure each leg twice so as to cut only once. He dragged his fingertips along the blanks enjoying the sensation of the wood grain, and even found he enjoyed the whirring noise of the table saw. The men worked in tandem without saying more than was required, moving as fluidly around one another as dance partners doing the tango. Eventually, Tinker had to go fetch Florence from her meeting at the church and Charlie got a break. He decided to FaceTime Nell.

She didn't pick up the call so he tried a second time, then a third. On his fourth attempt, she answered.

"What took you so long to pick up? I figured I'd catch you no problem on a Saturday."

"And hello to you too, Charlie. Do you think I just sit around waiting for your calls?" Nell immediately regretted her sarcasm. "Sorry. Let's start again. How are you?"

"I'm okay. Grandpa's keeping me busy in the workshop. How 'bout you?"

"Good, good. Flag football finals are this weekend. We made it to the playoffs, so that's a little exciting."

"Nice. And work?"

"There've been more layoffs. Oil prices are still low and people are worried."

"Oh crap. Is your job safe?" Charlie wanted her to have a job she loved, but if she lost it, she might have to come back to Cape Breton and that'd be sweet. Lately he'd been missing her more than usual.

"The mood's tense, but my job seems safe and I still like it."

Her face filled up his phone's screen.

"Your hair's a mess, girl. What gives?"

Nell self-consciously raised her free hand to her head and tried smoothing it down. "Oh nothing. I was just lying in bed, being lazy."

"That's not like you. You're always on the go. Isn't it, like, eleven o'clock there?"

"Gosh, it is. I better sign off and change for football. Say hi to your grandparents for me, okay?"

For the first time since he left Alberta, Nell hadn't asked when he was coming back or about his recovery. "Yeah, sure. Bye. Good luck in your game."

"Bye, Charlie. Thanks for calling."

Charlie's phone screen went black. He stared at it for a few seconds. He wanted to tell her about the Syrians and building the table for them. He wanted to see her face again and hear her laugh, to tell her that he loved her and that his withdrawal symptoms were improving. Yes, he still wanted to get high every day, but it wasn't a twitchy sort of craving anymore. It was an urge he could confront and resist. Nell was always there for him when he felt like talking. He thought about calling her back but hesitated. She was probably just distracted because of her football game. Their next call would be better.

NELL HAD FELT TELLTALE HIVES popping out on her neck as she'd FaceTimed with Charlie. She'd never been a good liar. Damn modern technology. In the old days when they all just talked on landlines, no one had to worry about their appearance. Nell hung up the phone and turned away from the window to face the other side of the bed. "We have to stop doing this, Rex. I have to tell him."

Rex lay naked, a twisted sheet partially covering his legs and torso. "Do we have to stop? Who's making us?"

"It's not cool." Nell buried her face in the pillow. Every time she'd been with Rex, she'd told herself it was the last time, but it kept happening. Her guilt was growing like a tumour. The right thing to do would be to end it with Rex, come clean to Charlie, and atone. For all he'd put her through, Charlie would forgive her this misstep, wouldn't he?

Rex lay beside her and stroked her hair. "I feel shitty, too. He was my buddy. But are you sure it's good for either one of you to try to hang on to what you had? Charlie wants you when it's convenient for him."

Nell couldn't disagree with that. Charlie had always set the terms of their relationship. She thought about the months when he was first in Alberta and she was in Cape Breton, only hearing from him sporadically, and how she'd worried and lost her confidence and followed him out to Alberta uninvited. And how badly it hurt when he left her yet again to move back to Cape Breton. But that didn't justify what she was doing now, did it? Nell was raised differently, named for the Charles Dickens character Nell Trent, who was portrayed as infallibly angelic in the book *The Old Curiosity Shop*. She loved that her parents chose this name for her. She read the book when she was thirteen, and pledged to always be as good and loyal as her namesake. And yet here she was, unfaithful.

Nell lay on her stomach with her face buried in her pillow. Rex started rubbing her back. Her mind was unsettled, but her body's willpower was waning, and she slowly began unclenching and relaxing to Rex's touch. His hand moved down her back to the top and then the insides of her thighs. When she flipped on her side to face him, she was struck by how intently he was focusing on her. She wasn't competing with anybody or anything for his attention. It was irresistibly attractive.

CHAPTER 40

Cape Breton, October 2015

FLO HELD THE PHOTO IN HER HANDS. IN IT, ALEX was wearing one of Tinker's old tweed ivy caps. The brim reached his eyes and he thrust his pointed chin upward so he was able to see from beneath it. Charlie had dressed Alex in an old beige trench coat. It draped down to his feet, and there was a coiled notebook stuffed in the breast pocket. Alex held a magnifying glass in front of him and Charlie stood just off to the side, grinning and pointing at his brother with both his hands. Flo couldn't stop staring at the picture. Her two grandsons, together with her and Tinker for one week. Such a short time. The boys had a bumpy start, but Charlie came around, as she'd figured he would. Alex was such a doll you couldn't help but love him. She pried apart a frame and fit the photo inside, planning to ask Tinker to hang it in the upstairs hallway later. She sat at the kitchen table with a cup of tea and a ginger cookie and sighed.

Flo retrieved a letter from the odds-'n-sods kitchen drawer and read it for the umpteenth time.

Dear Florence and Tinker,
First, thanks for caring for Alex for all these months. He needed it and so did I. We do okay on our own, just him and me, but I want more for us.

You now know what a fantastic boy he is. He's the best thing in my otherwise crappy life. In some ways it hurts me to share him with you since it's always been just us two, but he deserves more than just me.

Alex also needs your help. How much do you figure you spent raising Charlie? Doesn't Alex deserve his fair share, too? He is just as much Russell's son as Charlie is.

You're going to have to make this right if you want to keep seeing Alex. There's no way you didn't get a settlement when Russell died. I want to know how much and I figure a third of it is owed to us. I could be greedy and ask for half but I'm willing to compromise. We can divide three ways for yourselves, Charlie, and Alex. I suspect the courts would consider this more than fair if you want to drag it out that way but we'd all lose a lot on lawyers' fees.

When you're ready to settle up, you'll have Alex back in your lives for calls and regular visits.

Courtney

Flo folded it and put it in the envelope and tucked it back into the drawer. She recited the Lord's Prayer, focusing on the "as we forgive those who trespass against us" part. When she was less bitter she could admire Courtney's tenacity and the brilliance of her strategy. Courtney had left Alex in her and Tinker's care long enough for them all to fall hard for one another. But it infuriated Flo that Courtney used Alex as a pawn, and not knowing how Courtney was explaining this all to Alex. It would be beyond dirty if she was poisoning his mind against her and Tinker.

Flo worried about Alex to the point of obsession. Her blood pressure, which had been dropping, was once again elevated. She reached for her antihypertensive pills and swallowed two with her ghastly decaffeinated tea. She pulled out a pen and paper and began writing her own letter.

Dear Alex,
How are you enjoying school? Who is your teacher? Are you making new friends?
We sure miss you here in Cape Breton.
Are you still playing Snakes and Ladders? Charlie and Tinker won't

play with me and I think my skills are getting rusty. Next time we play I bet you'll win.

Did you get the parcel of books and letters I sent you? I hope you enjoyed them.

Be good for your mommy. I think about you every single day.

Love,
Grandma

Flo addressed the envelope for Tinker to mail on his next trip to town, but she wasn't confident Alex would ever receive it. Courtney held all the power. It was infuriating.

Too much time at home with her thoughts was not healthy, even though having Charlie back was a comfort, especially considering his health was visibly improving each day. Too bad his teeth wouldn't repair themselves the way the rest of his body would. She drummed her fingers on the table. The *Cape Breton Post* lay off to the side, but she didn't dare open it for fear of having to confront what fresh hell the Syrians were facing on this day. The world's suffering was too much to pile on top of her own at this moment. She knew it was a luxury to be able to turn away from the bad news in Syria while so many were living through it, and taking advantage of that privilege then made her feel guilty. Her nerves, clearly, were shot.

She walked to the basement. "What do you want, Florence?" Tinker asked, looking up from his desk as Flo entered the workshop. He had a notepad covered with columns of numbers in front of him. Tinker glanced down at it and without explanation, opened his desk drawer and tucked it away.

"Honestly, Tinker, that's how you speak to me now? I've just come for a hammer and nail." In the past fifty-odd years she'd rarely set foot in her husband's workshop. She'd heard the term "man cave" on TV recently and had chuckled, realizing her own home had contained one for decades before it became trendy. Well, too bad for the men. There was no reason Flo shouldn't be allowed to go in there. It was her home too, and she was surely capable of doing simple jobs around the house, like hanging a picture.

"Whatever it is, leave it be. I'll get to it after lunch."

Flo glanced around the workshop, noting its impeccable organization. Other than a pile of sawdust in the corner, it was completely tidy, and certainly the neatest room in their house. She'd lost the will to houseclean lately. "I'll do it myself." She extended her arm and waited.

Tinker knew when to give in. He walked over to a wall of hammers and lifted a small one off an S-hook. "Am I allowed to ask what it is you're doing?"

"I'm hanging a picture of our grandsons, if you must know. If I can't have Alex here with us, I get to at least look at him, don't I?" Flo didn't know why she was being argumentative. It all just felt like too much to bear. She lowered the hammer, realizing she had been swinging it back and forth as she spoke like she was about to clobber Tinker.

Tinker's face was pale. "You need to sit down." He rolled his desk chair toward Flo. She took a seat and a few deep breaths and let the hammer drop to the concrete floor. She crossed her arms in front of her chest.

"I can't go on like this, Tink. I have to talk to Alex. I need to know he's okay."

"He's fine. Alex is a survivor. And for all her faults, Courtney's a decent enough mother."

Flo was surprised to hear Tinker defending her. Courtney's ultimatum enraged him as it did Flo.

"I need proof, Tink. I need him to know we still love him. I know you're tired of hearing it, but I'm still inclined to meet Courtney's demands. To cash out Russell's settlement and give her some regular financial support."

"I don't enjoy being bribed," Tinker said. "I'm not saying no, just that this feels like a ransom."

"Do you have to look at it that way? He is our grandson. Our dead son's son."

Flo saw Tinker wince at the mention of Russell, but he appeared to consider her point before speaking. "She's got a job up there in Toronto, land of opportunity. She gets by."

"Tinker, Courtney's raising Alex by herself making hardly more than minimum wage. And the cost of living up there is outrageous."

"She needs to toughen up. Us Capers know how to overcome our problems and work hard to make ends meet."

"Oh, will you just stop." Flo stood up and crossed her arms in front of her chest. Though he was a foot taller than her, Tinker was intimidated. "You think people in Cape Breton hold a monopoly on hardship. People are struggling everywhere, Tinker. Not everyone can rise above their circumstances on their own. Sometimes they need a hand."

"I don't like that she's forcing *our* hand."

"She's desperate. People do desperate things in desperate times." Tinker sat on a stool and put his head in his hands. He'd been distracting himself by filling up his hours with even more odd jobs and projects than usual, but the ache of Alex's absence was becoming more acute by the day for him, too.

"I just want my grandson back in my life. If it means paying for that privilege, then yes, I guess I'm willing. Love makes people do crazy things—me included. But I also think we have an obligation to support Alex like we did Charlie." She felt her frustration morphing into resignation and looked hopefully at Tinker, unable to predict what his reaction would be. She feared he'd storm out and shut his emotions off entirely. He'd certainly done it before.

Tinker held her gaze for a full minute, then opened his desk drawer and pulled the pad of paper with rows of numbers on it back out. "Well, I was actually running some numbers when you barged in. If we're doing this—cashing Russell's settlement out—I'm sending Charlie to the dentist, too. He looks like a bum."

Flo held her breath and said nothing as Tinker made more calculations in his notebook. After a minute or two he put down his pencil.

"Call Gail at the bank. Let's set up a meeting."

"Maybe there'll even be a bit left over we could put toward the Syrian refugee fund?" Flo asked.

Tinker raised his eyebrows. "Don't push your luck."

Flo dropped it—for now. "Thank you for this, Tinker. Let me fix you lunch."

"Actually, there's a lunch ceilidh today at the Celtic Interpretive Centre I thought we might check out. Care to go?"

Flo retrieved the hammer and stood up from her chair. "Who are you and what have you done with my husband?" she asked.

CHAPTER 41

Turkey, October 2015

FOR AHMED, WAKING TOO EARLY, WHEN IT WAS still dark, meant lying like a corpse so as not to jostle his sister lying next to him, who in turn would jostle their grandmother. All three of them shared a mattress now, with baby Omar nestled between their parents on the opposite mattress. Sometimes after the baby cried out in the night and woke him up, Ahmed was forced to lie still for what felt like hours. Although his mother always rushed to calm Omar quickly, the infant's piercing cries never failed to rouse Ahmed and, despite his constant, bone-deep tiredness, when that happened he struggled to get back to sleep. His mind drifted. He thought about his home in Syria and the constant sounds of bombs dropping at night. He thought about his school closing, being sent home forever, and then reading at night by candlelight when the power was cut. His brain would flash him pictures of the faces of his friends, teachers, and imam he might never see again. And the worst of all was when he was unable to prevent his mind from replaying the night of his family's escape, slinking through the rubble that was once Aleppo like the thieves in *Aladdin*, scrambling through a ditch, cutting his hands, facing an armed guard.

But waking now, Ahmed could tell it was morning because of the light that seeped through the cracks around the tent's door. He was relieved he could get up.

His body was stiff from keeping still, so with slow, minimal movements, he grabbed his shoes, slipped outside, and found his father standing next to their canvas door.

"Good morning, Ahmed. I'm glad you're up," Sami whispered. "Can you pour water into my hands so I might wash my face?" He handed Ahmed a pitcher and Ahmed did as he was asked. He watched his father lather his face with soap, and then poured more water into his father's hands so he could rinse.

"Can I go now? I want to walk." Ahmed rubbed the sleep from his eyes.

"Yes, but don't be too long. Your mother will need help with breakfast."

Ahmed nodded and darted off, following his familiar route to the camp's makeshift playground. He and Abdo liked to meet and talk here at sunrise before it was overrun with smaller children. Early mornings were the only time of day Ahmed could describe as calm, before the din of daily life in crowded conditions began its crescendo.

He kicked the dirt up with his shoes as he ran, and when the playground came into view, he was relieved to see Abdo already seated on a swing.

"Hey, Abdo, have you heard who won yesterday's soccer matches?" Ahmed asked as he approached. They both were FIFA fans and followed their favourite teams' progress whenever they could get updates. Real Madrid was Ahmed's team, while Abdo preferred Barcelona. Ahmed sat on the swing next to Abdo and clasped his hands around the chains.

"No. I haven't heard. Did you bring any food?" Abdo asked. Ahmed noticed dark circles under Abdo's eyes, and his cheeks looked sunken.

"Sorry. I forgot." Ahmed often stuffed pita bread, nuts, or dates wrapped in paper into his pockets to share with his friend. Though Abdo didn't complain of hunger, Ahmed had deduced that while his own family had little, Abdo's family had far less. The soles on Abdo's sneakers had been flapping for weeks, and most of his clothes no longer fit him and had holes in them. Ahmed had never been invited into Abdo's tent but knew that if his tent was crowded with six people calling it home, Abdo's must be even more so with eight people living in it.

They started pumping their legs and swinging as Reyhanli Camp woke up. People emerged from tents, stretching their arms and squinting as their eyes adjusted to daylight. Soon water would be boiling for tea and people would be shuffling to latrines. No one hurried; each day here was much like the one before it. The swings creaked and moaned and their chains left red rust marks on the boys' palms.

"Have you heard when you're leaving Turkey?" Abdo asked. His usual exuberance wasn't there today, and his normally melodic voice sounded monotone. Often the boys played a game of seeing who could vault off his arcing swing and jump farthest. Neither boy suggested it now, and they gradually stopped swinging and sat still side by side.

"Not yet. We have to wait, and then there will be an interview and some health and security checks. I hate the waiting." Although Ahmed was eager to emigrate, it occurred to him now that when that day eventually came, saying goodbye to his friend was going to be terrible. "Hey, are you all right, Abdo?" Ahmed sensed something lay between them and he wasn't sure what it was. Maybe Abdo was jealous that his family had been officially registered to leave? Ahmed now turned to face him.

"I'm leaving Reyhanli Camp, Ahmed. This morning." Abdo scratched circles into the dirt with his toe.

"What? How?"

"We'll drive across Turkey today and board a raft at nighttime. We should be in Greece by the morning."

Ahmed stopped breathing. His only friend was leaving Reyhanli Camp—today. "Oh." Words escaped him. He'd be left behind.

"We won't stay in Greece. My dad says maybe we'll go to Germany. If I practice hard enough, maybe I'll become the next Thomas Müller. I can dominate the midfield, right?" Abdo climbed off the swing and began mimicking soccer moves, kicking an imaginary ball and pretending to bounce it off his knees and head.

Ahmed knew his friend was acting brave for his benefit. "Do you know how to swim?" he asked.

"No, but the Aegean Sea is calm. Lots of people have made this crossing. Thousands."

Ahmed understood why Abdo said this. Abdo had to think positively. But they both also knew that occasional storms blew in, causing rough seas and high winds. Stories of drowned refugees swirled through the camp. Everyone had heard of someone who'd died at sea. Dinghies were often overcrowded, got off course, and were known to puncture and sink. But the boys didn't speak of the risks. They also both knew even more stories about people succeeding in crossing, plus their current circumstances had conditioned them to live with hope. They'd already proven themselves to be survivors.

"I can't believe you're leaving." Ahmed had just assumed he'd leave Reyhanli Camp first. He wanted to be happy for Abdo, to congratulate him and wish him well until they met again, but the words didn't come.

"I know. Me neither." Abdo, normally a chatterbox, was also quiet.

"Wait here. Don't move." Ahmed ran as fast as he could back to his tent. He threw back the tent flaps and tore inside. He began scrambling through the piles of things along the tent's walls before locating it.

"What are you doing, Ahmed? Slow down. You're disturbing the baby," Amira said. She was seated on a cushion, feeding Omar, but he now detached from her breast and began squirming in her arms.

"Sorry, Mama. I have to do something. I'll be back in a few minutes to help with breakfast. I promise."

He ran back to the swing set where Abdo was waiting and thrust his prized Real Madrid soccer ball that he'd gotten for this eleventh birthday into his friend's arms. It was less shiny now and scuffed from being kicked down countless lanes in the refugee camp.

"Here. Take it with you. It floats, too, so hold onto it if you get thrown into the sea." Ahmed was breathless.

Abdo wrapped his skinny arms tightly around the ball. "Thank you, brother." They stood facing one another, unsure of how to handle their emotions and this goodbye. Abdo's shoulders started to shake. He turned away from Ahmed and walked in the direction of his tent. Ahmed watched him go, his head hanging low.

THE OLD MAN IN SKALA Skamnias, Lesbos, woke before dawn. As many times as he had seen it, the sun's ascent on the horizon and the yellow path it cut across the water's surface always took his breath away. He took a moment as he stepped out of his door to enjoy the fresh breeze on his face and the faint smell of salt in the air, then he began his slow walk to the beach. With more boats and bodies arriving every day in Greece, life jackets, dinghies, and debris regularly washed ashore. When he found boat wreckage or piles of cheap life jackets, sometimes stuffed with hosiery or plastic bags, he loaded them onto the back of his pickup truck and drove it to the local dump.

His thick white eyebrows and moustache stood out in contrast to his leathered face. He still enjoyed his morning stroll, but now it was an obligation, too. The authorities, who were at one time burning the piles of waste, had given up and now left it scattered on the beach. It was shameful.

He shuffled his sandalled feet through the dark brown sand and gazed out to the sea. It lapped peacefully at the shore, but a long lifetime of living on this bay had taught him not to be tricked by the apparent calmness. Storms blew in quickly, especially overnight, and last night as he smoked his pipe the wind had howled and rain beat at his windows. The water, now calm, would have been churning, and anyone out in watercraft would have been thrown about more vigorously than dice on a craps table.

Something bobbed along in the water: a round shape his aging eyes tricked him into thinking might be a human head. He watched more closely and deduced by its calm arrival that it wasn't in fact alive. As it came closer he was able to make out that it was a ball, and he kicked off his leather sandals, hiked up his cotton pants, and waded into the water to intercept it. He grabbed and held up the ball, recognizing the Real Madrid crest on it. He'd not add this to the pile headed for the dump; he would save it for his granddaughter to play with instead.

CHAPTER 42

Cape Breton, October 2015

VIEWED AT ANY ANGLE, THE OLD FARMHOUSE exhibited signs of neglect. Where once it had been white, it now camouflaged against the mottled grey sky. The chimney stood erect, but the roof was sagging and missing shingles. Prickly brambles grew up around splitting lattice on the sides of the front porch. Like other vacant homes in the area, it was as much a part of the landscape as the Gulf of St. Lawrence to its west, or the rolling hills where the leaves now fell to its east. If they noticed it at all, the people of Falkirk Cove thought it an eyesore.

Tinker wiggled the key into the lock but couldn't get it to turn.

"Here, let me try," Charlie said, jimmying the key until he heard the bolt slide. He thrust open the bloated door and they began their walk through.

Charlie grabbed the banister and tried wiggling it, but it held firm. Tinker managed to open a few windows, which emitted a loud groan as they woke from a long slumber.

"The floor and stairs need sanding and buffing." Tinker preferred a soft wall-to-wall carpet, but the trend these days seemed to be hardwood.

"True, but the wood's at least salvageable. Heck of a lot cheaper to refinish than lay new floors."

Sunshine pouring in through the living room's windows cast an ethereal quality to their inspection and they spoke in hushed tones. The light illuminated thick dust on every surface and dust particles doing pirouettes in the air. Their steps crunched mouse droppings on the floor.

"It's dingy, but there are sweet details," Charlie said, gazing up at the Grecian cornices in the living room. The fireplace contained a rusty grate with remnants of charred logs and squashed beer cans, and Charlie leaned over to pick up a few cigarette butts that were ground into the hearth.

"Damn squatters," Tinker said. Charlie was silent. "Overall it's not too bad, though," Tinker said. "I've certainly seen worse. Surely it'll be good enough for the Muslims."

"Meaning?"

Tinker stalled. He was trying to catch himself before saying such things, but this one had slipped out. "Just that it's got to be a step up from living in a refugee camp."

In the dining room hung a large chandelier missing a few glass teardrops. The kitchen wasn't updated but had solid oak cabinetry, and the appliances looked serviceable. They'd know more once the power was reconnected. Charlie turned on the faucet. It spluttered loudly and both men jumped backwards before it emitted an unsteady stream of brownish water. "We'll need the well tested," Charlie said.

"I'll add it to the list," said Tinker, grabbing a stubby pencil and notepad from his pocket.

The walls in each of the four bedrooms upstairs needed their peeling wallpaper stripped, and Charlie thought a fresh coat of paint would spiff these rooms right up. Each bedroom had a small closet and a window that pointed in a different compass direction. From the master bedroom Tinker could see his own house in the distance.

There was only one bathroom, with a cracked toilet, pedestal sink, and claw-foot bathtub.

"What do you think, Grandpa?"

"I think we've got a busy couple of months ahead readying this place for our Syrians."

Charlie was almost giddy at the prospect of getting started.

CATRIONA FLOPPED ON HER COUCH and flipped open her laptop. She hadn't checked Facebook for ages; it was a place for people who were accomplishing things with their lives, not for people like her.

Scrolling through her newsfeed, she quickly took in some highlights of what her graduating class was doing now. A few of her friends at university were grumbling about midterms while alternately posting pictures of themselves downing shots during happy hour at the campus bar. Another friend was at theatre school in Montreal, posting inspirational quotes like "All the World's a Stage." Seamus, whom she hadn't seen since prom, had been drafted into the Quebec Major Junior Hockey League and lived in Rimouski. It seemed everyone was chasing their dreams but her.

Her parents were disappointed and frustrated by her gap year, but she couldn't make herself go to school just to please them. She was almost nineteen and trying to figure this one out for herself. She wasn't sure she was succeeding, but that was the plan. At least the Syrian Refugee Project made her feel useful.

She "liked" a few photos and videos, added random innocuous comments like "Nice!" and "Happy for you!" so people would remember she was still alive, and then started creeping around. Charlie wasn't on Facebook, but Nell was. Catriona opened Nell's profile page where she shared lots of wilderness pictures from Alberta. It looked like she'd been to Jasper National Park recently; her pictures of Athabasca Falls were gorgeous. Catriona hovered above the "Like" button but decided against it.

There were no people in Nell's pictures—not even Charlie—but Nell was tagged by some big, bearded guy with gentle eyes called Rex, which led Catriona further down a rabbit hole as she then moved on to Rex's page. He posted a lot about flag football and had his arm around Nell's shoulder in a team photo. Interesting.

Catriona had a meeting with the Syrian Refugee Project today, which had nominated her to handle its social media. It was last minute but she wanted to have something to report. She started a page named The Falkirk Cove Refugee Project, writing a few sentences about the desperate plight of refugees and the group's goal of raising $35,000 to bring a Syrian family here. She sent out a request to all her Facebook friends to like the page. There. It was at least a start. She'd begin promoting Chase the Ace tomorrow.

CHARLIE AND TINKER CLIMBED INTO the Buick and drove toward St. Andrews Church. They'd have to ask Bob for a loan of his truck to haul building materials over to the McCormacks' house. Tinker handed Charlie his list of all the other things they had to borrow, buy, and do. They agreed winterizing the house was top priority. They'd need to check the furnace and insulation, repair the roof, seal windows, fill drafty cracks, and possibly re-side the exterior.

"Grandpa, you know I'm terrible with money, so correct me if I'm wrong," Charlie said, looking up from the to-do list at Tinker's profile as he drove. "The Project has so far raised about four thousand dollars. It needs thirty-five thousand for immigration. We need, what, another ten grand at least for supplies to fix up the house? We don't have near enough."

Tinker stared out the window at the familiar sights along Highway 19. How many thousands of times had he driven down this road? How many more opportunities remained in his future? Maybe it was time he started living in the moment. "Well, the fundraising should pick up, and actually, our family has a bit to contribute."

Tinker parked at the back of the church parking lot nose in, facing the graveyard. His son lay seven rows down, four headstones to the left. Tinker was now about twice the age Russell had been when he died. Right after the accident Tinker thought grief would kill him, too; he couldn't imagine how he was going to absorb the loss and manage the lingering pain. Yet somehow he had continued to live, to bury his grief and plod on.

"Your grandma and I have a nest egg, Charlie. We got a settlement from your dad's company after he died that we tucked away. With interest, it's grown some. We're cashing it out. Alex gets some. Some will go to our debts and repairing that house. And a portion will go to you."

Charlie stared out the front window. "Why didn't you ever tell me?"

"Dunno. Didn't want you to rely on it, I guess. Also it felt like hush money. Like your dad's life had a price tag on it. But a lawyer encouraged your grandma and me to take it, as we weren't inclined to sue your dad's company for wrongful death."

Charlie glanced at his grandpa's profile. Tinker had droopier jowls and less hair, but otherwise he was the same man who had taken him on long drives when Charlie was a boy. Charlie was grateful they were getting along again. He wouldn't take that for granted anymore. The people close to him had been loyal, but he'd pushed all of them to their limits. It was time for him to start doing right by them, and he'd do that with actions, not just words.

Tinker turned to face him. "Truth is, we'd tucked it away for your future. Well, that future has arrived but now you're no longer the sole beneficiary. Don't be letting that bother you."

"I won't. I'll be grateful for any amount, Grandpa."

"You're darn right you will. But will you squander it? Break our trust once again?"

Tinker's words hurt, but Charlie didn't have any right to get defensive. He answered softly, "No."

"Your portion will first cover the cost of fixing your damn teeth. I'm embarrassed to be seen with you with a mouth like that, boy." Tinker got out of the Buick and let the heavy door swing shut with a bang.

Charlie swept his tongue along the cracks and over the rough edges of the teeth he'd chipped. He'd not complained about the pain or humiliation but wasn't averse to fixing his smile, either. And Charlie had another purchase in mind after the dentist, one he knew would meet Tinker and Flo's approval. He was going to buy an engagement ring for Nell. It was about time he took things to the next level with her. He'd put her through so much but was ready to finally settle down.

Charlie caught up to Tinker. They paused briefly at Tinker's mother's grave and came to a full stop at Russell's grave beside it.

"I remember these headstones being so much larger. They either shrunk or I got bigger since the last time I was here," Charlie said. He burrowed his hands deeper into his hoodie pockets. "Listen, Grandpa, whatever you feel I'm owed, I'll use it to make a fresh start."

"Will you, Charlie? You don't know how much I want to believe that."

"I will. Thanks for believing in me, Grandpa." Charlie glanced at this father's headstone. "It helps me believe in myself. And I guess I ought to thank you too, Dad, for this money."

Tinker walked away to give Charlie and Russell a moment together.

CHAPTER 43

Turkey, December 2015

THE FAMILY ENTERED THE LARGE TENT IN THE centre of Reyhanli Camp. It was unofficially the camp office, where business was conducted. Even with his elevated status here, Sami had never before been invited inside, and he willed himself to control his nerves so he could relax and perform well.

Once they were all seated on cushions, the person on the computer screen in front of them began talking.

"Greetings to you all. May I see your passports?" she asked in accented Arabic. Sami was surprised and pleased that anyone in Canada spoke Arabic, accented or not. He opened their passports and held them close to the computer.

"You know that if your application is approved you'll need Turkish exit visas, right?" The immigration officer raised her eyebrows and Sami nodded. "They're notoriously hard to get," she said.

Sami shrugged. It was but one more hurdle.

"Well, why don't you tell me about yourselves?" she urged.

Sami introduced himself and his family members, explaining he'd had a family medical practice in Aleppo before they fled. He was as articulate and proud as he could be without appearing boastful.

Yasmine began squirming on her cushion and coughing. Amira shot her a look.

"And how is everyone's health?" the immigration officer asked.

Sami couldn't lie. "My daughter has asthma. It's worsened here in the refugee camp. I believe my mother-in-law is suffering from post-traumatic stress disorder and depression. She's also deaf." He gestured toward Fatima, who sat still and stared vacantly in the direction of the computer.

"The rest of us are in good health. Excellent health. Including the new baby," Sami said.

The immigration officer glanced toward Omar, slung across Amira's torso. "Do you know anything about Canada? What makes you want to come?"

The question rattled Sami. He just knew that it was far away and reportedly peaceful. He wanted to say something smart but froze.

"Canada is big. Canada is free," Ahmed piped up. They all chuckled.

"Have any of you ever been convicted of a crime?"

"No."

"What would you bring with you if you were allowed to come?"

"Only a few personal mementos. We have nothing else."

"Do any of you speak English?" she asked in English. "*Parlez-vous Français?*"

"I speak English little," Ahmed replied in English, making Sami proud.

"How long would you plan to stay in Canada?"

Sami and Amira looked at one another. He gestured that it was her turn to speak.

"We don't know for sure," she answered tentatively. "Maybe forever?"

ALTHOUGH SAMI DIDN'T LIKE TO get his hopes up too high, he had begun to imagine a new life for them all in Canada. He had even practiced sounding it out in English, twisting his mouth in an uncomfortable way to sculpt the word "Can-a-da."

The family had recently passed their first anniversary at Reyhanli Camp. Sami didn't draw attention to this, but it did affect his disposition. He was a patient man, but this was an extreme test. He'd mentioned it to Tareq when they met for tea last week.

"One year? That's nothing, Sami. There are families who've lived in refugee camps for many years," Tareq said, sipping his black sweet *shai* tea. "Sometimes even for generations."

Sami had never considered himself selfish, but he made a silent prayer to Allah that this wouldn't be his family's fate.

"The war has been brewing for years, brother. Like the flavour from these tea leaves, people have been seeping out of Syria and pouring into Turkey, Lebanon, and Jordan. Now they're muscling their way into Europe. Borders are closing. You read the news, right? Soon, I fear we'll all be trapped here."

"How did it come to this?" Sami asked rhetorically.

"We weren't raised expecting roses to fall from the sky, Sami. This is our lot in life," Tareq answered.

SAMI'S PHONE WAS RINGING. He heard it from inside the family's tent somewhere but couldn't see it in the dim lighting.

"Where's my phone?" he asked out loud to nobody in particular. Fatima sat on a cushion, oblivious. They'd been working on strengthening her leg muscles with short walks around the camp and to the latrine, but she had to be forced and would sit all day in a diaper if given the choice. "The phone? Anyone?" Sami again asked. Amira was out walking with the baby and Noor. Yasmine had had a poor night with lots of wheezing and was resting on a mattress. Ahmed was studying on the other mattress. No one got up to help Sami look. Sami cast his eyes around the piles of laundry, some washed but most of it dirty, with no success locating the ringing phone. It wasn't near the kettle or cooking supplies, either. In a space this small it was frustrating and bewildering to still lose things. It rang a seventh, eighth, ninth time. "Ahmed, help me look," he said, more sternly now.

Ahmed closed his book and plucked the phone from underneath a coat lying next to him. It was cold again in the camp, and their beds were once again piled high with all the donated clothes and blankets they'd received from an aid agency.

Sami snatched it, pressing "On" as he directed the phone to his face. Only Tareq called him regularly, but there was always the outside chance—the remote hope—that it would be the Canadian embassy.

"Hello?" Sami paced in tight circles around the only unobstructed floor space inside the tent.

Ahmed watched his father nod and look towards him. Sami pretended to write in the air with his finger, signalling his need for something to write with. Ahmed handed his father his pencil and worksheet. He turned around and Sami used his back as a writing surface.

"Okay, okay, I understand...Yes, we can do that...I've written it down. I understand...thank you for your call. This is most welcome news...*Insha'Allah*. I understand. I'll await your call and further directions." Sami hung up the phone and looked at his son.

"Is there news?" Ahmed asked, suddenly interested.

Relief flooded through Sami so powerfully he needed a second to collect himself and find his voice. "We passed our interview with the Canadian embassy. If we pass the health and security checks, the Canadian government will issue us a visa to move there." Sami pulled Ahmed to his feet and grabbed his shoulders.

"Grandma too?" Ahmed asked.

Sami didn't answer, not wanting to worry his son. They'd need to link Fatima's file with their own, and the health checks concerned him. Yasmine's asthma and Fatima's mental and physical health could be seen as a burden to any country's health-care system. Would Canada be merciful enough to accommodate them? "Things are in motion now, Ahmed. Go find your mother, but let me share the news, please."

Ahmed raced out of the tent and Sami sat on the mattress. His heart was pounding and he took some deep breaths to try to calm his nerves. There was no turning back now. It appeared his family would not be one of those poor families Tareq referenced, living indefinitely in a refugee camp, trapped in uncertainty and despair. God willing, they would start their lives over in Canada. This could be their second chance. It thrilled and terrified him, but he'd bury any doubts and uncertainties in front of his family. "Can-a-da," he said aloud. He gazed around the stuffy, dim tent and though it was shabby, he cared a bit less.

"What is it, Sami?" Amira asked as she re-entered the tent with Ahmed trailing right behind her. "Ahmed wouldn't tell me. He said I needed to hear it from you."

Sami swallowed, then stood up to face his wife. He grabbed both her hands. "We have tentative approval to move to Canada. It could really be happening, Amira."

Amira dropped Sami's hands and brought her own to her open mouth. "When do we leave?" she asked, glancing around the tent. She'd already started making a mental list of what she'd pack to take with her, and it wasn't much. Everything they owned was used up or worn out.

"It could be as soon as next month. We just need to pass health and security checks and then Turkey will have to issue an exit visa," Sami replied.

"So there are a few obstacles yet," Amira said, glancing at her seated mother and Yasmine, who still lay wheezing on a mattress.

"True. And I don't want you to worry, but your mother's file has yet to be linked to ours. We have private sponsors, and hopefully they'll be able to help us with that so we can all stay together." Sami couldn't imagine how Fatima could survive alone in a new country. None of them would entertain the possibility.

"We simply must go together," Amira replied. "It will have to be arranged that Mother goes with us."

"I know. We'll make it so," Sami replied, hoping this wasn't an empty promise he'd be unable to honour.

Ahmed piped up. "Ms. Hussain is from Canada. She showed me where it is on the world map taped to my classroom's wall. It's huge. I bet there are a lot of plants and trees there. Or is it always snowing?"

Sami chuckled. "I hope we'll find out for ourselves soon."

A small voice rose up from the mattress. "Are there cats in Canada?" Yasmine asked. "Because I want one, please." She coughed and crossed her hands on her chest. The coughing continued until she fell backwards onto the mattress. "Papa...what's happening...help!"

Sami rushed to her side. Her face was paler than he'd ever seen it and her lips were starting to turn blue. He cursed not having an inhaler to offer her and scrambled to think of alternatives. It was much easier to stay calm when patients weren't his own family members. Amira and Ahmed stood back, alarm visible on their faces. Sami propped her upright and encouraged Yasmine to take long, deep breaths as tears began streaming down her face. Her breathing was irregular, stopping altogether for five, eight, fifteen seconds. She stared at Sami with panicked eyes.

CHAPTER 44

Cape Breton, December 2015

LOTTERY TICKET SALES WERE GROWING STEADILY each week the ace wasn't pulled and the jackpot climbed higher. There were rumours that this week some people were coming from mainland Nova Scotia for a shot at the prize. Motels in Inverness County were booking up, which rarely happened after golf season ended. A story about their Chase the Ace in last week's newspaper made the Refugee Project Committee hopeful they might fill every seat in the Legion tonight. Catriona had started receiving calls from radio and television stations, too. She had a few interviews booked for that afternoon, but first she wanted to pitch in at the McCormack house.

"Charlie, you here?" Catriona tried the latch and found the front door unlocked. She let herself in.

"Upstairs," he shouted back.

Charlie and his helpers had repaired the roof and exterior walls first and now were working inside. The well had passed inspection and, after sediment was flushed from the pipes, the water was declared safe for drinking. The committee had to rent a new hot-water tank, as the one left behind wasn't repairable, but other things, including all the kitchen appliances, creaked and groaned their way back to life once power was restored. They weren't state-of-the-art, but they were serviceable.

Catriona took off her jacket and flung it across the polished newel post. It was a relief to now have a full oil tank and heat coming out of the radiators. She'd had to wear gloves working here last week just to keep any sensation in her fingertips, and when she took them off to strip wallpaper her nails turned bluish.

She mounted the stairs two at a time, excited to see what progress had been made since she was last here two days ago. "You in here?" Catriona asked, opening the door to the master bedroom. No one answered. The walls were now dove grey and the trim everywhere was a fresh white.

"How 'bout in here?" She moved on to the next room, one of the three smaller bedrooms. It now had pale lavender walls, but no one inside.

"Charlie?" Catriona shouted into the next bedroom. No one answered. "I'm getting the heebie jeebies. Where are you?" The smell of paint wafted all through the second floor, so she knew there was an open can somewhere nearby. She followed the scent into the final bedroom and pushed open the door.

A shrouded figure standing in the middle of the room said, "I am the ghost of Cape Bretoners past." Charlie threw off the white drop sheet draped over his head and let it fall to his feet. He was wearing paint-splattered overalls, and Catriona saw tiny white droplets had settled on the tips of his dark brown hair.

"You scared the shit out of me," she said, reaching out to punch his arm.

He caught her wrist in midair, pried open her fingers, and placed a paintbrush in her hand. "Stop slacking and get to work. We've got bedrooms to paint."

They worked steadily until Catriona heard a car coming up the gravel driveway. She looked out the window.

"Hey, the CBC's here. They want to do an interview about Chase the Ace and how we're using the money to bring over the Syrians. Do it with me?"

"An interview? *Moi*? Good thing I got my teeth fixed so I'm TV pretty. I'd bring shame to my grandparents' good name otherwise." He put his arm around Catriona's shoulders as they walked downstairs, leaving paint smudges on her work shirt.

"Don't mess up my clothes. I'm already going to come across like a huge dork. You're making it worse," Catriona said, opening the front door.

Charlie stepped back, crossed his arms, and looked her up and down. "Don't worry. You look adork-able."

COURTNEY AND ALEX BOARDED THE plane. Alex was becoming a pro at flying—settling into his seat, buckling and tightening his seat belt, even plugging his earbuds into the armrest so he could watch cartoons once they were in the air. Courtney had never even been on a plane until she was sixteen, so the fact that her son could do all this at only six impressed her. His teachers also told her he was smart. Despite missing kindergarten last year, he was keeping up with his peers and reading at an advanced level for his age. She knew she had Flo to thank for some of that. The books and letters she kept sending motivated Alex to advance his reading.

"Mommy, aren't you excited about our trip? I can't wait to see Grandpa and Grandma. And Grandma told me that they have a big real Christmas tree and Charlie's still there and we're going to make cookies and Santa knows that I'll be in Cape Breton so he's going to bring my presents there." Alex stopped talking when he ran out of breath.

"Mm-hmm. Listen to the flight attendant now, okay? He's going to teach us about the safety features." Courtney wanted to read *Us Weekly* and chew her nicotine gum in peace. Relations between her and the Gordons were improving, but she didn't share Alex's excitement about spending Christmas with them. Well, that wasn't entirely true. She did enjoy Flo's cooking.

"Are we going to crash? Where are the emergency exits? Do I need the oxygen mask? Will it fit me? If we crash into water, will I really get to slide down a big yellow slide?" Alex asked in rapid-fire succession.

"No, we won't crash. I'd never let anything bad happen to you. But it's polite to listen to the safety lesson all the same." Courtney turned to face the window and felt herself falling asleep as the plane took off.

NELL'S SUITCASE WAS OPEN ON the bed. She methodically folded T-shirts and underpants and neatly organized them in the same suitcase she'd arrived with eleven months earlier. Rex would be here to pick her up in forty-five minutes. She dreaded saying goodbye to him for ten days, but it was Christmas and she missed her family. And then there was Charlie. Their conversations lately were cautious and polite and made her feel they were further apart than ever. It almost would have been better if they'd fought. At least then it would have seemed real. He'd sounded good, so at least there was that. She'd always wish him well. She'd thought about telling him about Rex when they talked on the phone, but she knew she owed it to him to tell him where her head and heart really were when she saw him in person. Her stomach rolled over again at the thought of it. She'd woken with diarrhea—her usual nervous response. Her scalp itched, too, whenever she thought about having this conversation with Charlie. She put her hand to the skin beneath her hair and felt hot, angry welts. Terrific. She needed to not think about him, even just for a moment. She reached for the clicker and turned the television on.

"And in the next segment there's a story you're going to love. A small community on Cape Breton Island has come together to raise money for Syrian refugees." Nell's ears perked up when she heard "Cape Breton." "They've hit the jackpot, if you will, with a game called Chase the Ace," the newscaster said. "Stick around and after the commercials you'll learn more."

Nell was glued to the couch now. She couldn't believe her island was making national news. She'd not heard much news from home lately.

The ads ended and the TV showed a map of Cape Breton and zoomed into a dot beside the name Falkirk Cove. Now they really had Nell's complete and undivided attention. The voice-over explained how this small community had suffered from population decline in the years since the local fishery and area coal mines had closed. It was the same sad story Nell had been told her whole life. Frankly, she was a bit tired of her home being represented as a have-not place. But then the news piece became interesting. It explained the Syrian Refugee Project, and how popular some lottery being run out of the bingo in Inverness had become.

Charlie and Catriona appeared together on the TV. Nell dropped the remote control and the batteries spilled out and rolled across the floor. Nell let them scatter while she stared at Charlie. His teeth looked perfect again and he'd regained weight. He appeared healthy and was grinning. It was the version of Charlie she'd loved so dearly and for so long. Seeing him like this provoked a tenderness in her for Charlie that she hadn't felt in a long time. She was suddenly nostalgic for their early years together. A flutter of doubt entered her mind. How much did she still love him, and was she ready to let him go? Would seeing him in person make breaking up with him impossible? Both he and Catriona had paint smudges on their clothes, and they explained they were busy fixing up an old house for the Syrians to move into when they arrived. Catriona was doing most of the talking, but Charlie was gazing at her with what Nell could tell was admiration. Interesting.

CHAPTER 45

Cape Breton, December 2015

THE BINGO HALL FILLED UP EARLY. CATRIONA usually recognized every face in the room, but tonight there were a lot of newbies. People scrambled to find chairs together and complained when they had to sit apart. Catriona was trying to stay chill, it was only bingo after all, but the Legion felt charged tonight. Anticipation had mounted each week the ace wasn't pulled, and was reaching a new pitch. It might not have been Saturday night at a bar or nightclub, but it was the most excitement she'd felt in a long while and it made her frenzied and giddy. The best part was how well people were tipping. One guy even slipped a twenty-dollar bill into the waistband of her jeans.

"Snakes alive, do the jive, bees in the hive, all the fives, fifty-five. G55 is your next number, folks, G55." Jean had been calling bingo for twenty years—longer than Catriona had been alive—but had started having more fun with it since Chase the Ace began. Catriona teased her that she'd discovered a new musical genre: bingo rap. Charlie would have had fun riffing off her rhymes but he hardly ever came to bingo.

"Over here!" Hands waved to her as she sidestepped around peoples' backs and behind their chairs. She knew from experience to walk row by row and not be distracted or pulled in random directions; superstitious players would get annoyed and accuse her of potentially selling their winning card to someone else. People were so weird. Again, she longed for Charlie's company so they could laugh about it together.

It was so tight moving through the aisles her backside brushed up against some men and she thought she heard one wolf whistle. Uggh.

"Time for fun, forty-one. Let's get 'er done. N41. Let's hear those daubers, bingo players, N41." Pound-pound-pound. "That's the backbeat I was waiting for!" Jean was on a roll.

Catriona's legs were in constant motion responding to hands that never stopped shooting up into the air. The room was stuffy and getting hot with so many bodies breathing and sweating in it. Catriona felt her damp T-shirt sticking to her body and pulled off her sweatshirt to cool down. She tried tying it around her waist, but her belted money pouch was sagging, so she went to the canteen to unload. She noticed the guy who stuffed the twenty into her waistband following her with his eyes as she walked.

"Flo, help me organize?" Catriona dropped fistfuls of bills and coins from the pouch onto the canteen counter into two piles—card sales, and Chase the Ace sales.

Flo said "Oh my heavens" several times as she sorted and counted. She grabbed a large calculator off the table and started punching in numbers before looking up at Catriona. "Goodness gracious, we've done it. No matter what happens tonight, whether the ace is pulled or not, we've raised $35,000 for the Refugee Project. Our debt is paid."

Catriona felt herself grinning, but their celebration would have to wait. She needed to get out on the floor to sell more tickets. She tightened the laces on her sneakers and got back to work. The wolf-whistler was waving her over. Reluctantly, she approached him.

"Yeah?" She looked as disinterested as she could manage. He was about her dad's age and wearing a Hooters trucker hat. Gross. The eyes on the owl emblazoned on it started at her. She looked away and spotted Charlie entering through the back door. Well that was a bonus.

"Whatchaselling?" Hooters asked her.

"Bingo cards, Sherlock. How many you want?"

He reached out his hand as if to take a sheet, then quickly slipped it behind her and grabbed her ass.

She froze. Did that really just happen? There was so much commotion and no one else seemed to notice it. He was ignoring her now that Jean was calling numbers again. Maybe she imagined it. She shuffled farther down the row and tried not to think about it.

After all the cards were played, it was time for the main draw. Jean called Bob onto the stage to pull the winning ticket. He made a big show of cracking his knuckles, stretching his arms over his head, and doing a few jumping jacks to warm up for the task. Watching her grampie ham it up made Catriona feel better, and she caught Charlie's eye now too. They exchanged waves from across the Legion.

"You ready, Bob?" Jean asked into her microphone.

"Never been more ready in my life, Jean," he replied, plunging his hand into the bucket of stubs. A few people started slapping their hands on the bingo tables to imitate a drum roll.

"The winning ticket tonight is…" Bob was stretching it out for maximum effect. "Four thousand…three hundred…and…seventy…six." Groans could be heard around the room. After people realized they had lost, they waited for the winner to holler out. No one did. "Who has ticket number 4,376?" Bob asked.

Catriona heard a pair of sneakers squeak as they travelled across the back of the room. They made their way to the front. Roger's arms were swinging at his sides. He silently climbed the steps onto the stage and handed Jean his ticket, his head still drooping low and his mouth slightly agape.

"Roger? You have the winning ticket?" she asked.

"My ticket is number 4,376, Jean. That is the number Bob called. He called it twice. I double-checked. I have the ticket, Jean. I am the winner: 4,376."

Bob thumped Roger on the back in congratulations then returned to his seat, leaving Roger alone on the stage with Jean. People began cheering and chanting, "Chase-the-Ace! Chase-the-Ace!" Roger frowned and clapped his hands over his ears as the noise got louder.

Catriona hated seeing him distressed. She climbed up on the stage to see if she could make it better for him somehow. She put her hand over the mic. "Can you make them stop, Jean?"

"They're just riled up, Cat. It'll be fine." Jean turned to face Roger. "I thought you didn't like the odds in this game. You said it had terrible odds for the player."

Roger looked at the ceiling. "Terrible odds. Terrible odds. Less than one percent chance of winning. Somebody had to eventually win. Somebody was me."

Jean picked up the partial deck of cards and fanned them in front of Roger, face down. He paused, reached forward, plucked out a card, and looked at it. His mouth was a straight horizontal line and his face unreadable. He slowly handed the card to Jean while everyone else in the room was motionless and silent. Jean's eyes flew wide open. She held it up to show the crowd Roger's Ace of Spades. Loud cheers erupted.

Catriona smiled at Roger and said congratulations in his ear on her way back to the floor so she could begin tidying up.

"Hey card girl, c'mere." It was Hooters again, waving her over. Catriona ignored him. "Aw, don't be like that. Can't I get a smile? It won't break yer face, promise."

Charlie was by Catriona's side now. "Want me to deal with him?"

"I got it." She marched over to Hooters and stomped hard on his foot. "Oops. My big feet got in my way. You'll want to give me a wide berth from now on."

He shuffled out with the rest of the bingo players as she grabbed the push broom and began tidying up.

THE NEXT DAY, BOB AND FLO were talking about Roger's good fortune and speculating about what he might do with his winnings as Bob slid the blood pressure cuff onto Flo's upper arm and started pumping so it would tighten. He watched the needle on the meter rise to two hundred, then slowly let some air hiss out until he heard the first thump travelling through his stethoscope into his ears. The needle dropped and bounced, and Bob kept hearing thumps until it dipped too low and no more thumps were audible.

Flo distracted herself by looking around her living room. There were Christmas cards and nutcracker dolls displayed on the mantle. The Barra McNeils were singing "*Taladh Chriosda*," a Gaelic carol and one of Flo's favourites, on the radio. She didn't know what the words meant, but that didn't bother her. The harmony of their voices was so beautiful and reverent it made the hairs stand up on her arms.

A tall, dense fir tree stood in the corner, cold air and a sharp, refreshing smell still blowing off it. Decorations in faded, decades-old Simpson's and Eaton's boxes sat on the floor beside it so her family could trim it together later at their party. Courtney and Alex had arrived in Halifax yesterday and were on their way to Cape Breton now, Nell was home for the holidays, and of course Bob and Elsie would come over with Catriona and her parents. She'd extended an invitation to Cape Breton's newest celebrity, Roger (Courtney would have to button her lip if she didn't approve of his being included), and the other members of the Falkirk Cove Refugee Project, too, so the house would be full, just the way Flo liked it. They could toast their hard work fundraising and renovating the McCormack house.

"Well, Flo, I have to tell you that you're totally average. Nothing special at all," Bob said.

"What do you mean?" Bob never said an unkind word, so she was puzzled.

The Velcro made a loud ripping sound as he tore off the cuff. "Your blood pressure is 118 over 79, so within normal range. A couple more readings like this and you should talk to your GP about weaning you off the hypertensives."

Flo let out a whoop. "Can I start drinking caffeinated tea again now?"

"You drink that decaf dreck? Yes, you must stop. Immediately. Doctor's orders."

Flo sprang to her small feet and went to the kitchen to plug in the kettle.

"GRANDMAAAAAAAAAAAA!" ALEX OPENED THE DOOR and ran straight into her open arms while Courtney stood stiffly on the porch, then stepped through the open door with their luggage.

Florence peered up from the hug at Courtney. "Hello, dear. Welcome back."

Courtney nodded.

Flo took Alex by the hand, escorting him into the kitchen while Courtney drifted toward her usual spot on the living room couch. "How was your trip? Tell me absolutely everything while you roll out the cookie dough."

The dough was a bit like a big dried-up lump of old Play-Doh, and it took all of Alex's muscles to flatten it. After that hard part was done, he cut it into shapes like candy canes, trees, angels, and stars that they slid on sheets into the oven. He snuck in a few nibbles of dough, but not too much, because Grandma said the raw ingredients might give him a bellyache. Then Charlie came home with Catriona and promised the three of them would play Snakes and Ladders soon.

"C'mon, Alex, help me get the leaf for the dining room table. We have to make room for six," Grandpa said.

Alex grabbed his coat and headed toward the backyard, where he hoped he'd still be able to find a stray leaf. The trees were all bare now.

"This way. The leaf we need is in the basement. I'll show you."

When they all sat down for supper, Grandma said the little prayer she called grace, thanking God for bringing them all together at the table and for the food they were about to eat. They all passed around plates of ham, bowls of vegetables and creamy potatoes, and some mustard pickles. They ate together and talked and laughed—even Mommy.

After everyone was full and rubbing their bellies and telling Grandma how yummy everything was, Charlie picked up his fork and tapped it against his water glass. "I have an announcement," he said. "I've decided not to return to Alberta. Looks like you're stuck with me in Falkirk Cove." Grandma hugged him and Alex saw Catriona mouth a silent "yes" and pump her fist underneath the table. Alex thought it was just the best news, because he'd get to be with his brother during his summer vacation in Cape Breton.

Now, Alex was busy shaking snow globes and eating sugar cookies as more people started coming to the house. This was going to be a fun Christmas party. He was so busy and excited he forgot he was tired from the trip and surprised himself when he yawned. He'd better get busy decorating the tree like Grandma asked him. It smelled like the woods and was so ginormous the star on top poked the ceiling. He had to stop staring at it and get down to work.

ROGER TOOK EIGHTEEN STEPS UP the front walkway and knocked on the door six times. No one heard him. He saw lights on inside and the silhouettes of people and a big Christmas tree. He tried counting the people, but they were moving around, and some might have been in the kitchen and out of sight. His sack was getting heavy, so he rested it on the front step and stared at the red ribbon adorning the wreath on the door while he summoned the nerve to test the door handle. When he finally did, the door opened and he stepped into the foyer.

"Roger, please come in," he heard Flo say above the din of voices.

"Florence, you asked me once when I was born. I was born on a Friday. Friday's child—that's me—is loving and giving." Roger spilled wrapped gifts out of his sack and onto the floor before turning on his heel and leaving.

Alex rushed to the gift pile and began looking for a present with his name on the gift tag.

"Roger, come back!" Florence called from the front door, but Roger had already retreated into the dark night.

COURTNEY NESTLED INTO A COUCH in the living room and pulled an afghan over her legs.

"Here you are, dear," Flo said, handing her a cup of unsweetened tea. Courtney felt too lazy and settled on the couch to go to the kitchen to fetch some sugar. It was her third visit to Cape Breton, and she was hoping the third time would be the charm, that she'd come to feel even a smidgen of Alex's affection for the place, but something was still off. What? Dinner had gone well enough. They all talked and laughed without any awkward pauses or disagreements. Even grumpy Tinker looked almost jolly. Thank God they'd sorted out the money piece before she and Alex arrived. Alex was getting what he was owed—and it was about time—though not in a lump sum. It would come in staggered payments until he was eighteen. She wasn't thrilled about it but could live with that.

"Jingle bells, Batman smells, Robin laid an egg," Alex sang as he hung decorations on the lowest branches of the Christmas tree. Gusts of cold air entered the house with each person who arrived at the party, but inside it was cozy and festive. Still Courtney felt edgy. Probably now wasn't the smartest time to have quit smoking but she'd promised Alex, so she chewed her nicotine gum aggressively, sipped her tea, and tried to ignore her craving.

Though they were mostly strangers to Courtney, Alex looked up and said hello to everyone who arrived like they were old friends—even that creepy weirdo, Roger. He'd come in and just spilled presents from a sack like they were pieces of candy falling out of a busted piñata. There was a gift for everyone at the party except her, of course. She let Alex open his. It was child-sized binoculars and a package of red Twizzlers licorice.

It was strange for her to see that Alex had acquired his own life here outside of her own, but it was what she wanted for him, wasn't it? To have family beyond her, to be accepted and cared for and financially supported by Russell's people? Then why wasn't she happier? He was a lucky boy, and she'd made that happen. She couldn't wrap it up and put it under the tree, but it was probably the best Christmas present she'd ever given him. She wished someone loved and fought for her the way she had for him. She'd always be an outsider here and would have to watch that she didn't slag Cape Breton or its people once they got back to Toronto. It could be Alex's special thing. Maybe one day she'd find her own.

NELL STOOD ON THE FRONT step with her hand hovering in the air. She'd intended to call Charlie as soon as she arrived in Cape Breton yesterday. The hours had somehow slipped by as she avoided an inevitable confrontation by telling herself she first needed to catch up with her parents and brothers. Enough was enough. It was time. Past time. Way past time. She took a deep breath and grasped the handle and entered.

The Gordons' house was so familiar to Nell she should have felt almost like she was coming home, but she didn't. It felt more like walking onto a set. The people in the living room were like actors in a play, assuming the roles of merry townsfolk. In the backdrop Alex was there as though central casting had sent up an impish freckly faced redheaded boy on cue. He was crowding brightly coloured balls onto the bottom half of a tree while the top half he couldn't reach remained bare. While the other adults mingled, drank, and popped chocolate peanut-butter balls in their mouths, Courtney sat fidgeting on the couch. Nell hadn't seen her since the welcome party over a year ago at the Celtic Interpretive Centre, but it was easy to pick her out of the crowd; she was nothing if not distinctive here. Someone was playing "Lark in the Morning" on a fiddle in another room, a tune Nell had once known how to play herself before giving up her lessons and selling her fiddle. A few people seated were tapping their feet. She listened for a moment, waiting to feel a rush of nostalgia, but instead she felt lonely. Maybe there would be dancing later. She didn't think she'd be here long enough to see it.

Flo approached Nell and wrapped her arms around her tightly. "Nell, darling, you made it. Let me take your coat."

"Thanks, Flo, I'm going to keep it on. Sadly, I can't stay long." She looked over her shoulder and saw Charlie walking down the hallway toward her. "Excuse me Flo, please." She met Charlie halfway.

"Charlie." She kept her arms by her sides.

"Nell." Charlie looked nervous. He extended a glass of punch.

Nell accepted the punch and set it on a side table. "Can we go somewhere private to talk?"

Charlie directed her up the stairs. They slipped away unnoticed except by Catriona.

ALEX STUCK HIS HAND IN the cardboard box and pulled out a homemade decoration that was less fancy than the others. It was a square made out of green and red Popsicle sticks, with a Polaroid picture glued on top. He took it to Tinker. "Who's this?" he asked his grandfather.

Tinker took the decoration in his hand and spent a few seconds looking at the picture before speaking. "That's your father, Alex. He made it at school to surprise your Grandma and me. I believe he was about your age."

Alex gently took it back and turned to face the tree. One branch just in the middle stuck out a bit farther than the others. It was strong and had a small nub at the end. Alex had been saving it for a special decoration. He hung his dad's picture on it. There. Now the whole family had come home for Christmas. Alex would have to leave again in a week, but he didn't want to be sad about that now. He'd be back for two whole months in the summer.

NELL AND CHARLIE SAT SIDE by side on the bed with an arm's-length distance between them.

"I know I've been bad at communicating, Nell." Charlie looked at the floor. "I've been focused on getting better, but that's not a good excuse. Please know I was thinking about you all the time."

Nell scratched her neck. "Charlie, there's something I've got to tell you."

Charlie grabbed her hands and took them in his own. He forced himself to make eye contact. "Please, can I go first?"

Nell nodded.

"I've done a lot of thinking. We've grown apart."

"We sure have."

"Well, that's on me. But I think I can fix it." Charlie pulled a small box out of his jeans pocket. He opened the lid. "Nell, let's get married. Let's stop living separate lives. Move back to Cape Breton and become my wife." His face was white.

Nell looked at the ring.

"It's a Claddagh ring. The heart, crown, and hands symbolize love, loyalty, and friendship. Grandma helped me pick it out."

"It's beautiful." A diamond sparkled inside the heart. "I'm gobsmacked."

"I want to do right by you. I owe it to you. I love you."

Nell took a minute to collect her thoughts. "Charlie, our problems can't be solved with a wedding. You must know that."

His face slackened. "Are you saying no?" He snapped the box shut and put it back into his pocket.

"You took me for granted, Charlie." Nell stopped herself from saying more. "I didn't want to give up on us. I thought we could we could weather the distance; we'd done it before. But this time we drifted too far apart."

Charlie began pacing around the small room, raking his fingers through his shaggy hair and pulling it at the roots. His voice was raspy when he finally spoke. "Is it the drugs? 'Cause I've been clean for months. I'm done forever."

"That's fantastic. And you look well. But no, this isn't about the drugs. And it isn't all on you. I've done something, too."

"What?" He stopped pacing and looked expectantly.

Nell swallowed. "I've been with Rex."

"Been with Rex? Been how?"

Nell's hives began popping out on her neck, and she sat on her hands to resist scratching them.

"Rex? Really?" Charlie asked, staring at the floor. "Once?"

"More than once. I'm so sorry." She clutched her gut. "But it's about more than just Rex, Charlie. It's the other secrets and distance that crept between us." She slouched and then sank lower until she collapsed backwards onto the bed. She stared at this ceiling for what was to be the last time. A long silence ensued.

"You cheated on me with my friend," Charlie said, the pain audible in his voice.

"I know. That was a shitty thing to do. You're right to be mad." She stood and cupped Charlie's face in her hand. "I wish you well, Charlie Gordon, and I'll always love you. I just can't be your person any longer." Nell turned and rushed downstairs and quietly slipped out the front door.

CHAPTER 46

Turkey, December 2015

"A FEW MORE STEPS, MOTHER, YOU CAN DO IT."
Amira coaxed her mother forward in the camp along the dusty pathway. Fatima grabbed her daughter's forearm as they moved past the tents, but Amira refused to bear any of her mother's weight. Their pace was so slow Amira thought she'd become an old woman too before they reached the toilets. She was trying not to let her frustration at her mother's willfulness show.

"We're almost there. Just a little farther." Amira spoke though she knew her mother couldn't hear her words. Fatima was able to walk greater distances now with minimal assistance, but that didn't mean she wanted to, and she made no effort to mask her displeasure at being forced to rehabilitate. She sulked as Amira urged her forward.

They arrived at the latrine and Amira guided her to a stall. Fatima grimaced and turned her head away, objecting to the odour. "Here you are. I'll wait just outside the door." Amira opened it for her mother and swatted away a few flies. Amira had decided a week ago that she was done diapering her mother, and now she, Sami, and Ahmed took turns walking Fatima here. It was new and uncomfortable for Amira to stand up to her mother this way, but she simply had too many people to care for. She needed everyone in the family to do as much for themselves as they could, especially as they prepared to leave. They'd already passed their security checks, as Amira suspected they would, but today's tests were more worrisome. Today they had their health checks. She wanted her mother in the best physical shape she could possibly be, and prayed that Yasmine wouldn't wheeze during her examination. Poor Yaya had given them a terrible fright with her last major asthma attack. She'd stopped breathing altogether for about fifteen terrible, infinite seconds. Amira now lived in daily terror that if Yasmine didn't get an inhaler and move somewhere with better air quality soon, her next big attack could be even worse—possibly even fatal.

"All done? Good. Let's walk back."

"Why are you tormenting me this way?" Fatima asked her on the way back to their tent. She didn't often speak, but when she did her words were barbed and her voice was raspy from lack of use.

"Because I'm an insufferable, mean daughter," Amira replied, emboldened by her mother's deafness.

SAMI LAY ON HIS MATTRESS. He had been up much of the night worrying about Yasmine, but now his emotions had shifted to something rare for him: pity for himself and his family. He wallowed in the misery of their not belonging anywhere. He usually tried to stay brave and optimistic for the family, but the truth was they were drifters, refugees, displaced persons. They not only had no real physical home, they had no sense of the security nor comfort the idea of home carried. They had no medicines. Would they find those things in Canada? It was incredulous to Sami that a community had raised money and furnished a house for them. It let him reclaim a smidgen of his faith in humanity—but then doubts crept in. They'd fail their physicals. Turkey wouldn't issue them exit visas. Their airplane would be hijacked or would crash because as Tareq once told him, people like them weren't raised to expect roses to drop from the sky. He'd not fully trust in the recent bit of good news they'd received that a community on the east coast of Canada was actively working to bring them there until his feet stood on Canadian soil.

Sami saw his wife and mother-in-law in the tent's door. "Good, you're back. It's time to go for our health checks." He scooped a wriggling Omar up from where he lay beside him on the mattress, and waved the elder two children outside. When his eyes were able to focus on Amira's face, he noticed the strain it held. She was no longer the docile, contented young woman he'd married who loved to read, visit the souk, and meet friends for coffee and conversation. But she was a survivor, and he admired her new fortitude.

"It's almost over," he told her as he exited the tent.

"It's just beginning," she replied.

FATIMA SAT DOWN ON THE carpet, crossed her legs, and folded her arms in front of her chest.

"No, no, no. We must go now. We cannot miss these appointments." Amira extended her hand to help her mother to her feet. Fatima swatted it away, turned her head sharply to the left as far as it would rotate, and squeezed her eyes shut.

Amira grabbed her mother's arm and tried pulling her to her feet while Sami and the children waited outside. "I'm begging you to cooperate, Mother."

Fatima began thrashing her arms and wailing like a wounded animal, trying to shake Amira off her.

Sami popped his head back inside the tent. "Everything all right?"

Amira was at her wits' end. "Take yourself and the children to the health checks. I'll catch up." Amira squatted and placed her hands on her mother's shoulders to try to calm them both down. "Do not do this. It's our only chance to get the clearance we need to leave. Without the health check you'll be stuck here in Turkey." Amira noticed that she didn't say "we'll" be stuck here.

Fatima turned to face Amira and opened her eyes. "I'm not going. Leave me alone."

Investing any more time in this argument meant Amira would miss her own health check. Her mother's standoff could derail all their carefully laid plans. Exasperated, Amira took her hands off her mother, stood up, and took a step back. Her mother now barely resembled the proud, intelligent, and loving woman she had been before the war. Amira had been waiting for that person to re-emerge, but maybe she was gone forever.

With an inner strength she didn't know she had, Amira made a resolution. If forced to choose, she'd pick Sami and the children. May Allah forgive her. She exited the tent and ran to her appointment.

A few minutes later, Fatima also exited the tent and went in the opposite direction. She was strong enough now to walk to the camp entrance without drawing attention to herself. She started down the road toward town, unable to hear the cars honking their horns at her as she weaved farther into the lane.

TAREQ WAS DRIVING BACK TO Reyhanli Camp when he saw a few cars parked on the rough shoulder opposite. Several men were standing and pointing at something in the ditch. Tareq pulled a U-turn and joined them. "What is it?" he asked.

"A body," someone answered.

Tareq walked briskly toward it. He leaned down to pick the woman up but fell to his knees and clasped his hands in front of his chest when he saw her face. He gently closed her eyelids with his thumbs and said a quick prayer before scooping Fatima into his arms and carrying her back to his taxi.

"I know her family. I'll return her to them," he told the men standing roadside.

Happy that someone else was dealing with this headache, they all returned to their cars and drove away.

AMIRA WENT THROUGH THE MOTIONS. She washed her mother's body three times and braided her hair. She silently acknowledged Noor's entrance into her tent with a glance and a nod before letting Noor help her dress her mother in an ankle-length sleeveless dress Noor had brought. Sami and Tareq then entered and lifted her mother onto a sheet. Amira picked up her mother's left hand and laid it on her chest, then laid her mother's right hand on top of her left and folded the sheet around her, pausing for a last look. Even through her numbness, Amira registered that her mother finally had a peaceful look on her face that had long been absent. Sami secured the shroud with ropes he tied above her head and below her feet, then lifted Fatima. Cradling her in his arms, he exited the tent.

The children met them outside. Ahmed carried Omar, but a whimpering Yasmine took Amira's hand as they all walked slowly to the main camp office tent together. The setting sun cast an ochre glow on the family like a spotlight following them. People in the lanes and emerging from their tents saw the procession, turned to face Mecca, and began reciting the *Salat al-Janazah* funeral prayers, creating a growing chorus of voices. Amira drew strength from it, straightened her back, dropped her shoulders, and lifted her head. Fatima's grave was being dug as they walked.

A WEEK LATER, AMIRA CLUTCHED the coveted Turkish exit visas in her hand. Yasmine's asthma was noted on her file, but she had passed her health screening along with the rest of them and they were all issued Canadian visas. Things had then started moving quickly, and the Turkish exit visas arrived, stamped by immigration, within days. She tore the one issued to her mother into tiny shreds and stared at the rest until she imagined her eyeballs might burn holes in the paper. How strange to think they'd once worried they wouldn't be allowed into Turkey, and more recently worried they wouldn't be allowed out. It distressed Amira that her mother's remains would be here for eternity but, at the same time, knowing her mother's soul was at last reunited with her father's soul in the afterlife comforted her.

The day had arrived. Amira shooed the family outside and closed the flap on their now-empty tent for a final time. A new family would move in, perhaps tonight or tomorrow. They could have it. Emotions flooded over Amira as she adjusted her hijab, clutched their passports tightly in her hand, and made the final walk through Reyhanli Camp.

Noor and her children were weeping, and Amira choked up as she bade her friend farewell with kisses on her cheeks. "When I needed you the most you were always there," she told her. Noor promised to visit Fatima's grave and stay in touch.

Many people whom Sami had helped when they were sick and traumatized stepped forward to thank him. Amira experienced equal measures of guilt and relief to be moving on as they all stayed behind. She acknowledged her privilege, but that didn't mean she felt lucky. The war had taken both her parents from her. Every day without them was a trial. She acted brave and as normal as she could for the children's sakes but was panicky and short of breath when they weren't watching and she imagined her mother lying dead in that ditch, or her father suffocating under rubble. Her compounded grief was like a yoke around her neck, dragging her down. She reflected back on her final days in Aleppo, when she'd thought things couldn't get much worse. How wrong she'd been.

She'd thought her life was at a low point then, but it had sunk much deeper since. Rationally she supposed she'd smile and laugh again at some point in the future, but that seemed a long way off yet. For right now, she was just trying to get through one day at a time.

AHMED HELD YASMINE'S HAND as they walked past the white tents. He saw the swings he'd not sat upon since Abdo left and heard them creaking now under the weight of other children. He saw the paths on which he and Abdo spent countless hours kicking a soccer ball back and forth, and dragged his toes to draw a line in their bumpy surfaces a final time. He wondered if Abdo thought of him, too, wherever he was, and if Abdo had made a new best friend to play soccer with. He kind of hoped Abdo had, but he also kind of hoped he hadn't.

Ahmed felt sad about his grandmother and wished she hadn't died. She'd been so unhappy and unwell at the camp that it felt like she just gave up on life. It didn't really seem fair that the rest of them got to move to Canada and start over but neither she nor his grandfather would have that chance. Their bodies would be in the Middle East forever, and who would visit their graves? He wished they were at least buried side by side. Ahmed also noticed that since his grandmother died, sometimes his mother went very still and stared at nothing for a few seconds at a time or longer. It worried Ahmed when she froze like that and he prayed these spells were temporary.

Walking on, Ahmed saw the school he loved, where he made art, solved math equations, read the same small selection of books over and over, and learned more English words than the rest of his family knew combined. He stood inside the school's door and waved at his teacher. Ms. Hussain interrupted her lesson to see him off.

"Listen to me, Ahmed," she said in English, speaking slowly and clearly, enunciating each word. She laid her broad hands on his narrow shoulders and Ahmed felt the warmth of her strong palms radiate beneath his T-shirt. "You are smart, kind, and brave. Go make a full life in Canada. Never forget you are Syrian, but let yourself be Canadian, too."

Ahmed only partially understood the English words she was saying, but he inferred their meaning and nodded gravely. He pulled away before his tears fell.

THE INTERNATIONAL ORGANIZATION FOR Migration booked a driver to take the family to the airport, but Sami declined, choosing to have a final private ride with Tareq. Words seemed redundant at this point, so they drove in wistful silence.

Sami told himself they were fortunate to be moving somewhere peaceful, and resolved to focus on that rather than his nerves about starting all over in a completely new culture where he didn't know the language. He'd also have to accept it was, if not the end of his medical career, the start of a long hiatus.

They'd learned they would have financial support for a year while they settled into Canada and learned English. He was a quick study but a year was not long. He doubted his English would be sufficient by then to start the lengthy doctor recertification process. He'd take whatever job he could find. There were so many unknowns. The only certainty was how much he was going to miss practicing medicine—and his friend Tareq. They reunited with the family on the tarmac.

"Bye, Uncle Tareq. Come see us in Canada," Yasmine said, waving goodbye. She was the jolliest of them all, ready for whatever adventures were to come. Her shock over her grandmother's death dogged her in nightmares, but in the daytime her temperament was as lively as ever. Her brown curls bobbed as she spun her head toward the chartered airplane that would fly them out of Turkey.

"Remember, you are my brother," Tareq told Sami, grasping his shoulder tightly and squeezing it. "For the rest of our lives we are family. No ocean between us changes that."

A flight attendant guided them onto the plane and they took their seats. Into two small suitcases Sami stored overhead, Amira had packed her family's meagre belongings: her beloved Quran wrapped carefully in a hijab, a few spare clothes and diapers, some spices she feared she'd not be able to buy in Canada, olive oil soap, and the family photos of her, Sami, and her parents on her wedding day, plus the baby photos of Ahmed and Yasmine.

Sami shoved his medical bag, which was empty except for a stethoscope, below the seat in front of him. It seemed like a lifetime ago that they'd fled Syria in the night with little more than the clothes on their backs. He flashed back to walking down streets littered with rubble, riding with the smuggler, scrambling through the ditch, and confronting the armed guard at the border. It made him shudder. He hoped this would be their final escape.

They all buckled their seat belts, and as the plane took off they strained to look one last time at the land they were leaving. Leaving, hopefully, for better, and leaving for good.

CHAPTER 47

Cape Breton, late January 2016

CHARLIE TRAVELLED ALONE TO SYDNEY WITH thoughts of Nell swirling around in his head. He kept glancing over his right shoulder, wanting to see her in the passenger seat. Even though they hadn't spent much time together recently, he was struggling to accept her absence in his life as permanent.

He turned on the radio, but every song provoked a memory of Nell so he snapped it off. Were they really finished for good? He'd been so certain they would always be a couple—maybe a little too certain. Nell was right. He'd taken their relationship for granted.

He'd thought about fighting for Nell and trying to win her back but when he mentioned this to his grandma, she was firm. "No. Leave her alone now. She gave you an answer." Grandma had always rooted for them as a couple in the past.

Charlie understood now why it was called a broken heart. There was an ache in his chest that just wouldn't go away.

A bell rang over the door as he entered the shop after parking across the street.

"Can I help you?" a short, round man asked from behind the counter. He reminded Charlie of the roly-poly Weeble toys he played with as a boy.

Charlie plucked the box out of his jacket pocket and opened it with cold fingers. He looked at the Claddagh ring he'd bought with so much hope six weeks earlier. What a damn fool he'd been. "How much will you give me for this?"

The shopkeeper pulled out a loupe and peered at the ring closely. "I'll make you a good offer: five hundred"

Charlie scoffed. "Buddy, I paid triple that. It's never been worn. That's a half-carat diamond in there. Help a fellow out."

The Weeble ran his tongue across his teeth. "Eight hundred. It's my best offer."

Charlie appreciated that at least the Weeble didn't ask why he was selling a never-been-worn diamond ring. He'd probably seen this sort of thing many times before: dumped losers trying to recover a buck and a shred of dignity.

The Weeble unlocked a drawer, counted out eight hundred-dollar bills and extended them in his pudgy hand toward Charlie.

He took the cash and left the store, relieved that was done but not particularly excited about the money. It helped him understand why Grandpa was so squirrely about his dad's settlement money. Money sometimes came your way on a wave of sadness.

There was a bar on the way to the parking lot. Charlie stopped and looked up at the neon OPEN sign. The bills were folded neatly in his wallet, which bulged in his back pocket. It was bitterly cold standing on the pavement, but it would be warm inside the bar.

CHAPTER 48

Cape Breton, February 2016

YASMINE WOKE UP WITH HER HEAD ON HER father's shoulder. She forgot where she was at first and felt a familiar tightness in her lungs, but she wasn't scared. Glancing around, she made out the silhouettes of her mother holding her baby brother in the window seat on her left, her father on her right, and Ahmed in his seat across the aisle. The seat next to Ahmed's, which was supposed to be their grandmother's, was empty. Everyone was still and the only sound was the hum of the plane's engines.

Yasmine mumbled, "Where are we, Papa?" She was rubbing her small hand against a soft blue blanket someone had draped over her midflight and wishing she could to get back to her dream, in which she'd been patting a fluffy black cat. The cat had been purring and trying to crawl onto her lap. Yasmine glanced around the cabin, still sleepy, hoping briefly the cat had been real and was hiding now under some seats. She focused on the blob in front of her father's feet, but it was his medical bag.

"Shhhh. We are somewhere over the Atlantic Ocean. Try to get more sleep, Yaya. You'll need your energy later."

Yasmine closed her eyes and snuggled in closer to her warm Papa but remained awake. Her breathing became shallow and her mouth was dry.

"Papa, can I please have some water?" She knew better than to request an inhaler. She hadn't had one for a long while.

Sami pressed a glowing button and just like that, a smiling lady in funny tight clothes appeared at his side. The lady wasn't wearing a hijab, and Yasmine tried not to stare at her yellow hair. It was twisted into a circle on top of her head. The lady's skin was so white she seemed almost to glow in the cabin's low light. Yasmine wondered if her own hair would turn yellow and her skin would turn that white once she was living in Canada.

"My daughter has asthma and I fear the air pressure might trigger an attack. Can she have water, and do you have oxygen on board in case there's an emergency?" Sami asked.

The flight attendant shook her head and raised her shoulders, an apologetic grimace on her face. Yasmine understood her father's words, but this lady didn't speak Arabic. She watched her Papa smile and nod in apology, then raise his hand and pretend to drink from an invisible glass. The lady left and reappeared a moment later with a plastic cup of water that she handed to Yasmine, and a chocolate bar she gave her with a wink. The water felt cool sliding down Yasmine's throat, and when she was finished she handed the cup back to the lady, who smiled kindly at her before walking away. Yasmine looked to her Papa and, once he nodded his approval, she broke off a piece of the chocolate bar and popped it in her mouth. It was the first chocolate she'd eaten since leaving Aleppo. She'd never tasted anything more delicious.

When she finished swallowing, Yasmine practiced counting her breaths the way her father had taught her: one-two-three inhale, hold, one-two-three exhale. The tightness in her chest went away and she slid back into sleep.

CHARLIE LOOKED DOWN AT THE yellow "NA" key tag dangling from the ignition. Nine months in recovery. He'd gone to a Narcotics Anonymous meeting in Sydney the day before where he he'd declared the length of his sobriety and was awarded the yellow key tag. He even walked by the bar with the neon OPEN sign and once again managed to not go in. The pain of his breakup with Nell was starting to dull and he felt, if not content, then at least better than he had since Christmas.

He heard a horn toot-toot and saw Catriona's car parallel to his in the left lane. She smiled and made a duck face before tucking ahead of him in the right lane. He laughed. They had a rest stop planned together just up the highway about thirty kilometres away. Charlie would be glad to stretch his legs and grab a coffee with his pal. Talking with Cat was always easy and light. It was nice to have a friendship without a ton of baggage or strings attached.

They sat down with coffees and a box of Timbits. Charlie placed the chocolate and white powdered sugar ones on a napkin for Catriona because they were her favourites. They talked about their plans for the future. Charlie was bidding on all the building projects he could find and had recently made the decision to get his carpentry papers, and Catriona had been accepted into a community studies degree program at Cape Breton University. In the new year, they'd be carpooling into Sydney together.

"It's funny, am I right, how no matter what you and I do lately our paths just seem to keep crossing?" Charlie asked.

Catriona took a sip of hot coffee and fanned her mouth for a few seconds before answering. It must've been piping hot, because her face turned red. "Right? Stop following me around like a bad smell, Charlie Gordon."

Charlie was staring at her and reached across the table to grasp her hand briefly before letting it go and popping a sour cream Timbit in his mouth. He didn't mention the icing sugar around her mouth but had a sudden urge to lick it off her lips. What was happening? He tilted his gaze and it struck him how lovely she was. How had he never noticed it before? Plus he could be totally himself around her and she still seemed to like him—maybe more than as a friend.

"What?" she asked.

"Nothing," he said, chuckling. "Do you even know how cute you are?"

Catriona's face went redder still.

WHEN YASMINE AWOKE THE NEXT time, the plane's wheels were touching down on the runway. Her eyes flew open at the jolt, and this time she knew immediately where she was—in her new homeland, Canada.

The lights were all on inside the plane and a voice coming out of some hidden speakers was saying things she couldn't understand. She leaned and waved her arms to get Ahmed's attention from across the aisle. "What's the man saying, Ahmed?"

"It's the pilot. He says welcome to Halifax. I think he's also saying what the weather is like here. I can't understand much," Ahmed replied. "I only learned *some* English words at Al Salam School, Yaya. Not all of them."

Amira opened the blind covering the window next to her seat, and Yasmine leaned across to try to see outside.

"Watch baby Omar," her mother cautioned. Yasmine's baby brother was awake in his mother's arms. Omar was squirming like a little inch-worm and starting to grunt.

"Sorry, Omar!" Yasmine replied, quickly planting a kiss on his fore-head, then grazing him as she leaned to look out the window. There wasn't much to see except trees, but the terminal was like a beacon at the end of the runway pulling them closer.

The plane came to a full stop and two beeps rang out before there was another announcement Yasmine couldn't understand. People started taking off their seat belts and standing up, so she did the same. Now her legs were restless and she had the urge to jump, dance, or run but no space in which to do so. She glanced at all her family members as they gathered up their things. Her father's stethoscope rattled in his medical bag as he lifted it.

"So much better than our last border crossing, wouldn't you say? You have our passports, right?" Sami asked Amira.

Yasmine wished her father wouldn't talk about their last escape. She didn't want to remember the night they left their beautiful home in Aleppo and snuck out of Syria. They'd gotten a drive from a stranger, but he couldn't take them the whole way and they'd had to walk through a scary ditch in the dark to reach the checkpoint. They'd heard bombs dropping in the distance. Yasmine had tried hard to be brave and not let the others hear her cry that night. She'd worked hard trying to forget that ever happened, but the memory often surfaced anyway. When it did, or when she remembered her grandmother was dead, she played the game Ahmed taught her. She found five good things that made her feel safe and happy. Looking around now, she listed to herself: my baby brother, my first trip in an airplane, the soft blue blanket that kept me warm and cozy on this trip, the chocolate the lady with the yellow hair gave me, and…she struggled for a fifth and thought again of her grandmother… ears that can hear even if they can't understand the words yet.

"Of course, Sami. All our identification papers are in hand," Amira replied.

The lady with the yellow hair waved goodbye as Yasmine skipped through the plane's doorway. A cold tunnel connected them to the airport, and the five of them followed the other passengers into the arrivals area.

"Are you Sami and Amira?" a young man asked, approaching them as they walked through a sliding glass door. He was speaking slowly and Yasmine's parents recognized their names. They nodded.

A tall girl held a tablet and spoke into it slowly. She turned it toward the family and clicked the Go button so they could hear the Arabic translation: "Welcome to your new home, Canada."

A small group of people with balloons and posters approached them. Yasmine didn't know who they were or why they'd come to the airport. Was it to meet her and her family? They were talking and shaking hands with everyone, big smiles on all their faces. Some people were taking pictures and walking around with notebooks. Were they famous now? Why? A woman next to them was talking into a big microphone and looking into a video camera. Yasmine suddenly felt special. Meanwhile, a man in a uniform but without a rifle was trying to move them all forward into a small office. Yasmine didn't know if she needed to be nervous or excited, and she froze for a second. The tall older girl with the tablet crouched down low and talked to Yasmine at her eye level.

"My name is Catriona, but you can call me Cat." She pointed at herself and said, "I'm…Cat."

Cat was one of the few English words Yasmine knew. Yasmine was confused by this girl who thought she was a cat, but decided they could be friends. After looking at her parents and receiving their approval, she took the hand Cat had extended into her own.

THEY PULLED UP TO THE renovated house in two separate cars. Charlie had driven Amira, Ahmed, and baby Omar. Catriona had Yasmine and Sami in her car. The sponsors couldn't talk directly with their passengers, but both Charlie and Catriona had pointed at things outside their car windows anyway as they drove from the Halifax airport to Falkirk Cove on this cold but clear winter day. They each made a big deal of the overhanging WELCOME TO CAPE BRETON sign on the Canso Causeway, eliciting polite smiles and nods from the oblivious Syrians.

"How'd it go?" Charlie asked Catriona as they both exited their cars in the driveway.

"Okay, I think?" She wished she'd had an interpreter so she could ask the new arrivals questions. But despite the language barriers, she liked these people, and she didn't want to admit it, but she already had a favourite—little Yasmine and her bouncy brown curls and long eyelashes. Catriona kept peeking at her in the rear-view mirror as Yasmine hugged and petted the stuffed cat she'd given her as a welcome gift.

Catriona watched Sami help Amira to her feet and regretted that the family wasn't yet outfitted with boots, as the ground was frozen and slippery. Despite that, they all made it to the front door without falling. It flew open as they approached.

"Come in! Come in! We've been waiting for you," Flo said. She and Tinker had stayed back in Falkirk Cove to warm up the house and stock it with basic groceries. The Syrians stood awkwardly in the foyer of their new home, their few bags at their sides.

"It smells fantastic in here, Grandma," Charlie inhaled deeply.

"Well, was I ever relieved to discover there's at least a small selection of Middle Eastern foods and Halal meats at the grocery store," Flo said, gently waving them all into the dining room where they were directed to sit at the table Charlie and Tinker built.

TINKER SEATED HIMSELF AT THE head of the table, then thought better of it. This wasn't his home. He moved to the side, standing up when the Syrians entered the room. The parents and boy were smiling and said hello in English. The daughter squirmed behind her mother's legs the same way Alex had when he first arrived.

Tinker pulled out chairs for them and motioned that they should sit. Florence had made Tinker learn their names and he ran through them in his head as they settled in. When he caught Amira's gaze she looked away quickly, but the dad, Sami, held eye contact with Tinker.

Flo and Bob brought in bowls of chicken soup for everyone, and there were plates of pita bread cut into triangles passed around. Tinker preferred a nice fresh brown bread, but had to admit the pita was a decent-tasting alternative, if a little flat.

Over homemade cookies and squares they all drank cups of strong tea; the Syrians took it black while the Canadians drank theirs the proper way, with milk. The Syrians nodded appreciatively and Ahmed said thank you on their behalf every time food was passed their way. Amira held the baby in her arms the whole time, though several people gestured that they'd like to take him so she could eat more comfortably. She declined their help, which Tinker could understand. Trust took time to build.

A few other community members hung back in the living room, not wanting to crowd the newcomers. Bob had learned how to say hello in Arabic and was being a bit of a show-off using it over and over, "*Marhabaan!*" The family repeated it back each time and began laughing.

When their meal was finished, Flo offered to walk them around their new house. They appeared confused, so Catriona typed, "Come see the rest of your house" on her iPad. She showed the translation to Sami and Amira, who nodded and rose to their feet. The children trailed along.

They went from room to room, pointing out obvious things like closets, beds, and dressers that they'd partially filled with donated clothing. The children's eyes grew wide when they saw their own rooms with toys and books in them.

"It's all ours? Everything?" Sami asked into the iPad. When the translation came forth Tinker assured them yes, it was.

They weren't going to include the basement on the tour, but at the last minute Flo suggested they go down so she could show them the laundry room. The committee had splurged on a new stackable washing machine and dryer that Tinker and Charlie had installed only the day before.

Flo showed them where the laundry soap was and demonstrated how to turn the washing machine on. Tinker watched Amira stare at it like it was a lemonade stand in the desert. She even handed the baby to her husband so she could open and shut the washing machine's door and run her hands down the front of the dryer as though she were caressing it. It was both amusing and telling. He hadn't seen basic appliances provoke so much obvious delight since his mother traded in their wringer washer for an automatic in the 1960s.

The children were laughing now and running room to room. Their delight was spreading and everyone's steps became bouncier. Ahmed found a soccer ball and was dribbling it down the hallway upstairs like a pro until his mother waved her index finger at him. Even without understanding Arabic, the meaning of her admonishment was clear to Tinker. The mood was changing from awkward to festive. Tinker was sure if someone had brought a fiddle they'd be playing by now and turning this into a proper party. Then again, no one wished to tire out or overwhelm the family that had just come from so far away. He and Flo put on their coats and got ready to leave, with promises to check in on the Syrians the next day. They'd have to help them settle in, but that would be manageable. Besides, now that Tinker had met them, they seemed like decent enough folks.

Tinker watched Catriona link arms with Charlie as they all walked down the front stairs.

AHMED LAY IN HIS NEW BED. He stretched out his arms and felt nothing but smooth sheets. He listened for sounds but only heard a faint grumble from the furnace now and again, and a pinging in his radiator. He inhaled deeply but smelled nothing. He looked around but saw only walls illuminated by moonlight. Restless, he went to his window and opened the curtains. The barren, frozen fields lay still under the starry sky, dotted with the silhouettes of leafless trees. The road was an empty black stripe. The moon was full and he wondered if Abdo was looking up at it too, wherever he was, thinking about him. He feared never hearing from his friend again and began to tremble.

He climbed back into bed and willed sleep to come. His whole family was in the house, but he felt alone and unsettled. What if he hated it here? What if the children at his new school thought he was weird or ugly? Would they be his friends?

There was a knock at his door. "Come in."

"Can I sleep with you, Ahmed?" Yasmine had one hand on his doorknob and the stuffed cat in her other hand. She looked tiny and lost.

Ahmed was glad for her company. He lifted the covers on his bed and patted the empty space next to him. "I suppose so, if it will make you less scared."

Her body was still warm from her bubble bath, and her new flannel pajamas felt soft, but she'd walked across the hardwood floor with bare feet.

"Don't touch me with your cold toes!" Ahmed warned, so Yasmine purposely pressed them against his legs and giggled.

"Do it again and I'll make you sleep alone in your room."

Yasmine withdrew her feet. "I don't like these high beds. What if I fall out?"

"You'll get used to it." Ahmed spread out a blanket on the floor beside Yasmine just in case.

Baby Omar had been nursed and finally settled into his new crib after a bout of fussiness. Sami and Amira now appeared in Ahmed's doorway. When they saw the children were still awake, they came and sat on the foot of Ahmed's bed.

"What do you think of our new home?" Sami asked. He grabbed Amira's hand.

Ahmed lay on his back with his head on a pillow. "It's big. Bigger even than our Aleppo home. It's nice but just so different."

"Change is hard, Ahmed. Even change for the better." Amira tucked the blankets up around the children's shoulders.

"I feel like we're guests here and we'll wake up back in Reyhanli Camp. But I hope not."

Amira leaned forward and kissed both he and Yasmine on their heads. She was so rarely affectionate they both stiffened and said nothing, but secretly enjoyed it.

"We're safe here. We're together. I thank Allah for that," Amira told them. "The rest will fall into place."

Yasmine was asleep before her parents had time to tiptoe out of the room. Ahmed watched her chest rise and fall, certain he'd be awake all night, but it wasn't five minutes later that he, too, drifted off for his first sleep of many thousands in his new homeland.

EPILOGUE

Cape Breton, February 2016

AHMED SAT ON A TOBOGGAN ON TOP OF THE snowy hill. He'd never touched snow before moving to Canada and was still in awe of it. Snow was like a cold blanket covering everything. It was packable, both soft and hard, and sometimes it fell from the sky like diamond dust. On weekdays, after the long bus ride that brought him and Yasmine home from their new school, they made snowballs and snow angels in their front yard until their parents called them inside. On weekends they stayed outside even longer, exploring. They had a tree of their own here, too, but this tree grew pinecones rather than olives. The children liked climbing its low branches to look into the distance at the cold blue ocean, then turning around to gaze at the vast hills behind them. The cold shocked them at first, but with layers of warm clothing on, it didn't bother them. Ahmed thought often of Abdo and imagined how, if his friend were here, they'd pack the snow tightly into a soccer ball. They'd then kick it around until it broke apart.

Yasmine walked with Catriona over to her brother. Though she'd made friends her age at school and loved her classroom and teacher, she still considered Catriona her best friend. Catriona wasn't the furry feline friend Yasmine hoped to have in Canada—she was better. Yasmine looked up, asking, "Yes, Cat?" for approval before climbing on the toboggan. Catriona said yes, and Yasmine flopped down in front of Ahmed on the wooden sled.

It was their first time using it since their neighbour Roger bought it for them, and Ahmed admired how strong and sturdy it felt underneath him as he stretched his legs out beside his sister and extended his feet into the graceful arc at the end. Roger had also dropped off new ice skates for the children, but they hadn't had a chance to use them yet. Their sharp-as-knives blades made them nervous. Ahmed wrapped his arms tightly around Yasmine's waist. "Are you ready?" he asked his sister in Arabic. "On three." He switched to English. "One. Two. Three!"

Sami stepped forward and firmly pushed Ahmed's back and they started sliding down the hill, their squeals accelerating along with the pace of their descent. Their small voices trailed off as they slid away from the adults. Yasmine lifted a small pink-mittened hand to touch the snow spraying up from either side of the coasting toboggan until they skidded to a stop. Immediately they sprang to their feet and Ahmed grabbed the yellow rope and began hauling the toboggan back up the hill. Yasmine trailed rosy-cheeked behind her brother, her lungs strong enough today that she could almost keep up.

Tinker, Catriona, and Charlie mirrored the children's smiles as they got closer. Ahmed's face was relaxed and open, and Yasmine's eyes were wide and sparkling.

ROGER STOOD ON THE HARD SNOW. He looked down at his feet, now tucked into fleece-lined rubber boots instead of white sneakers. His socks were drooping and it agitated him; so many things about winter were difficult. Like dusk at five o'clock. His daytime walks had to be precisely timed.

He wanted to count snowflakes but knew it would be futile. He'd taken a tablespoon of sand from the Falkirk Cove beach last summer and attempted to count each grain as the first step in a sample analysis but hadn't been able to complete even that, and sand didn't melt. Some things apparently just didn't want to be counted.

Good thing he had new neighbours to distract him. He could count the Syrian family easily; there were five of them. Once they got more words he'd ask them their birthdays, but for now, he just liked watching them come and go into what had long been an abandoned house. He could see four of them in the distance now, along with Tinker

Gordon, Charlie Gordon, and Catriona Libbus. He shoved his mittened hands in his parka's pockets to warm them up.

The father, Sami, caught sight of him and waved him over. Roger didn't respond. It wasn't because they didn't speak English or weren't from here. Those things didn't bother him a bit; in fact, he liked them more for those reasons. But he was keeping an eye on his small house, which was a speck in the distance, to make sure no one entered it. His money pile was thankfully diminishing, but he still had several thousand dollars to spend before he'd feel comfortable leaving it alone. He knew about banks, but his experience with them wasn't good so he was keeping his Chase the Ace winnings in his microwave until they were gone, thank you very much.

"TOO BAD ALEX ISN'T HERE too, eh, Grandpa?" Charlie asked.

"Sure is. But he'll have new friends to play with when he visits this summer," Tinker replied. He was discovering that the more he got to know them, the more he actually liked the Syrians.

Since the refugees had arrived, with the help of Google Translate on Catriona's iPad and an ad-hoc system of hand signals, together the long-time community members and new arrivals had worked out some rudimentary methods of communicating. Charlie turned to Sami and Amira now, wrapped his arms around himself, and said, "Brrrrr?" to ask if they were cold.

Sami shook his head. He was bundled in a down parka and boots, and Amira had pulled a touque down over her hijab. She stamped her feet and smiled but was secretly anxious to leave. It was the first time she'd left baby Omar with anyone, and she was feeling acute separation anxiety even though Flo was so gentle and kind with the baby and they were only to be gone for an hour.

Despite the welcome they'd received in Cape Breton, Amira had been intermittently sad since arriving. While she loved her spacious new home and especially the washing machine and dryer, the reality of all she'd left behind was catching up with her. She missed her mosque, Noor, books, and speaking Arabic to people other than her family. She'd never been able to say goodbye to her father and didn't even have a memento of his. Plus she carried guilt about fighting with her mother on her last day. If she'd been more sympathetic and gentle with her, would her mother still be alive? Was she complicit in her death? Amira watched her children having so much fun sliding down the hill and tried to imagine her mother living here with them. She would have hated it. Her mother meant it when she said she'd rather die there than leave. Amira would feel her mother's absence for the rest of her life, but after giving herself the customary forty days to mourn her, resolved to then turn her attention to learning English and understanding Canadian culture. Her life carried on.

Sami looked up at the sky. It was hard to believe this sky, which cast a steel blue light, was connected to the Syrian sky, whose light was a warm yellow hue. Even if they lived here for the rest of their lives, and they did intend to apply for Canadian citizenship, Sami would never stop being Syrian. He'd been warned that some people in Canada might fear or dislike him, or even confuse him for a terrorist, but it hadn't happened so far. The family's sponsors had been nothing but welcoming, but he knew they didn't represent everyone living here. There could be animosity or discrimination against his family for their traditions or religion still to come. These were early days yet. Sami hoped he could show any skeptics or doubters that he'd come to Canada to contribute, not take from the community. He just needed time to adjust and learn the language.

"One more time?" Ahmed asked Sami in Arabic.

"Ask Mr. Gordon, he is our driver," Sami replied. Until Sami got a Canadian driver's license and car the family was dependent on others for all their transportation. The dependency bothered him. There was little here within walking distance.

Ahmed turned to Tinker, his head cocked to the side. "Again? Please?"

Tinker nodded. This time it was he who stepped forward to push the children off, igniting the ache in his arthritic shoulder. More painful still was the memory it triggered of a year and a half earlier, when he was on the beach pushing whales into the ocean while learning that Charlie would be leaving him for Alberta.

"G'bye!" he yelled at the children's backs. "Come back soon," he added quietly, and of course they did climb right back up the hill after one final slide before piling into the Buick so Tinker could drive them home. After an ordeal Tinker couldn't really wrap his head around, these Syrians were now Cape Bretoners, and he was okay with it. They'd come so far and it struck Tinker that he had, too, without ever leaving Cape

Breton. Wasn't it Roger who told him that as Thursday's child he had far to go? He'd scoffed at the time, content as he was to stay in his little corner of Cape Breton, but maybe there was some truth in what Roger said. For an old guy set in his ways, he now surprised even himself with his new attitudes. Sure, some other people had left him, but those who were meant to had come back. Plus, it turned out there was room here for newcomers, too. Some people might move again, and he wouldn't like it much, and he'd probably grumble about it, but he would try to accept and make the most of it in the future. No matter the journey, however long or fraught, he hoped they'd make their way home.

ACKNOWLEDGEMENTS

THANK YOU TO THOSE WHO HELPED ME BETTER understand life in a refugee camp and the immigrant experience: Fr. Russell Daye, Boghros Barbouri, and Steve Law at the Immigrant Services Association of Nova Scotia.

Thank you to the International Writing Program at the University of Iowa, my teachers, and so many writers who have inspired me.

Thank you to my students at Mount Saint Vincent University, the Writers' Federation of Nova Scotia, and the Nova Scotia Community College, who taught me more than I ever taught them.

Thank you to my beta readers, Anne Louise O'Connell and Susan Heinrich, who read early manuscripts and suggested necessary adjustments.

Thank you to Whitney Moran at Vagrant Press, who gave me generous feedback and said yes(!), and to my editor, the incomparable Stephanie Domet, who was direct, specific, kind, tough, and warm in equal measure. Thank you to Ahmed Danny Ramadan, for reading the manuscript through the lens of a Syrian person who came to Canada and performing a sensitivity edit. Whitney's, Stephanie's, and Danny's suggestions and endorsements mean the world to me.

Thank you to wise friends and cheerleaders inside and outside of writing, editing, and publishing businesses, particularly Kat Kruger, Jay and Hazel Millar, my fellow Ravens book club members, my mom, Diane Lane, Adriane Abbott and University of King's College colleagues, Lola Augustine Brown, Angela Trainor, Danielle Cordon, and Monica Arab—for living through this with me, for invaluable conversations, and for also giving me time and space to write.

Thank you to my immediate family, Manfred, Curtis, and Eric Gangl, for understanding and indulging my need to write, and even more so for inspiration, focus, laughter, and love.

And saving the most heartfelt for last, thank you to my writing group, who read each chapter multiple times: Jill Hamilton, Susan Church, Cheri Wilson, Carol Moreira, and Mary Lou Petersen. I simply could not have written this book without your encouragement, criticism, and friendship. You showed me that writing doesn't have to be lonely or isolating, but rather it can be a team effort. When I got a new job and had three weeks in which to do a total rewrite and was full of doubt that I'd be able to do it, you all gently said, "Yes, you can. Now get to work." I am eternally grateful.

MANFRED GANGL

ALISON DELORY is a writer, editor, and teacher living in Halifax. She has been writing stories for newspapers, magazines, and digital platforms for twenty years. She's also written two children's chapter books and contributed to several anthologies. *Making it Home* is her first novel.